WELCOME TO MAMMOTH

TALES OF HORROR IN NORTHEASTERN PENNSYLVANIA

DEAN ALAN CONRAD

eBook ISBN: 979-8-9904560-6-8

Print Edition ISBN: 979-8-9904560-7-5

ACKNOWLEDGMENTS

For my grandsons Connor, Archer, and Colton

FOREWORD

Why is Mammoth home to so much paranormal activity? Who knows? Maybe it's the water or the air. These eleven short stories are all set in and around the fictional city in the heart of Pennsylvania's hard coal region. Named after a forty-foot-thick vein of anthracite that helped fuel the new country's industrial revolution, it is the type of place where almost anything can happen. Buy a home and you might find the place is haunted. New neighbors could have a circus sideshow oddity that comes to life. Somebody down the block might own a ghoul or belong to a blood-swilling cult. Go out at night and you surely will run into a vampire. Just for fun, you might find a reincarnated serial killer. The list goes on and on.

The Mammoth vein exists. So do the abandoned coal mines and cemeteries that are featured in some of the stories. Some characters and places appear in more than one story. Enjoy!

LIVING WITH THE DEAD

I STARTED TO COMMUNICATE WITH THE DEAD AFTER THE third time I died. For most people dying once is enough and it's actually quite easy, but I had to do it the hard way. After all, everyone who has ever lived either died or can expect to die. Of all the great thinkers through the ages who pontificated on life, recorded history, delved into the complexities of their times, unraveled the secrets of time and physics, none was able to cheat death. War, disease, murder, stupid mistakes and—for the few lucky—old age, all take their tolls. The high, the low, the intelligent, and foolish all take a last gasp, whether their lives were happy or miserable. The famous are written about in history books, the not-so-famous became footnotes, and the vast majority who were never recorded and were forgotten after they passed. Some lived many years; some were cut down early. Others fell somewhere in between. I am somewhat unique because I died three times and am still here to talk about it. Yes, clinically dead, even though briefly. Unexplainably, I lived through death. I don't know why I came back but I did. There might be a purpose to my life that I don't understand. Someone or something might have pushed or pulled me back into the realm of the living. Perhaps the devil was too busy to take me immediately on my traumatic exits from this world, although I don't think I deserve to be sucked to hell for eternity, if there is a hell.

Was God preoccupied with the death of a saint, a mass shooting, or a multitude of earthquake victims to call me home, if there is a heaven? It's possible I'm on a back burner, too insignificant for anyone to notice my comings and goings from this world to the next and back. When the fourth time comes, will I be so lucky? Who knows. Eventually, my time will run out and I will remain dead, as a cat does after it exhausts its nine lives. I don't fear that ultimate death, whether it's the fourth or hundredth time I expire, although I doubt my body can take much more abuse of the kind it has already endured in dying. Death is not always kind, especially to me.

The First Time (I don't mean sex.)

The first time I died was on a warm, idyllic summer day that was warm and had a cloudless sky. I sailed down the highway on my Harley Davidson Sportster, doing the speed limit in the middle of some rather heavy Sunday afternoon traffic. The Sportster was just the right size for a thin, smaller than average guy. I wasn't exactly the biker type. After all, I wore a helmet and shaved every day. No hair stuck from underneath my helmet. The bike's customization was limited to a set of black leather saddle bags on the back filled with rain gear, a few tools, a bag of trail mix, and a water bottle. I felt comfortable riding and didn't look to get noticed. I rode for the sheer pleasure of it.

My direction west dipped and curved, rose and fell, and at places opened to two lanes for a few miles and then narrowed again to one. I enjoyed leaning into the turns and feeling the air rush by me. It was exhilarating. At times I sped up, when there was an open road in front, and then backed off the throttle when traffic appeared ahead. There were fields and woods and farmhouses about with pastures dotted with horses, cows, even goats grazing. Occasionally there was a small church with a graveyard behind it on a hill. Hallowed ground that was chosen because it was not suitable to till, I imagined. Too steep or too rocky. The old gravestones, thin as crackers, leaned at various odd angles.

There was no destination in mind that day. If I met other bikers along the road, I might follow them. If not, I'd drive until hunger set in, stop somewhere for a bite to eat—I loved diner food, especially the daily specials that stuck to your ribs—with some flirting with the waitress if she was young and pretty, and then return home before there was any threat of an evening thunderstorm, and especially before it got dark. I hated driving even a car at night.

At some point, when the road widened to two lanes, a dark, smallish SUV pulled along the left and began an agonizingly slow attempt to pass. Our speeds remained constant, and for a while we seemed to hover in the same space, neither changing positions. We were on a long straightaway, and I missed the opportunity to wave to half a dozen bikers driving the opposite way because the SUV blocked my vision, but I heard them roar by. There was a little girl, possibly eight or nine, with longish blond hair in the SUV's back seat next to the door. She had just peeled a banana and started to take a bite. I drifted closer to the car than I found comfortable and returned my gaze to the road and moved back into the right lane's center. I looked again to the left and smiled. She might have been scared when I drifted close, I thought. However, she seemed not to have noticed and mouthed the banana, now fully peeled, sliding it in and out of her mouth with her lips clamped softly around it. She looked out the window and noticed me watching her. She pulled the banana from her mouth, licked its length, and sucked its tip.

I wondered how she learned *that*. I had seen enough and roared ahead until the road returned to a single lane, and they left my sight in the rearview mirror around a curve. Within minutes, traffic slowed, and they were on my tail again. Now the parents were visible in their front seats through my rearview mirror. They were thirtyish. He was dark-haired, spectacled, somewhat peevish-looking, and sported what appeared to be a new scraggily goatee he stroked with his free hand. She was blond, like the girl, and looked wistful as she peered out the side window, coiling strands of hair around her finger. Her shoulders were slim and bare. As soon as the road opened again, the SUV passed, this time with more determination. The little girl slipped by slowly, with the late afternoon sun on her face. She raised her hand and waved, holding her palm still and curling and uncurling her small fingers. I smiled for a moment as the SUV slipped ahead. Then she showed her middle finger and laughed. Dad turned on the gas, and they were gone, back in front as the road narrowed again, choking me with exhaust fumes. This time, the SUV pulled out of sight, but before long, they were some twenty-five yards ahead. The road dipped, rose steeply, turned sharply right, and then flattened out. They sped up, and so did I.

A pale, thin arm emerged from the SUV's right rear window, now open, with a flapping banana peel held in the girl's fingertips. It looked larger than it was, with its waving yellow segments, as if it were a giant octopus chasing prey across the ocean bottom. The girl rolled her wrist several times and tossed the peel. It fluttered like an undulating starfish and seemed to hang there forever. I was so mesmerized I didn't see Dad slam on the brakes. In the blink of an eye, I crashed into the SUV and was hurled through the rear window into the interior.

I was dead, at least for a while, and don't remember what happened next. According to the police report and witnesses happy to spill their guts to the local newspaper about the gruesome event, it seemed Dad was mesmerized, too, by a groundhog seeking greener pastures across the highway, and slammed on the brakes. I ended up with my face over the rear seat, my ass in the air outside the vehicle, and my legs in the cargo space. The groundhog escaped to greener pastures, the newspaper noted—no corpus delicti was found—apparently unconcerned about the mayhem it caused. The banana peel landed on the guard rail braided wire, where it baked in the sun the rest of the summer and transformed into a dark glob that looked like a malformed spider. It was still there when I returned to the accident scene after months of rehabilitation.

State police, local police, and firefighters responded to the scene. The highway was closed temporarily. I crashed through the SUV with such force the SUV occupants were transported by ambulance and then helicopter to a trauma center to recover. The SUV was draped with white canvass to prevent rubberneckers from seeing the vehicle's grisly interior, although my skinny ass managed to remain visible, even in the newspaper's front page Monday edition. Everyone knew I was dead, and I remained in that humiliating position for some time, until the coroner arrived, torn away from a fundraising picnic for his re-election, where a pig turned on a spit and there was plenty of ice-cold draft beer, to pronounce me and the little girl officially dead.

Upon impact, my helmet struck the back of her head and split it open, hence the SUV's grisliness. In addition to the little girl's body, I was saved by a cargo area packed with tents, sleeping bags, a mound of soiled clothing, and sacks of souvenirs, mostly stuffed animals. The word *saved* is used rather loosely because any number of police and firemen, no strangers to these kinds of gory scenes, found no pulse in my neck or wrists. Neither did the coroner, who stood shaking his head, picking strings of pork from his teeth. Much of the gore was presumed erroneously to be mine. After all, how much gore can a little girl hold?

Eventually, I was pulled from the SUV. The brain-encrusted helmet was removed. Firemen held up another sheet while I was extracted and placed inside a body bag as black as my bike's saddle bags, which in the accident were catapulted over the guardrail and into the river, where they floated downstream to some unknown destination.

The sense of *being* was the first to return. I don't remember breathing. I felt no pain. I couldn't talk. I saw because my eyes were open. My hearing worked, despite some ringing. The first memory after the accident was the sound of the body bag's zipper closing. Two cops joked whether there would be an open-casket funeral with my ass pointed in the air as it ended up in the SUV?

"Good thing we bagged him before rigor mortis set in," the one cop quipped.

The other cop laughed and punched him lightly in the arm. "You're too much, man."

I screamed. I cursed, but it had no effect. No one noticed. I tried to thrash about but couldn't move. The zipper inched upward, over my knees, my groin, my navel. Someone adjusted the bag. I was completely inside. The black interior loomed above my face. There was a sickening, visceral smell. Was it from the bag, was it from me, or was it from the girl who was being placed into a similar body bag on a similar gurney next to me? The same tarp shielded us both from the roadside and traffic. I could hear her body bag zipper close smoothly and quickly along with the cries from her distraught parents in the background. Cries of pain and anguish. I wanted to vomit but couldn't. I wanted to breathe and shout but couldn't. I wanted to say I was sorry. Would I ever see them again? The noise from my zipper continued. Eventually, the bag closed over my face. Everything faded away. Between the top of the zipper and the body bag's rubbery material, an infinitesimally small hole admitted a pinpoint of white sunlight.

THE SECOND TIME

I can't say whether that body bag trapped me—my spirit, my soul—in this world and blocked the path to the next, but at some point in the slow ambulance ride to the morgue—It was a slow afternoon in the ambulance business, and the EMTs had time to kill before supper—I started screaming and clawing. I screamed and clawed as best I could for someone who had shattered both legs and hip, broken my right arm and collarbone, cracked three vertebrae, and as many ribs, and punctured a lung. Now I felt pain. Hot, searing pain.

The scream was more of a whisper. The whisper was deadened by the body bag material. Then there was the ambulance radio cackling, a stream of unintelligible, static-laden voices. My calls for help sounded loud enough to me, as frantic as I was, but it took minutes for the EMT riding shotgun to notice the body bag moving.

He was busy telling the driver about an operating room nurse he met the previous night after delivering another DOA to the hospital. A gunshot victim in a drug deal that went south. The girl and I were his third DOAs in a row, he said nonchalantly, as if we weren't close to breaking the DOA record, but the nurse had seemed interested and gave him her telephone number. She was pretty enough, he said, but she had a child and so did he. It was a relationship that could prove expensive and complicated by their ex-spouses, ex-in-laws, their extended families, and a multitude of friends who still liked the ex-wife, but, after all, I was a dead guy, and it was none of my business.

The relationship sounded like more problems than the EMT wanted to deal with, but he found a bigger problem when the ambulance hit a pothole, and the nerves in my shattered body sent a wave of pain through me. I screamed. The EMT either heard or turned around to ensure the ambulance's equipment was secure.

"Fucking wow, Ted! We got a live one!"

The ambulance lurched from side to side when Ted learned

the news, causing me more excruciating pain. "This guy was supposed to be dead, Matt," Ted said.

"I checked him myself," Matt said.

"Me, too!"

"Well's he's back. Looks like a fish out of water."

Matt rushed to my side, unzipped the body bag, and started to take whatever vital signs lingered. Ted radioed the hospital to report they no longer had a DOA. He turned on the siren and sped off, leaving the little girl's ambulance in the distance. Within moments Matt inserted an IV in my arm and attached a heart monitor and blood pressure cuff. I couldn't tell what else he did. Wracked by pain, I drifted in and out of consciousness.

"Stay with me, buddy. You got it made," Matt screamed in my ear, which caused more pain. "We're going to take good care of you. You'll be in the ER in a minute. The doctors are waiting. Don't leave me."

Now that my heart was pumping, I was oozing blood everywhere. I pissed my pants. My legs were wet and cold; blood was in my throat and mouth.

I tried to talk, but mouthed words that made no sound. Matt put his ear to my mouth. "What do you need, buddy. Let me know. You're okay."

That was easy for him to say. "I'm cold," I managed to whisper. The taste of blood was strong in my mouth. I smelled his shampoo. I wished I were back at the point where I had no senses.

"Hold on, chief. We'll have you in some nice PJs as soon as we get to the hospital. It's only a couple of blocks. Hang in there. They have some nice, heated blankets for you."

"PJs? Get me out of this fucking bag."

"Yeah. That's not exactly the place where you want to be. I understand."

Perhaps he thought of the nurse and weighed the possibility of a dinner date.

The ambulance pulled up to the hospital, where doctors and nurses waited at the door. The body bag was transferred to a gurney as gently as I suppose was possible, but it hurt like hell. I grimaced and groaned. The gurney rolled through the entrance and down the hospital hall. Ceiling lights passed overhead. Faces loomed over me. I recognized one from the ambulance.

"Are you Matt?" I said.

"I'm with you, chief. All the way!"

"Thanks." I tried to smile but even that simple motion hurt.

Matt's hands were on the gurney side rail, helping catapult me through the hospital to an unknown destination—the operating room, morgue, or PJ sizing shop? I didn't care. In one brief moment of clarity, I saw Matt share a glance across the gurney with a red-haired freckled nurse. She was attractive. Even in this dire condition I looked toward Matt and whispered, "Is she the one?"

"You heard?"

I blinked my eyes. Matt took it for a *yes*. He and the nurse traded another look, as they realized I knew more than I should for a dead guy.

The gurney rolled through a set of open doors and a new set of faces covered with masks hovered over me. "I'm Doctor Wormwood. We're going to take a look at what's hurt and then fix it."

"Everything hurts," I managed to say.

"I understand. You'll be fine," the doctor said. His mask moved as if a small creature moved inside as he sucked in and expelled breaths. "Stay with us, son."

Did doctors always lie to the dead or dying? I lost consciousness when they moved me from one gurney to another. I regained it briefly when I sensed the sound of scissors. My new leather chaps and jacket were cut off. Those clothes were expensive, but at that point I didn't care. I had the vague feeling I wouldn't need them. No matter what happened I would never ride a motorcycle again.

At first there was a sense of nausea and dizziness. Then I had no feeling. I left my body and hovered over it, always in motion, drifting side to side, up and down, more like I was bobbing on a lake's rough water as the last remnants of clothing were cut and stripped off. I had no sense of having a body as I drifted overhead. There were no arms or legs, fingers or toes visible on this floating being. I wanted to propel myself, as if swimming through water, but couldn't. All my concentration was focused on the body below.

Battered, bloody, bruised, and naked, I was a bloated, pitiful example of what I once had been. It was difficult to see this gruesome corpse, bloodlessly pale, as the gowned doctors and nurses dipped and bobbed over me, cleaning, suturing, and filling my leaking body with bags of blood and plasma and saline, while from the other arm they drew vials of blood for the laboratory.

There was no sense of desperation on their part or mine. They exhibited teamwork at its finest. Instruments were ready before they were called for. I merely watched. I was not hot or cold, hungry or thirsty. There was no hurry to go anywhere.

There was no sense of time. I don't think I could have left the room had I wanted. To be honest, I was content to remain where I was and watch the proceedings below. I even found it entertaining. It was like I finally got to see the missing footage from a medical show deemed too gruesome for viewers at home. An invisible tether seemed to connect me to the body below like some long umbilical cord. I watched from above as a completely disinterested observer. I didn't even have the effort to root for the surgical team. My life draining out on the floor had no more effect than the greasy stain of a bug splattered on the motorcycle wind screen.

Suddenly, urgency surrounded the operating table. The gowned figures talked hurriedly, exchanged worried glances, barked orders. I couldn't understand what they said. I floated off, parallel to the ceiling, among its lights and spiderlike medical machinery, to the end of the operating theater, stopped at the wall, and slowly drifted back over my body. Below, the doctors and nurses removed their masks and gloves. Everyone moved away, except for the freckled, red-haired nurse I had seen at the gurney. She lingered, held my hand, and wiped my forehead with the mask she had worn.

I wondered what that red hair would look like, blown by the wind, if she sat behind me on the motorcycle. I, of course, wouldn't be able to see it, unless I could leave my body again and hover above the motorcycle cruising down the highway. She would have her arms wrapped around me, and her helmet would occasionally tap mine, as if we were clinking wine glasses or trading a message in Morse Code.

Just then I rose, melted, and passed into the ceiling. I was part of the ceiling for a moment and found interesting the rebar, concrete, and a conduit holding cables. There was a noise below, a scream, so distant I could hardly hear it. I dropped down through the ceiling, curious, although I still had no control over my motion. There was one brief glimpse of the room below. The doctors and nurses had returned to the operating table. They shouted and applied electric paddles to my chest. I felt nothing, melted, drifted through the ceiling to a room above, an office, where a woman filed her nails. A small bottle of polish sat on the desktop. Continuing upward, I entered a patient's room, floated through a mattress and urine-soaked pad toward the ceiling.

A mottled old woman was surrounded by a family as corpulent as she was, venting their anger and tears. A young priest administered the last rites. It appeared the old lady was exiting this world, too. She lifted an arm toward the ceiling. Apparently, near death herself, she saw me. Of course, no one recognized me as they followed her finger, preoccupied as they were, but she smiled, mouthed, "Have a good one."

I floated upward and through the next ceiling and another foul mattress pad. This time a young woman was tethered to the bed. She writhed and screamed. Nurses and orderlies tried to calm her. A young nurse was determined to insert a catheter. Normally, in a corporeal state, I would find this scene somewhat erotic, but I merely watched, without concern, vaguely interested. Without a penis I could sense, I had no interest in this young woman and her gaping shaved vagina.

I felt I was already dead because who wouldn't be aroused by a naked young woman, even though she appeared to be a drug addict? She had dark circles under her eyes and rotted teeth. Needle marks on an arm. The nurse tried again to insert the catheter into the writhing body.

"Hold her! Hold her!" the nurse shouted.

For an instant, she turned her head, as if looking at me, her brow beaded with sweat, then immediately returned to her task. "Damn it! Do you want your bladder to burst?"

But the girl's only intention was to escape. What monsters she must have seen in her drugged, delusional state. She struggled under the weight of the orderlies. Despite her restraints, she clawed and bit. I watched completely detached, not caring whether the medical staff was successful in inserting the catheter or her bladder exploded. Eventually, I moved slowly downward, through the patient rooms and office, into the operating room.

"We have a pulse," the redhead said.

I sank back inside my body and sweet oblivion. After days in an induced coma, and later with the help of opioids, I managed to sit in a bedside chair and then a wheelchair. My cracked ribs were the most painful condition, because it hurt to breathe. After two months in the hospital, including inpatient therapy and two more operations, I was discharged and walked with a cane. By then, the redhead and I were an item. Things with Matt the EMT didn't work out.

When I said Red—Her name was Margaret O'Reilly—and I were an item, more accurately, she looked in on me, shopped for groceries, helped with laundry, and cut my hair when it needed it. We weren't intimate yet, but she promised someday we would be. Another reason to live. Luckily, I could still get aroused when we kissed and petted like teenagers on my broken-down sofa. I could no longer do my job in a machine shop as a tool and die maker, so I cashed out my 401K, reinvested it, and eventually took a job as a telemarketer, working afternoons and evenings, calling people just home from their own shifts while they cooked dinner and fed their kids before soccer practices.

Needless to say, I wasn't popular. If they answered, I connected their phone to a prerecorded message. Then some evenings I would give them the spiel myself, looking for donations to this group or that, try to sell them a new credit card for which they probably wouldn't qualify. My work was easy, both physically and mentally, but boring. It didn't pay nearly as much as the machine shop gig, but I was able to collect a partial disability check and the corner market accepted food stamps.

When I returned home, Red was usually waiting. She liked to shower at my place so she wouldn't infect me with any microbes from the hospital. She had an amazing immune system but worried about mine. I never knew her to be sick, not even a sniffle. She'd be naked under my robe and cup her hand in my groin.

"You're still alive, babe. After your experiences, it's the only way I can tell, unless you're on top of me."

She called me *Babe*, and I called her *Red*. She had mostly moved in with me at that point, leaving her daughter more and more with her mother. We pieced together the details of my first and second deaths, from what I remembered, what we gleaned from newspaper accounts, and what she witnessed when I died on the operating table. As I grew stronger, we walked in a park and decided to go on a picnic one day in the early fall. We stopped at Bag It, a convenience store near the park, for a few things. I liked the Moon Pies that the store sold. The robber was already inside ahead of Red in the checkout line, a mask to ward off the COVID virus covering most of his face, we all presumed.

"Give me the cash," he demanded, brandishing a pistol as he stepped up to the counter. The cashier emptied the cash drawer in a paper bag and handed it to the thug.

"Where's the rest?" he demanded.

"That's all there is, man," said the cashier, a wide-eyed high school boy on the verge of tears. He stammered, "They collect the cash twice a day and just took the money."

Not content for this meager haul, the thief turned and grabbed Red's purse. She raked her fingernails across his face, and he sprayed three bullets into her chest. I ran for him from the magazine rack, with cane clutched overhead like a club. Holding the gun sideways, he sprayed more bullets in my direction. The robber fled on foot. Before passing out, I raised my head enough to see Red on the floor leaning against the counter, eyes open, blood and pinkish foam on her lips.

THE THIRD TIME

The bullets that hit me were slowed by the metal shelf, a bottle of olive oil, and my wallet concealed inside a denim jacket but still managed to enter my chest and kill me by the time I reached the operating room. I don't remember leaving my body the third time, but they told me later I was shocked back to life, thanks again to Dr. Wormwood.

The Mammoth Sentinel published the following brief newspaper article on Sunday:

MAMMOTH — A Mammoth Hospital operating room nurse died in a robbery and shooting at the Bag It convenience store on Milton Street late Saturday morning as she stood in line to check out.

Police said Margaret O'Reilly, 29, died in the hold-up. After emptying the cash register, the gunman also tried to steal O'Reilly's purse. She fought back and he shot her in the chest three times with a 9 mm. handgun. O'Reilly died at the scene, police said. Also shot in the melee was the nurse's boyfriend. Police have not released his name. He was taken to Mammoth Hospital. His condition was not available at press time. The investigation continues, police said. This was the third fatal shooting in the city this year.

I missed Red's funeral. Her family never liked me or contacted me after the robbery, claiming as a cripple I monopolized time Red should have spent with her daughter, who was now virtually an orphan. I found out later through Dr. Wormwood, of all people, on one of my interminable post op visits to his office that Red's ex had threatened to kill me, bully that he was, if he ever found out who I was. After a third brush with death, I wouldn't be much of a match against such a guy, or anyone for that matter, so I used my tool and die skills and an old co-worker's workshop when he wasn't home to fashion a new cane, one that concealed a stiletto knife, razor sharp, inside the shaft. A button on the handle's side allowed me to pull out the blade in a mere second. I practiced this move endlessly. In addition, I bought a small pistol, applied for a conceal permit, joined a shooting range, and learned how to shoot the gun. I wouldn't spray bullets like a Hollywood gangster but aim carefully at my target. I wasn't afraid of Red's serial philandering ex —he didn't seem to have much drive—but I planned to hunt down her murderer, crippled or not.

Another long, painful recovery ensued. I had my previously broken hip repaired and was on a ventilator for more than a week after an infection set in. This recovery was aided by a morphine pump implanted in my abdomen. And Madelyn Johnson, the girl I killed on the motorcycle. She sat on the hospital bed when I regained consciousness and wore a light blue sundress and sandals. Her hair was parted in the middle and held in place by matching daisy berets. Her fingers and toenails were painted. It appeared her mother had fussed over her with care, perhaps for a birthday party she would never attend. Her spectral hand rested on mine, although I couldn't feel it. She hummed a childish tune I didn't recognize.

"So, there you are," she said in her chipper, spectral, little girl voice when I stirred painfully. "It's about time. It seems I've been waiting here forever."

"How would you know what forever is like?" I managed to croak, doubting I could communicate with this diminutive phantom.

"Actually, I can tell you. Don't forget I'm dead."

She evaporated when nurses entered the room, apparently alerted that I was awake by the numerous monitors connected to me. Madelyn's sudden appearance did not surprise me. I'm a connoisseur when it comes to pain, and even if she wasn't a drug-induced delusion, she didn't appear especially malignant.

When I told the older nurse about Madelyn, she smiled, patted my arm on one of the few places that wasn't either bruised or had an IV said that I probably had ICU delirium, which should go away on its own.

The problem with Madelyn was that she never let me forget she was dead and tended to materialize at odd moments, sometimes out of thin air, often through a door or wall, without notice, already talking, so it seemed I missed the first part of what would be a conversation. If I whispered her name, she might or might not appear. When I woke, it was not unusual to see her on the edge of the bed. She even visited me while I was on the toilet. It appeared the dead had no sense of decorum, at least from my limited experience. That might be enough to unnerve the average person, but I took it for granted. After all, I had experienced death three times, be it ever so briefly.

After I got out of the hospital, Madelyn visited often. She wasn't much help around my apartment, but she was company. By now I was considered morbid and weird, a guy who died three times and talked too much about it and his murdered girlfriend. My family lived in another state and found it convenient to let me recover in peace now that I was out of the hospital. I could not drive yet and needed rides, so my friends found it more convenient not to invite me to get-togethers from which I would need a lift home. The only living person I saw regularly was Eddie, the delivery boy who brought groceries from the corner market. Even he beat it out of my apartment as fast as possible. When I wanted to see if I still had a job, it took a half hour for someone at the call center to answer. Imagine that. It seemed almost all calls were outgoing, but the manager said the turnover was so great there would always be a job for me, but I had to be ambulatory. In the meantime, I had Madelyn.

On one of her ghostly visits, I said, "I wish you could bring me some bourbon. You can take money to pay for it. Go in after hours, leave the money and bring a bottle back."

"Have Eddie do it. Buying booze is a little beneath me. Technically, I'm not old enough."

"He's not old enough, either."

"If you weren't so cheap, you'd have him buy two bottles of bourbon and let him keep one. That would make you both happy."

"The other thing is I scare him.," I said.

"You scare me, too, the way you limp around with that cane that has a knife inside. Don't forget, I'm a kid. If I were alive, everyone would say you're a bad influence. What if I brought back the wrong bottle and pissed you off? What if it was Scotch? I don't know what Scotch is, but my dad drank it. Now he drinks it more. My mom, too. I never tasted alcohol. You made sure my life experiences were limited. I can go through a wall, but I can't take a bottle or money with me. I can't even move a bottle across the store. I need more *time*."

"You're not much help."

"I'm learning. You'll see. As I grow stronger, you'll find me very helpful."

"As time goes on, I'll get stronger and won't need you."

"When you don't need me, I'll go away."

"Is that a promise?"

"That's a promise."

Then I didn't see Madelyn for a while. I didn't know whether the ICU delirium cleared, she was pissed, or she decided I no longer needed her help. Maybe she watched over another, like got a job as a guardian angel. Was it possible that jobs were handed out in heaven? I had regained enough strength to walk outside, do my own grocery shopping, even though I still depended on my cane. Eddie, the delivery boy, disappeared into a back room when he noticed me enter the market with my little cart, as if he feared I might ask him to help carry my bags, even though I was a good tipper.

With the help of the Mammoth Bus Line, I rode downtown and bought my own bourbon. It rained and I got soaked, but I enjoyed the two fingers I allowed myself. I missed Madelyn, though. She hadn't delivered on the "very helpful" she promised, but then she was just a kid, even if she was a dead one.

I was responsible for two deaths, Madelyn's, while I watched an undulating banana peel float through the air, and Red's because I wanted to go on a picnic, insisted on Moon Pies for dessert, sit on a blanket on the grass, and watch her hair shimmer in the sun. On Dr. Wormwood's advice, I went to counseling because the two deaths affected me greatly. Eventually, I realized there was nothing I could do now about either and quit the sessions. I was determined to find Red's murderer and scoured the newspaper and the television for police reports. I even bought a police scanner.

I walked through the Mammoth Arboretum one day. Upon emerging, I saw Madelyn at the playground across the street sitting on a motionless swing, as if waiting to be pushed. I crossed the street and stood outside the fence, motioning for her to join me. There were other children running around inside, laughing and smiling under their mothers' watchful gazes.

"Come here," she said. "Give me a push."

"Come out here and sit on a bench with me. It'll look creepy if I'm alone without a child and pushing an empty swing."

She considered my request for a moment, jumped off the swing, and walked toward the fence. I hobbled toward the gate to open it for her, but she disappeared into the fence and materialized on the outside. "You owe me a push," Madelyn said.

"Showoff," I said.

She giggled.

We sat on a bench across the street, facing the arboretum.

"I haven't seen you lately, Madelyn."

"I've been busy."

"Doing what?"

"You wouldn't understand. Stuff."

"I wish I could hold you."

"I can sit on your lap, but you wouldn't feel it. I'm lighter than a feather."

"That's okay, then. It wouldn't be the same. I wanted to apologize for killing you. If you hadn't thrown that..."

"That's okay. I know you didn't mean it and suffered for doing it afterward. It's different being dead. I miss my mom. There's so much I never got to do, but now I understand so much. Do you know what I mean?"

"No."

She smiled. "You couldn't."

As usual, when we talked at length or on a serious subject, Madelyn appeared almost solid in form. Today she wore a pink coat, a knit hat, jeans, and boots.

After an uneasy pause, I said, "I've been meaning to ask you. Have you seen Red in your...travels? I miss her."

She thought for a moment, watching my eyes fill with tears. "No, I haven't," Madelyn said. "I can tell you, though, she's at peace."

"How would you know? She'll miss watching her daughter grow up, get married, have her own kids, be a grandmother."

She twisted her mouth as if she wanted to continue, but said, "I can't express it You wouldn't understand. That's how it is. Unfortunately, that's how life is. Sometimes, we don't get to do the things we wanted to do, things that should have been accomplished, to have what we think is a full life. There are some things I can't talk about, and you wouldn't understand. Trust me."

We stared at each other from opposite sides of the bench. "I watched you walk. It looks painful."

"It is."

"The morphine doesn't work?

"It does, but not completely. The doctor said he might try a different drug."

She looked skyward for a moment and cocked her head. Then she looked into my eyes and smiled. "I'll talk to you soon," she said, and evaporated in front of me. I sat on the bench and cried.

Days passed without a sign of Madelyn. I whispered her name at night, hoping she would appear in my apartment as she sometimes had. I walked by the playground every day, hoping to see her. I desperately wanted to push her on the swing just to give her pleasure, make her feel like a real little girl. Once I thought I caught a glimpse of her in the sandbox, but it turned out to be a real girl. People are ridiculed for seeing ghosts. I felt foolish imaging a real girl was a ghost. Of all the times I felt she was a pain in the ass, babbling on about being dead, the friends she had, missing candy and cake, telling me endlessly what her favorite things were. Now I missed her desperately.

On one occasion we argued.

"Cake and candy would have decayed your teeth," I said.

"That's what dentists are for."

"All life isn't happiness, Madelyn. I can tell *you* from experience."

"Look at all I'll miss."

"You'll never have acne or be sick."

"I'll never have another birthday party. There're cool toys I'll never play with. I'll never have friends again."

"You have me."

"A cripple with a machete in his cane."

"It's not a machete."

"I'll never have a sweetheart. Go to my prom."

"You'll never have a broken heart, menstrual cramps."

"I'll never have sex. From what I heard through the wall, my mom liked it." She pointed a finger at me. "And so did Red."

Time passed. Eventually, I returned to the call center and fell into the old routine. Most of the other callers had new faces, but there were a few crips, like me, who remained because they couldn't find better jobs. Still, most people avoided me during their free time and whispered behind my back. The manager smiled and said little. Then one chilly night, Madelyn appeared at my desk. It had been months since I saw her.

"Come outside," she said. "I want to show you something."

"I'm working."

"Now!" she insisted in the little girl's voice that only I could hear and stamped her foot.

It must have appeared that I talked to myself, because the other callers sniggered and waved to their friends to watch. Surely, they thought my anticipated meltdown was about to unfold, and they wouldn't miss a second of it. A few pulled out their cell phones, ready to record the incident. I rose stiffly and followed Madelyn outside, leaning heavily on the cane with the pronounced limp that remained after the holdup.

"I'll be back," I called to the manager and made a motion over my lips indicating I needed a cigarette.

She knew I didn't smoke and worked through most of my breaks. She looked morose behind her desk and nodded. "Are you okay?" she mouthed.

I smiled back and nodded my head.

Madelyn walked through the call center glass doors and reached the sidewalk before me, where she waited. I followed and almost bumped into a man who walked quickly, a hoodie obscuring his face.

"Watch it, asshole," he said, "or I'll break that fucking stick over your head."

Although it had been almost two years, I recognized the gruff voice. "You!" I said, reaching for my pistol.

He turned around and looked at me, backing away. "I thought you were dead."

His face exposed, I saw he was Red's murderer. White lines remained on his face where Red had clawed him. He reached inside his hoodie and pulled out a gun. My pistol was already out and pointed. We traded shots, both emptying our guns like we were in a movie version of the OK Corral. I was hit in my left hand and chest. He was hit in the stomach, hip, and shoulder. People on the sidewalk fled, screaming. Workers in the call center crowded around the door to see what happened. The heavyset manager wormed through her employees and locked the door from the inside. I was screwed.

The man staggered toward me, punched my face, and choked me. I felt myself falling forward, released the cane's handle lock, as I had so often practiced, let the cane clatter to the sidewalk, and plunged the stiletto knife between his ribs. He gasped, staggered back, a look of surprise on his face, and fell. I collapsed on the sidewalk, propped myself on one elbow, a better position from which to breathe and watch him die. He raised himself but slumped immediately. I knew he was dead from the glazed eye stare he gave me.

Madelyn appeared at my side, no longer looking like a child but as a solid illuminated figure, still small but gold in color. She wore a knight's armor. I heard the call center door unlock and the employees spilled onto the sidewalk in hushed disbelief.

"For God's sake, somebody call 911!" the manager screamed. "Doesn't anyone have a phone?"

The crowd that fled surged back to surround me.

"Help me, Madelyn," I managed to croak.

She looked at me, sorrow in her eyes. "I'm sorry. I can't."

The man's body oozed a viscous fluid, dark and oily, putrid-smelling, not blood. It steamed on the sidewalk. His torso shook violently, his dead eyes rolled, and a long, forked tongue whipped about. Slowly a dark creature separated from the body. It was hideous with long snout, sharp teeth, and flailing tail. The creature bled puss where my bullets hit. and where my blade punctured his ribs. It appeared to grow stronger as it pulled away from the corpse and stretched its grotesque, malformed limbs. Some of the call center employees returned inside, nonplused by the event. The thing pulled out my blade and dropped it to the concrete.

Madelyn stepped forward with a golden sword and pierced the thing through its center. The beast howled and spit, its venom making small smoking puddles that bubbled the concrete. It screamed in an ancient, incoherent dialogue.

"Abomination, spawn of hell, return whence you came!" Madelyn cried in a voice that was now a woman's. She raised her sword and the creature impaled on it above her head. The demon shrieked in pain at it were pulled apart by invisible hands and disappeared in an instant into the night sky. Madelyn turned to me, leaned on her little sword. Then Madelyn, too, evaporated. The pus from the sword dropped to the sidewalk with a hiss. The little pile smoked and evaporated, too.

There was a sudden calm over the street. I heard sirens in the distance. The call center manager called from the door, "Won't someone help the pour man."

I felt someone loom over me. I turned and saw Red. She kneeled and took my hand.

MAMMOTH — A disabled city man was called a hero after he died in a hail of gunfire Saturday, but not before killing a man police said made bombs in his apartment and who allegedly shot and killed the hero's girlfriend two years ago in a local convenience store.

Police said Martin Sohl, 32, traded gunshots with Jerry Zola, 36, Mechanicsville, at about 7:30 pm outside the Maxim phone call center on Centre Street. Both men emptied their guns at each other before becoming embroiled in a fist fight. During the melee, Sohl pulled a homemade knife from his cane and stabbed Zola through the chest. Both men died at the scene, police said, Sohl of bullet wounds and Zola of bullet and knife wounds. Sohl was a call center employee. It was not clear whether Sohl worked Saturday night.

Police said Zola was the suspect in a two-year old robbery and murder investigation at the Bag It convenience store on Milton Street. Margaret O'Reilly, a Mammoth Hospital operating room nurse, died in that hold-up when Zola allegedly shot her three times. Police said they found bombs and bomb-making materials in Zola's apartment after the incident at the call center. The state police bomb squad and canine unit were called to locate and defuse the bombs.

Police said a block around Zola's apartment was evacuated temporarily while the bombs were dismantled and removed. Police said the bombs had the potential to be devastating. Included with the arsenal was a map detailing where charges would be set and detonated. Police said Zola became a suspect in the Bag It robbery when his DNA was

DISCOVERED ON THE VICTIM. POLICE SAID ZOLA MOVED OFTEN AFTER THE ROBBERY WITHOUT LEAVING FORWARDING ADDRESSES AND FELL OFF THE GRID. IT WAS ASSUMED ZOLA LEFT THE AREA, POLICE SAID. THE INVESTIGATION CONTINUES.

THE GHOUL

The meeting was set at midnight, inside the old cemetery in the caretaker's cottage a hundred yards behind the main gates, a location near the border between the Italian and Latino gang turfs. Tony "The Hook" and Joey "Freeze Pop" sat in their Lincoln waiting for the rival gang members to arrive. The engine purred. The night was cold, and the car's heater steamed the windows. The tailpipe sputtered small clouds of exhaust into the night air. Both men wore dark, heavy, overcoats and fedoras. Clouds crossed the nearly full moon in long ragged ribbons. Tony had been a less-than-successful boxer in his youth. Now, at seventy-two, Tony The Hook had a nose that could land a marlin, one he couldn't breathe through very well after one too many pummeling.

Joey had been a punk hitman before he rose through the ranks, a guy who liked to freeze his victims temporarily until he made them disappear. Their frozen grimaces, gnarled hands, and grotesque positions had always amused him. Joey Freeze Pop liked watching them thaw, waiting for a limb to finally move. Sometimes he snapped off a frozen finger or two just for fun. He would have kept such trophies on ice, or at least photographed them, but, after all, the stiffs and all their parts were supposed to disappear. No evidence.

The windshield fogged more when the old friends sighed in unison. Occasionally, they glanced at each other. They had worked together so long no words were necessary. They checked their revolvers *again*, worked the cylinders between their meaty fingers, and returned the guns to their coat pockets. Joey pulled out a flask and passed it to Tony, who took a swig and handed it back. Joey drank and replaced the flask inside his coat. Something rustled in a wooden crate on the back seat.

"It's okay, Fang," Joey said, softly. "Soon enough. You must be hungry. I think it's been a while since you ate."

The men smiled at each other.

Just when they thought the Latinos wouldn't show, and their night would be ruined, along with weeks of negotiations and delays, a loud car with shaded glass bounced into the cemetery in the distance, rolled up, and stopped beside the Lincoln going the opposite direction. A whimper of expectation came from the backseat. After a lengthy pause, all the Latino's car doors opened and four men stepped out quickly, as if the move had been choreographed. Both Italians reached for their guns.

"What the fuck," Joey said. "They were supposed to be alone."

"That's why Rocco's in the woods," Tony said. His deformed schnoz left him with the voice of a head cold sufferer.

"Still. Alone was the agreement," Joey insisted. "I don't like when they throw a curve. Ehhh!"

"What does it matter in the long run," Tony said and sniffed. "What's two more?"

"You bring enough meat?"

"Sure."

The Latinos' bling blazed in the dark even without much light, from their gold chains and medallions to the jewel encrusted Glocks stuffed in their waistbands. The two men who had been in the front seats, short and squat, wore oversized jeans and plaid shirts buttoned to the neck. They sauntered toward the Lincoln; their baseball hats cocked to the sides. Their car doors hung open. Hip Hop music blared.

Joey rolled down his window and hollered, "Hey, Carlo, how about turning that shit off. You'll wake the dead; God rest their souls."

"Watch what you say, Joey," said Carlo, the Mexican who had been a passenger up front. He looked around the dark cemetery. "It's no laughing matter." The man cocked his head toward one of the back seat passengers, who hurried back to the interior and turned off the music and shut the car doors.

"You two were supposed to be alone," Joey said. "What's with that?"

"We brought them to play cards with the guy you got in the woods. The one with the shotgun." The Mexican smiled. His gold teeth gleamed. "We saw him get out of your car. We've been here a while."

Joey crawled from behind the driver's wheel. Tony struggled out the other side. Both Italians were overweight and soon winded by their exertions. Joey coughed when the cold night air hit his lungs.

"Let's go inside the office," Tony said. "It will be warm. I had Iggy the caretaker make a fire."

"Your guy in the woods?" the Mexican said.

"He can stay there."

"My guys?"

"I don't care," Tony said. "If they're cold they can come inside."

"And the thing?"

"Backseat. Have your guys carry it inside," Joey said.

"I don't know if they'll do it. Superstitious." Carlo grimaced and cocked his head.

"They'll have to learn. Let them be useful."

Carlo nodded his head toward the backseat passengers. One man opened the Lincoln's back door, but recoiled immediately, slammed the door, and cursed in Spanish.

"He says it stinks inside," Carlo said. "Like the dead."

"You'll get used to it," Joey said. "Come on. I'm freezing my nuts out here."

Joey and Tony walked slowly, side by side, like an old couple, their shoulders touching at times, toward the cemetery office with a light on inside. Carlo and his driver followed. Their heavy shoes crunched over the frozen ground. The other two Mexicans hauled out the oblong box, some four feet tall and some thirty inches square and brought up the rear. As they approached the office, Iggy the cemetery caretaker, opened the door and let them all into the cemetery office. He led the way down a dark hall to his living quarters. The only light came from the kitchen with its grimy metal cabinets and was cluttered with newspapers, magazines, and dogeared paperback novels. An ancient vacuum stood in a corner. The cast-iron sink was full of dirty dishes. Shirts, pants, and coats hung over chair backs. The place smelled of dirty clothing and tobacco.

"Full house. I didn't expect a full house," Iggy said. "It's not even card night." He gathered the clothing in his arms and threw the pile on his bed. Then he waved the men to sit at a table over which a single light bulb with a metal shade hung from the ceiling. The Latinos placed the box on the floor near the Italian capos.

"Is this all the light you got, man?" Carlo said.

"Don't need much," Iggy said. "Just enough to eat and read by." He shrugged his shoulders. "I have cold beer. It's Corona."

"I'll try one," Carlo said. "And one for my men." He squinted at Iggy. The caretaker returned a blank stare.

"Not a problem," Iggy said. "I have lots. Like the stuff myself." He hurried to the refrigerator and opened the door. His long arms in their shabby sleeves disappeared inside the ancient cooler and pulled out a handful of bottles cradled between the fingers of his big, workingman's hands.

"Your hands are dirty, man," Carlo said. "No wash?"

"I was working in the garage before you came," Iggy said, somewhat embarrassed. He lowered his shaggy head and scratched his gray face stubble with grimy fingers. "There's always lots of work."

One of the Mexicans said something in Spanish.

Carlo turned, nodded at the man, and responded in Spanish. Then Carlo returned his gaze to Iggy. "Is that grave dirt on your hands?"

Iggy thought a moment, as if he tried to recall where his hands had been all day. "It could be," Iggy chuckled. He opened his arms. "When you think about it, almost all the dirt around here is grave dirt. It keeps getting turned over. I dig a grave, pull the dirt up, and fill it in. The dirt on the bottom ends up on the top. When it dries out the wind blows it around. Just now, before you came, I was working on the backhoe bucket. This afternoon, that backhoe bucket dug a grave. So, you tell me if it's grave dirt. I don't know."

Carlo's eyes grew wide. "We don't want no fucking beer touched by grave dirt." One of his henchmen, who had sidled up to the counter for beer, backed off and returned to his seat. They moved the chairs to the wall, away from the table before they sat.

Tony The Hook and Joey Freeze Pop traded amused glances.

"That thing stinks," Carlo said. "It smells like a mass grave on a hot day."

"I don't smell nothin'" Tony said.

"That's because you have a cold in the head," Carlo said.

"I don't got no cold," Tony said. "What's your problem?"

"You sound like you have a cold in the head," Carlo said, his voice rising. He rested his hand on the Glock in his jeans. "Stay away from me with your cold germs. I don't want to be sick."

"He always sounds like that," Joey said. He shrugged. "That's the way it is."

"That's the way it is," Iggy repeated. "Boys?"

"I'll take a beer, Iggy," Joey said. "Hand me one for Tony, too."

One of the Mexicans exclaimed something in Spanish and they all crossed themselves when the Italians took beer bottles from Iggy. Iggy sniggered.

"It's ice cold, gentlemen," Joey said after taking a swig of Corona. He raised the bottle toward them "You sure?"

The men shook their heads.

Joey shrugged.

After a long silence verging on uncomfortable, Joey said, "All right. Here's the deal. Through our intermediaries you should know that Tony and I want to retire. We're old, we're tired of the business. Prostitution was—I don't know—an honorable business years ago. Now, you have all this other stuff. Fentanyl, for instance. Put it this way. Years ago, you could sample the merchandise. Imagine spending an evening with a nice young lady. These drugs can kill you. I had a godson die from an overdose, rest his soul." Joey and Tony crossed themselves. "Nineteen years old. You would think he would be smarter."

"The point is?" Carlo said. He sounded annoyed. His tattoos and pockmarked face shined under the glaring light, appeared wet from sweat, despite the temperature outside.

Joey continued. "The point is we want to retire, live near a nice body of water, fish, enjoy life, watch our grandkids grow. We have enough money for several lifetimes. We don't need the business, and the business don't need us.

"We have one problem, though. Fang here," Joey said, pointing to the box. The box moved and the thing inside whimpered, as if it recognized its name. "Fang was entrusted to us for our safe keeping many years ago. We got the job because we were young men at the time. We had ambition. We don't know if *Fang* is its name. We don't know if it has a name. We call it Fang because when it breaks or loses a tooth, another grows back—almost immediately. There are rows of teeth inside its mouth waiting to move forward and chew. You'll see. Ever see inside a shark's mouth? Same thing. Now, we don't know how old Fang is."

"We suspect it is *very* old," Tony said in his nasally voice, nodding his head. His pendulous ear lobes swayed. "It seemed already old when we became Fang's handlers. But Fang looks the same today as he did the day we got him." Tony shrugged, twisted his mouth.

"You should have said no, go to hell, fuck you, when they gave you this creature," Carlo said. "That is what I would do."

Tony cleared his throat and took a swig of beer. "In our line of work, the words *no, can't, won't, I don't want to*...are not an option. We were given Fang to care for. *It was an honor.*"

"We don't even know if it's a male or female," Joey continued, after shooting Tony a glance. "You can't tell by looking at it. But it doesn't matter. Nobody ever, ever, man or woman, wanted to fuck it." Joey stared at the Latinos for a moment. "And Fang never seemed to want to fuck anything else, human or beast. Not once did he grab my leg like a dog. In fact, I never heard of another one like him, either, because I spent years doing research, especially after the internet came along."

The Mexicans tittered but fell silent when the beast rattled the box again.

"It got no sex organs," Tony interjected. "None. Nothing. All it got is an asshole to get rid of waste."

The Mexicans stared at the box's dark interior and seemed to marvel at the silent creature.

"I don't know," Carlo said. He stood and walked toward the box, a hand resting on his Glock. He peered inside the cage but soon returned to his chair at the table. "I don't see nothing. I don't know if I can take this. It's too supernatural."

Joey shrugged his shoulders. "Fang doesn't talk, *but* it understands most of what you say. You give him a command, he does it. For example, you say, 'Get in the box,' he gets in the box. You say, 'Get out of the box,' he gets out of the box." Joey raised an index finger in the air. "The important thing is it listens. It's very obedient."

"Obedient, huh?" Iggy said, smiling, patting the top of the box. "That's nice."

The Mexicans watched Iggy warily.

Joey continued. "The best thing about Fang is that he's a problem solver. I'm sure your organization, like ours from time to time, runs into a problem. You end up with a dead body."

The Mexicans sprang to their feet, shouted various oaths in Spanish. "What you talking about?" Carlo hollered. "We have no problems. No bodies. We're honest businessmen. Not like you guys."

"Take it easy, Carlo," Tony said. "Take it easy." He rubbed a finger across his great, rubbery nose, then raised his hands in front of him, as if surrendering. "Okay. Just suppose that sometime in the future you have a *problem*. Fang will fix it."

"How's he fix it?" Carlo said. "He dig graves?"

The Italians smiled at Carlo. "When Fang first came to our family many years ago, before Tony and I took care of him, before we were born, Fang was called a ghoul. Do you know what that is?"

"I know what a ghoul is," Carlo said, matter-of-factly. He stared at the Italians. "A ghoul eats bodies."

Tony smiled. "Now you see."

"Fang does such a good job being a ghoul, you'll have no evidence to take care of. Nothing. I repeat. Nothing. He will lap up the blood and body fluids, so the cops won't detect any with their ultra-ray lights, or whatever it is they use."

"Truly?"

"Truly, Carlo," Joey said. He placed a palm over his heart. "A couple of times we thought our asses were cooked."

"Cooked," Tony interjected, his breath whistling through his crooked nose.

"Cooked!" Iggy repeated, with more emphasis.

"We thought our asses were cooked," Joey continued. "In fact, the cops brought in their forensic team. Scraped the floors, walls, even the ceilings for samples. Dug splinters from the floorboards. Picked up crumbs with tweezers. Pulled threads from the carpet. They shined their special lights everywhere. There was nothing. Not even a fingerprint. Fang likes the oil on human skin. He can smell it a mile away." Joey raised a beefy hand and rubbed his thumb across the tops of his other fingers. His diamond-encrusted pinky ring shined in the light.

"Maybe more," Iggy chimed. "Maybe more than a mile."

"But..."

Joey continued before Carlo interrupted. "All you do is have to hide Fang. After he's finished with a cleanup, move him someplace where the cops won't find him. He fits in that box. He's been in it as long as we have him. It's the same box he came in. It doesn't take up no room. The box is sturdy. Never needed repair. Fang hasn't grown an inch in the whole time we have him. We never weighed him, but I'd say he never gained or lost a pound, except temporarily just after he feeds. The best part is he's dormant most of the time. Just sleeps. Wake him when you need him. He's always ready to go. He's always ready to eat."

"Almost too good to be true," Iggy said, sitting on the bed amongst his foul-smelling clothes. He scratched at his long, greasy hair.

Carlo said, "Exactly how often does he eat?"

"As far as I can remember," Tony said, looking toward the ceiling for a moment, scratching his flabby neck, "Fang went more than a year without eating that one time. But, if you have multiple problems, he can take care of that, too. Immediately. His capacity is amazing."

"Something must be left behind," Carlo said. "Something."

"He shits," Tony said. "Just like you and me."

"I'll bet he shits," Iggy added. "Does a bear shit in the woods? That's what I want to know." Iggy winked at the Mexicans along the wall. They whispered among themselves.

Everyone looked at Iggy momentarily. He cleared his throat and looked down.

"Listen, after he feeds, he shits the next day or so," Joey said. "He'll let you know. He has a special whine. Very high pitched. You let him out of the box and show him the bucket. He squats on the rim and shits. You dump the shit. Flush it down the sewer. Rinse out the bucket."

"It comes out like gravy," Tony said. "Not a lump. But, oh, does it smell!" He pinched the end of his great, curved nose with a thumb and index finger. "So, you got to flush it fast. Flush a few times to clear the drain out. Spray the area, too."

"This is not possible," Carlo said. "I can't do it. No matter how good Fang is. However, we will still take your turf...so you can retire to the water. Catch your fish. Despite our past problems and disagreements, we want to see you happy with your grandkids. Maybe you will have a need for Fang in the future. With a neighbor. There is always a problem."

"It doesn't work like that," Joey said, leaning toward Carlo, grinding his teeth. "Fang comes with the turf. If you're not interested, we will make the offer to somebody else. Out of respect, we asked you and your people first. After all, there was a time when a sit down like this wouldn't have been possible. There was trouble. Always trouble. We lost guys. You lost guys. Good men. Then we set a boundary. We agreed, and you agreed. Since then, we have had no problems. Not with the community. Not with the cops. Not between us."

Tony reached inside his overcoat. The Mexicans sprang to their feet with guns drawn.

"What the fuck!" Tony screamed.

"You go for your gun!" Carlo pointed his Glock at Tony's head.

"I got no gun," Tony said.

"We never pack," Joey said, spraying spit on the table. "We're above that. Besides, we're both felons. Having a gun could put us away for the rest of our lives."

"Look. I got a nice soppressata. I'm going to pull it out," Tony chimed, smiling at the men. Slowly, Tony pulled out a large, sausage-like piece of meat and lay it on the table. "Hey, I thought we'd have a little something to eat. This is imported. Good stuff. Iggy, you get the cheese board like I told you?"

Iggy approached the table slowly, raised hands above his head, and lay down a large wooden wheel covered with various cheeses. He showed the men his hands, palms and backs. "Clean now. I washed," Iggy said. "This is from Marcos, over in

Little Italy. Just like you told me, Tony." Iggy nodded and backed away.

The Mexicans approached warily, looked over the food. Meanwhile, Tony pulled a penknife from another pocket and stripped off the meat's casing. He worked deftly, like one accustomed to handling a knife and cutting food. He sliced the meat and fanned it out next to the cheese like it was a stack of playing cards.

"Help yourself, boys," Tony said.

The Mexicans backed away from the table.

"It's salami. You know sal...a...mi," Tony said. "Everything's imported."

"We're here for business," Carlo said. "Not food."

"Suit yourself. More for me," Tony said. He ate a piece of meat. Then he deftly used his knife blade to raise a slice of cheese to his mouth. His great hooked nose whistled like an oboe as he chewed in silence.

"I understand you might be intimidated by Fang," Joey said. He chuckled. "That's what a prosecutor said about us—me and Tony—years ago in court. We intimidated witnesses."

"Did you?" Carlo asked. He raised his eyebrows.

"Of course not."

"Did he put you away?"

"Not a chance," Joey said. "Fang put *him* away."

The two Italians traded glances and laughed. Tony choked on his cheese. His nose sounded like a flute.

Carlo smiled. "Can we see this Fang?"

"Of course," Tony said, regaining his composure. He blew his nose, snorting out a chunk of cheese.

Joey rose stiffly, walked to the box. "Here's the latch. Fang can open it himself from the inside when he wants to come out and stretch, but he prefers to remain inside. In the dark. He likes the dark."

Joey released the latch. The door swung open. A long-nailed claw grasped the door top. The Mexicans recoiled to the wall again. First one, then two clawed feet and thin, hairless legs stretched across the floor. Fang hoisted himself from the box.

"Diablo! Diablo!" the Mexicans repeated in whispers. Carlo backed away.

"He's harmless," Joey said. "Fang, say hello."

Fang looked at the Italians, then the Latinos, and made a guttural noise. Fang scratched its mostly hairless, dark brown body. The creature had amazingly thin arms and legs, with large hands and feet with sharp claws. Its head was big with a flat forehead, pointed ears, and large mouth. It stretched and yawned, revealing the rows of developing teeth behind its serrated first set. Fang looked blankly through two slits for eyes, reptilian looking.

"Maybe I kill this freak," Carlo said, pulling his gun, pointing it at Fang.

Fang showed no reaction.

"I don't think you can," Tony said. "I shot him myself years ago. The bullets had no effect. Twice we got caught in crossfires, once with the cops and once with some...competitors. He was hit again. Once in the head. Here he is today, good as new. When he was hit, the bullet pushed out after a day or two. You'd hear it hit the floor. Then the hole, wherever it was, healed over. Didn't even leave a scar."

"I don't like him," Carlo said. His men grumbled in Spanish with the words *diablo* and *fucking* sprinkled profusely.

"Fang's a little bit to take in all at once," Joey said. "Come here, Fang. Get up on the table, show Carlo what you look like."

Fang obeyed and stretched out on his back, exposing his stomach.

"He's going to want you to scratch his belly," Tony said. He laughed. "He loves it."

"Fuck that," Carlo said.

Fang stretched again. It watched Carlo. Then it turned its head toward the other Mexicans

"Hey, he's going to roll over your cheese," Carlo said. "He'll eat your imported salami."

"He's not interested in people food," Tony said, with a grin. "Just people."

Joey said, "Years ago we had a job at a funeral home. It was a busy place. Lots of burials. All legit, too. There was an accident. Somebody...died unexpectedly. The guy in charge of the funerals got nervous. He owed us a favor."

Tony sniggered. His nose bobbed up and down. He batted it back and forth as if to bring it under control.

"There was going to be a stink, so Fang was called in," Joey said, rubbing his beefy hand over the creature's stomach. Fang closed its eyes and sighed with pleasure. "We were watching this woman getting embalmed. Never saw such a thing before. She wasn't so old and had a big rack everybody wanted to see. Nobody was watching Fang, and he climbs into a casket and starts eating the stiff, hours away from the wake, embalming fluid and all."

"We didn't realize how hungry Fang was," Tony said, popping a handful of cheese slices in his mouth one at a time. "It was a while since he was fed."

Carlo looked at the Italians in disbelief.

"That's when one mess became two messes," Joey said, as if fondly remembering some childhood prank. "We had a hell of a time getting Fang off that corpse and out of the casket. He tore the liner to shreds."

"That's when *we* went to work," Tony said, picking at the end of his nose, pulling off a small scab, examining it closely before flicking it away.

Iggy watched the dried blood sail to the floor.

Fang licked its lips.

Joey looked at Tony and smiled like a loving old husband. "By the time we got Fang off the corpse, the only thing left was the head and part of a shoulder. To make a long story short, we put the embalmed head on the body Fang was *supposed* to consume, redid the casket liner, and put a big cover over the *new* body just as the grieving family arrived to see the corpse before the wake."

"In the end, everybody was happy," Tony said. "Fang gets results."

A man against the wall piped up, said something in Spanish.

"He wants to know what happened to the second head," Carlo said.

"Fang," the Italians said in unison and then smiled at each other.

"I don't believe your story and I don't believe *you*," Carlo said. He was agitated again and so where his men. "I don't think we have a deal. I don't think this foul thing eats bodies."

"No?" Joey pursed his lips for a moment. "Are you ready, Iggy?'

"Sure, boss," Iggy said. "It's time for the demonstration."

Iggy sang softly, "The thigh bone's connected to the hip bone," as he passed the table, patting Fang's head. The Mexicans followed him with pointed guns. Iggy returned to the refrigerator and pulled out a femur. The Mexicans along the wall recoiled and crossed themselves. Iggy took the bone to Fang and let the creature sniff it.

"That human?" Carlo asked.

"Sure thing," Iggy said. "Dug it up today."

"How long was it in the ground?"

Iggy twisted his mouth and scratched his head. "Not sure exactly. He didn't have a headstone. He had a special plot. Like the man says, this guy was buried on the QT."

Fang took the thigh bone in its hands and licked at the ball that fits in the hip joint. He mouthed the end and took a ferocious bite, as if the bone had been a celery stalk. The Mexicans scattered. One man fled down the hall and outside. Fang, meanwhile, chewed methodically, almost thoughtfully, as if trying to confirm a delicacy's ingredients. rolling the mashed bone around inside his mouth. Occasionally, Fang's large, flat tongue appeared between his lips momentarily to pull back an errant shred. After the bone was pulverized, Fang swallowed and took another loud bite. Iggy giggled. The Mexicans cursed. Within a minute, Fang popped the last of the bone inside his mouth, chewed, and swallowed.

"On a fresh bone, Fang will bite off both ends and suck out the marrow," Iggy said. "Then he'll bite down the bone shaft, split it open, and scoop out what marrow's inside with his tongue. He does enjoy the marrow. I'd say that's his favorite part. He also likes the brains and organs. Sometimes saves them for dessert." Iggy pointed a warning finger at Carlo. "Watch that tongue. Don't let him lick you, because it has little barbs that'll tear your flesh open. He did that to me once. It was all innocent, but I got a nasty infection. *Our* doctor said it was worse than MERSA. Took forever and a skin graft to clear up."

"I remember," Tony said, using his little knife to convey another slice of meat to his mouth.

Fang stared blankly at Carlo, then licked its lips.

"Why does he look at me like that?" Carlo said.

"He always looks like that," Joey said.

"Always," Iggy added. "We don't know if it's thinking or something else. Maybe he doesn't think at all."

Carlo approached Fang. "I can touch him?"

"Please do," Joey said. "He doesn't..."

"Bite?"

"Watch," Joey said. He waved his hand at Iggy.

Iggy approached the beast, placed his arms around him, and lifted Fang off the table. Iggy and Fang embraced. Fang nuzzled his head against Iggy's shirt. Iggy scratched its back. Fang closed its eyes again.

"All lovey dovey," Tony cooed. "Fang's better than any dog or cat. Low maintenance. Problem solver. Good company. No special foods. No vitamins. No veterinarians."

"Won't touch your soppressata," Carlo said.

"Exactly," Joey beamed. He picked up a slice of meat, offered it to Fang, then chucked it into his own mouth. "No people food. Only people."

Carlo approached Iggy and touched Fang. Fang arched his back.

"He likes your touch," Joey said, with a laugh. "You're a natural."

"He's warm, soft," Carlo said, examining his fingers.

"Always is," Iggy said. "You can take a bath with him, you know. If you're ever in the mood. Just have to watch he don't claw your jewels by accident. He moves his legs a lot in the water."

"That's doubtful," Carlo said."

"Well..." Joey stopped.

"Fang likes television," Iggy said, laughing, until his shoulders shook. "I plop him down and turn on reruns of *Green Acres*. Fang likes Arnold the pig. Gets all excited when the pig grunts. I was thinking maybe Fang understands pig talk."

Carlo eyed Iggy warily.

"I grunt for him, like Arnold grunts, and Fang gets excited about that, too. Claps his hands," Iggy said.

"Suppose I take this Fang," Carlo said. He looked at the other Mexican. One man shook his head no.

"Sure," Joey said. "You get Fang, the box, the shit bucket, and a dolly to wheel around the box after it feeds."

"So, Fang gets heavier after he feeds," Iggy said. "If he consumes a guy who weighs one fifty, he'll weigh an extra one fifty until he shits it out. That's what the dolly's for. If he eats a couple people, you wouldn't be able to lift him or the box. Put the box on the dolly first and let Fang crawl in the box. Hell, I'll even throw in some *Green Acres* CDs for him to watch. I seen 'em a million times."

"What if I decide I no longer want Fang?" Carlo said. "Suppose I no longer need him. What do they say? Down the road."

"That's simple," Tony said. "You give him to someone new. The way I am giving Fang to you. The same way Joey and me got him. Just make sure the new owner will have a need for Fang's *talents*, so he has food."

Carlo looked at the Italians. "Fang won't mind you give him to me after so many years, and maybe then I give him away again?" Carlo asked.

"As long as you find him a body occasionally, he won't give a shit," Joey said. "Like I said, he sleeps most of the time."

"We're definitely going to miss Fang," Tony said. His face looked sad.

"Definitely," Iggy repeated. "He's a good friend. Almost like a brother."

"And when do I take over your turf?" Carlo reached across the table and took a piece of soppressata. He raised an eyebrow and nodded as he chewed.

Iggy nuzzled Fang and whispered in his ear. Fang lay his head on Iggy's shoulder. The creature appeared to smile.

"Immediately," Joey said. "You walk out this door with Fang and our turf is yours. My people will get moved elsewhere. Supposedly, they're already packed. Tony and I retire to our beech houses. You establish the turf with your folks. Run it the way you want to run it."

"It's that easy?"

"It's that easy," Tony said.

"Too easy," Iggy said.

Carlo thought for a while. Inclined his head toward the glaring light bulb. "Okay. We take the thing," Carlo said. To one of his henchmen, he added, "Find Manny. He's outside. Get the car ready. Call my cousin. We'll need his car, too, for Fang."

The Mexican picked up a handful of cheese, stared down the Italians, walked down the hallway, and went outside. Iggy dropped Fang on the tabletop. Fang groaned, but Iggy kept a hand on the creature's shoulder. Iggy kneaded Fang's neck.

Joey walked toward the refrigerator. "All this talking makes me dry. Anyone else want a Corona?" The Mexican in the corner raised a hand, smiling. Joey opened the refrigerator door, slowly pulling the revolver from his pocket. "Where's your opener, Iggy?"

"I got it." Iggy released Fang.

Joey spun with amazing speed for a fat, old man, shot the Mexican in the corner. The bullet entered between the man's eyes and exited with a splash of blood and brains on the wall. A shotgun roared outside. Two quick shots. Fang tore out Carlo's throat in an instant. It pushed the chair over, climbed on Carlo's chest and slurped up the spurting blood. Fang stopped a moment, turned to Tony, seemed to smile, before returning to the drug dealer's corpse.

The fourth man stood frozen in fear. Tony pulled out his gun and shot the man at point blank range.

Joey pulled out two bottles of beer from the cooler, sat down next to Tony, and handed him a Corona. Iggy giggled.

Joey said, "We're going to need the dolly, Iggy. Want to get it from the car?"

"Well, old friend, it looks like we're back in business," Tony said, turning his attention to Joey who sliced more meat with his tiny knife.

Fang snapped off rib bones and chewed methodically.

"You have a banquet tonight, my little friend," Tony said, slipping on one of the dead Mexican's rings.

"Eat some cheese," Joey told Tony. "Don't let it go to waste."

"Back in business," Iggy said, smiling.

LAST DANCE

It had been an unusual winter, periods of severe cold and unseasonably warm temperatures. Spring arrived with torrential rain and more chilly weather. Warm temperatures finally moved in for Memorial Day. Flags, daffodils, and iris bloomed. At David Broomhill Cemetery in Mammoth, the First Brigade Band arranged their chairs on the paved road behind the cemetery's massive arched main entrance for its annual concert. The group, men and women of all ages and a few promising high school students wore crisp white shirts, black trousers, and old-fashioned baseball hats, even the women. Volunteers from the Presbyterian Church's various guilds stood in the sun to serve coffee and cake, soft drinks for youngsters, and bottled water. In addition, there were cakes and pies for sale, as well as various other souvenirs, histories of the cemetery, replicas of old-fashioned postcards, pamphlets about historical Mammoth, and the anthracite mining industry that put the city on the map.

There had already been soup, spaghetti, and hoagie sales the previous week. Proceeds from the annual fundraiser helped with the historic cemetery's upkeep. Captains of industry, coal barrens, heroes of the Civil War, as well as Mammoth's hoi polloi were buried on the rolling lawns dotted with century-old trees and a large variety of cemetery statuary. Tombstones reflected tastes in mourning and remembering the dearly departed for more than a hundred years. Obelisks and fenced in plots identified the wealthiest families' resting places. Among all the graves there appeared to be too many lamb and dove monuments, indicating children were interred. Some stones lacked names. Here and there were benches and shrubs, as well as mausoleums with locked doors. A shallow pond occupied the cemetery's lowest point. It was choked with water lilies and surrounded by cattails. Still, the flash of bright-colored koi was visible among the water plants. All the cemetery's run-off collected in the pond and eventually evaporated, soaked into the ground, or drained through some other unknown means.

On Sunday, there was a special church service in the cemetery chapel. Monday would bring the mayor with his patriotic speech on the holiday. Last year, a columbarium was dedicated outside the chapel to hold cremains. The old cemetery had become crowded, and it was difficult to dig new graves among so many large trees with their roots, and with nearby fragile old headstones. As a result, this year a new section was dedicated on flat land east of the pond. The new section had not been popular with some cemetery caretakers, because the ground remained wet for most of the spring. However, with space at a premium the cemetery council approved the addition and the land was cleared. A few graves already occupied it by Memorial Day. In such cases, death could not wait for the dedication.

Adjoining the cemetery 's new section was a Mammoth Area School District soccer field and a section of High Street. While the old cemetery was quiet with its trees and shrubs and cool grass, the new section, despite its seclusion, was sunbaked and noisy. Traffic was bothersome. Soccer games and practices were raucous. Kicked balls sometimes landed in the cemetery. In addition, the high school band practiced on the field, marching endlessly back and forth. At night the area was a haven for teenagers parking, booze parties, and drug deals. In short, the grass was tromped to dirt in many places.

Despite the noise and general soggy conditions in the new section, there was still some importance in being planted in the historic David Broomhill Cemetery, within a long stone's throw from, say, a Civil War general or a captain of industry, and the new plots sold briskly. After they were sold, the plots filled, too, as might be expected. Old age, disease, tragic accidents, and now fatal drug overdoses never took a day off.

AMONG THE DIGNITARIES present for the speeches on an overcrowded and haphazardly constructed dais were Earl Stoudt, owner of Stoudt Funeral Home, and Elmer "Digger" Bennington, owner of Bennington Home for Funerals, two of Mammoth's oldest institutions. The morticians moved from the dais, collected paper plates with cake, plastic forks, and Styrofoam coffee cups, and moved inside the chapel where it was cooler. Both wore dark suits and plain, dark ties. The two men seldom saw each other. They were rivals, really, as the city's only two morticians, although Digger got most of the Catholic dead and Earl buried most of the Protestants. It was a toss-up for Jewish deaths. So it was for nonbelievers.

"They ought to tap a couple half barrels," Digger said. "Charge by the glass. They'd have all the money they need to keep the cemetery going."

"Well, that's the thing. It's the church and you won't have any of that," Earl said. "But I'd rather have a pint of Chesterfield ale than this coffee. It would help straighten out this hangover."

Both men grinned. Digger pulled a flask from his suit's inside pocket, unscrewed the top, and passed it to Earl. The First Brigade Band started to play a crisp Sousa march.

"Irish?" Earl said.

"Embalming fluid. Aged seven years underground in an old whore."

The men laughed. Earl took the flask, drained the coffee from his paper cup, and poured in a generous helping. Earl passed the flask back to Digger and slapped him on the back. Digger poured the remainder of the flask into his empty cup.

"How was the cake?" Earl said.

"What cake?"

The men chuckled, looking around warily, not wanting to seem disrespectful inside the chapel.

They touched cups in a toast. "Cheers!" Earl said.

"To the new section. May we never run out of room."

The undertakers sipped their drinks.

"Speaking of embalming fluid," Earl said, "was there a salesman at your place last year or so trying to sell embalming fluid?"

"I bought a shitload of it," Digger said. "At half the price, you can't go wrong. The guy said it was developed for the military, for soldiers who died overseas."

"That's what he told me, too," Earl said. He raised an eyebrow. "Now that a lot of the troops are coming home, the manufacturer had a big surplus. Wanted to get rid of it."

"I have bodies embalmed with it already. In fact, they're in the new section," Digger said, pointing his Styrofoam cup toward the chapel door. "You use any yet?"

"I got some planted down there, too," Earl said.

"How's it working for you?"

"Fine. I didn't notice anything, but you know I took my niece into the business. She claims the corpses *feel different.* Their skin texture."

"I didn't notice anything," Digger said. "After all, they *are* dead, and I wear gloves."

"We all do. You can't feel the skin." Earl took a sip of whiskey. "Nobody's going to see an acne outbreak among the dead unless they decide to crawl out of the ground."

Earl laughed. "Well, my niece just got out of mortuary school. You know what that's like. She's still trying to reinvent the wheel. I suppose a more natural *feel* to the skin is better for the families who are all touchy feely with bodies. Had one last week where the family wanted to make sure I put on underwear they gave me for the body."

Digger smiled. "Was it there?"

"It was there. Boxers with red hearts. Go figure. Like I'd keep them for myself."

———

THE FOLLOWING MEMORIAL DAY, Earl and Digger again met in the David Broomhill Cemetery chapel over cake and coffee. Each had gained a few pounds, and their stomachs rested comfortably over their belts. The day was cool. The recently mowed grass was still wet after overnight rain. The new section had more forever occupants. The First Brigade Band played in the distance. A few women danced to a Benny Goodman tune, *On the Sunny Side of the Street*. A crowd listened to the band or walked among the tombstones on guided tours. Here was a Civil War hero's final resting place. A cannonball took off a leg at Gettysburg. Over there was a coal baron allegedly killed by the Molly Maguires.

"Still using that new embalming fluid?" Digger asked. He dropped his paper plate and plastic fork on the back pew.

"Sure. I even got more of it. Say, did you remember to bring your flask this year?"

"No, I had to cut back," Digger said, rubbing the small of his back. "My fucking liver's in rough shape."

"That sucks."

"Tell me about it."

"Better take care of it or somebody'll be pumping that happy juice into your veins. Get you ready for your forever home."

"Yeah. Got to take it easy on the hard stuff."

"What a mess on High Street," Earl said, pointing out the door toward the distant road. "They have it chopped up for weeks after the water main broke. I wouldn't want to live near here. No water at times. Jack hammer's blasting all day. Heavy equipment going in and out. The band marching all over that field, playing new tunes. Then soccer practice in the evenings.

Cars rolling in and out. Even the dead don't get any rest. I wouldn't want to be laid to rest there."

Digger swirled the remains of his coffee before draining the Styrofoam cup. "I hope they don't care," he said. "It's a mess all right. I thought the damn street was fixed, and then we got a funeral procession caught in it on Friday. People laying on their horns, screaming at one another, all so they can get the funeral over faster, go to the funeral dinner, and get drunk at the open bar."

"Same thing happened to me on Wednesday. Got a flat tire on the hearse trying to turn it around. I can't imagine anything worse. People were getting nasty. Thought I might pick up some new clients by the end of the day."

"I can think of something worse. Did you hear?" Digger said. "When that high pressure water line broke it blew out the side. Washed away the dirt underground, as far away as into the cemetery, before it broke out through the top and water spouted out on the street. Like a friggin' geyser. Part of that new section is undermined. It's going to cost a fortune to fix. I heard they have to probe for sink holes, then collapse the ground when they find one, and bring in fill by the truck load."

"I heard the same thing," Earl said. "I'm glad I'm not on the cemetery board anymore. I put my time in."

"Some of these graves might need to be exhumed and reburied. I wonder what the legal ramifications are," Digger said. "You know who's going to come out on top?"

"The lawyers, that's who."

"Look, there goes old Fenster. Let's get him over here and get his opinion."

"Who?"

"You know. Hal Fenster. He's only the senior partner in the city's largest law firm. Hey Hal, come here a minute," Digger called down the chapel steps. Then he said to Earl, with a wink, "We'll get this cleared up."

"Jesus Christ. Hal's dead. I planted him six months ago," Earl said.

The old barrister turned and staggered toward the undertakers, who stood frozen in disbelief. Fenster wore a dark, pinstriped suit, with the coat split up the back. He had been among the first to buy plots in the cemetery's new section after the cemetery board closed all burials in the old part, even though some family plots had unused graves. Fenster died about a year later.

Screams from below the chapel broke the undertakers' spells.

The first walking corpses to arrive at the fundraiser scattered one of the tour groups below the chapel as the undead staggered and lurched along the drive from the cemetery's new section. Their skin and clothes were soiled and shredded from digging to the surface through dirt and tree roots. Their eyes were milky orbs; their eyelids hung in tatters. The only noise they made came from their shuffling gaits.

Fenster locked on the two men in the chapel doorway. His mouth moved in noiseless words.

Digger took a step back into the shadows. Earl followed.

"It looks like he's trying to talk," Digger said.

"He's saying 'Quiet'," over and over again," Earl said.

Digger looked at him in disbelief.

"I learned to read lips when I was a kid," Earl said. "My brother is deaf."

Suddenly, a woman ran by screaming and it shifted Fenster's attention. She wore a brightly colored sundress and sandals. He lunged after her and in falling caught her leg and tripped her, bloodied her knees on the asphalt. She screamed louder. Fenster held her by the leg as she scrambled to stand, crawled up her body, flattening her to the ground, and bit a large piece of flesh from her bare shoulder. She screamed until he tore open her neck with his teeth. More dead attacked the screaming living. People ran in every direction with the dead in shambling pursuit. Soon the ground and gravestones were sprayed with fresh blood.

"Look at that," Digger said, pointing. "Lykens! He lost both legs below the knees to diabetes. Then he went blind. Look at him go now! You'd think he was on crutches."

Lykens chased a screaming girl of about ten, until running uphill she increased the distance and Lykens lost interest when she stopped screaming to catch her breath.

"He's chasing the noise," Earl said. "They're not eating the living, they're trying to shut them up. Don't you see—they want quiet! They all came from the new section. They're all embalmed with that army fluid we bought."

The men stared at each other in disbelief with open mouths and sweating faces.

Meanwhile, members of the First Brigade Band scattered. Most still carried their instruments. Their crisp white shirts were blood-spattered. Earl ran to the bottom of the steps and waved to anyone who would notice to come to the chapel. Some saw him and zigzagged among the tombstones and the dead to follow his directions. Others ran for the wall that ran for blocks along Market Street and climbed over it to safety. The large main gates had been closed, and a white tarp was attached to it to serve as a movie screen for an after-dark showing of famous Disney cartoons. The screaming crowd was left to exit the cemetery through a smaller gate, single file, while the dead picked them off. Soon, fleeing people had to clamber over their own dead to escape the cemetery.

"Over here! Over here!" Digger called.

"Quiet, Digger. You'll attract the dead. What are they, anyway? Zombies?"

His call did attract the dead, but it also convinced the remaining living to run toward the chapel. The young outran the dead easily, jumped over those who writhed on top of the living, and climbed the chapel steps. The elderly were cut down summarily and bitten savagely until their screaming stopped. Most of the band was able to thread their way among the dead. Even a tuba player, red-faced and panting, was able to escape with his instrument. As the living became fewer, either through escape or murder, the dead turned their attention to the chapel.

Earl herded the last of the living up the chapel steps and inside. Then he and Digger pulled the wooden doors closed and locked them from inside. The living sobbed. Some called to lost family members. A few were reunited, but most were left to scream in anguish, in disbelief. Others kneeled in the pews and prayed.

"Quiet. Quiet, everyone," Digger called with his booming voice. "I need your attention!"

The crowd silenced, although a few who sat on church pews continued to sob. Even the prayerful looked up at the men.

"Everyone knows Earl," Digger said, pointing. "He has an

idea I want you to hear. He has a deaf brother and knows a lot about acoustic stuff."

Earl stepped forward. He pulled his tie loose from his throat. "This might seem a little farfetched, but unless anyone has an explanation, I think these dead people weren't too happy with the new section."

"Do you think they cared?" one man said.

"No," Earl said. "I don't. But I imagine most bought plots down there before they died. What they didn't anticipate was all the noise from the soccer practices, the band, the traffic, the partying at night, you name it. Then we had the water main break and all the noise and confusion associated with that. I think that was the icing on the cake. That water main break."

"That's ridiculous," a woman said, nursing a bite on her elbow. "Have you men been drinking?"

Others in the crowd voiced their disbelief.

"Just listen," Digger boomed. "Earl can read lips. He thought old Attorney Fenster was saying 'Quiet' repeatedly."

Jeff Partridge, head groundskeeper, peered out a window. "They're all standing around the bottom of the steps. Maybe twenty of them. Their mouths are moving. I can't read lips, but they seem to say the same thing. It looks like it might be *quiet*."

Earl spoke up again. "What I'm proposing is we stay as quiet as possible. They might go away. Let the authorities round them up. Who knows? Put them back in the ground. They're already dead."

Several people piped up, saying they had called 911.

"What I don't understand is what brought these folks back to...*life*, if you can call it that," Jeff said. "What animated them."

Digger looked at Earl, gave him an elbow in the ribs.

"We don't know," Digger said.

Jeff continued his watch out of the window. "And what about the people who got bit. Are they going to turn, like what happens in movies?"

There were gasps among the crowd. Individuals inspected bite marks on their arms and legs. Showed them to others.

"Don't go jumping to conclusions," Digger said. "This isn't a George Romero movie. Not that a bite can't get infected like any other bite. But nobody's going to *turn*."

The crowd breathed a collective sigh of relief. A few even applauded.

Suddenly, a horn tooted. A fifteen-year-old Brian Farber turned crimson, admitting his guilt. "I wanted to make sure my clarinet wasn't broken. I dropped it twice out there. My mom would kill me if I broke this thing. It's practically new."

A few in the crowd tittered.

"They heard it," Jeff said. "They stopped mouthing. Try it again."

Brian played a few notes of *Eleanor Rigby*.

"They like it," Jeff called, grinning. "They're actually smiling. Play some more. See what happens."

A half dozen band members, their uniforms torn and splattered with blood, huddled together near the main doors, started to play *Eleanor Rigby*. As soon as the music started, Jeff called, "They're shuffling their feet. They're backing away from the steps."

"Keep playing," Digger boomed. "Let them have it!"

"They moved to the asphalt turnaround out front," Jeff said excitedly. "I think it's working. The dead aren't attacking anymore. Their letting the people get away, those that are still alive."

Digger and Earl moved to the chapel door and opened it a crack. The dead had paired up and stood facing one another, as if waiting for something new. Digger opened the door fully. "Over here," he called to the band members. "Play over here in the open door."

"Try some dance music," Earl said. He opened the other chapel door, making a large space. Reluctantly, the remaining band members crowded into the open doorway. They looked at one another furtively. Whispered back and forth. Shrugged. Nodded.

One voice called out, "Okay. One, two, three."

———

THE BAND STRUCK UP *STOMPIN' at the Savoy*. The dead looked in unison at the chapel, smiled, nodded to their partners, and danced. It wasn't pretty as they leaned against one another and staggered in circles. Some couples were paired as men and women, others as two women or two men. They moved slowly, laboriously, grinning. Couples bumped into each other and went spinning off like colliding pool balls. Their heads and elbows bobbed. Even Lykens had found a diminutive child partner and whirled around the outside of the assembled dead at a faster pace, his short legs moving furiously, grinding on the asphalt, leaving a trail of bone, flesh, and embalming fluid.

Earl and Digger stood behind the band members and looked at each other with relief. Multiple sirens were audible in the distance. While the dead danced the murdered lay bloody and scattered about the cemetery grounds and were piled in a heap near the small gate they tried to escape through. The bloody bitten limped and crawled to safety.

When the song finished, the band huddled again to select another tune. *Don't Be that Way.* The members were amazed at the rapt attention their playing received. The band played on. The dead danced. Their clothing—not meant to be worn by the ambulatory—sloughed off the bodies like skin shedding snakes. Soon, most of the dead were naked, revealing postmortem incisions, surgery scars, disease-wasted torsos. Most of the survivors looked away. Finally, before the band could agree on the next song, the dead walked away from the chapel in unison, traveling in a slow-moving, shuffling herd, back to the cemetery's new section. They dispersed once they reached the parched lawn and dropped to their hands and knees. Crawling the last few feet, they slipped into the holes they emerged from and disappeared, clawing at the loose earth to cover themselves. Some scratched their heads, pulling off wigs that fell to the ground, as if trying to remember what graves they came from.

A few dead had escaped the cemetery, following potential victims who still screamed. One lay flattened on the street like a dead squirrel after it was struck by a box truck. Another was two blocks away walking up Tenth Street toward Sharp Mountain, her split funeral clothes sloughing off, apparently seeking the quiet she couldn't find in the cemetery. Or was she returning to a home whose memory still lingered in the dead but animated brain cells? Others may have escaped, too, now on their way to new *lives* among the living. How long they would remain animated was impossible to tell.

THE BUS STOP

It seemed like ages since I talked with my father, so I decided to stop and see him. The best place to find Dad was in the tavern he owned on Oak Street in Mammoth. Dad was married to his business and was always there. The bar was open for long hours Monday through Saturday. On Sundays he cleaned and let in a few of the regulars who wanted to play pinochle. Dad joined them when they needed another hand, which pushed his cleaning back into the evening hours. I arrived on a cold night made chillier by blustery winds. It was already dark, and the place looked closed as I viewed the front from across the street. However, as I approached the building there appeared to be a sliver of light above the drawn curtains, an indication Dad was still there. Dad closed early some nights when business was slow. He would rather clean up than wait for a few barflies to nurse their drinks in the hope some generous patron would come in and buy them another round. As Dad always said, some guys could drink any *given* amount.

Dad was a stickler on cleanliness and organization. I always thought years in the Army had ingrained those qualities. The bar surface was never sticky. The floor was always clean. His glassware sparkled. The bathrooms were spotless. The shelves that held assorted spirits were dusted and the bottles wiped, lined in perfect rows. Even the unseen coils through which the draft beers were cooled as they wound around and around on their way from barrel to tap were cleaned weekly. Everyone loved his beer's exceptional, clean flavor. Dad's bar was the type of place a woman alone could stop after work for a drink and not get hassled by some pick-up artist. The F-bomb was frowned on, especially when women were present. The regulars all knew this. It was an unwritten code. A stranger was put in his place if he swore in the company of women. Members of the Mammoth Ladies Club, all dolled up, often stopped for a drink and a chat after their monthly meetings. The juke box sat in a corner and played big band tunes and love songs by such artists as Dean Martin, Andy Williams, Patti Paige, and Perry Como. In short, the atmosphere was always friendly and inviting.

I climbed the four concrete steps and found the door locked. Luckily, I still had a key on my keyring. The lock was a little sticky, something Dad had intended to fix for years, but he was the only one who opened it and, I suppose, over time got accustomed to the stickiness. With a little key giggling, the lock opened. I pushed open the door. It was sticky, too, and needed some extra force to move. A shot of WD40 on the creaky hinges wouldn't hurt. I would tell Dad as soon as I saw him. Inside, the light was low, illumination from the light across the street. I called Dad, but there was no answer. I thought he might be in the basement changing a kicked beer barrel. However, the basement was dark when I opened the door to the steep steps that led down. There was an electric breaker box inside the basement door that controlled most of the lights. I flipped a few breakers, and the bar lit up. Afterall, I had helped Dad run the place for a while a few years back after he had his first heart attack. What was supposed to be a short-time gig tending bar turned into a long-term one until he could return to work full time, so I knew where everything was and how it worked.

With the lights finally on I was shocked to find the bar an incredible mess. The floor was dirty. The bar top was dusty. The bottles of spirits behind the bar were gone. The shelves were grungy. Some were sticky looking, as if bottles had tipped and their contents spilled. I opened the beer taps, but nothing came out—not even air. A taproom without beer. Glasses on the sink were begrimed. Some had lipstick and fingerprints. Several were tipped over on their sides. One was broken in the sink. And there was no water in the faucets.

I called Dad again and still got no answer. I noticed the beer cooler and Dad's antique cash register, which printed out a thin strip of paper with each transaction, were gone. Had Dad been robbed and the bar trashed? The juke box was even gone and, in its place, a rickety wooden stepladder leaned against the wall. Then I noticed it was cold inside, even with my coat on, although not as cold as outside with the wind that howled around the door.

The stoker must be out, I thought. That's why it's so cold. Dad let the fire go out. I returned to the basement door, flicked on the light downstairs, and made my way down the old wooden steps. A single light bulb illuminated the basement, hung from the low ceiling. The boiler was cold. No fire. The tenants above the bar would be furious. You could never please them. Old Mrs. Hendricks was always cold. Mr. Campion was hot, kept his windows open all winter. Dad controlled the heat in the apartments from a thermostat in the bar. Dad babied that old boiler. I can't understand how he let the fire go out. Now I'd have to make a new one. I turned to the coal pile but found there was little more than a bucket's worth of coal there. Dad was slipping. He hadn't ordered coal. Or beer. The usual line of kegs was missing. I returned upstairs and turned off the basement light.

There was a knock on the front door just as I reached the bar again. Normally, Dad never opened the door unless someone knew the code—three fast raps, three slow ones, and then two fast ones. It could be a state Liquor Control Board agent intent on slapping a fine on Dad for some idiotic impropriety, whether real or imagined. Still, I went to the door and opened it a crack. Two men in long overcoats and hats stood there.

"You open?" asked the smaller man.

"No. Not now," I answered.

"Can we come inside for a few minutes," the taller man said pointing an arm across the street. "We're waiting for the bus and it's so cold out here."

"I suppose," I said, reluctantly, "but I plan on leaving in a few minutes. Actually, I was ready to go when you knocked."

"Just for a minute, sport?" the shorter man said, removing his hat, almost reverently, as if he had just entered church, revealing a bald, shiny head. "Until we get warm. We'll leave when you want to go. We won't hassle you. I promise. The bus should be here any minute. Probably before you turn off the lights."

"It stops across the street at the corner," the taller man said.

"I know where it stops. Over by the bench," I pointed.

"We were on the bench," said the shorter bald man with a bulbous nose. "But it was like a wind tunnel." He thought a moment and tugged on his nose with its large pores and blue veins. "It's funny you didn't see us."

"Did you see me?" I asked. "I'm here only a few minutes."

"No. Can't say I noticed you," the short man said replacing his hat. "It's like a tempest directly from the arctic and blowing dirt in your eyes and garbage and leaves along the sidewalk. It gives a grown man the willies."

"That's the truth," the taller man said, wiping his long, dripping nose with a nicotine-stained finger. "Say, do you suppose we could get a little brandy or a schnapps to warm our bones?"

He smiled with worn, yellow teeth. When he unbuttoned his coat, I imagined for an instant his stomach and chest were covered with bullet holes and blood seeped through his clothing, but he folded his arms almost immediately, which closed the overcoat. No one could walk around, seemingly painless, riddled with bullets. My eyes were playing tricks on me, I thought.

"It appears to be all gone," I said. "I don't think there's a drop in the place. I can't even offer you water. Even that's turned off. Sorry."

"Not a problem," the big man said. He walked to the window and parted the curtains an inch to look out. "The bus will be along directly, I suppose."

"It's noted for being punctual. That's what I was told," the shorter man said, with his own decayed smile. "Are you waiting for the bus, too? How'd you get in here anyway?"

"My father owns the place. I was looking for him. Just to chat. But he's not here."

"I see," the shorter man said, as if there might be a more sinister reason why I was in the building, a bar without booze, not even water. He raised his head to look at the ceiling but lowered it almost immediately. For a second his throat appeared to have deep, red ligature marks. I blinked and his neck appeared normal.

"Where are you guys off to?" I said, more interested in changing the subject than I cared about their destination. After all, they looked a little suspicious themselves, two seedy looking middle-aged men traveling together, with or without death marks on their bodies, although the short one seemed harmless, even dull. The taller one, however, seemed to be plotting something. His reptilian eyes darted around the bar, as if in search of something valuable he could carry away.

The men looked at each other and then back at me. The tall man opened his mouth, as if to speak, when there was a knock on the bar's back door, which led to the yard, an alley, and the street behind the building, an entrance only a regular would know. However, there was no familiar coded tap. I walked to the back door cautiously, wondering if in an instant it might be kicked in. There was a small diamond-shaped window about eye height in the door with a wooden cover that attached to the door at the top with a screw. The cover could slide to the left or right to see who stood outside. I moved the cover, but it was dark outside. I flipped on the outside light and discovered a man, woman, and a girl standing bundled against the cold. The girl, who was about twelve, I imagined, lifted her mittened hand to knock on the door again. The muffled rap was barely audible inside.

"Who is it?" the larger man wanted to know, as if people outside might cause him a threat.

"It's a man, woman, and child," I said. "A family."

"Aren't you going to let them in?" the shorter man said. "The kid must be frozen."

"I'm really ready to go," I said. "I can't stay here all night while you wait for a bus. I don't want to deal with more people."

"Maybe they need help or want to make a phone call," the shorter man said.

"There was a pay phone there, but it's gone now. You can see the mark on the wall where it was," I said, pointing.

"Think of the kid," the short man whined. "The bus will be here soon. So, it's a little late."

"Maybe someone handicapped got on board," the tall man said. "You know. It takes a while to get a handicapped person on a bus. The steps are hard to climb. Maybe it's someone who has a walker or a wheelchair. That takes even longer to get someone like that on a bus. Sometimes the driver has to get off and help the person, take care of the walker or wheelchair. That can take several minutes. And sometimes the driver isn't in the greatest shape. He'll need to catch his breath. That all adds to the time. Every stop he makes a little time is added. The next thing you know the bus is behind schedule."

"I don't know," I said. "This doesn't seem right."

"What kind of kid is out there?" the tall man asked. The men joined me near the back door.

"What do you mean?"

"Boy or girl?" They tried to look around me through the little window.

"Girl."

The tall man lifted his eyebrows and smiled at the shorter man. "Girls are usually quiet," the tall man said. The short man nodded in agreement. "I doubt she'll be any fuss. No loud talk. No running around like a boy might do. You know how boys are."

I stared a moment at the two men smiling at me. I didn't smile back.

"What could it hurt?" the short man said. "By the time you find out what they want, the bus will be here."

"I'd bet on it," the tall man said. "Are you a betting man?"

The three people outside were already walking away when I opened the door. They turned quickly and came back to the door. "We're looking for the bus stop," the woman said.

"Which bus?" I said.

They looked confused.

"There are several. There's the local loop and the long haul."

"The long haul," the man said. "We're not staying local."

"The stop is across the street," I said, pointing toward the front of the bar. "How did you find this way in?"

"We got lost. The directions we got were confusing," the man said. "Make a left, a right, another left, then finally a right. We lost track. We were walking in circles." The man moved his hands in circles in front of him. We saw two men sitting on a bench. We were going to ask them for directions, but they disappeared. We walked some more and then Mary saw a pinpoint of light in the distance through your door. So, we came here. A point of light in the dark is reassuring. It gave us hope."

"You saw us," the short man said, excitedly, pulling his rubbery nose with one hand and pointing his thumb on the other hand at his partner. "We're waiting for the bus, too. You *were* at the bus stop. This gentleman left us in to wait inside out of the cold. What a prince! The bus should be here shortly. You can wait, too. Right, chief? They can wait?"

"Thank goodness," the woman said, rubbing her gloveless hands, pushing by me without making eye contact. The man and girl followed quickly. "Mary is frozen! So am I. Thank you so much. You are too kind."

"Thank you, sir," the man said with a laconic nod of his head.

The man turned his head toward the men, and for a moment I thought a part of his skull was blown out behind the left temple, but it was dark near the door and when he stepped into the light his hair merely seemed ruffled by the wind.

Mary moved to a table, pulled out a chair, wiped off the dust on the seat, and sat. The rest of the family followed.

"There's a lot of dust on those table and chairs," I said. "I hate to see you get dirty."

That's okay," Mary said. "I feel like we've been walking forever. I really need to rest. I can't wait to get settled into the bus. They always have such comfortable seats."

"I hope it has a good heater," the girl chirped.

The two men smiled and sat at the table next to the family.

"I'm sorry. I can't offer you a drink. The place is empty. Even the water is turned off. And the bathrooms..."

"Not a problem," Mary's father said. "We're happy to be out of the cold. Maybe the bus will have a bathroom."

"Maybe it will," the short man said, pulling at his nose again.

"I must tell you, I didn't intend to stay here this long. I have things I have to do tonight."

"The bus will be here directly," the tall man said. He pulled a handkerchief from his back pocket and dabbed at his nose. The cloth appeared to be blood covered.

I blinked and the handkerchief appeared yellow again, as it had at first. He returned the cloth to his pocket. The tall man stood, walked to the window, and parted the curtains to look outside, revealing a dirty mark from the chair on the back of his overcoat. Mary sniggered and looked at her mother. The short man smiled and suppressed a giggle. He winked at the girl. Mary's mother raised a finger to her lips. Her coat sleeve rode up her forearm, revealing a large, whiteish scar on her wrist. I looked at Mary and imagined for an instant her right eye was missing, a black hole in its place. I blinked and Mary's eye was back. Mary smiled at me, conspiratorially.

"What is this place?" Mary asked in her sweet, high-pitched voice.

"It's, or it was, a tavern. A place where adults would go..."

"To drink alcohol?"

"Yes. And to talk and play music. Sometimes they played cards. There was a juke box over there that had records. Mostly oldies."

"I like oldies," Mary said. She looked around, scanning the four walls and ceiling, a smile on her face as if she were enchanted by the place. "I've never been in a real tavern. And I've never had alcohol."

"You have time for that," I said, smiling at the girl.

The short man tittered. Mary's mother coughed. Her father made a short, strange sound.

"Is this your tavern?" Mary said.

"No, it belongs to my father," I said, my voice trailing off at the end, as if perhaps I had been caught in a lie.

"And where is he?" Mary smiled again.

I thought for a moment. The group looked expectantly at me. "He's ... dead. He died some time ago," I said, finally. My head felt strange, and I had to rub it. First my scalp, then my eyes, and finally the back of my neck.

"That's too bad," Mary said.

"You didn't tell us that," the tall man said, turning from his lookout post at the window.

"I believe I just realized it now. I feel somehow dazed."

"It looks like it was quite a place," Mary said.

"It was. It was the kind of place you could leave your troubles outside, whether it was from work or home. You could leave money on the bar, say a twenty, go to the bathroom, and return to find your money in the same place. There were no political arguments. Period. You could bring a girl or your wife in and not worry they'd be offended by something someone said or did. No crude jokes, unless they were whispered to the person next to you. You could spend the night talking or sit quietly with your thoughts. People respected that. They respected your mood."

"It sounds like you could bring a kid here," Mary quipped. She smiled broadly.

"It was. Dad had a big selection of soft drinks, root beer, and even sarsaparilla. I pretty much grew up here. All the regulars knew me. Knew what kinds of grades I had. Knew my batting average when I played baseball. They were like family."

For a moment I imagined the tavern was filled with all the old customers. There was laughter and music played on the juke box, Tennessee Ernie Ford. A Phillies game was on the television, the sound turned down, the announcer's words typing out on the screen bottom in closed caption letters. Dad was behind the bar, white haired, white shirted, tapping a draft beer. The glass he held sparkled. The floor was clean. Members of the Mammoth Ladies Club sat among us at the tables, their drinks resting on paper coasters on clean white linen table-cloths. Dad served the beer, collected money off the bar, and rang up the sales on his antique cash register. He scanned the bar for empty drinks. Finding none at the moment, he sat on a barstool he kept behind the bar and smiled broadly. These people had come here because the place was friendly, the beer ice cold, the taps and coils clean, and the bathrooms spotless. Their kind of music played on the juke box. Frank Sinatra crooned now. No one was out of line.

I smiled at the thought. A tear welled in one eye. It had been a long time since I thought of all these people my family called friends. All gone now. Dad waited on them for years. Even on a slow night when he was occupied with his crossword puzzles and cryptograms, he kept an eye on the glasses and rose to fill them as soon as they were drained.

"She's here!" the tall men shouted, his voice echoing off the bare walls for a second.

The others, except for Mary, rose stiffly and filed toward the door. I hurried around them, unlocked, and opened the door. They passed by me, again thanking me for the chance to wait for the bus out of the cold. The bus stopped across the street. Once outside, they stood on the sidewalk looking at me. Mary's eye was gone again. She smiled at me. The bus driver opened his side window and beckoned them with his arm.

"Points west," the driver called. "Come on. Can't wait all night. I'm already behind schedule."

The tall man winked at me. "What did I tell you. A handicapped passenger. I should have made a bet. They should sit up front, but they're always huge and want that big bench seat in the back. It takes them a year to walk back the aisle. Have to squeeze through. Jostle the other passengers. The bus must wait until they're settled. It's the law, I think. The bus can't move until everyone is seated." He made a clicking noise with his mouth. Blood dripped from the holes in his torso and fell on the ground.

The group edged toward the curb. The bus waited. The driver beckoned again with his arm. I walked down the steps to the sidewalk to say goodbye.

"Will you come with us?" Mary said, spritely. "You can tell me more about your father's tavern." She blew on her fingers and pulled on her mittens. The streetlight overhead was out, but the one farther down the block cast a wan illumination over the group, making their lethal wounds visible again.

"I have to close up here and build a fire in the boiler. There are tenants upstairs. Order more coal for tomorrow."

"Really?" Mary said.

I walked toward her to inspect the hole in her head.

She pointed back to the building.

I turned and saw an empty lot where the tavern had always been. The ground was leveled, except for the occasional brick or stone that stuck out at an odd angle. Pieces of paper blew across the flat surface. I looked back and found Mary's eye was back in place. She was pale and smiled.

"What the heck. I'll ride along for one stop." I laughed suddenly. "You know, I don't remember how I got here. I'd have to look for my car. I don't see it anywhere on the street."

The others in the group, even Mary, threw back their heads and laughed, as if they believed I didn't have a car. The short man patted my back. "You can ride as far as you want," he said, warmly. "We better get going before that driver pulls out. We don't want to walk on a night like this. Who knows when another bus will come along."

There was no traffic within sight, and despite the driver's encouragement, we took our time crossing the street. Just as the tall man had predicted, there was a mangled wheelchair in the aisle by the first seat we had to squeeze past, and a large man spread out on the bus's back bench seat. He was silent and glared at us. The tall man gave me a nudge in the ribs with his elbow and made the clicking sound with his mouth. We found seats up front. Mary's parents sat together. Mutt and Jeff sat behind them. The shorter man was brushing dust off the taller man's overcoat with his hand. They seemed excited to finally be underway. Mary and I sat across the aisle from each other.

"I have a million questions to ask you about your father," Mary said. She turned toward me and pulled off her mittens. The hole in her head was back.

"All aboard?" the driver called, smiling.

"Will there be other passengers?" I asked the driver.

"Indeed. I expect the bus will be full eventually."

He raised his head to see me in the rearview mirror, revealing a swollen, mottled face and neck. He lowered his gaze to the road, closed the door, and pulled the bus from the curb.

STICKIES

The stairs to the attic wound upward like a corkscrew, narrow and steep, creaking under every footstep, eventually opening on a large unfinished space. The stairwell sides were covered with peeling wallpaper, streaked brown with age and stains. Light poured through the clear, blue, and green windowpanes upstairs with old wavy glass that distorted objects outside. A mourning dove on the roof peak appeared grotesque as it rested outside one window. Jill Benning missed the bird and smiled at the large space.

"You know, *if* we open a B&B, we could put another room up here and still have space for storage," Jill said. "It would be a climb but look at the view. You can see all of Mammoth."

Dave, the home inspector, added, "That pipe over there is the plumbing vent. That would be a good place for a bathroom."

"Oh, yes," Herm Benning said. "We'd need a bathroom up here. Otherwise, we'd have to pay guests to stay up here if they had to climb up and down these steps to use a bathroom."

Gwen Babcock, the Bennings' Realtor, chortled. "Once *you* start paying guests this third floor will be booked all the time. You definitely need a bathroom up here. Nobody shares bathrooms anymore. Not even at home. Really! I can't imagine sharing a bathroom with my husband." She paused for a moment and pressed a pen to her lips before continuing. "I can recommend a good contractor. He does all my work."

"I'm not crazy about this colored glass" Jill said. "It gives the place an eerie look. Dave, what's up with these stains?"

"They're old. Don't worry. You'll find bumps and bruises all over. Don't forget, this place must be 150 years old. The longer you're here, the more you'll notice them. To be truthful, to find them all I should move in for six months, flush the toilets multiple times a day—mostly at night, unfortunately."

The little group laughed. Dave pulled out a small device and touched the plaster, pressed in two small pins. He moved the device from place to place over the largest stains. After an initial beep when he turned it on, the unit remained silent. "This is a moisture detector. Very sensitive. It would chirp like crazy if the plaster was wet. It's all dry now. These stains are old. I wouldn't worry about them."

Dave replaced the moisture detector in the pouch he wore around his waist and crawled on his hands and knees toward a cubby and opened its door to look under the eaves. After he disappeared inside, dust apparently made him sneeze as he moved around. All three followed the noise with interest. Gwen checked her watch and pressed her pen to her lips again. Dave was still inside the cubby for a moment and then said, "That's interesting."

"You find some spooks in there?" Herm wanted to know. "Maybe a skeleton?"

Gwen chortled again, hugging a soft briefcase to her body. "All skeletons must be in closets." She was twitchy and picked at her face with long, lacquered nails. "A place this old has to be haunted."

Dave emerged from the cubby, wiping cobwebs from his head and blowing more from around his mouth. His palms and knees were black from decades of dust. "It appears there was a fire here at one point." He showed the trio his black palms. Then he returned to the attic center and moved some insulation overhead with the end of his long flashlight. "See here? Just as I thought. The rafters are charred. Some were replaced, others were sistered with new wood to make the roof strong again."

"Is that a problem?" Jill said. She looked worried.

"Probably not," Gwen said. "Remember, the place has been standing 150 years. That's what Dave said. Right, Dave?" She laughed again and looked at her Fitbit watch.

Herm looked worried. They had searched for a long time for a large, old home, now that he and Jill were retired. Owning a B&B was a dream they had long talked about. The quest for the perfect home had taken months while the real estate inventory shrank. Gwen was their third Realtor. A little pushy and now nervous in her tight suit, short skirt, and heels. This place had enough space for guest rooms and bathrooms, ample parking, and a location on the crown of a hill with a view of historic Mammoth —the city in northeast Pennsylvania named after a forty-foot-thick vein of anthracite, coal that helped fuel the country's industrial revolution and provided back-breaking jobs for generations of immigrant laborers. Mammoth had been home to coal barrens, bootleggers, and the Molly Maguires. This home had a stone foundation and brick construction. Most of the exterior trim and shutters were original. It was everything the Bennings wanted. Plus, it had been recently painted, inside and out.

"The roof seems sturdy enough," Dave said, adjusting his jeans after crawling on the floor. "I was on it before you got here. Some people get squeamish when they see me on a roof, that's why I like to arrive early and get the roof inspection out of the way. I'd say the fire happened long ago, because the roof decking was replaced with wood planking. A newer roof would have plywood or OSB."

The Bennings smiled.

"Did you hear that?" Jill said.

"I didn't hear anything," Gwen added quickly. "I was texting. It's quiet as a...grave up here." She chortled again.

"It sounded like a child tiptoeing down the steps to the second floor," Jill said.

"My hearing's shot," Herm said. "Worked around too much heavy equipment, explosives all my life."

"I wasn't paying attention," Dave said, "but old houses make all kinds of noise. Heating pipes clank. Drafts rustle curtains. Wood makes noise when it expands and contracts. That can sound like footsteps. Be prepared. You might hear mice in the walls."

"Not in this house. I had an exterminator go through last week. It's clean. Guaranteed." Gwen nodded her head, affirming the pest-free home, and smiled. "If you smell a dead mouse, it'll dry out in no time." She pointed a highly lacquered finger at Herm. "No termites either. Dave, himself, did that inspection."

"I heard it again," Jill said, walking to the top of the steps. "I don't see anything, though."

"Just like I said. Old homes have all kinds of noises, especially at night it seems," Dave added.

Gwen excused herself, saying she had to make a telephone call about a property closing in trouble of collapsing. "All the stuff I need is in my car. Come get me if you have any questions." The realtor scrambled down the steps. They heard her heels click and her short steps in the tight dress all the way to the first floor. A moment later, the front door slammed.

Dave laughed. "All realtors get spooked by strange noises in old houses. Especially the females. No offense, Jill."

"None taken. I spent twenty years in the Army. Four tours overseas. It takes a lot to scare me."

"You ever see anything *spooky?*" Jill said, wiggling her fingers like an old witch at Dave.

"Not me. I heard weird stuff, though. One time there was a bird trapped upstairs in a house. The buyers thought the place was haunted after they first viewed the home, but they were okay with ghosts, because the noises didn't seem malevolent, so they said. It took us half an hour with all the doors and windows open in January to chase that grackle outside.

"There was a time when I first went into business, that I'd take random photos in a place like this, hoping to catch a spirit, in attics and big, empty rooms, and especially on stairs. Supposedly, a lot of ghost activity happens on the stairs. But nothing ever turned up on my camera. And I've inspected homes where there were murders and suicides. I inspected a few funeral homes, too. I've seen old blood stains and what looked like devil worship, black basement walls and pentagrams painted on floors, old dusty candles and melted wax everywhere. But I never seen a ghost. Had some scares when I caught my own reflection in a mirror I didn't know was there. That will stop your heart for a second. Especially when you see an ugly puss like mine grinning."

They laughed at Dave's stories and a basement room with stone walls and a creaking old heavy door that reminded them of a dungeon. Gwen never returned inside. They found her outside in her locked Mercedes. They laughed about that, too. The Bennings liked Dave and gave him a twenty-buck tip for his thorough home inspection and stories.

———

THE PROPERTY SALE closed three weeks later. Jill and Herm stood outside the home holding hands, watching movers carry in their furniture, collected from around the world when they both made careers in the Army. When the last table lamp was set in place and the last drawer slid in the bedroom bureau, the couple returned outside to examine the landscaping, even though many boxes remained inside to unpack. The exterior had been mostly neglected during their previous walk-throughs. There was rain on one occasion and chilly temperatures on another. Now a cherry tree bloomed, and the maples showed green buds. A koi pond would go near the proposed fire ring. Day lilies there and hostas in the shade. Herm measured for a backyard hammock he was eager to try. English ivy would cascade over low rock walls, remnants from a long gone shed. There would be a little garden to provide fresh herbs for the kitchen. Jill loved to cook. The backyard focal point would be a fire pit surrounded by Adirondack chairs equipped with cupholders. They had already bought an iron hoop made by a blacksmith to hold wood.

The B&B was not etched in stone. Two more bathrooms were required for second-floor guest rooms and a partition to section off the Bennings' living space. Jen wanted a bigger kitchen stove and a restaurant-grade refrigerator. Her guests would be amply fed. Then there was the third floor, a project that would not be tackled until the hostelry showed a profit.

However, during the walk outside they noticed a rotted windowsill someone had painted over. Dave could push a finger into the soft wood. Suspect molding near the peak was already discolored, despite the fresh paint. There was a loose tread on the back steps to the kitchen that "someone could break a neck on," Jill said. Surely there would be other defects that remained unnoticed on their eager mission to find the perfect B&B.

The couple returned to the front yard and porch. A leaf rake leaned against the wall near the front door. They entered the home and found a tall, older man in the hall, wearing a pork pie hat, peering into the living room.

"Excuse me," Herm said.

The man spun around. He pointed a thumb over his shoulder. "Sorry, folks. I'm Jack from next door. I rang the doorbell and knocked. This place is so big I thought you didn't hear me."

"We saw your rake on the porch."

"That's mine." Jack was tall and thin, brown from the sun. Still, his narrow face flushed. "I didn't want to bring it inside and get grass on your floor."

Jill looked at Jack's muddy shoes and smiled. "That was considerate of you."

"I wanted to introduce myself." Jack rubbed the sleeve of his plaid shirt across his nose.

Introductions followed. Jill walked to the porch, leading Jack outside, spreading her arms as if she herded animals. She didn't like this nosey neighbor. If Jack were outside raking, he must have seen Jill and Herm in the yard before he came over, a slimy way to get a quick peek inside.

"It will be nice to have neighbors again," Jack said, grabbing his rake and leaning on it. "This place has been empty for years, so long I can't tell you how many."

"I wonder why?" Jill said. "It's quite beautiful and in good shape."

Jack laughed. "Nobody told you? It's supposed to be haunted. Old Gustus, the guy who sold me my home twenty-five years ago, told me. Not that I believe in that sort of thing. But some people do.

"There was a veteran moved his wife and son into the home in 1948. Old Gustus was here—that is, where I live now—and remembered them." Jack pointed vaguely across the street. In 1949, there was a fire, and all three perished. The vet had survived D-Day and the Battle of the Bulge. Lost some toes to frostbite. Walked with a limp, so old Gustus said. Then he was in an airplane crash. Survived that, too. Shattered the leg with the good foot. He used a cane after that. But the fire did them all in. Wasn't even that big of a fire. The house still stands. Old Gustus said the smoke got them in bed. All three were in one bed. Police figured the little boy might have had a bad dream and crawled in with his parents."

Jack looked toward the sky and mused, "Maybe the little man had a premonition. Who knows?" He smiled at the couple. "Eventually, the flames got to them, too, and all three were burned up good. Not exactly a cremation, though. Even the little guy was substantially there, but not recognizable. None of them were. They could tell who they were by their...relative sizes. Old Gustus said the home sat vacant for years. Then a man named Barker moved in with his wife. She died after a while, supposedly of a heart attack. They had a dog jump through a second-floor window in the middle of the night and die when it hit the brick patio out back. Then Barker took a walk on Sharp Mountain and killed himself with a Nazi luger he brought back from the war. He was a vet, too. That added fuel to the fire about the haunting."

The couple looked at each other but Jack plowed on through his story, seemingly to relish the grisly details.

"So, the place sat empty again. Another buyer never lived here but tried renting it. That didn't work out, either. I think the place's reputation preceded it, so to speak. If you know you're moving into a haunted house, you expect to hear and *see* creepy things. That's how I think."

"Like you're telling us," Jill said.

"Well, you asked," Jack said. "Old Gustus said some people didn't last a single night inside. He kept track. Old Gustus was that kind of a guy. Eventually, a third owner couldn't find renters, and the house was foreclosed on. Ended up in some kind of trust or estate. The house sat empty again, but eventually somebody got ahold of it to unload it fast. One of those home flippers like you see on TV. They replaced the shingles on the roof, painted it all nice inside and outside. Rewired the whole shebang, so there wouldn't be another fire. Even had a new furnace installed.

"And now," Jack concluded.

"Here we are, ready to move into a haunted house," Jill interrupted, forcing a smile.

"Don't take what I told you seriously. After all, I don't believe in that kind of thing."

"Neither do I," Herm said, smiling at Jack.

"Never heard one iota of trouble from this place in all the years I'm here. Not a peep. This is a nice neighborhood. You'll see."

The Bennings unpacked enough boxes to go to bed and make breakfast in the morning. Fresh towels and soap were placed in the bathroom. Clothes were laid out. The coffee maker was filled and ready to turn on. Herm snored. Jill couldn't sleep and watched the nightstand clock's illuminated numbers change minute after minute.

At 2:30 am, Jill smelled charred wood. She wondered if the smell came from the burned rafters in the attic. Did they forget to close the attic door? That couldn't be, though. The rafters didn't smell when they were in the attic. They certainly wouldn't leave an odor this far away from the floor above. She climbed out of bed and went to the door. She thought she heard a child tiptoeing up the steps from the front hall downstairs. Then the footsteps stopped and there was silence. The refrigerator emptied ice cubes with a clatter in the kitchen. The smell of charred wood became stronger. To that was added the odor of burnt flesh, a sickening, sweetish, rotten smell. It burned Jill's nose and made her sneeze. She returned to the bedroom.

Then came the howling, high-pitched, frantic, filled with

pain. The wailing continued and separated into three distinct voices. One was deep, the second was higher pitched, and the third, although not as loud, was even higher in pitch, painful to hear. The cry of a child. Herm woke with a start and sat up. He shouted, "I smell smoke!"

Jill returned to bed and hugged Herm. "There's no fire, Herm. It's just a smell."

The screams moved through the house. They passed the bedroom door, went downstairs through the rooms, roared back to the second floor and continued to the third floor, then returned to the second floor and burst into the room. A black cloud moved toward them and split into three parts. The burned faces of three people emerged from the sooty blackness. Each face howled with a gaping mouth. The faces became more distinct. Red eyes like coals burned in the skulls. Just as they were about to collide with the Benning's the three forms peeled off and went over and around the couple. The inky cloud withdrew from the room.

Herm and Jill stared at each other. After a moment's silence, the wailing started again. This time the cloud entered the bedroom immediately and broke into three parts. Jill and Herm screamed. The entities stopped in front of them and howled with pain filled voices, as if hot irons were held to their flesh. The little one's shriek was painful to hear. Again, the entities peeled off and left the room. Each time the cloud re-entered the bedroom it brought a stronger smell, until Herm and Jill choked. They pulled pillows over their heads, cried, and screamed. They were punched, scratched, and bitten repeatedly. The sheets were torn to shreds. After an hour, the house became quiet. The odors dissipated. The

Bennings stripped the bed of the shredded sheets, which now were wet with fetid smelling secretions black and charred. They held each other, shivered, and sobbed, remaining in those positions until morning. In the morning, their bodies bore bruises and black smudges, as if from charcoal, and teeth marks.

———

JILL AND HERM fled the home in the morning—no showers, no breakfast, and no coffee, in the clothes they wore when they moved in. Next door, Jack was raking his front lawn and waved as they sped away. He pulled off his pork pie hat to shield the morning sun from his eyes to watch the Bennings.

The couple checked into a motel outside Mammoth, high on a hill above the main highway. It was a cheap room with mismatched secondhand furniture. Gwen Babcock didn't answer their repeated calls. Something had to be done. There must be a way to break the sales agreement. They poured over an old phone book that lay in a bedside drawer. The Yellow Pages contained scores of attorneys under such categories as wills and estate planning, workers' compensation, bankruptcy, criminal law, family law, DUI and traffic offenses, real estate, and wrongful death.

The Bennings sat side by side on one of the room's single beds. "In our case, what kind of lawyer do we need?" Herm said. "Real estate or wrongful death."

"Would anyone take us seriously?" Jill said. She looked at her husband and swallowed. "Can we afford a lawyer? Would one take our case?"

"Lawyers will take any case if they smell money," Herm said.

Jill thumbed through the old phone book nervously, shaking her head. "If only we knew what to do? If only we knew someone in town besides that realtor and our new neighbor."

"Let's think about it over something to eat." Herm said.

They drove north to The Four Stars, an old train-car-style diner with a large dining room added. The Bennings sat in a booth, away from patrons that lined the counter. Charlene, their waitress, was broad and limped. She wore a peculiar stone necklace and had a pencil stuck in her stiff-looking beehive hairdo.

"Is it too late for breakfast?" Herm asked.

"You can have breakfast or lunch any time, but don't ask for anything on the dinner menu, because it upsets Cooky. He's not set up for dinner this early," Charlene said. "Ask for something now and it puts him in a mood, especially if he's hungover. He chased me out of the kitchen with a knife last week when I asked him for liver and onions at 10 a.m. We'll be serving his liver if he doesn't stop drinking."

"Cooky sounds like a tough customer," Herm said.

"Not really. He made the liver and onions," Charlene said, with an eye roll. "He just had to put on a show first. Bang the pots and pans around. Curse a blue streak. The usual stuff."

When the Bennnings didn't acknowledge the joke, Charlene added, "You folks seem troubled. Everything all right?"

"We just moved to Mammoth, bought a home, and had a rough night," Herm said.

"Spooks?"

"How did you know?" Jill said.

"Mammoth is the kind of place where almost anything can

happen," Charlene said, nodding knowingly. Then she added, "So they say."

"We had to move out with the clothes on our backs," Herm said. "Know a good lawyer who can break a real estate sale?"

"You like the house?"

"We loved it," Jill said.

"You don't need a lawyer, hon. You need a medium. You must cleanse that house. Get rid of the evil inside. Then move back in. A home's a big investment."

"Do you know a medium?" Jill said.

"My sister. I'll get you one of her cards."

Charlene limped to the cash register, returned with a card, and handed it to Jill. "Don't call her in the morning. She can be a little testy. Wait till the afternoon. I imagine she's confabulating with the spirits half the night, so she tells me." Charlene shrugged and rolled her eyes again.

"She keeps cards at your cash register" Jill said.

"I let her put them in. Like I said, Mammoth is the kind of place where almost anything can happen," Charlene said. "You can go directly to her shop after you eat. She should be open by then. The address is on the card."

Jill examined the card. "This looks like a vape shop." She looked up at Charlene in disbelief.

Charlene said, "It's more than that. White magic. Black magic. Voodoo. Whatever you're after. She has it. My guess is she can cleanse that house. She's done others. I used to help until my hip slowed me down too much to make a quick exit, if one was needed. Get my drift? I can just about hobble around this place."

The Bennings nodded. They ate, paid their bill, and took

their time driving back to their new home. Everything seemed quiet. Their neighbor Jack sat on his front porch, noticed their car, and raised his coffee cup with a wide smile. They were afraid to go inside, even to get fresh clothes. Should they go to a lawyer or try the medium? It was now afternoon, and they decided on the medium. With daily hours printed on the card, they shouldn't need an appointment.

The Cauldron Occult Shop was on Second Street, a narrow, thoroughfare with tightly packed old homes. The street was strewn with litter and the sidewalk was dirty. They found parking a few doors above the shop. People on neighborhood porches watched them with interest as they approached the shop.

Sleigh bells jingled when Herm pushed open the shop door and rang again when he closed it. The interior was small, old, and dimly lit. There were vaping supplies, cigarettes, and video games inside glass cases. A cooler with soft drinks hummed against one wall. Another wall was covered with video game posters. The third wall had three classic pinball machines. The room smelled of tobacco.

"I think we're in the wrong place," Jill whispered. "This looks like a hangout for juvenile delinquents."

"But the sign outside," Herm said.

She shrugged her shoulders. "Maybe it closed."

"But the waitress gave us the card with this address."

Jill shrugged her shoulders again.

A beaded curtain behind the cases parted suddenly, and a small woman, barely five feet tall, limped into the room. "I can see you are here for spiritual advice. I am Tatianna. How may I help you?"

"We bought a home in town, and *it* has ghosts," Jill said.

The woman looked around the empty shop. "Follow me, please," she said, parting the beads and limping into the adjoining room, a larger space with black walls, ceiling, and floor. It was illuminated by small lights hung in strings from the ceiling and walls. "We can talk privately back here."

Jill and Herm traded glances and followed. The larger room appeared equally deserted.

The place was crammed with counters and shelves. On display were candles in all colors. Some had etched carvings of pentagrams, stars, and witches. There was incense in sticks, vials of oils, other liquids in small, dark bottles, and packets of coarsely ground dried herbs, each with handwritten labels and prices. Statues of all sizes were displayed: Egyptian, Indian, cats, wolves, bats, reclining goddesses, and medieval knights swinging swords or maces. Some human forms were made of wax and had wicks. Pestles and mortars lined one shelf, from miniature to large. Small cloth packets tied with ribbons held shapeless contents. In one corner were hooded robes with wide sleeves displayed on mannequins, some with embroidered stars and comets, and others were plain black. Witch and conical sorcerer hats abounded. Here and there were human and animal skulls and long bones, as well as complete skeletons. A full human skeleton in a bowler hat and loincloth sat at an old upright piano. Its hands rested on the keys, as if the macabre set of bones, wired together, was ready to play a request. A bony foot rested on a piano pedal. In addition, there was a large collection of crystals and small polished stones, necklaces, and rings. The occult shop had an overpowering smell of incense and candle wax, some of it unpleasant.

Jill found it difficult to breathe. "Impressive," she managed to say, stifling a cough.

"This is quite a collection," Tatianna said. "Black magic, white magic, voodoo. We have it all. Some items belonged to wizards or high priestesses and aren't for sale." She tilted her head and smiled again. "The stuff out there pays the bills," she said, sweeping her arm toward the other room, "but this is my sanctuary. I keep it away from the kids who would steal love potions and curses. I don't need trouble with the police over a dead kid.

"Now for your ghosts. You saw them or heard them?" The old woman looked at them intently. She wore a mauve turban and a long paisley dress. A black fishnet shawl hung over stooped shoulders. Thick ankles were visible below the dress hem. She showed an uncanny resemblance to the waitress from the diner.

"We saw them, we heard them, we smelled them, and the little one bit us. The two bigger ones punched and scratched us," Jill said. "It was an outright attack. I'll show you the teeth marks."

Jill raised her arm, exhibited the small teeth marks above her wrist. Herm leaned toward the old woman, pointed to a bruise forming below his right eye.

"Ah, yes. You bought the old Benedict home, the place that had the fire. I've heard of this activity. What do you want done?"

"We retired and wanted to open a bed and breakfast there. We had plans," Herm said. "I can't believe I'm saying this, but I want those spooks removed from our home."

"Yes, I understand," Tatianna said. "I will have to visit it first. There will be a cleansing fee, of course."

"Of course," Jill said. She looked at Herm. He nodded. She returned her gaze to the old woman. "Whatever it takes. When can you come?"

Tatianna moved to an ornate desk crowded with papers, sat down with a sigh, and turned pages in an appointment book. "Anyone out there when you came in?"

Herm said no.

"Good. Then we can go now. You are lucky. I have a rare free afternoon," Tatianna said.

"Really?" Jill said.

Tatianna turned toward Jill, raised her arms toward the ceiling. "Really. Usually, I'd be too busy. Depends how the stars are aligned. You said the little monster bites. I can protect you against that." She opened a nearby display case and pulled out a board arranged with an assortment of crystal and stone necklaces. The small stones were affixed to braided necklaces with thin wires, twisted and arranged ornately on the pieces.

"These amulets won't stop the ghost activity, but they will protect you from them doing harm," Tatianna said with a knowing nod. "No more biting or punching. I made these myself and placed protective spells on them. You must wear them next to your skin until we cleanse the domicile."

Jill and Herm each picked an amulet and Herm paid for them with a credit card. Tatianna added other items to the bill. "You will need these, too," she said with a wink.

When they exited through the vape shop, Tatiana said, "You might want to grab us some cold drinks. I can tell you from experience, ghosting will parch you."

Herm bought a six-pack of soft drinks.

"You folks gamers?" Tatianna said, waving a bare, flabby, tattooed arm at the video games, as if hoping for another sale. Herm said they did not play video games. Tatianna drew her lips into a frown.

Once outside, the neighborhood porch dwellers watched intently. One man called "Witch!"

Tatianna pulled a crooked stick from the worn satchel she carried and pointed it at the man. She unleashed a loud string of incomprehensible words. The porch dwellers vanished inside their homes and slammed the doors.

Tatianna cackled. She leaned toward the couple conspiratorially. "You'll never have a break-in when the locals think the worst of you. They say I breed hellcats and get blood from the morgue to feed them. It's a little rumor I started myself. I have some old glass pint bottles, the kind hospitals used to store blood for intravenous transfusions. I leave them on my porch at night a few times a month, as if they were milk bottles waiting for pick up."

"That's crazy," Jill said.

"It works."

"I didn't see cats," Herm said.

"Don't have any. I'm allergic, but they don't know that." The old lady cackled again.

Tatianna climbed into the car's back seat and sat in the center, obstructing Herm's view in the rearview mirror. She chugged her Coke on the short ride to the Benning's home, burped loudly, and excused herself, flushing slightly. Jack waved from his front yard, where he was trimming the hedge that bordered his sidewalk. Once inside, Tatianna donned a black robe she pulled from the worn black satchel and moved through the first-floor rooms carefully, carrying the satchel and pointing the gnarled stick, as if it were a potent weapon.

"The problem is upstairs," Jill said. "I think..."

Tatianna stopped her with a raised arm and continued her investigation. Eventually, she replaced the stick inside the satchel and dug out some bound, dried plants, which she ignited with a Zippo lighter. The stalk flared briefly and glowed red after she blew out the flame. It smoked and emitted a pungent-smelling odor. Jill coughed.

"This is sage. It's a potent cleanser," Tatianna said. She continued her slow progress through the downstairs rooms. She waved the glowing sage stalk over her head and mumbled as she walked, spilling ash on the floor. Occasionally, she'd say "I see," talking more to herself than to the Bennings. They followed her closely. Tatianna asked no questions. When Herm or Jill talked, she raised a hand to quiet them immediately. With the first floor covered, Tatianna, with some difficulty, climbed the stairs to the second floor and peered inside the various rooms.

"This is where you were attacked," Tatianna said, pointing to the bed and the shredded sheets on the floor.

"This is it," Jill said. She spun to the door suddenly and said, "Did you hear that? It's like a..."

"I hear it. Like a child on the steps," Tatianna said. "It's the little creature." She waddled down the hall, paused a moment to look toward the attic, and hauled herself up the circular stairs. "This is where they hang out. They're standing in the corner near that old pipe."

"That's where the bathroom goes," Jill said. "Maybe." She

stepped forward and Herm moved behind Tatianna. "You there! We have plans for this home, and just because you died here doesn't mean you're entitled to *live* here. I mean haunt us. We bought the place and paid the taxes for a year. You have no right to—"

Tatianna turned to the couple and raised an eyebrow. "You shouldn't have said that," she whispered.

The smell of charred wood and burned flesh returned to the attic. A black cloud formed in the corner and fanned out into three parts. The wailing started immediately. The entities howled and circled the trio, coming ever so closer with each pass. Their charred faces came into focus, with gaping black holes for mouths and red eyes. The mouths seemed to spray the stench of death. The fiends' features were more distinct in daylight. They circled faster and faster around the trio, but there were no punches or bites. Tatianna pulled a large crucifix from her black satchel and raised it above her head.

"Be gone, vomit from hell!" she screamed, spraying spit. "Infest not this home or these people in the name of God and his holy son, Jesus Christ our Lord!"

The three Benedicts formed one cloud, the individual forms no longer visible, retreated to their corner for a moment. The cloud paused for a moment, gathered into an undulating mass, suddenly charged across the attic, and steamrolled into Tatianna's midsection. She managed an "Ophff," and dropped like a rock to the floor. The cloud gathered in the corner with the vent pipe and disappeared.

Jill rushed to Tatianna's side.

"Holy shit!" Herm said. "Is she dead?"

"Knocked cold," Jill said. "I feel a pulse."

"I see her breathing. Thank God," Herm said. "We have to get her and us out of here."

"There's a bottle of ammonia under the kitchen sink. Get it and a rag and bring them here."

"The kitchen?

"The kitchen! We can't leave her in the attic, and we can't carry her down the steps. We gotta revive her. Look. The sun is setting. You have your amulet."

"What about her?" Herm said, pointing to the prone Tatianna.

Jill felt the old woman's neck and found no amulet. "She's not wearing one," Jill said, looking at Herm incredulously. "Hurry. I think the amulets work. You'll be safe and I'll be safe."

Herm returned with the ammonia and a rag, pumping his arms as he ran up the creaking circular steps. Jill poured a small amount on the rag and held it under Tatianna's nose. The woman coughed and woke slowly. She was groggy and, after a few minutes, was able to stand with help and slowly traverse the steps back to the first floor. The Bennings sat Tatianna in a dining room chair. With her elbows on the tabletop, she held her head in her hands and moaned.

"Do you want another soda?" Herm said. "You look... parched."

Tatianna turned her head and looked at him through the corners of her eyes. "Have anything stronger?"

"I have some good bourbon, and I know what box it's in," Herm said.

"That'll do," Tatianna said. Herm rearranged a stack of boxes across the room and rummaged through one until he produced the bottle. From another box he pulled three glasses and poured drinks for each of them.

Tatianna drained her glass and slid it across the table for Herm to refill. "Good stuff," she said in a hoarse voice as she inspected the amber liquid in the glass.

"Are you sure you're okay?"

"This isn't my first rodeo, son. I've been overwhelmed before, but I was younger when it last happened. I'll be fine." Tatianna smiled and cackled.

"You weren't wearing an amulet," Jill said, "after you charged us $150 for ours."

Tatianna cackled again. "Oops. Forgot it. You had better take me home. I have to plan our next step. These three have gained a lot of power since they died. They thrive on your fear. It gives them their strength. They grew stronger through everyone they scared out of here."

Tatianna rose stiffly, grabbed the nearly full bottle of bourbon, stuffed it and her gown into the satchel, and limped toward the front door. The Bennings dropped off Tatianna at the Cauldron Occult Shop. They went back to the diner and weren't alarmed about upsetting Cooky with their orders. They had seen enough for one day. After eating, they went to Mammoth Mall to buy some basic clothes to hold them over, returned to the motel, showered, and fell into bed with amulets around their necks.

———

AT 2:30 AM, the howling began. The Bennings sat upright in bed to the stench of rotting flesh. The screaming spirits circled the couple and disappeared into and reappeared from the walls and ceiling. They pressed the amulets to their chests. Jill wanted to scream but couldn't. Someone hammered at the room door, but the couple was paralyzed with fear and couldn't answer. After an hour, the room became quiet. In the morning, the couple expected to see the walls and ceilings damaged where the spirits entered and exited the room, but there was none. The motel manager kicked them out and told them not to return. He said he believed they were haunted but did not want the entities remaining in his motel. Hauntings were the kinds of things you'd expect in Mammoth.

The Bennings, with no place to go, returned to their home, showered again, and changed clothes. Jill made breakfast. They washed the dishes together and walked through the home gingerly, avoiding the attic, and eventually sat in the dining room until early afternoon, when they returned to the Cauldron Occult Shop. They went directly to the back room, where they found Tatianna at her ornate desk, nursing a black eye and bite marks on her wrist. Herm's bottle of bourbon sat empty on the desk. Jill told her about the night in the motel.

Tatianna thought a moment, tapped an index finger on her chin, and said, "I believe the Benedicts are what we call *stickies*. They have attached themselves to you, even though they died in that home. When you ran from the home, they followed you to the motel. If you leave on a plane tonight and go to, say, Arizona, they will follow, and every morning at 2:30 sharp—even in a different time zone—they will attack you. At least we know what we're dealing with. Stickies. Your story about the couple from years ago—the woman who died of a heart attack—probably scared to death. The husband killed himself. Probably mad with grief and the realization he had no hope to escape the spirits."

"If you can believe a guy named old Gustus," Jill said. "What about this home cleansing?" Jill said.

"I don't think that will be possible," Tatianna said. "The Benedicts are too strong. They have gained strength from the old couple who died at the home and the renters they scared off. Especially from the suicide, even though he didn't die in the home. Even school children who pass the home and shiver feed their energy. You two have added to it."

"But our home?" Jill said.

"I'm sorry," Tatianna said. She lowered her head.

"What if we called a priest for an exorcism," Jill said. "I want to fight for this home. What about another medium, one stronger than you? Maybe younger. I would think you have connections."

"The Catholic Church is not interested in exorcisms anymore," Tatianna said. "You can have a priest bless the home, but that won't chase the Benedicts and possibly make them worse. They believe they died wrongly. They are angry. The house is still theirs, so they think. The amulets make them angrier because they can't hurt you. Always wear those amulets. Don't get caught without them. Just for your information, there is no medium stronger than I am. It's not how it works. Your only chance is to sell the home and move away."

"We don't want to move," Jill said.

"I agree," Herm said. "It took months to find this place."

"I understand. Your only recourse is to live with the Benedicts. Your amulets will protect you from physical beatings and bites. I can place objects to keep them out of your bedroom. But they will own the home every day between 2:30 and 3:30 am. That must have been the hour during which they died. You will be safe but will lose sleep every night."

"How will we ever have a B&B?" Jill cried. "Will we compare bites at breakfast? Offer a prize to the one who got the least sleep? Good God! What if somebody got rabies!"

"A B&B is out of the question," Tatianna said. "These entities are dangerous. You already know that. Move back in until you sell the home."

"I can't go back," Herm said.

"They will follow you no matter where you go," Tatianna said. "They're stickies."

"Then we'll go back until we can sell the place," Jill said. "Then we'll find another home."

"There is one caveat," Tatianna said, raising her finger and smiling wryly. "You must tell the buyers the place is haunted. You don't have to be specific. You don't have to say the Benedicts died there and will haunt you every night for the rest of your lives."

"What!" Jill screamed. "No one told *us.*"

"Are you sure? Someone must have."

Jill thought for a minute. Her eyes darted back and forth. "Yes. Both Gwen and that nosey Jack told us."

"Yes," Tatianna said. "Someone told you. It might have been innocently."

Jill said, "It was such a casual mention. No one put a finger in my face and said the place is haunted."

"That's all it takes. You tell buyers the home is haunted. Besides, most people won't believe you. They don't have to believe you. Make it sound like a joke, because it's an old house."

———

THE BENNINGS MOVED BACK into the home. They worked inside and outside the home during the day, trying to give the place as much curb appeal as possible. Herm fixed the back step, dabbed more paint on the rotted windowsill, mended the stone wall that had toppled stones in several areas. They shopped, ate out, and went to the movies. It appeared they were the average newly retired couple. Jack waved from his front porch as they came and went. At night the couple huddled in their bedroom protected from the Benedicts by Tatianna's amulets and foul-smelling charms, stacked in each corner, enduring the howling that took place daily, the smell of burned flesh and wood, footsteps racing up and down the stairs, noises in adjoining rooms and attic, and the terrible pounding on the bedroom door. Still, the Benedicts did not enter the bedroom and physically attack them. As the months wore on, Jill checked the placement of home-for-sale ads placed in the Mammoth Sentinel and straightened her own yard sign. They dragged through the days, feeling drugged by lack of sleep. Dark circles appeared under their eyes. They felt ill.

Herm replaced the bedroom door three times, swapping the original cracked and oft pummeled door with others down the hall. He tightened the door hinge screws on the jambs every morning and watched for cracks in the heavy, solid door panels. They didn't trust the old door locks and moved heavy furniture from downstairs into the bedroom to place against the door at night, even though it seemed Tatianna's charms kept out the Benedicts.

The doorbell rang one day while they sat in stupors over coffee in the dining room. Jill answered the door. A couple stood outside clutching a handful of papers. They said the home belonged to them and the Bennings would have to move. They were tall and thin. Looked like marathon runners. Both had dark, slicked hair, wore sunglasses, black clothing.

"This is impossible," Herm said, as he moved behind Jill. "We bought this home and it's ours."

"Here's copies of the deed from the courthouse," the man said, thrusting the papers through the door. "We'll be back to claim our property, if need be, with a constable."

The couple turned and walked toward a black SUV parked at the curb. They climbed into the back seat and the vehicle roared off downhill into Mammoth.

Jill and Herm looked at each other in disbelief. They returned to the dining room table, where it seemed most of their recent important decisions had been made and poured over the paperwork. Jill ran upstairs to the small safe stashed in their bedroom closet and returned with the deed they had. The documents were identical, except for the names.

"What will we do?" Herm said. "I don't understand."

"We paid cash for this home. They're not taking it away," Jill said.

"What about the stickies? I can't take more of this. Every night. Neither of us sleep."

"That's what you said when you were defusing bombs," Jill said.

"I remember you saying that when you were cleaning corpses for shipment back home," Herm added.

The Bennings drove to the courthouse. After passing through a metal detector at the entrance, they walked up two flights of steps to the Recorder of Deeds office. Inside the office, the first clerk examined the two sets of deeds against the papers on file.

"Officially, Mark and Jody Foster are the homeowners," the first clerk said. "The copy you have must be a forgery." The clerk examined the deed, holding the papers close to his face. "I must say it is a good forgery. It even has my signature and seal affixed."

"I don't believe this," Jill said. "We signed these papers. I can't believe you don't remember us. It's not that long ago."

The clerk looked at the couple. "Sorry, you don't look familiar. You can't imagine how many people I see in a single day. Did you inherit this property?"

"We live in it," Herm said, throwing up his arms. "Our furniture is inside."

"This deed was recorded months ago," Jill said. "We have title insurance."

The first clerk chuckled. "I'm sorry, but the deed recorded here is the official one. You can always get a lawyer and go to court, but I don't think you have a leg to stand on."

"We've been living in the home," Jill said. "The Fosters showed up at our door this morning and said they were taking over. That we'd have to get out."

"When?"

"I don't know," Jill told the clerk. "They didn't give a date. They threatened us with a constable."

"Well, when they show up, you'll have to vacate. As far as I can see, the Fosters are in the right."

"What if the forgery occurred here," Jill said, "and we are the rightful owners? The fact is we are the rightful owners." Jill waved her hands in circles. "It's incredulous that someone changed the names on the deed here in your office to get rid of us and take over a home that's paid for and all fixed up."

The clerk said, "I've lived in Mammoth long enough to know it's the type of place where almost anything can happen, but in this case, I highly doubt it. They'd have to come in at lunchtime or when we have a union meeting. Then the office might be empty, but only for a short time. And that is highly unlikely. Plus, they'd have to know exactly where to go and what to do."

"These Fosters could be professionals. Maybe they steal homes for a living," Herm said.

The clerk remained silent.

"There was that bomb threat," a secretary said. "Remember? The whole courthouse was evacuated for two hours while they brought that canine unit in. Such cute dogs."

"I don't know," the clerk said and returned to his desk.

Herm looked at the clerk and said, "What about the gho—"

Jill gave him a sharp elbow to his ribs. She glared at Herm and then the clerk. "Okay. We'll go home and think this thing through."

"Your best bet is legal help," the clerk said, craning his neck to smile at them. "I'm sorry I can't do more."

The Bennings drove to the Cauldron Occult Shop to consult with Tatianna and returned home with more charms. They sat at the dining room table, where they burned candles and odiferous incense. They spread out their important papers, bank statements, and investment records.

"The Fosters are crooks," Jill said. "They even look suspicious. They're stealing our hoe out from underneath us, and we don't deserve it. But I'll get even if it kills me."

The next morning the Fosters rang the doorbell again and stood silently outside on the porch in their black clothing. The SUV purred at the curb. Jill answered the door and said, "We've been to the courthouse and were told you appear to be the rightful owners. I don't know how you did it, but we're ready to move out."

"I knew we could make this amicable," Mark said, smiling. His teeth were very white. He waved away two large men standing next to a second black SUV. "We'll give you a month to move. I think that's reasonable."

"We'll be out in two weeks," Jill said. "We've already started plans to move our furniture. To be honest, we've had enough of Mammoth. Would you like to come inside?"

"Sure would," Mark said, grinning at Jody.

The Fosters came inside and sat at the dining room table. The Benning's papers had been returned to their safe.

"What's that smell?" Jody said wrinkling her nose.

"We like to burn incense," Herm said. "Got this stuff specially made."

Jody made a face. "You can take *that* with you." She laughed. "It's not my style. What about the furniture. Are you taking *any* of it?"

"Yes," Jill said. "We have a mover and a storage place to keep everything temporarily. And your plans? Will you live here?"

"For a while," Mark said. "At first, we thought it would be longer until we fixed the interior, but it appears the home is ready to move in. The ultimate plan is to sell it and move on. After a while."

"Of course."

"What was that?" Jody said. "Are there children here? It sounded like a child on the stairs, creeping down from the second floor. A light step."

"No children," Jill said, smiling. "We were both married before. Herm has a grown son who doesn't bother with us. And we never had children together. My first husband was a drunk, beat me up, and caused a miscarriage."

"So sad," Jody said. She turned her head toward the hall and wrinkled her nose. "That's weird. I could have sworn I heard a kid." She stood and walked to the stairs to investigate.

"You know these old houses," Herm said. "They're always making noises."

"So they say," Mark said. He smiled.

"Would you like a drink?" Herm said. "I just replaced a bottle of good bourbon."

"No thanks," the Fosters chimed together.

"It's a little early," Jody added. "We're not really what you would call drinkers." She smiled at Mark. Jody raised her eyebrows. "I suppose that's it, then."

"There is one more thing," Jill said.

"And that is?" Jody looked across the table at the couple and smiled again.

"The house. It's haunted," Jill said. "Just so you know."

"Oh."

"The boy you heard on the steps. He's one of them," Jill said.

"One of who?" Jody asked.

"One of the ghosts," Jill said.

"You know it's a boy?" Mark said. He raised an eyebrow.

"Yes. He likes to bite, too," Herm added.

Mark and Jody looked at each other and burst out laughing. "That won't change our minds," Jody quipped.

"I hoped it wouldn't," Jill said.

Herm and Jill laughed, too. The couple stood and walked to the front door. "That's a good one. Ghosts! Biting ghosts, no less! I never heard that one before. I didn't know ghosts have teeth. We'll be back in two weeks."

"If we're already gone, we'll leave the front door key under the mat," Jill said. "The rest of the keys we'll leave on the windowsill inside the door. There's a warranty on the roof and other warranties on some of the appliances. They were mostly new when we moved in. We'll leave them here, too. On the kitchen island."

"Do the ghosts come with the place?"

"Naturally," Herm said. "No extra charge. They died here."

The Benedicts traded glances and laughed again. Their white teeth gleamed. Jody wiped away a tear. Both couples laughed.

"Where do we find them?" Jody said, shaking her head, as if what she just heard was unbelievable. "The ghosts, I mean."

"Don't worry. They'll find you."

WHAT A NIGHT

A WEEK BEFORE HALLOWEEN ALLISON CLARK DECIDED she and her boyfriend Jeff Barney had to get costumes for the party another lawyer, a partner in the firm where they worked, was throwing at an abandoned home he had purchased for an investment. A knock-down, drag-out affair was planned for the joint, no holds barred, before workmen gutted the structure in mid-November for a complete rehab. In fact, the wrecking crew had already "seasoned" the house for the party by loosening floorboards and knocking holes in walls to add to its spookiness.

Any valuable furniture had been sold. What remained was junk and could be trashed, along with anything else there. The invitation to law firm employees said mayhem was expected. The floors will run with blood and vomit. The party would have pranks, a fortune teller, zombie bartender and waitress, creepy music, and lots of booze. Everyone was under orders to get annihilated. The firm had just won a massive wrongful death suit, and its percentage of the take was in the millions. Therefore, a brain cell killing event was in order. Everyone was to let down his or her hair. No exceptions. A limousine and Uber drivers would be provided rides to and from the party. Guests were told to leave their vehicles at home.

A paralegal in the firm told Allison her cousin's friend's neighbor was a Wiccan and knew the Caldron Occult Shop sold great costumes. The partner throwing the Halloween shindig was going to great expense and effort and expected everyone to have a costume that told a lurid tale. No off-the-shelf vampire or mummy getups. No rubber masks. The office conference room had a sign-up sheet. Every invitee had to list his or her costume. There could be no duplicates. No excuses for non-attendance would be accepted.

It was after dark when Allison and Jeff arrived at the Caldron Occult Shop on Second Street in Mammoth. Even though most of the homes appeared abandoned, the couple had to park a half block away and walked the distance to the shop holding hands. It seemed everyone owned a car nowadays. The evening was windy and blew leaves and papers and dust up the narrow, winding street. A crushed plastic water bottle skidded along the dirty sidewalk, making a surprising lot of noise. Allison jumped out of its way and squeezed Jeff's hand.

"I bet it's creepier inside than outside," Jeff said. "Wait and see."

"I hope so," Allison said. "We must get some *great* costumes. Get noticed. You want everyone talking about us until the new year. We need to be more popular, more noticed with the partners. The way it is now, I hardly see them. I'm tired of doing amicable divorces and sending threatening letters. I could have done that in high school without a law degree."

"Copy that. I was on the Sullivan case last year but only as a gofer."

The couple had met and started dating after they were hired as junior lawyers in Mammoth's largest law firm. They moved in together about six months later, almost a year ago now. Allison thought Jeff would make a fabulous trial lawyer. He was aggressive and liked being the center of attention. She imagined him running for public office someday, possibly as state senator or even governor. She wanted to focus on family law, elder law, perhaps, railing against an ever-growing society bent on taking advantage of senior citizens. There would be notoriety there, too.

Jeff's grip felt moist, as it usually did, holding Allison's smaller hand. In fact, he seemed moist to her everywhere, especially around his thick hair line. He sweated profusely under the arms and rarely took off jackets to expose the wet half-moons under his arms. His hats and shoes smelled damp. She hid air fresheners in the closet where he kept his clothes, a hall closet outside their bedroom.

They climbed old wooden steps to a porch outside the shop. Jeff almost kicked a half dozen bottles near the door. "Look at that," he said. "Old glass bottles that held blood for transfusions. Someone probably dropped them off."

"Maybe they're out here to get refilled," Allison said, raising her eyebrows.

"You wish, Mrs. Creep."

"Ha. Ha. Mr. Creep. Wait and see."

Sleigh bells on the door announced their entry and continued to jangle a moment after the door closed. An old woman, short and squat, looked up from behind the counter.

She wore a kelly-green turban at an odd angle, as if she might have been scratching her scalp, paisley dress, and a long, black fishnet shawl. Heavy, dark makeup covered her eyes and was smudged after a long day of who knew what. Two teenagers played old pinball machines at the end of the room. The woman sat behind the glass counter that might have held candy years ago but was now filled with vaping supplies and cigarettes. Other display cases around the room contained video games under glass. She rose from her seat slowly, stiffly.

"Good evening," the old woman said. Dark teeth showed through her smile. "I am Tatianna. How can I help you?"

The teenagers stopped to listen.

"We need Halloween costumes," Jeff said. "Special costumes for an important party."

The old woman shot a look at the boys. "You kids, scatter. Get home. And watch my milk bottles on the porch when you leave."

"Okay, thank you, Tat," one boy said as they hurried by her, watching warily.

She cackled with a laugh that seemed stuck in the back of her throat, and they moved faster, slamming the door after them, making the bells jingle furiously.

"Those boys get on my nerves," she said. "Instead of doing homework, they're bothering me. Just what I need. They'll end up sitting on the porches all day, just like their parents, no work, no drive, the only future the one the government gives them."

Jeff looked around the store. "We were told you have Halloween costumes."

"Really? By whom?" Tatianna looked at the couple as if trying to see whether they told the truth.

"It was a friend of a friend sort of thing," Allison said, moving her hands as if she were juggling balls. Then she rested her hands, palms down, on the display case's cracked glass top.

"Oh, my," the old woman said, raising a small hand to her chin. Her fingers were curiously dirty. Not nicotine stains. Something else. "Come this way. I'll show you I have no Halloween costumes."

The couple introduced themselves and walked between a gap in the counters and followed the old woman through a door with strings of beads. After they were through, the beads clicked and clacked as they collided, swinging back into place. Dimly lit, the room had an overwhelming smell of incense, many fragrances combined. Allison stifled a cough. The room's ceiling, floor, and walls were flat black. The place was crowded with candles, statuettes, stones, crystals, jewelry, pestles in mortars, salves in tins, potions in small burlap bags or cellophane, knotted decoratively with ribbon. Allison was drawn immediately to a corner where life-sized mannequins without faces modeled sorceress robes with wide sleeves, hoods, and belts made of rope. Some of the attire was plain black. Others had embroidered shooting stars and comets. There were also tall and short witches' conical hats.

"That's perfect," Allison said, with glee, zigzagging through shelves and counters to the robes. She pulled off her coat and tossed it on a selection of candles in the shape of humans, grabbed a robe with shooting stars, and tried it on. She laughed when she thought the rope belt tightened around her waist by itself.

She looked toward Jeff. "It's perfect. I want a tall hat, too."

The green-turbaned woman limped after the couple. She

said, horrified, "They are not for theme parties. You must be careful. They have powers." She picked up Allison's coat and folded it in half. "Please. Take off that robe."

Allison winked at Jeff. "I'm wearing this until after Halloween. Even to work."

Tatianna inspected the candles where Allison had thrown her coat.

"You broke this one," Tatianna said, annoyed. "It has a powerful spell. Now it's ruined."

"You probably broke it yourself. I don't care. Add it to my bill." Allison whirled in a circle.

Tatianna squinted. "Very well. I will sell you the *costume...* and the candle."

"Plastic?"

"Of course." The old woman smiled. A cackle began in her throat but died immediately.

Allison wondered if this was the woman's first sale of the week, other than the coins the boys had pushed into the pinball machines. "Now, what do you have for my sorcerer?" Allison said, spinning again, laughing, making the robe's hem spread into a wide cone to match the sleeves and hat.

"I can't wear the same thing," Jeff said. "It's against the rules. We'll need something different, just as spectacular. Something with a history."

"So, you are going to the lawyer's ball," Tatianna said in disgust. "A night of reveling on a holy eve. You should be careful."

"You know about it?" Jeff said. He looked at Allison and smiled.

Tatianna grinned back. "I do. A lawyer came in last week.

Tall and thin. Gray and mostly bald. An aura of dishonesty about him. He wanted me to read palms at this party. I told him I wouldn't. He offered me a thousand dollars for the night. Said all I had to do was make things up for the crowd's amusement. Wear the same clothes I had on. Especially my shawl and turban. Tell all the guests something horrid. You know." She raised her palms and shrugged. "They had an incurable disease. Someone close will die mysteriously. That kind of thing."

"What did you say?" Jeff asked.

"I pointed an amulet at him, told him to hit the bricks, or I'd make him impotent."

"And."

"He left in a hurry." Tatianna cackled.

Allison and Jeff looked at each other and burst out laughing.

"Old Fenster on the run from a place like this," Allison said, laughing nasally. "That's rich. His girlfriend wouldn't be happy with him impotent."

"Neither would he, the randy old fool. The only thing worse would be if his wallet ran out of money," Jeff said.

Tatianna's eyes narrowed again and looked at Jeff. She said icily, "Well. Let's see if I can do something for the gentleman. Follow me, please, young man."

Tatianna gave Allison her coat and limped to the opposite end of the shop. Allison watched Jeff follow the old woman, mocking her gait. Allison sniggered and poked among the relics, statuettes of Egyptian gods, medieval knights, demons with the legs of animals, cloven hooves, standing or seated on thrones. amulets, and representations of the Holy Grail. Eventually, she picked up an old-fashioned walking stick with a peculiar handle.

"I need something with a *lurid tale*, if that's any help," Jeff told Tatianna as they meandered through the merchandise. He looked over his shoulder and motioned for Allison to join them.

Tatianna reached a rack of old clothes, mostly dresses, some long, some short, all black, and from among them pulled out a dark woolen pinstripe suit.

"I have plenty of suits," Jeff said. "What's special about this moth-eaten gem?"

Tatianna smiled. "It is special and has a lurid tale. Just what you need."

"Now you're getting somewhere," Allison said as she joined them. "Looks like it will fit, too."

"It will fit," Tatianna said. "They all fit."

"Well?"

"Do you know of Woodrow Hearst?" Tatianna asked.

"Of course. The Mammoth serial killer. I did a paper on him in law school," Allison said.

"Killed eight people in the '40s and '50s," Tatianna mused, smiling, holding a begrimed finger to her chin, as if recalling fondly some old childhood story. "Now, some of the people he killed were worse than he was, but it was murder none the less and the state caught him, convicted him, and electrocuted him. I think it was 1954. They said he got to like killing so much during the war, that's World War II, he couldn't stop when he came back home. I think he was always insane. Another story says he just happened to get caught in Mammoth."

"Anyway, he was buried in this very suit. It was his best. Look here." Tatianna removed the coat from an old metal hanger, laid it out on a counter, and flipped open the lapel. The name Woodrow Hearst was stitched inside. "This suit was a custom job. It cost plenty. Look at the back. This is where the undertaker split the seam open to fit over the corpse in the casket. They say he gained weight in jail. Somebody stitched it up again at some point. Did a nice job, too, even if the pinstripes don't line up exactly."

"But how did you get it if he was buried in it?" Jeff said. He swiveled his head toward Allison and rolled his eyes.

"I'm getting to that," Tatianna said. "Keep your pants on." She was annoyed again. "Run out to the front and get me a Diet Coke from the cooler. I get parched when I tell stories."

Allison and Jeff traded glances. Jeff retraced his steps to the vape shop, picked out a drink from the cooler, and returned to the women.

Tatianna took a long pull on the soda's plastic bottle, cleared her throat, and continued. "After he was electrocuted, at some point, officials decided to exhume the body and investigate more. Who knows what for? The story I got was that his clothes were thrown in a pile in the morgue while he was in the cooler. Then they decided to exhume a couple of his victims. While they did *that* Woodrow Hearst remained on ice. Somebody got tired of looking at that suit and tossed it, but eventually—after some years—it found its way here. You'd be surprised. A lot of unusual items find their way here. I've had it for years. Couldn't give it away."

"So, the suit is free?" Jeff winked at Allison as she wandered away to look at more merchandise, still carrying the cane.

"Hardly," Tatianna said with a cold stare. "This item is valuable. It has a *lurid tale*. Plus, it might not be legal to possess as it came from the morgue, and all. That's a problem I'll leave to you, the expert in the law."

"When was it cleaned last?" Jeff asked.

"Cleaned? Never!" Tatianna cried. "That would ruin its... *charm.*"

"You're not putting that suit in my closet," Allison said with a scowl.

"Come on, babe," Jeff whined. "I'm sure it got aired out." He looked at Tatianna for an answer.

"As far as I know, the suit's only time outside was on the trip between the morgue and here. Anything you put outside to air in this neighborhood would be stolen in a second. That's why I put those old bottles outside. The neighbors think I get stale blood from the blood bank to feed the hellcats I raise. House is swarming with the fiends, don't you know." Tatianna cackled in her odd voice. Then she coughed until she washed it away with more Coke. "Every once in a while, I haul an empty box with holes cut in the side to my car. That looks like I'm sending a hellcat to a client. That's what they believe anyway. The neighbors, that is. Nobody'd dare to enter this place, except for the boys who want to show everyone they're macho by playing pinball and drinking soft drinks in the front room."

"The suit has aired in this room, bathed in various incense and potions and spells all these years," Tatianna said, with a knowing smile.

"Is it safe to wear?" Allison said, walking toward them. "I don't want Jeff to get lice, or God knows, some skin disease from a corpse. After all, we sleep together, and I don't want him infecting me."

"I'm sure any bacteria, viruses, microscopic bugs—you name it—would be long gone," Tatianna said, with a smile. "Even fleas and bedbugs. Everything alive has to eat."

"Does the suit stink?" Allison said. "How long was it underground? We can always have it dry cleaned before the party."

"Not on your life," Jeff said. "Fenster would die if I wore an uncleaned corpse's suit. Talk about getting noticed."

"Hearst was buried more than a year before he was exhumed," Tatianna said. "The story I got was the suit was wet when he was dug up, something about him buried in soggy ground and the casket leaking. Old Woodrow was floating when they brought him to the surface. The casket weighed a ton. The weight almost tipped over the crane. As for the suit, it dried on the floor in the morgue. I can't say what other *fluids* might have mingled with the fabric. But the suit was dry when it came to me." Tatianna raised a hand and inspected her nails. "A little stiff, but dry."

"You can sleep on the sofa until after the party," Allison said. She took a step closer to Jeff. "If you're so insistent on the suit, *this* will complete your costume. She raised the cane. "A walking stick for a serial killer."

"Oh," Tatianna said. "I didn't intend to sell this."

She reached for the cane, but Jeff took it from Allison.

"This is perfect," Jeff said. "So dapper. Too bad the handle isn't a wolf and silver like the one in *The Wolf Man* movie. Lon Chaney, Jr. killed a werewolf with the cane and then was killed himself by it." He lifted the cane and pretended to smash it over Allison's head. "But the handle is an eagle, I think."

"No. It's a vulture," Tatianna said. "See? There are no feathers on the bird's head."

"Maybe the head feathers were worn off over time, from holding the handle," Jeff said.

"I don't think so," Tatianna added quickly.

"A vulture's better," Allison said. "Make sure you point it out to Fenster."

"Let me see," Tatianna said, taking the cane from Jeff's hands.

"I want this," Jeff said, letting the cane go begrudgingly.

"Just be warned," Tatianna intoned mysteriously. "This cane was custom made, too. It killed a man. Watch." Tatianna pressed a small button and twisted the vulture's head. The handle separated from the cane, revealing a long, stiletto knife attached to the vulture's head. "Be careful. The blade is razor sharp."

"More serial killers?"

"The story I got was that one person was killed," Tatianna said. "Stabbed through the chest. The man who made the cane was killed, too. The cane was in the police evidence locker. It got in the way and disappeared. Eventually, it made its way here. So, it might not be legal to possess this either, although the case involving it must surely be closed."

"How long ago did this all happen?" Allison said.

"I'm not sure," Tatianna said. "But considerably more recent than the Woodrow Hearst case."

Jeff reassembled the cane with care. He took it apart again and replaced the knife. Then he pulled it out suddenly and pretended to lunge toward Allison. Allison cried and stepped back.

"You asshole!" she said.

Unaffected by the sudden move, Tatianna watched Jeff with narrowed eyes.

He picked up the suit and offered it to Allison. "Take a whiff. See if it smells like anything."

Slowly, gingerly, she bent her face toward the folded jacket.

"Ouch," she cried. "I got shocked. It hurt."

"Static," Tatianna said. "Must be static. What else could it be?" The old woman smiled.

"Static," Jeff said. "What else could it be?"

"No. It actually hurt." Allison touched the end of her nose and then wiggled it gingerly.

Jeff picked up the coat to sniff and he recoiled. "I got shocked, too. Son of a bitch. It did hurt." He looked at Allison.

"See?" Allison said. She touched the end of her nose again.

"That's a lot of static," Tatianna said. "Most unusual." She raised her painted eyebrows. "My little shop is most unusual. The suit should be discharged now. Had I known it held so much electricity I would have run some lights off it." She cackled again but stopped suddenly and said, "What did it smell like?"

"I don't know. I was too busy getting shocked," Allison said.

"Me too. I'll try again."

Jeff raised the coat to his nose, careful not to let the fabric touch his face. "It smells like incense. Like the interior here. But there's something more. Something under the other scents. More subdued. Subtle, like drinking good Scotch. I can't put a finger on it."

"There you go," Tatianna said smiling. "I wouldn't mind a snort of good Scotch myself about now."

Allison smelled the coat fabric. She screwed up her face. "There is another smell, but I can't tell what it is. It's not nice, though." She held the coat at arm's length, inspecting it, front, back, and lining.

Tatianna scratched at her turban, blew out a sigh. "You

should have an amulet to look the part of a witch." The old lady smiled and pulled a small amulet from her throat under the shawl.

"Indeed," Allison said. She moved along a counter and picked up a brown stone, polished as if it had been plucked from an ancient riverbed. The stone was fastened to a necklace woven with thin copper wire, ornately twisted. Allison smiled at the object and held it up to her throat.

"Not that one, dear," Tatianna said. She limped to the counter's other end. "Try one of these. You've already found love. You need protection."

"Really? From whom? Jeff?" Allison inclined her head toward the old woman.

Tatianna raised her eyebrows. "From whatever could inflict harm. We live in dangerous times."

"I imagine these are more expensive."

"They are, but for you they are the same price," Tatianna said, smiling, exposing her dark teeth.

Allison perused the amulets, taking her time, trying on several before eventually finding one she liked. It was not the one Tatianna recommended.

Tatianna consulted her wristwatch and said it was closing time. They moved to an old cash register where she totaled a bill and handed it to Jeff. He, in turn, gave her his credit card. While they waited for the electronic transaction to complete, Jeff scanned the bill.

"Jesus Christ," he said. "You charged me for the soda you drank? And three percent for the card?"

Tatianna shrugged her shoulders. "You wanted to hear a story, and I was parched. The credit card company charges me three percent on transactions. I'm in business to make money."

The couple gathered their purchases and left the Cauldron Occult Shop. Allison was careful to keep her robe and hat away from the suit. She wore her new amulet around her neck.

Before they left, Tatianna raised a finger and said, "This lawyer's ball. This house *he* bought to remodel. He gave me the address when he thought I'd tell fortunes. It's the place where Woodrow Hearst lived. The place where they believe he did most of the killing. I thought you might want to know."

"That's interesting," Allison said with a smile. "I wonder if Fenster knows. I'll have to dig out my old paper. I remember saving notes and newspaper clippings. That will make another lurid tale." The young couple smiled at each other. "What a night this will be."

Outside on the sidewalk, Allison said, "Did you believe all that?"

"It's bullshit," Jeff said. "Like the old woman said, we wanted to hear a story, and she told a whopper. No wonder she got *parched*. Two fifty for a fucking Coke. I ought to sue the old bitch."

The pinball boys were on the corner when the couple walked to Allison's car. They smoked cigarettes and giggled as the couple approached. The taller boy said, "Hey, you buy a hellcat from her?"

"No, I'm allergic to cats," Allison said. "How about you? You have one?"

"Fuck no! They're evil," the smaller teen said.

"She show you any?" the taller boy said. He looked nervous and moved his weight from side to side. There was worry in his eyes. "We always ask to see one, but she won't how us. She says it's too dangerous. All she does is laugh."

"We heard them," Jeff said, conspiratorially, looking around before he continued. "It sounded like there was a litter upstairs and a litter downstairs in the basement. You can't mix hellcats from different litters."

The boys nodded in agreement. "What did I say?" one of them said.

"Go on YouTube," Allison said. "Look up hellcats in South America. An old witch in Peru was breeding hellcats. Got the litters commingled. Most witches..."

"Or warlocks," Jeff interjected.

"Only raise one litter at a time. The hellcats tore the old hag apart. Wiped out the entire village. Drained every drop of blood. Even from the chickens. The hellcats grew huge." Jeff raised his arms over his head. "Their teeth were like razors. Their bellies were so full they drug on the ground when they walked. They were so full of blood. One of the policemen who investigated shot a video. Showed the villagers' bodies. The wounds. And a hell cat slinking off into the jungle. Their bellies swayed back and forth."

"I think YouTube took that video down, Hun."

"Really? Well, it's worth a look," Allison said, smiling at the teens.

The boys wagged their heads in unison.

"Tat gets old blood from the hospital to feed her hellcats," the older boy said.

"I saw the bottles on her porch," Jeff said. "Someone must pick them up."

"They do. Fills them in the middle of the night and puts

them back in the same place. My Nan says she can smell the blood in the morning. It's heavy in the air."

"With two litters feeding, I don't know whether the hospital can supply enough blood. Tat might need fresh blood," Allison said. "Fresh blood is more nutritious. You better be careful around her."

"I'm not afraid. Tat can suckle them herself, as far as I care," the taller boy said. "My Nan says Old Tat has at least a half dozen nipples. She seen some of them. The old witch takes moon beam baths. My Nan gets up to pee at night and she seen the old witch in the full moon, in the nude, in her little backyard that's full of weeds and snakes and rats. The city always sending her notices about the weeds. I know 'cause I take her mail when I can."

"Interesting," Jeff said.

The tall boy laughed. "We got a couple of her water bills, and the city was here to turn off the main. There was a big argument here in the street. But nobody turned off the water because she got connections. Most of the people at city hall are witches."

"Those moon beam baths give a witch they power," the shorter boy said, knowingly. "Can even make them pretty for a time, but Tat's so old nothing would help her."

There was an awkward moment when the boys and the couple traded stares and smiles. They had escaped Tatianna's hell cats and lived to talk about it. Finally, Allison said, "It's getting late. You guys must have school tomorrow."

"We do, if we want to go," the taller boy said. "Usually, we find other stuff to do."

"Interesting," Jeff chimed. He expected to meet them again, possibly as clients.

Allison and Jeff arrived home and climbed the stairs to the second-floor apartment they shared. "Keep that suit in your closet," Allison said. "I don't want it infecting my clothes."

"It's just an old suit, babe. Probably came from some thrift shop. Not the morgue."

They passed in the hall outside their bedroom, and Allison laughed. "You should see your nose. It's bright red. You must have a zit."

Jeff looked up. "So do you. It looks like a burn from the shock you got."

He touched the tip of her nose and she recoiled. "Christ! That hurt."

"Mine is sore, too," Jeff said.

They went to the bathroom and peered into the mirror above the sink. Both sported red noses at the tips. Allison touched her nose gingerly. Jeff pushed his from side to side, grimacing. They took turns leaning their faces toward the mirror. Both retrieved their glasses to see better. They moved their heads this way and that. Finally, they stepped away from the mirror and looked at each other.

"It's not a zit," Jeff said. "Feels like a bad case of sunburn, but only in a small place."

"Mine's no zit, either. I haven't had a zit since the eighth grade. Feels like the burn I got on my thumb baking cookies with my grandmother. She put butter on my thumb."

"Put butter on your nose and you *will* have a zit."

They washed their faces carefully and brushed their teeth. Once in bed they turned to kiss and bumped noses. Each recoiled in sharp pain and rolled over. "I am so going to hurt you, Mr. Creep," Allison said.

"I'm going to cut off your infected nose with the knife in my new cane, Mrs. Creep."

"I never looked at your nose that close. Your pores are really large."

"Do you have a problem with that?" Jeff said. He rolled over to face her back.

"Not now. Maybe in thirty years."

Their noses were still red in the morning, and Allison dabbed powder on them to hide the burns. Who would believe they got burned by an old coat? Static electricity? They drove to work and sat in their separate offices, more cubicles to be accurate. They could always use one of the conference rooms if they needed privacy with a client. After a morning staff meeting, Jeff planned to do research in the courthouse's recorder of deeds office. Allison had an appointment with clients in the afternoon. An amicable divorce.

Allison googled Tatianna but found no references to the old woman or her magic shop after reviewing page after page of results. The Cauldron Occult Shop apparently had no web site. The vape shop, tobacco products, and video games all drew blanks. Who wasn't online these days, despite their age, Allison wondered? She sat over her computer, dabbing her sore nose.

Fenster appeared at her cubicle, tapping lightly, smiling broadly. "I see you and Jeff finally signed up for the party," he said, rocking back and forth on his heels. "I noticed Jeff's 'exhumed man's suit'. And you, a cauldron stirring witch. Good stuff."

"We expect to be a real hit," Allison said, giving him her charming smile. The best smile she could muster.

"Wonderful. What a time I had getting a fortune teller. Had some old crone lined up, but she backed out. Threatened to put a curse on me. Imagine that!"

"If you need help?" Allison said. She suppressed a giggle and had difficulty making eye contact with him.

Fenster raised his palm. "You have your own work. Everything's arranged now. Got a fortune teller that's really quite cute. And young. I thought it would be a different spin on the old hag I had planned. This girl was signed up to be a waitress. Has a degree in theater or some such thing. She said she can act the part. A little makeup, a wart or two on her nose and chin, a few scarves, some jewelry, and she'll fit the bill. The best thing is she couldn't put a curse on a monkey."

"I'm sure the party will be fun," Allison said.

"It will be ghastly," Fenster proclaimed, raising an index finger toward the ceiling.

That night after dinner, Allison searched the internet for capital punishment in Pennsylvania. Hanging was replaced by the electric chair in 1913. In 1990, a new law replaced the electric chair with lethal injections. In 2015, Governor Tom Wolf signed a bill placing a moratorium on the death penalty.

Old Hearst was fried in 1954. His name was among the almost thirteen hundred executed while the electric chair was in service. The executed had electrodes placed on their head and left leg. The areas were shaved to ensure better contact. As much as two thousand volts of electricity passed through the convict's body for up to twenty seconds. If that was not sufficient, a second jolt was administered. The shock cooked the inmate's insides. In some cases, the convict smoked, Sometimes the eyeballs popped out. After execution, it was necessary to let the body cool to conduct a postmortem. Allison found the information lurid and fascinating. There were internet photos of postmortem electrocution victims, with their scalps burned black and red, their facial muscles twisted in gruesome grins. Jeff watched football on television and did not accept her requests to view the dead.

The rest of the week seemed interminable. Gradually, their noses healed. The redness and pain subsided. After sleeping in on Saturday, Halloween, they rose, scanned the Mammoth Sentinel over breakfast, and ran through the Mammoth Arboretum. The next part was tricky. Should they eat during the day to absorb alcohol at the party, or should they get wasted quickly on empty stomachs? They decided on the empty stomachs route. After all, Fenster promised catered food after midnight, and no one was driving to or from the party.

They showered, made love, and napped. Saturday afternoon in bed was a luxury. Now it would be cut short by the party. They showered again and Jeff shaved.

"If it were up to me, I'd take a pass on this shindig," he said, walking into the bedroom naked. "In the end, this night is going to be a poor remake of *House on Haunted Hill* without Vincent Price."

"Taking a pass will be impossible," Allison said, pulling a brush through her hair. "I'm sure Fenster will take attendance."

Jeff pressed himself against Allison, took the brush from her hand, and continued to stroke it through her hair. She closed her eyes. He kissed the back of her neck and massaged her shoulders. "What were you saying about a pass being impossible?"

"Do you know how Woodrow killed his victims?" she said, dreamily with her eyes closed.

"No." He smelled her neck and perfume, licked her skin with the tip of his tongue.

"I looked through my notes from the paper I wrote," she continued with difficulty and a light moan.

"Well?"

"Well, the ones he got inside his house he drugged, stripped their clothes off, gagged, and tied up. Then he patiently waited for them to regain consciousness. While they watched, Woodrow sharpened a straight razor—his father was a barber—on a strop. Apparently, shaving with a straight razor was der rigueur. The more the victims struggled, the more excited Woodrow became."

"Like this?" Jeff dropped the brush and wrapped his arms around her, pressing himself harder against her.

"That's what he told the police eventually, after he realized he was a goner," she said in a halting voice. "Male, female, they excited him equally. There was nowhere to go. No way to scream."

Allison freed herself from his grip, turned around, and kissed him on the mouth. He pulled off her bra. She stepped out of her panties. Then he backed her onto the bed. It was dark and they lay on their sides staring into each other's eyes. Saturday afternoon had not been wasted.

Suddenly, Allison jumped up. "Shit! The Uber will be here in a few minutes. She got her clothes together and dressed. Jeff rolled over slowly and sat on the bed a moment before standing.

He pulled on his underwear and a white shirt, then went to his closet for a tie and the suit. After he pulled the tie knot against his throat, Jeff pulled on the suit trousers.

"Wow," he said with a startled voice.

"What is it?"

"Feel these pants. It's like more static, except it's not a shock but tingling up and down my legs."

"Your leg's asleep." Allison cocked her head. "You're imagining it."

"No. This is different."

A horn sounded outside. "It's the Uber," Allison said. "I'm ready."

Jeff pulled on the coat. He reacted immediately. "There it is again. Tingling all over. All through me. It makes me shiver. I can't take it."

"Stop fooling around. Here's your cane, Mr. Creep. Save the theatrics for the party."

Jeff pulled the knife from the cane, faster than he had at the Cauldron Occult Shop. He grabbed Allison's wrist and spun her around. He was behind her, pulled her by the hair, tipped back her head. He placed the stiletto knife at her throat, high against her chin. She couldn't talk.

"I'm going to cut your throat," Jeff said, in a voice she didn't recognize. "But first I'm going to slit you open and crawl inside among your innards."

Allison struggled in his grasp. She was frightened. She needed a weapon to escape. There were scissors on the nightstand. She had used them to cut stray threads from her sorceress robe. Her fingers fumbled across the nightstand, squeaked on the waxed surface. She knocked over the lamp. Finally, she felt the scissors handle, but Jeff jerked her around, lifting her momentarily off her feet, and her hand pushed the scissors off the nightstand and on the floor. Jeff laughed maniacally and pulled the knife tighter against her throat. He licked her ear.

"I love the smell of your fear. Your panic," he said in the voice that was not his.

Allison lunged toward the nightstand. Raised a foot and planted her heel in his groin. She fell forward. Her palm covered the amulet on the nightstand. She closed her fingers around the stone. Immediately, Jeff released her.

"Not so rough, babe," he said, his normal voice back.

"You fucker."

"I was just playing."

"You cut me." Allison put a hand on her neck, pulled back blood on her fingers.

"I'm sorry, babe. Let me see. It's just a scratch. I'll get a bandage."

Jeff tried to put his arm around her.

The Uber beeped again.

"Get away from me," Allison said. "I'm not wearing a bandage on my neck to a Halloween party. For Christ's sake. It'll look like you gave me a hickey. That will be another lurid story!"

Jeff applied his styptic pencil to the cut, and it stopped bleeding immediately. They finished dressing and hurried downstairs to catch their ride.

"That's some cane you got there, boss," the driver said, as the couple climbed into the back seat.

"My lady bought it for me," Jeff said.

"Good taste," the driver replied.

Allison remained silent on the ride to the party. The driver seemed to pick up on the tension and was quiet for the rest of the ride.

Allison's mood improved when they got inside. A sign at the door over a garbage can read, LEAVE ALL YOUR CASES HERE. An arrow pointed toward the garbage can. Other colleagues had already arrived, as well as some of the firm's well-heeled clients. Most crowded around the bar. There was laughter, hand shaking, and back slapping.

"Look at this place," Allison said. "I wonder who decorated. It looks like a prom. Balloons and streamers? Really?

"You'd think we were at a nudist colony," Jeff said. "See how all the creeps are checking out everyone's costumes?"

"What do you expect? Get me a drink."

Jeff got two Manhattans from the bar and returned to Allison. She linked her arm through his.

"I'm sorry about tonight," Jeff said. "I thought I was fooling around, but then it somehow got serious. I couldn't stop. Maybe it's the cane."

"Maybe it's the suit. Let's forget about it. We'll get rid of all this shit tomorrow. You can take it back to the old lady or throw it in the trash, but I don't want any of it in our apartment."

Allison heard skates rolling down the long hall behind her. She turned. It was Fenster on skates, dressed as an old-time mortician in top hat. The skates, tight-fitting suit, and hat made his already tall frame frightening. A thin pencil mustache was drawn above his wide lips. He held a drink in one hand and a polished black cane in the other.

"Welcome! Welcome! Ha. Ha. I see you found the bar."

"Our first stop," Jeff said.

"Well done. Good stuff. I see you have a cane, too."

"A vulture's head."

"Impressive."

"Now watch," Jeff said. He stepped back, pressed the secret button, disengaged the knife, and waved it in front of Fenster.

"It's quite wonderful." He laughed. "Oh, what good stuff!"

"I was told it was used in a murder. Just one, though. A stab through the chest." He thrust the knife through the air.

"Through the heart, most likely." Fenster feigned swooning.

Someone called Fenster from the bar and motioned him to join a group.

"I must skate on," Fenster said. He stabbed a finger into Jeff's shoulder blade. "Don't forget. I want to examine that cane later. Drink up. The caterer arrives at midnight. The fortune teller is making her rounds. We have a large sheet cake, too. A graveyard with white chocolate tombstones. Wait until you see it. In the meantime, explore this place. What do you think? Looks like a fucking prom. What a gas! Later, everyone will get the chance to tell a lurid tale about his or her costume."

Just as the old man prepared to propel himself away, a clump, clump, clump echoed in the hallway. It was Fenster's girlfriend—live-in, as he called her around the office, as in, "If my live-in calls, tell her I'm in court."—approaching on stilts.

"Maggie, nice of you to join us," the old barrister intoned sweetly. He introduced Allison and Jeff. "Maggie had a job hanging wallpaper. She papered my foyer. You ought to see it. A work of art. She was employed by a painter and learned her trade on stilts. No hauling around heavy ladders and scaffolding for this kid. She papered my foyer in the morning, made me an omelet for lunch. We were in bed by quitting time.

"Steve," Maggie said, resting a hand on his shoulder, digging in her fingers.

"We decided to show skills from our pasts," Fenster said. "I was an avid roller skater in my youth."

Maggie was incredibly thin and frenetic looking. Her long, dark hair made her look older than she was, but still young enough to be Fenster's daughter. "I want another drink," she whined.

Fenster smiled. "I'll race you to the bar, dear."

He glided off smoothly with hands clasped behind his back, as if he were a long-distance Olympic ice skater, still managing to hold his cane and drink glass. She clumped awkwardly after him, bent at the waist, dressed as Little Bo Peep, complete with an odd-looking bonnet.

"I told you they were circus people," Allison said, poking Jeff in the ribs.

"Can't wait to see them after a couple more drinks," Jeff said. "What do you say we get another drink and explore this place. Who knows? Woodrow Hearst might be home."

The couple got two more Manhattans and walked room to room on the first floor. The carpenters knocked holes in walls, removed plaster to expose old lath, ripped up sections of the floor and re-laid the loose boards. Piles of plaster and wood lay everywhere. The dust made Allison sneeze.

"What a dump," she said. "There's even plaster on what little furniture is left. You can't sit anywhere. What possessed Fenster to let all this shit lie around?" She swung her arms around to point out the debris. "I hope somebody falls and sues him."

"I'm sure that party sign-up sheet now is attached to a disclaimer that would prevent that," Jeff said. He smiled at her.

They walked upstairs and Allison used the bathroom, which looked like it was remodeled in the 1970s. The bathroom floor was covered with green carpet stained red in places. "What a creepy place," she said when she reentered the upstairs hall. "I wonder if those stains are blood."

"Probably Fenster or one of his workers put food coloring on the floor."

The bathroom was at the back of the house. Bedrooms lined the halls moving forward. The largest room was at the front, still furnished, and looked out on Brown Street. More holes were punched in the walls. They walked gingerly down the hall over loose floorboards. The attic consisted of three rooms and a half bath with toilet and sink.

"Originally, servant's quarters, I would think," Jeff said. "Today, a proper man cave. Sports memorabilia. Flat-screen TV, bar, beer fridge."

"You wish, Mr. Creep. All this place will be apartments. It's such a shame."

Music filtered up to them. It appeared the DJ had arrived. "I want to get a piece of that graveyard cake" Allison said. "You know I can't resist white chocolate. I haven't had a piece in ages."

"Me neither."

"You bastard. I'll give you a piece when we get home."

"Let's check out the basement, Ms. Sweet Tooth."

They returned downstairs, picked up more drinks at the bar, and went to the kitchen to find the basement door. A few people danced. More hung out at the bar. Most were getting wasted, standing unsteadily, talking in small clumps. They could hear Fenster and Maggie gliding and clumping room to room. Occasionally they'd hit a spot of loose floorboards and caused a racket. It seemed the circus duo was above them when they reached the bottom of the basement steps. Dust filtered down from the ceiling. Allison sneezed again.

Dim lights barely illuminated the large basement. Water seeped through the stone foundation in areas. Mold grew in green and white spots on the massive beams overhead. Light streaked through where floorboards were pried up and replaced loosely. The dirt floor was uneven and covered here and there with piles of plaster and debris. An old laundry sat unused for years in a corner under the kitchen.

"This place is immense," Allison said. "There's more rooms down there." She pointed into the darkness.

"Something stinks."

"It smells like that suit," she said after a moment. "I couldn't put my finger on it before. It smells like a dirty, musty old basement."

"The suit did smell like the air down here," Jeff said. "Probably sat in a place like this for years. There was never a body. That old crone at the occult shop is crazy."

She took his hand while they continued slowly toward the home's front. She fingered the amulet with the other hand. They explored room by room, finding piles of junk, rusting bicycles, smelly carpets laid over the dirt floor, cast-off furniture, broken tables and lamps, exercise equipment, and toys, all left over the years by a succession of owners and tenants. A dump. One room appeared to be an old dark room where photographs were developed from camera film. There were trays, tongs, old brown glass bottles, and a wire overhead with clips to hold drying photographs. A photo enlarger stood on a bench. Next to it was a small egg timer covered in grime.

"You never finished your story about Woodrow," Jeff said, inspecting the darkroom equipment, moving items with a set of the tongs. "How did he kill his victims? He squeezed her hand.

"A few he killed out in the country. Just stabbed them and let them lie. Out in the open, too. But most he enticed in here and had his way with them. Once they were bound and gagged, and he made them watch him strop the razor, he ever so slowly and painfully cut them apart at the joints, severing muscles and tendons. He started with fingers and toes, then worked himself up to the bigger joints. After he had a joint loose, he'd bend it backward until it snapped off. He took his time. Loved the agony he caused. When someone passed out, he sat and listened to big band records until they came to. He was careful to keep their wounds clean and stop the blood. He even cauterized the big veins so they wouldn't bleed out. It appeared some of the torture lasted for days, when he could keep them alive and coherent. As he dissected and deboned, he laid out the bones carefully, like an anthropologist who found a skeleton from thousands of years ago. It was very gruesome. Even the most hardened police officers couldn't take it. Even the ones who had been through World War II.

"He didn't try to hide the bodies. He kept the bones on display. They were all here in the basement. He said he never thought about being caught. He decided to go on dismembering people until someone stopped him. It was like having a hobby, taxidermy, maybe."

She stopped and turned to Jeff. Looked him in the eye. "He

didn't fight when he was caught. Was very compliant. Didn't complain about the electric chair. Asked for a diaper so his last meal wouldn't make a mess for the guards. The prison staff found him very considerate. Of course, the families of the dead didn't see it that way. They wanted him put down in the most painful way possible. One guy offered to vivisect him. The newspapers had a field day."

Jeff interrupted her. "I'm starting to itch from sweating. It must be the wool."

"Oh, God. Are your gym clothes in the car? What if it's scabies."

"We didn't bring the car."

"Oh. That's right. The only way we have out of here is an Uber."

"It doesn't itch that bad. Really. I'll get a shower after we get home."

"No shit."

"Let's go upstairs. Maybe a drink will calm me. At least it won't hurt."

"Good idea." Allison led the way, retracing their steps until they climbed out of the basement.

They were no sooner through the door and in the kitchen when Fenster glided by, followed by Maggie clumping after him, trying to keep up. Fenster returned to the main room and had the DJ announce it was costume story time. Everyone gathered around. Each attendee—some were drunker than others—stepped forward and told his or her lurid tale. The crowd laughed and applauded. Fenster, among the drunkest, roared.

Jeff was the last. He recounted serial killer Woodrow Hearst was buried in the old suit he wore and later was exhumed. The suit had never been cleaned since it was separated from the corpse. He even turned around to show everyone the coat's back seam split by the mortician but later stitched by an unknown person. He opened the coat's lapel to expose the custom label with Hearst's name stitched inside. The crowd oohed and awed with each grisly detail and crowded around to inspect the suit and its lining.

Then in an inebriated flourish, Jeff unlocked his cane handle and withdrew the stiletto blade. He waved the knife around his head for everyone to see.

The crowd cheered.

Allison clapped and was proud.

"Excellent! Good Stuff!" Fenster roared. "What a night!" He was out of his roller skates and wearing slippers. He had transitioned from maniac on wheels to tipsy, avuncular host, with a whiskey glass in one hand and a dapper cane in the other. His stove pipe hat sat on his head at a rakish, precarious angle. He seemed completely satisfied with himself. Maggie, still dressed as Little Bo Peep, had lost her stilts and shoes. Her bonnet sat at an angle, perhaps from bumping her head on door frames chasing Fenster between rooms. She stood next to Fenster in white stockings, teetering, applauding. Her beer glass rested on the floor between her feet.

Jeff's exertions caused him to sweat more. "Holy shit! I itch like crazy," he said.

Allison looked at him. "You're red. It looks like hives."

"Benadryl?"

"In my big purse." She gave him a look. "At home."

"I'm going to check out this rash upstairs in the bathroom. Want to come?"

Allison followed Jeff up the stairs. It seemed the partygoers had not noticed Jeff's condition. They were reeling, laughing, refilling drinks. The bartender and fortune teller were drunk, too. Her cards spilled on the floor. The kerchief she wore on her head slipped over one eye. The bartender called her a pirate.

Fenster slapped his hand on the bar. "Good stuff. What a night!" he roared.

The bartender passed out behind the bar. Partygoers started to mix their own drinks.

Upstairs, the bathroom was clear. Once inside, Allison locked the door. Jeff took off his tie and opened the white shirt. His chest was red and finely pimpled.

"Oh, man," he said.

"You must be allergic to something. Maybe all this plaster dust. Who knows what they mixed with it years ago?"

"Maybe it's the suit. The wool. I itch like crazy."

Jeff looked in the mirror, turning his head this way and that in the dim light. "Look. My skin's peeling." Jeff rubbed his forehead near the hairline and pulled off a long strip of skin.

"It looks like a burn. Sunburn," Allison said.

"It can't be. The only time we were outside was on the ride here."

Jeff turned on the cold tap, cupped his hands under the stream, and splashed water on his face and hair. He shivered when the water hit the coat. His mouth grimaced. Jeff shook violently. Mumbled. Drooled.

"Electricity!" he managed to stutter. "Shocked! Help!"

Allison grabbed his arm and recoiled with a scream. She shook her hands violently. "You're being shocked. How?"

Jeff's body tensed. He looked stiff as a board, unable to

move. Allison unlocked the bathroom door and threw it open. She grabbed his arm again, screaming in pain, and pulled him as hard as she could. They toppled into the hall. Allison rolled off him. Jeff convulsed on the floor, foaming at the mouth.

"Please stop pain!" he managed to call. "Oh, help me!"

Allison grabbed his shoulder and was knocked backward. She shook her hands to stop the intense tingling. "What is happening," she cried. "This can't be a prank."

Downstairs, the DJ started a new set of dance music, louder than ever, "In the Mood" by Glenn Miller. Fenster was in his skates again, sailing in great exaggerated loops among the downstairs rooms with Maggie in a hot pursuit, clumping in her stilts. Allison saw them flash by when she regained her feet.

She called for help, but no one heard. "What will I do?" she called.

Jeff was in excruciating pain. He moaned. His limbs were rigid and shook. His face was contorted. His eyes bulged. Thin smoke lifted from his hairline.

Every time she touched Jeff she received a terrific shock that bowled her over. She wrung her hands again. She pulled up a dusty painter's tarp from the floor and laid a corner on Jeff's hands.

"Grab the material," Allison told him. "I'll try to pull you way from this spot.

Slowly, painfully, Jeff closed his stiff fingers on the cloth. He cried in pain. The tarp burst into flames as soon he closed his grip. Allison yanked the burning cloth from Jeff's hands, fell to the floor, jumped up, and stamped out the fire.

Meanwhile, Fenster and Maggie glided and stomped below. Maggie screamed for him to stop. Fenster looked up the stairwell at her for a second and howled. Then he was gone. Music thumped. A glass smashed. Laughing, shouting were audible below. Suddenly, Jeff relaxed. Allison knelt beside him, touched his chest cautiously. There was no discharge. She touched his cheek, combed her fingers through his damp hair, pulling away ribbons of skin and clumps of singed hair. He regained consciousness slowly.

Jeff smiled. "What the fuck just happened," he said. The voice was a whisper, all he could manage, and sounded raspier, deeper than normal, as it had earlier when he grabbed her in their apartment.

She leaned over and kissed his mouth. She thought his breath smelled of tobacco. "Let's try to stand. You can sit on the bed at the front for a few minutes. Then we'll get the fuck out of here. We'll take that Uber to the ER."

He struggled to his feet. "I don't know if I can walk that far. Where's that cane?"

"In the bathroom," she said. "Lean against the wall while I get it."

Allison hurried away and returned with the cane. Slowly, unsteadily, he moved down the hall to the front bedroom, dragging his left leg, Allison propping him up. He sat heavily on the bed, pulling Allison with him, stirring up a great cloud of dust.

"Allison, you should get help," Jeff said in his raspy, smoker's voice.

Jeff caught Allison's wrist as she rose, used her weight to pull himself up, and swung her violently in a circle ninety degrees and let her go. Allison slammed into the open closet and slumped to the floor. Jeff closed and locked the door. For good measure, he pushed a straight-back wooden chair under the doorknob.

Jeff hobbled down the hall, leaning on the cane. Maggie emerged from the bathroom, holding her stilts in one hand. "What happened?" she said. Maggie leaned the stilts in a hall corner and moved toward Jeff.

"You look like hell," Maggie said. She pulled off her Bo Peep bonnet.

"It's Allison. Hurry. She's on the floor!"

Jeff let Maggie pass him in the hall.

"In there. The front room. I think she hit her head."

Inside the bedroom, Jeff was behind Maggie. He closed the door.

"Where?" Maggie said bounding up and down. She turned to Jeff. Her eyes were wide with excitement.

Jeff grimaced. He fingered the secret cane button and unsheathed the blade. The cane fell on the floor. He backed Maggie onto the four-poster bed and straddled her. Dust rose around them. She tried to scream but he covered her mouth with his palm. The other hand, holding the knife, rose and fell repeatedly, stabbing Maggie. With each stroke he seemed to gain strength. Maggie lay limp, blood oozing from her torso. Her eyes stared. Her mouth hung open, as if in a violent, soundless scream. Jeff climbed from the body and stood on the floor, breathing heavily.

He turned and took a step toward the closet but suddenly pivoted and jumped back on the bed, plunging the knife into Maggie's lifeless body again and again. He sawed through flesh and muscle. Then he removed the head. He held Maggie's head in front of his face and kissed the lifeless, bloody lips. Jeff smiled. He wiped a hand across his face, licked his lips, tasted her hot blood. He held Maggie's head for a moment and carefully impaled it on one of the bed's four posts.

Again, he stepped toward the closet. There was noise in the hallway. Marcy Brennan, the paralegal who told the couple about the Cauldron Occult Shop, knocked at the bathroom door.

"You in there, Maggie?" Marcy called. "Girlfriend, I thought we were going out to burn one. Can't imagine Fenster doesn't want anybody smoking in this dump. Does he have insurance? Maggie, you there? I refuse to go outside this creepy house by myself."

Jeff, his suit and shirt bloodstained, opened the bedroom door and called for help. Marcy, dressed as a short, plump half-eaten zombie, bounded down the hall. Jeff slit her throat as she passed him in one clean swipe. Marcy collapsed immediately with a thump. Her body gurgled through the deep incision that almost decapitated her and spilled blood on the loose floorboards. Jeff giggled. He removed Marcy's head and impaled it on another bedpost. He wiped his bloody hands on the suit jacket. His body tingled again.

Jeff looked in the bureau's mirror, coated with dust, distorting his image, and said, "Call me Woodrow Hearst. It's good to be back." He smiled and admired his reflection. Jeff returned to the closet and removed the chair from the door.

Downstairs, Fenster took a break. He was back in slippers, savoring a bourbon by the bar when a drop splashed on the top of his bald head. He looked up to see a red spot fanning out on the ceiling. He touched his head with long, tapered, manicured fingers and pulled back a red smear on his fingertips.

"What the hell? Maggie! Where's Maggie?" he called.

"She went up to the bathroom. Marcy went up, too, but they didn't come back. I was waiting to go out for a smoke with them." This was Greg Barner, who had the hots for Marcy according to office gossip. Barner was incredibly thin. Fenster called him Jack Sprat, who could eat no fat, and Mary his wife who could eat no lean. Barner was dressed in a loose-fitting toga and was supposed to be Caligula.

"Where's our muscle," Fenster shouted. "Where's Jeff and Allison? We must go upstairs. Something might be wrong."

The partygoers talked in hushed whispers, trying to account for everyone. One person went outside to search for smokers. A few people had left because of young children and babysitter curfews. Al Zukowski pushed forward. He was trashed. Zukowski had played football, a center for a division II college. He was large and intimidating, always called in for meetings when it was thought clients might become hostile. His size had a calming effect, Fenster said. Zukowski was dressed as The Flintstone character Bam-Bam. The rest of the partygoers stood in a circle, swaying, amazed, fixated on the ceiling's spreading spot, but still managed to avoid its drips.

"We're going upstairs," Fenster shouted, as if a commander in a war movie. "Apparently, we have some missing guests. How apropos on such a night."

"So maybe they went home. Called their Ubers," Zukowski slurred."

"Nonsense. The night is young. Maggie is among them," Fenster said. "We need to go now. I believe they are hiding. Ready to jump out. Good Stuff!"

Fenster led the way to the staircase in his slippers but

stopped half up to let Zukowski go first. A few intoxicated souls lined up to follow Fenster. They too were pushed ahead to allow Fenster a chance to adjust a slipper and bring up the rear. Zukowski marched up the stairs, unafraid. The rest followed with trepidation. Fenster allowed a space to grow between him and the office secretary dressed as Marie Antonette with a high wig. When she looked over her shoulder, Fenster called, "Nothing to fear. I just want to see where everyone is. Take a head count. Maybe Maggie found a secret passage they're exploring. I hope they're not smoking up there. Don't want to set this place on fire, especially after I started the renovations."

Jeff unlocked the closet door and pulled it open a few inches. Allison was still unconscious, curled on the floor, her robe hiked up her bare thighs. Jeff smiled. "In good time, Allison. I'll get to you."

While the search party stole down the hall silently as it could over the loose floorboards, pressed against one another, Jeff dropped behind the bed. Zukowski opened the partially closed bedroom door and peered into the dark room. The small group of four pressed closer. Fenster remained at the top of the stairs at the hall's other end with a clear view of the front room. Zukowski fingered the wall inside the door, found the light switch, and flipped it on. The heads staked on the bed posts, the bodies on the bed and floor, were illuminated. A collective gasp issued from the group. They began to retreat, crying, screaming. They rushed down the hall. Fenster stood frozen at the top step; his fist clinched at his mouth.

"Maggie!" Fenster cried.

The group passed Fenster and flew down the steps.

"Call 911," Zukowski called from the bedroom door.

While Zukowski's head was turned Jeff rose from his hiding place. Fenster crouched and pointed toward Jeff. Zukowski looked back to the room. Jeff approached the door with a knife covered in blood. Zukowski stood silently inside the bedroom door. Fenster stood and moved down the hall, his eyes fixed on Maggie's head with its open eyes and slack mouth.

"Poor kid," he mouthed in a whisper. "She was having a swell time."

He touched the top of his bald head, as if expecting to find more blood. Fenster carried one of Maggie's stilts across his chest, retrieved from the corner near the bathroom. He swallowed with difficulty. His breathing was fast and shallow.

Zukowski was focused on Marcy's face, her mouth twisted open, one eye closed, as if in a lecherous wink. The closet door opened. Allison stumbled out, bent over, one hand on the back of her head. She stepped on the cane shaft, which flew across the room. Her feet went out from underneath her and she dropped heavily on the floor as Jeff stepped forward and swung his knife in a wide arc, missing her head by inches. The knife penetrated the closet door. Jeff wrenched the knife, but broke the blade, leaving him a sharp point on the vulture's head handle. Allison crawled away. Zukowski roared and slammed into the smaller Jeff, driving him into the wall. One big hand closed on Jeff's throat. The other caught the hand holding the knife and repeatedly smashed it on the wall.

Jeff grimaced. Choked. He managed to pass his free hand across his body and catch the knife he dropped from his smashed hand. With the knife free, Jeff slashed Zukowski across his muscular chest, and drove the small blade repeatedly between his ribs. Zukowski coughed up blood, sprayed it on

Jeff's face, backed up releasing his grip, and slumped to the floor. Fenster was at the bedroom door. Jeff turned on him and snarled.

"Uncle Fucking Fenster," Jeff said. His voice was raspy and didn't belong to him. "You know, that's what we call you in the office. Everybody does. *Uncle Fucking Fenster.* How nice of you to drop in on my humble abode."

Fenster launched the stilt like a javelin. The foot pad hit Jeff squarely in the chest and hammered him back into the wall, driving the air out of him. The two men eyed each other.

Downstairs, the partygoers had spilled into the street and clustered in a group. Some walked away, deciding to take their chances in Downtown Mammoth. Others waited nervously for their Uber drivers, hoping to escape before the police arrived. The caterer, who had just delivered and set up the food as the commotion upstairs started, was even more quickly refilling his truck. Police sirens were audible in the distance.

Fenster backed into the hall. Jeff approached him slowly, stooping to pull the broken blade from Zukowski's ribs. The dead man moaned as his wound expelled air. The room smelled of blood and eviscerated entrails.

Jeff grinned. "There's plenty of knife left to slice you, Uncle Fucking Fenster. You and dear Allison. We'll have to flip a coin to see whose heads can get *posted*. Where is dear Allison, in her little witch's robe with almost nothing underneath?"

Allison crouched in a corner inside the bedroom. Her head hurt. She held her amulet with one hand. The cane shaft with the other. Jeff blocked her retreat. He turned to find her.

"My little muffin," Jeff cooed in his raspy voice. "Let's make love with Maggie on the bed. Do you mind if I don't get undressed? I rather like this suit, itch and all." Jeff looked up at Maggie's grinning head. "What's that? Maggie says she doesn't mind if I leave the suit on." He smiled his apparent approval.

Allison, still squatting, backed against the corner wall. She held the cane shaft in both hands.

"Allison first. Uncle Fucking Fenster next," Jeff said. "You've been fucking me for years, Unc. Now it's my turn."

Fenster ran to the end of the hall and brought back the second stilt.

"No!" Fenster screamed, standing in the doorway with the stilt. Jeff turned toward him and laughed. Allison launched herself from the corner. She thrust the cane upward with a cry. The metal tip pierced the soft flesh between Jeff's jaws, crushed the roof of his mouth and sinuses, passed through his brain, and blew through the top of his skull.

Jeff stepped back, cocked his head, and said "Babe!" He collapsed on the floor.

Fenster ran to Allison. Hugged her and led her from the room. He looked into her tear-flooded eyes and said, "What a night!"

THE THING IN THE WALLS

It was hard to trace the start of the rat problem on Hazel Street. It was even harder to explain its sudden disappearance and what came later. Charles Barton, however, who had lived on Hazel Street his entire life, thought the local nightmare began when the circus people moved into the brick row home in the exact middle of the block, the side with the even house numbers, six doors above his home. Instead of retiring to Florida, like most carney folk, the Headstrongs settled in Mammoth, Pennsylvania. It was thought Forrest Headstrong had family in the region, possibly the state prison, although Headstrong was an uncommon name in and around Mammoth and he had a distinct southern twang to his speech. Pennsylvania winters could be brutal, the summers hot and humid, although not as bad as Florida. Pennsylvania winters were enough to send most retirees packing. That's why most Hazel Street residents thought the Headstrongs arrival rather odd.

However, Mammoth was the type of place where almost anything can happen. The city was the county seat and named after a forty-foot-thick vein of anthracite whose coal helped fuel the American industrial revolution. The black gold was heaped on barges, pulled by mules when necessary, and otherwise floated down the Schuylkill River to Philadelphia. Coal barons made fortunes on the backs of immigrant labor and built mansions in Mammoth on its highest hill. Hazel Street, an entire block—both sides—of brick row homes, was built in the 1880s at the city's lowest geographical point for families who worked in the old Mammoth brick works, which used coal to fire its kilns. The brick works died out eventually with the coal industry, its land consumed by the growing city, but Hazel Street and its sturdy houses remained. The Hazel Street abodes were thought to be good starter homes. Only fifteen feet across, from side to side, the homes also were an alternative for older people who wanted to downsize. The original builders were unconcerned about the immigrants who moved in and didn't bother incorporating firewalls between the structures. Common walls between homes were studded and layered with wood lath and plaster. Therefore, the fear of fire was ever present. The thin walls also allowed sound to travel, and before long most people on Hazel Street knew the Headstrong's business, anything the family discussed above a whisper.

The Headstrongs had operated a sideshow of human and animal oddities under the auspices of a larger circus, the Kingpin Brothers Menagerie. When they retired, the family sold off most of the attractions, retaining a three-armed mummy, one arm appearing to be an enormous, bandaged erection growing from its lower abdomen. The mummy was scandalous when first introduced at the turn of the 20th century but delighted tittering crowds even into modern times.

The Headstrongs also kept an assortment of barnyard and human deformities preserved in large jars, but the centerpiece was a legless vampire, complete with three-fingered hands, a short, reptilian-like tail and an ornate stake through its heart. Old posters claimed the vampire was staked at the moment it transformed between human and giant bat. The withered torso was greenish black, leathery, and dressed in a white shirt, white waistcoat, and black tuxedo coat complete with a dried red rose in the lapel. The clothes were now discolored, frayed and dusty. The white fabrics had turned yellow and had stains. The trousers were missing. The large claw-like hands were crossed over the creature's chest. The face was dark and sunken with a pig-like snout. According to the poster, the creature had been staked by a famous European vampire hunter—not Dr. Van Helsing of Bram Stoker fame—with a *silver* spike that had an ornate handle with inlaid gold. The creature lay in a small coffin, possibly a child's, because it was no more than four feet long. The coffin was lidless and appeared ready to disintegrate at any moment, which gave neighbors a good look at the abomination when the Headstrongs moved in. It appeared Forrest retained a carney mentality, because he stood on the sidewalk and barked details about the grisly little corpse as it was lifted from the moving van and carried inside. He also showed the ever-growing crowd the six fingers on his own right hand, each encircled with a silver ring. There were skulls, devils, and curious gems on the rings, including one that looked like an eyeball. He claimed to have six toes but did not remove his box-like right shoe, much to his new neighbors' disappointment.

Charles Barton was superstitious. He stood among the crowd, watched the pickled monstrosities, the mummy, and the vampire taken inside, slowly and carefully with just a little fanfare, and was glad he lived six doors away from the Headstrongs. He knew no good would come from their addition to the neighborhood. Charles's dog Kona sat by his side, growling at the circus people and their freakish exhibits.

Forrest approached Charles, leaned to pet Kona, but the dog showed his teeth. Charles jerked the leash to break Kona's attention on the man.

"Don't want to lose a finger," Forest said, smiling. "Especially the special one." Forrest wiggled the deformed sixth digit and chuckled. Forrest was a tall, thin man, pale and wrinkled. His hair was long and appeared dirtier more than gray.

"Sorry," Charles said. "He usually doesn't act like that. It must be the crowd."

"Of course," Forrest said. He rubbed his hands together. "What kind of dog is it? I love the brindle coat. It would make a lovely vest. Just kidding, of course." Forrest chuckled so his thin frame rose and fell.

"He's part Plott Hound and who knows what else. We rescued him from Florida. Plott Hounds were bred down south to hunt bear."

"Indeed. I'm sure we'll make good friends." Forrest inclined his head toward Kona, but the dog recoiled and growled again. Forrest laughed. "We'll try again another day when there aren't so many people around. I usually carry treats, but with the move I believe they were mislaid in the packing."

With the Headstrongs, the carney oddities, and their sparse furniture transferred safely inside, the crowd dissipated, and Charles returned home to his mother Viola with whom he lived. He decided not to tell her about the Headstrongs other than that they were retired circus people. Viola had a weak heart and at eighty-five ventured out only for visits to her doctors or to sit on the small front porch. Pastor Johnson visited monthly to offer her Holy Communion. Charles figured his mother would learn soon enough about the strange new people down the block. He wanted to prepare a story to calm any fears she might develop.

Charles did the cleaning, shopping, and cooking for his mother. She doted on him, her only child, and was thankful a middle-aged son would attend to her so attentively. They wore matching colors when he took her out, even to the doctor, as if one might get lost and later more easily be identified.

Within a few days of the Headstrongs' arrival on Hazel Street, immediate neighbors on both sides complained of smells from their home, deciding the bodies they brought home were decaying and might contain diseases. Perhaps even a mummy's curse. The Mammoth Health Officer visited the Headstrongs. Forrest ushered her and the complaining neighbors and their children into the house. Although boxes remained to be unpacked, some clearly marked *circus*, a séance room, and a computer were already set up. Miriam, Mrs. Headstrong, bought and sold various items on eBay. She warned her new neighbors that there would be frequent deliveries and pick-ups at their home. The dusty mummy and vampire, displayed in the smallest bedroom on the second floor, along with an assortment of boxed circus oddities and memorabilia, were found to be odorless. Everyone smelled the two corpses, and even the children dared while Forrest looked on smiling, apparently approvingly.

Donnie Savitsky, age twelve, who lived next door to the circus family, took a couple of sniffs and then tugged on the vampire's stake, but Forrest brushed his chubby, dirty hand away.

"Young man, don't you know that if you remove a stake from a vampire's heart, the creature will return to life and hunt down *first* the person who removed the weapon?"

Donnie laughed. "You gotta be kidding. That thing is so dried out I bet the stake is holding it together."

"I wouldn't want to try it," Forrest said sinisterly, closing one eye as he stared at the boy and pointing two of his six fingers at him. "We don't know whether the vampire hunter impaled the thing while it was transformed to bat or back to human."

"Go on," Donnie said.

"Of course, the vampire could decide to remain in its present state, if that fit its purpose. You can never tell with vampires."

"What's a stake like that worth?" Donnie said.

Forrest and Miriam smiled. "It's priceless," Miriam said. "Can you imagine the trouble a vampire on the loose could cause in this community? It would drain everyone dry of blood." Miriam raised an eyebrow and smiled at the boy. "It could decide to turn some into vampires. Then you'd have more than one creature and no place to hide. It would be a plague. That stake, my boy, is priceless."

"I don't think it's real. My dad says you're a fake and your stuff is fake."

"The doubting public always amazes me," Forrest said. "I wouldn't lie to a neighbor."

"I still don't believe you. Is that thing male or female?"

"I don't know, Donnie. Let's have a look," Forrest said.

Donnie smirked.

Forrest flipped the coat and shirttails away from the torso.

"A cunt! Will you look at that? It's an old shriveled up cunt."

"Donnie!" Mrs. Savitsky cried, blushing. "I never. If your father heard you talk like that!"

The rest in the group sniggered or coughed nervously. Forrest dropped the clothing over the torso and smiled. "Question answered. Mystery solved."

Forrest said, "Well, suppose I show you the rest of the house. You know, we don't have it arranged yet, and Miriam wants to do some painting and papering before we're ready for company, but it won't hurt for you to take a peek. We have nothing to hide. Nothing."

As if on a museum tour, the group visited the bathroom, kitchen, and basement, Forrest leading the way pointing here or there to describe circus attractions or future renovation projects. They found no odors in any of the drains, closets, or cabinets.

"We might have been mistaken," Mrs. Savitsky said. "It's been so hot. Sometimes we get a sewer smell in *our* basement. I'm sorry for any inconvenience we caused, especially while you're still unpacking, and I'm sorry for Donnie's behavior."

Forrest raised an eyebrow. "That's all right. Boys will be boys." He reached out and touched Donnie's shoulder with his six-fingered hand. Donnie flinched.

Charles and Kona were inseparable and walked every night,

weather permitting, after Charles returned from his job on the maintenance staff at Mammoth Hospital. It was a good way to get some time alone away from his mother. Neighbors gave Kona treats and pet him. Kona wagged his tail. Over the next few days Charles noticed Kona refused to walk by the Headstrong home, including on the opposite side of the street, even though he had a canine friend, Gypsy, at the end of the block, who always proffered her backside for a good sniff. As soon as Charles pointed Kona in the Headstrong's direction, the dog lay down on the sidewalk and refused to move. However, Kona would rise and resume walking as soon as Charles tugged the leash in the opposite direction.

Charles was worried. Viola was worried, too.

"Do you know those circus folk have a mummy and a vampire, dried up like old prunes, in they home?"

"I know, Mom. I seen them. There's nothing to worry about. The Headstrongs are just plain folk. Maybe a little different from working in the circus all those years. I don't believe they attractions are real. Just fakes. Like movie props."

They're evil," Viola said. She stood and touched a crucifix hanging on the wall. "God help us. Jean Savitsky was through the place. Did you know they have a séance room? She told me all about it. And that man having six fingers. It just ain't natural. No good will come of that. Predicting the future and talking to dead souls. Interrupting they eternal peace."

Charles said, "So I heard, but it's just a little table with a crystal ball on it. The crystal ball is probably a decoration. Maybe Mrs. Headstrong tells fortunes and reads palms. Maybe it's one of those snow globes and doesn't see the future. What did I tell you about Jean Savitsky? When they is no trouble, she makes it up. You just remember your heart. I don't want you upset and getting a spell when I'm at work."

"Upset! I'm going into pray. That's when I'm at peace. Let me know when supper is ready. Maybe you could give me butter on my bread. An extra pat of butter might calm me some."

"No butter, Mom. Too much salt. Too much fat. I been talking to the dietician at the hospital, and she gave me some ideas to lower your cholesterol. You have a doctor appointment end of the week."

"You worried about cholesterol when they's a vampire up the street! Do you think that thing cares how much butter is in your blood?"

The next day, Jean Savitsky told Viola the Headstrongs had left for Florida. A friend from the circus, a sword swallower, had died. Perforated stomach and peritonitis. They would be gone at least a week, maybe two until they drove down and back and visited with other circus folk.

Many residents on Hazel Street didn't realize the flimsy common walls between homes had unfinished space in the attic cubbies under the eaves that allowed someone small enough to crawl from home to home undetected. The evening after the Headstrongs left for Florida, Donnie Savitsky and a friend named Jeremy Brothers, went upstairs and crawled into the Headstrong attic while Donnie's parents were on their deck smoking dope. Donnie was big for his age and just managed to squeeze through the unfinished lath wall near the floor.

Inside the Headstrong's, the boys made their way down to the second floor, moving carefully because the attic steps creaked and were littered with boxes destined to be carried upstairs. In fact, before the Headstrongs left for Florida, Donnie had volunteered to move the boxes in the hope he would get another look at the vampire. They stopped to look at various things—a sequined gown, gawdy jewelry, a blue fez, an old tuxedo, a turban of gold fabric. Eventually, they reached the room where the sideshow artifacts were displayed.

The boys marveled at the two-headed human baby, pale in pickling brine, a fine white film covering the jar's bottom, and a misshapen cow, and an equine-looking specimen with six legs. Donnie dared Jeremy to touch the mummy's cock, but he wouldn't. They giggled and whispered because they feared the Barkers, the Headstrong's other immediate neighbors, might hear them. The boys moved toward the vampire. It was warm in the room, and they sweated profusely. Donnie's dark hair was plastered to his forehead. His fat cheeks were flushed. They took turns feeling the vampire's dusty coat.

"You can tell it's good material," Donnie said.

"How would you know?"

"Don't worry," Donnie hissed. "I know my stuff. I tell you it's good material. Expensive. It's a tuxedo."

When Donnie touched one of the leathery hands that crossed over the cadaver's chest, Jeremy recoiled. Both were breathless in the heat and near darkness. The room's single window had been covered completely to prevent light from entering.

Donnie nudged Jeremy's ribs. "Look. No sunlight."

The boys nodded to each other. "It's a real vampire. Not a fake," Jeremy whispered.

"Look at the stake," Donnie said, nervously. "It's solid silver.

And that handle, the yellow stuff is real gold. It must be worth a fortune, and it's ours."

Donnie touched the end of the handle, slid his finger down the smooth, silver shaft.

"What will you do with it?" Jeremy asked.

"Either take it to the pawn shop downtown or that occult shop on Second Street. Whoever gives the best price." Donnie wiped his sweating hands on his jeans. "You'll get half."

Jeremy smiled and took a turn touching the stake.

"I'm going to pull it out," Donnie said. "Then we're going to beat it."

"You can't pull it out. That might bring the vampire to life."

"Nothing could bring this thing back to life."

"I'm telling you. You must put another stake in, even if it's wood, back through the heart. Find something else to use for another stake. Even that mummy's dick."

"How do you know?" Donnie said, arms akimbo. Jeremy looked scared.

"Because I watch Svengoolie on Saturday nights. I've seen plenty of vampire movies."

"Unreal," Donnie said, shaking his head.

"No. Undead," Jeremy hissed, turning his face toward Donnie. "I'm telling you, if you pull that stake out the thing will grab you."

"Okay, use the mummy's dick if you want a replacement stake."

"No way. Are you nuts? That might bring them both back to life."

"Let's see." Donnie looked at Jeremy, grabbed the stake handle, twisted the shaft, and pulled it from the corpse. Both boys jumped back with a start. Nothing happened. They laughed. Then they heard a noise in the Barker home.

"Let's go," Jeremy said. "Before they hear us."

"Wait a minute. They're probably going to bed. Maybe they'll go at it. Newlyweds screw like rabbits. I heard my dad tell Mr. Barton. They're always going at it. It's funny. We could listen."

"I'm getting out of here," Jeremy said. He turned toward the door.

"Wait for me. Stay a minute, just to see if they get started."

"No way."

Jeremy left the room and Donnie followed reluctantly. As they reached the hall, it sounded like a long moan came from the room.

"Vampire!" Jeremy said. He ran toward the attic.

"No. Barker came already. I knew they'd go at it," Donnie said. "I've heard that sound before." He trotted toward Jeremy.

"It sounded like it came from inside the room," Jeremy said.

"Couldn't have. I'll prove it. Go look, Jeremy."

"Not on your life."

Donnie tiptoed back to the room, peeked in through the open door. He turned back to Jeremy. His face was white.

"The fucking thing is gone!"

Jeremy backed away a few steps, knocking over boxes, and ran for the attic steps. Donnie followed. He dropped the stake halfway up the stairs and it clattered end over end to the bottom. Donnie raced back down, grabbed the stake, and sprinted up the steps as fast as his chubby legs carried him. Jeremy was already in the cubbie, scrambling on hands and knees toward the hole in the common wall without regard for the noise he made. Donnie came after him. Inside the Savitsky attic, they covered the hole in the common wall with suitcases, boxes, anything they could pile against the opening.

They went to Donnie's room and fell on his bed. Donnie's parents were still on the deck. The boys were breathless and sweating. Donnie burst out laughing. "That thing didn't move, you goof. That noise had to be the Barkers. That's what it sounds like when you come. We hear it every night. They have a lot of sex."

"Did you see the thing in the coffin? You looked in the room."

"I didn't have to see it. That thing looked like it was hit by a truck."

"You prick. You scared the shit out of me."

Donnie smiled at his friend. "Our next move is to see what we can get for this stake. Remember, we can't act like a couple kids with a stolen thing. We have to be, what's the word, nonchalant, like we sold other stuff in the past."

Donnie handed the stake to Jeremy. "You hold onto it. Sometimes my mom snoops around my room. I don't want her to find it before we unload it."

"I don't want it."

"Take it. What could happen?" Donnie said.

———

THE NEXT DAY, a Monday, Donnie disappeared, and rodents moved into Charles Barton's home and the houses between the Headstrongs' and his. The neighbors were on the street arguing. Someone was responsible for feeding the vermin, or someone had pets that escaped and their population exploded. Police combed the city for Donnie and had few leads. The health inspector returned on Tuesday morning to Hazel Street and confirmed mice or rats were running with abandon through the walls and above the ceilings in most of the homes on both sides of the Headstrongs'. She would put poison in the drains and seal them to prevent the vermin from escaping back into the houses.

"The circus people have brought a plague to us, the same as the one God descended on the Egyptians," Viola shouted. "Not locusts, but rats." She started holding prayer sessions on her front porch because she was afraid the vermin from hell might attack her inside the house.

The Barton home sounded like a stampede in the walls and above the ceilings as seemingly hundreds of little paws raced back and forth frantically. The noise was so distracting that Charles and Viola could not watch television. Occasionally, they caught a glimpse of a rodent scurrying across the carpet along the wall or felt one run over their feet. The rodents squealed, seemingly in terror as if chased by something unseen. Kona leaped from the sofa to give chase, knocking over end tables and almost upsetting Viola's prized curio cabinet.

Charles set thirty traps and sticky strips in the home on Tuesday night. He was afraid to use poison. There was Kona to think of. Charles had already seen a tail flapping in Kona's mouth briefly before the dog swallowed one of the rodents. Rats that died inside the walls would stink for days, if not weeks. The next morning, all the traps were filled with dead or dying rodents. Charles returned to Home Depot and bought more traps, set them in the same places, and caught forty-five more by Thursday morning.

Kona caught and killed a few, swallowing the little ones whole. Then Charles set fifty traps on Thursday evening. Other neighbors claimed they caught similar numbers in their traps. Garbage bags with trapped rats lined the sidewalk awaiting trash day pickup. Charles and Viola had difficulty moving through the home, clinging to furniture to keep their balance, fearing the spring traps would break their toes, the sticky strips would attach to their feet, and tear off their skin. Kona was confined to the kitchen. However, the next morning, Friday, all the traps were empty. A whole jar of peanut butter was wasted on the spring traps.

Viola sat on her bed and prayed. Charles vacuumed up rodent droppings. Kona lay on the kitchen floor, waiting to pounce. Then they listened for rodent activity, pressing their ears against the walls. There was no noise. Charles scooped up the peanut butter coated traps and dropped them in garbage bags, put them outside.

Friday evening, Charles conferred with other neighbors who had gone through similar experiences. They gathered in the street, talking in hushed voices, as if the varmints would hear their plans. The rodents had disappeared. Now some neighbors blamed others for using poison on the vermin. Soon their homes would be filled with the stench of death. However, no odors materialized through the weekend, and the walls and ceiling remained silent. Charles and Viola lay in their respective bedrooms for hours straining their ears to hear rodents scrambling overhead. They even refrained from using their ceiling fans. The house remained quiet as a tomb.

On Monday morning, once more, neighbors gathered on the sidewalk outside the Headstrong home. They rejoiced for their apparent victory over the vermin. They believed all the rats were caught. They bumped fists and high-fived. However, they were saddened by the fact that Donnie Savitsky had not returned home. Women sobbed. Men shook their bowed heads in disbelief. Along the crowd's fringe, Jeremy moved between people, trying to take in everything. Viola led more prayer circles on her porch. The crowd filled the porch and spread to the sidewalk.

After supper on Monday, Charles finished the dishes, and Viola sat at the kitchen table reading her Bible.

"Are you sure you feel okay, Mom. I've been worried about you. I know how the rats and the Savitsky boy have distressed you. You seem too quiet."

"I'm fine, son. The Lord tests even old folks like me. My faith in Him has carried us through a lot more. Remember when your father was taken."

"I'd like to take your pressure, just to make sure."

"There's no need. I feel calm as a church mouse...I mean a purring kitten when I have the Book in my hands."

"I know you do, Mom. That's a good thing." Charles went to the table and kissed her on the cheek. "You're the best mom in the world."

"And you're the best son. Your devotion to me is...What was that? Did you hear it?"

"I didn't hear anything, Ma."

"It sounded like the rats are back."

"You couldn't tell, Ma. You put the TV on so loud that the windows rattle. How you think you're going to hear a little rat in the wall?"

"Must be my nerves then."

"We had a trying week."

They retired to the living room to watch *Family Feud*. Charles had to return to work the next day. Viola was exhausted and nodded off before the first set of commercials. Charles turned off the television and roused his mother so they could go to bed.

During the night Viola screamed. "Help me, Lord! Save me!"

Charles leaped from bed and ran to his mother's room, flicked on the overhead light. Viola was curled on the bed with the covers wrapped around her. She pointed at the wall. "Something's in there. No rat. No pack of rats. Something big!"

Charles heard it immediately. It sounded like something large moving through the wall slowly, with difficulty. To his amazement, a bulge appeared on the wall and moved toward the corner, knocking to the floor a picture of Christ and the palm fronds braided neatly and attached to the wire holding the picture. The palm came from church on Palm Sunday and was replaced each year. As the thing moved, wooden lath cracked, nails popped, and plaster crumbled and fell inside the wall. The thing whistled, a single, high-pitched long note, but it was barely audible through the wall. The bulge moved slowly until it reached the corner and disappeared. However, the sound continued. Charles ran to the next room, his bedroom, where the bulge reappeared and moved across his wall. Lath cracked, nails popped, and old plaster crumbled, falling inside the wall, leaving cracks across the room. Charles thought it had to be a cat; a feral cat that feasted on mice for so long it got huge and now got stuck in the walls.

"Don't worry, Ma. I think it's a cat in the wall looking for mice. It's looking for a way to get out. It'll be gone as soon as it finds an exit."

"I am worried," Viola shot back. "Ain't natural for a cat to climb through the walls. Don't matter how hungry it is."

The bulge traveled from Charles's room to the bathroom and into the kitchen ceiling below. It moved down the wall and over the back door frame. Charles ran outside. He saw dust and mortar fall from between the bricks on the back of the home. He turned on the back spotlight and watched the thing's progress until it entered the next home. Charles ran inside, turned off the light and locked the door. He went to his mother, who sat quaking on the bed.

"You okay, Ma? Whatever it was—I think it was a big feral cat—is gone."

Charles got Viola a drink of water, straightened her bed covers, and tucked her in.

———

THE NEXT MORNING, Charles went outside to look for damage on the brick wall. Ned Barker was outside on his deck several houses away. "You know your basement window is open. I saw a big groundhog come out and run to the next street."

"Groundhog?"

"It was something. Had a white face, pointy snout, and sharp teeth." Ned pulled up his upper lip over his own canine tooth. "Real sharp." He wore sunglasses and drank a glass of tomato juice.

"Tail like a...snake," Chole Barker said. She pressed against her husband and giggled. She appeared to be wearing only a sheet wrapped around her like a toga. She held a mug of coffee in her free hand.

"That sounds like an opossum," Charles said.

"It was squeezing through our walls last night, whatever it was, whistling like a tea kettle. Made a hell of a racket." Barker adjusted the crotch of his shorts. He was shirtless.

Charles thought a moment. "Probably looking for rats. Probably ran away this morning, like you said, when it didn't find any. I think an opossum would eat a rat. A groundhog wouldn't," Charles said. "I thought it might be a feral cat. A big one."

"Cats don't whistle," Chole said. "None that I ever saw." She giggled, adjusted her toga to show Charles her bare shoulder.

"It might if it got stuck on a nail in the wall."

"What ran through your yard this morning *wasn't* a cat," Chole said. "I can guarantee that." She raised a bare foot to examine her sole. "I got a fucking splinter from this deck. Ouch. Ned! It hurts. I thought you were going to paint this wood."

"Better wash it off good," Charles said, looking over the distance between their decks to see her raised begrimed sole. "That thing that was in the wall might have crossed your deck. It might have rabies. Animals like that, used to the wild, don't normally come around people and houses unless they sick."

"Well, it's gone now, I think," Ned said.

"I'll tell my mother. She'll be relieved it's gone. She was pretty shook up last night. We both were."

———

THE THING RETURNED THAT NIGHT. It whistled and clawed, pulling itself through the voids in the walls, pressing out bulges on the interior living space, cracking plaster, breaking the lath underneath. It made one pass through the Barton home and disappeared.

With his mother shouting instructions from the top of the basement steps, Charles tiptoed down holding a broom and a flashlight. He leaned the broom in a corner at the bottom of the steps and picked up a shovel. Charles figured the shovel gave him more killing power. The basement window was closed and locked, just as he left it after talking to the Barkers. He remembered opening the window to help ventilate the basement, which tended to get damp, and forgot to close it. He listened intently for noise. There was none. He explored the basement cautiously, fanning the beam of his flashlight this way and that. The floor remained clean. There were no new droppings after he swept it yesterday.

The next day, Charles bought a crossbow and a half-dozen bolts on his way home from work. His mother would never allow a gun in the house, and he didn't like the idea of owning one. Even if the thing never came back, the crossbow would provide protection for Viola and him. After dinner, Charles and his mother watched *Family Feud*. They always rooted for one family over another and howled at Steve Harvey's antics. Except for Donnie Savitsky's disappearance, it appeared quiet had returned to Hazel Street. Other than the noise from the television, the Barton home was quiet. They had the crossbow for protection against any animal that might have rabies. There was no commotion on the street like when the creature moved among the homes and their frightened occupants fled to the sidewalks in their pajamas.

The Bartons were tired. Viola was always tired by evening. Charles had spent most of the day on ladders at the hospital, changing fluorescent bulbs in ceiling lights. He was happy to turn in early. He walked behind his mother up the steps. She climbed slowly, one step at a time, pulling herself up with one hand on the rail.

After going over the steps necessary to arm the crossbow, Charles rested it against the wall next to the bed. The bolts fit on a holder attached to the weapon.

Charles had just dozed off when he woke to the whistling noise and turned on the light. His mother screamed in her room next door.

"Save me, Jesus!" Viola shouted. "Are you there, Charles? Do you hear the fiend in the wall? Help me, Sweet Jesus! The devil is back!"

Charles watched a bulge move across his bedroom wall that separated his and his mother's bedrooms. He heard claws gripping and pulling the beast through the voids. Wood cracked. Plaster fell. Plaster dust rose into the room. The creature whistled. The crossbow was armed in seconds. Charles sat on the bed and fired. He missed the bulge, but the bolt hit a stud and stuck in the wall. He fired two more bolts in rapid succession. Each missed its mark and disappeared into the plaster. The fourth stuck in the wall under the first. He reloaded, walked resolutely to the corner, and fired the fifth inches from the bulge. The arrow disappeared into the wall. The beast shrieked so loud the house seemed to shake. It was a long high-pitched howl of pain, far louder than the whistle had been.

The creature convulsed inside the wall. Plaster cracked. Lath snapped as the creature seemed to spin inside the wall. Dust spilled into Charles's room. A black, viscous fluid seeped from the fifth bolt hole and trickled down the wall. It was foul smelling and Charles recoiled back to the bed and covered his nose. The thing clawed at the plaster, as if intent on breaking through the wall into Charles's bedroom. It shrieked in pain. A long, yellowish curved talon pushed through the old plaster, raising more dust. Then a second and a third claw emerged and pulled back the plaster into the wall, making a larger hole. Another hand reached through and pulled off more plaster and lath, the wood snapping loudly. Finally, the creature's head was visible.

Charles saw a green, bat-like head, its leathery skin engorged with blood. It snarled, showing sharp teeth. Charles stood and aimed the crossbow. He intended to make the shot count now that he knew what he was fighting, but the creature withdrew inside the wall in an instant. Charles fired. The arrow disappeared into the hole. The thing moved easily through the wall now, the void expanded by its writhing, and was gone.

"It's the fucking vampire!" Charles screamed. "It's no opossum. It's no rabid cat. It ate all the rats. Hundreds of them. Thousands of them. Millions of them! It's full of they blood." Charles dropped the crossbow and held his head in his hands, sobbed.

The home was suddenly eerily quiet. He tried to pull out the two bolts stuck in the wall but they were seated too deeply in the studs. He was afraid the creature would come back if he made more noise. Then Charles thought of his mother. She was quiet. She had stopped screaming. What if she had a heart attack? Her medicine was next to her bed. She knew what it was and where it was.

Charles ran to his mother's room. The door did not open. The creature's violent gyrations inside the wall had moved the studs, pinching the doorframe. He had to put his shoulder against the door before it sprang open, causing him to fall into the room.

His mother sat on the bed, slumped over, legs dangling over the side. One bolt had hit her in the abdomen, another in the chest. A third caught her between the eyes. Charles kneeled at her side and sobbed.

"What did I do? What did I do?" he cried.

A noise brought back his attention. Someone pounded on the front door. He stood shakily, went downstairs and to the door. It was the Barkers. Ned was shirtless, wearing only pajama bottoms. Chole had on a short silk robe, belted so tightly it revealed she wore nothing underneath.

"It sounded like World War III. Is everything okay?" Ned said.

"The vampire attacked us. I just killed my mother!"

"I don't believe it," Chole said. "That's impossible. You must have had a dream."

"I shot through the wall with the crossbow. I was trying to hit the thing in the wall, but three arrows hit my Ma."

"Are you sure she's dead?" Chole said, putting a hand on Charles's arm.

"She is," Charles said. "There's no doubt."

Chole led Charles into the living room and had him sit on the sofa. Ned ran home for whiskey.

"We still have to call 911," Chole said.

Charles shook his head in agreement. "I'm going to jail."

Ned returned with a bottle of bourbon. He scavenged noisily through kitchen cabinets until he found glasses. He returned with glasses and poured two drinks. He handed one to Charles. Chole grabbed the second. Then she called 911.

"You better have a look upstairs," she told Ned.

"I don't think I can," Ned said, over his shoulder, retreating to the kitchen for another glass.

The second floor shook. Wood snapped. Plaster dust streamed down the steps. Chole covered her nose and ran to the base of the steps. The noise stopped. Chole looked at the men. Ned refilled his and Charles's glasses.

"Aren't you going up?" Charles said. He looked up at Ned with tears in his eyes.

Chole mounted the steps cautiously. Her legs disappeared when she reached the second floor. "Fuck!" Chole screamed.

She limped down the steps. "I stepped on a fucking nail in the hall."

"You saw Ma?" Charles said.

"There's no one up there," Chole said. She limped down the steps, hopped on one foot to the sofa. "I didn't go in the room because I stepped on this fucking nail. I was impaled, had to pull the fucking nail out of my foot. I did see partly inside. Maybe she was stunned and walked away."

"Not in her condition," Charles said, sobbing. "Even without the arrows, she wouldn't go far. Her heart."

"Ned, if you're not going upstairs, give me your flip-flops. We need to find Mrs. Barton."

Chole drained her whiskey glass, grabbed Ned's, and

finished it off, wiped a sleeved arm across her mouth, and slid into the flip-flops several sizes too large.

"The crossbow's in my room, but I shot all the arrows," Charles said. "Be careful."

Chole walked up the steps slowly, nervously. The flip flops slapped against her soles."

Ned poured another drink.

Charles followed Chole at a distance. "I can't believe I killed my mother," he moaned. "What judge and jury gonna believe me. I shot at a vampire in the wall and killed my mother."

Chole was halfway up the steps. There was a noise from Viola's room that sounded like someone being dragged across the floor. Chole tiptoed down the hall, the flip flops snapping against her feet. She peered into Charles's room. The crossbow lay on the bed. She went inside and picked up the crossbow, saw two bolts in the wall, and approached the wall's damaged section. There was a large hole, Shards of sharp lath protruded. Clumps of plaster hung from the old horsehair used to bind it. A long bulge of cracked plaster proceeded across the wall and disappeared at the corner. The two bolts would not budge from the studs inside. Chole carried the crossbow back through the door. She continued down the hall, pressing herself against the wall.

Charles was at the top of the steps. She turned and indicated he should be quiet, placing an index finger on her lips. She reached Viola's bedroom door. It was partially open and wedged into the floor, where Charles had forced it open. She heard the dragging noise again. Chole tried to open the door more to get a better look inside, but it wouldn't move. She heard more dragging. Chole looked around the door and saw the creature inside the wall pulling Viola Barton the last remaining few feet to the wall.

The creature looked up, hissed, and dropped Viola's arms. It cocked its head a moment at the noise of approaching sirens and then returned its gaze at Chole. It had shed its tuxedo. The leathery skin had a hole in the shoulder, from which a black viscous goo, mixed with plaster dust, seeped down its torso. Chole recoiled when the foul odor reached her nose. She backed into the door and it slammed shut. Chole dropped the crossbow and tugged on the doorknob. It came off in her hands.

The creature started to pull itself from the hole in the wall, intent on adding Chole to its victims. It licked its bloodied lips. Viola's blood. Chole picked up the crossbow and pointed it at the creature. The vampire shrieked, grabbed Viola's arms, and pulled her into the wall. In a moment they were gone. The creature and Viola raced through the wall. Wood exploded. Their trail spewed plaster into the room, raising dust Chole choked on. She dropped the crossbow and pounded on the door. Charles was at the door in a moment.

"Stand back," he called, before putting his shoulder into the door again. The door opened and Chole ran, crying into his arms.

"Ma?" Charles said, not seeing his mother in the room.

"It took her. Pulled her through the wall." Chole motioned with her head to the damaged plaster and the hole. A trail of Viola's blood ran up the wall to the opening. She choked more on the dust that rose around them.

Downstairs, Ned opened the door for police and paramedics, a whiskey in his hand, the bottle under his arm.

"It's upstairs," Ned said, pointing to the stairwell, where more dust filtered down the steps. His words were slurred. "Somebody might be dead or missing. I'm not certain. I...I...I can't go up there."

Police raced up the steps and met Charles and Chole. They all returned downstairs. Then the police went back up.

It was a long night. Everyone gave statements. Ned fell asleep on the sofa, the whiskey bottle cradled against his side. The officers were skeptical. Charles and Chole swore they saw the creature. Charles admitted shooting his mother by accident, intending to hit a vampire in the wall. Chole claimed she saw the creature pull Viola's body into the wall. Officers shined their flashlights into the cavities behind the plaster, saw trails of blood disappear inside. Crime scene investigators swabbed Viola's blood, the creature's black goo, collected fabric shreds stuck to wooden lath. They photographed Charles and Viola's rooms in detail, as well as the damaged walls. They measured footprints in the plaster dust and lifted fingerprints. They confiscated the flip flops Chole wore, which had managed to pick up blood on their soles. Chole thought it was her blood from the nail she stepped on. Then they went to the Barker home and investigated wall damage there.

The investigation ended temporarily at the Headstrong's home, which was empty and where the doors and windows were locked. The noise, the sirens, and flashing lights brought most Hazel Street residents to the sidewalk, where they mingled and spread gossip of the night's activities on the warm, humid air. It was agreed that a vampire had been identified and moved through the Hazel Street homes, ate rats, and then turned on Donnie Savistsky and Viola Barton.

Perhaps even the Headstrongs had been murdered. After all, they were missing, too. Worst of all, the fiend was still at large. It could be holed up in anyone's home, in some dank corner of an attic or basement, waiting for the chance to strike again.

None of this rumor missed the ears of Jeremy Brothers, Svengoolie aficionado and self-proclaimed vampire expert, who milled around the crowd in his pajamas, the sliver stake concealed under his belt. The next morning, he knocked on the Barker's front door, pale, and lips quivering.

"I told Donnie the vampire would come for him first if he didn't replace the silver stake with another one. Even a knitting needle I told him." Jeremy looked from Ned to Chole. "Donnie pulled the stake out. We were going to sell it. Get new bikes and baseball gloves. Go to the movies for a year. Extra butter on our popcorn. Then we heard a moan, and we ran. Donnie said, 'That's the Barkers going at it in bed.'" Jeremy blushed and lowered his head. He talked toward the floor. "'We hear them all the time.' That's what Donnie said. I live across the street and don't hear nothin'," he concluded with emphasis, raising his head to look at the Barkers again.

Chole smiled, suppressed a giggle. Ned left, returned with his whiskey bottle and a glass.

"Did you see the vampire?" Chole asked.

"We saw it. We crawled through the opening in the attic between Donnie's house and the Headstrong's. All the homes on this block have them. We touched the vampire's clothes and the stake. Donnie even touched its hand when it was still dead, with the stake through its heart."

"Clothes?

"It had a white shirt and tuxedo coat. She had no legs so there was no pants."

"She?"

"It was a girl vampire. Donnie lifted the shirt to show me. It had sexual parts," Donnie said, lowering his head again.

"It had no clothes when I saw it," Chole said. "I don't remember legs or a...because it was inside the wall."

"It was in a little coffin when I saw it. And I'm telling you it had no legs."

"I believe you, Jeremy," Chole said, reaching over to touch his hand.

Reluctantly, Jeremy reached inside his belt and pulled out the stake. "This was the thing Donnie pulled from the vampire. We ran down the hall after he pulled it out. We heard the moan. Donnie said the noise came from your house, but I knew it came from the room. The vampire came back to life. Just like John Carradine when he played Dracula. I saw it on *Svengoolie*."

Ned put down his whiskey glass and took the stake to examine it. "If this is really silver it would be worth a pretty penny," he said.

"That's gold in the handle," Jeremy said. "Donnie and me had plans. We were going to be rich. Buy anything a kid wanted." He was quiet for a moment. His eyes filled with tears. "Who would have thought a vampire would want that old stake in the heart, no matter how much it's worth. Then we realized the Headstrongs would know it was missing. They'd call the police. We weren't thinking at first. We'd be in trouble. We decided to put the stake back, but the vampire was gone. There was no place to put it. So, we held on to it."

"Is that when *it* got Donnie?" Ned, said, turning the stake over and over in his hands, feeling the point's sharpness, finally holding it tightly by the handle.

Jeremy was silent. His eyes filled with tears again.

"Did you see it happen?" Chole asked. She touched Jeremy's shoulder.

"Donnie ain't dead. He's at my house across the street. Hiding in my attic. I bring him food and he uses the bathroom at night when my mom's asleep."

"You didn't tell anyone?" Chole said in disbelief.

"We were afraid. What if the vampire heard people talking? We were worried. Maybe it understands English. Maybe it doesn't."

"Can you imagine what you put your parents through? I don't believe you kids!"

"We were scared. The longer it went on, the worse it got."

"We're calling the police," Chole said. "Right now."

"You can't! We gotta kill the vampire *again*. It might turn a man like Ned to be its love slave forever. Then we'd have to stake Ned."

"What are you talking about?" Ned said in mid-pour.

Chole reached for her cell phone. "How would we even know where to find it...*her*?"

Jeremy stared at Chole. "Because I know where it is."

"Where?" Chole said.

"At the Headstrongs," Jeremy said, raising a finger like Peter Cushing as Van Helsing on the trail of Christopher Lee's Dracula. "The thing has to sleep during the day. The Headstrongs put the coffin in the middle bedroom, same as mine, where there's only one window, and that was covered, so no light comes in. Sunlight would kill it. The Headstrongs knew what they were doing." He looked back and forth between Ned and Chole.

"But it was already dead when they moved in," Ned said.

"A technicality. We can crawl through the opening in the attic and stake it during the day while the Headstrongs are still away. We'll use *that* stake just to be sure. After all, it worked once. Drive it through the same hole it came out. If the hole healed, which it probably did, there might be a scar. We'll add another hole."

"It's too dangerous," Chole said. "I'm calling the police."

"Do you think they'll believe us. If police go into the Head-strong's it could get more people killed. Nobody'd be safe."

Chole paused, put down her phone.

"Donnie won't look so bad when it's all over," Jeremy said. "He'd be a hero. We could say he killed the vampire. Sent it back to hell."

"Was that Donnie's idea?" Chole asked.

"Well, I think it might have been. After all, he has the most to lose."

"What about his poor mother?"

"She doesn't know anything," Jeremy said.

"Sounds like a plan," Ned said. "I'll be happy when this is all over, and we can get back to normal."

"There ain't nothing normal in a place like Mammoth," Jeremy said.

"No. Too much can go wrong," Chole said.

"Think about it. Too much can go wrong if we get the police involved. Don't forget, we might be on the hook for Mrs. Barton's disappearance." Jeremy's eyes filled with tears. "Please. Let me look in the Headstrong's house. If the vampire isn't there, we'll call the police. We can go in tomorrow morning. The thing should be so full of blood from Mrs. Barton it won't move for a couple days. We'll get it at its most vulnerable time."

Chole looked at Jeremy, the freckles on his nose and under his eyes. "I'll have to think about it."

"What's one day? The time to hit is now, when it is sleepy, groggy. If you wait until it wants to feed it will be at its strongest. Then we'll be up shit creek."

"I want to talk to Charles. Get his approval. He's faced this thing. It was his mother after all. Maybe he'll come along. You, too Ned."

"I don't know," Ned said. "Vampire hunting is not my cup of tea."

"We'll need his crossbow," Chole said. "Better not to get too close to that creature."

The three of them went to Charles's home. Pastor Johnson was leaving. Charles wanted a memorial service for his mother. It had been among her final wishes. She had picked out her favorite Bible readings and hymns. Even without a body, Charles had laid out Viola's favorite dress and good underwear and shoes for a funeral.

After Pastor Johnson was gone, Charles said," How you doing, Jeremy? I suppose you miss your friend."

"We have a plan to kill the vampire," Jeremy said. "We know where she is. We want you to come, and we need your crossbow."

Charles backed up and sat down suddenly on his sofa. He stared at the trio. After a pause, he said, "I shot all my arrows. I broke the two in the wall I could see, trying to get them out of the studs. The other arrows must still be in my Ma. Or the police have them. I suppose we could buy more."

"We have something better than arrows," Ned said, producing the silver stake. "We have this son of a bitch."

Charles examined the stake, turning it over in his hands, feeling the weight, touching the point. "It might work, but my aim isn't good. I shot six times at close range and hit the thing only once. I shot my Ma three times, and I couldn't even see her in the next room, but the arrows flew through the plaster."

"It was an accident," Chole said.

"That's what the police said, but they don't believe me. There's blood but no body. They smirk when I mention vampires. They want me to go for a psych evaluation. How do you think that's going to go? Vampires in Mammoth. Nobody's going to believe me."

"In Mammoth? Really," Chole said.

"They'll believe *us* when it's over," Jeremy said. "They won't have a choice."

The four sat in Charles's living room making plans for the following day's assault on the Headstrong home. Charles and Chole would crawl through the attic to the Headstrong home with the crossbow loaded with the silver stake. Jeremy would take a position in the Savitsky home attic at the hole, armed with a sharpened broom handle should things go awry. Donnie would hold his cell phone ready to call 911.

The plan was foolproof.

Jeremy assured them the vampire would rest in its coffin and be powerless during daylight hours. All they had to do was approach the sleeping fiend and either push or shoot the stake into its heart. The pathway to the heart was already there. The stake would find its own way in. The vampire was allergic to silver. It might squirm and scream, but that was normal, Jeremy said, nonchalantly. Expect it. Then they would call the police. Donnie would reveal he had been in hiding. All that was left was to smile for the newspaper photographer.

The next morning, while it was still dark, Jeremy and Donnie crept across the street to Charles's house. Donnie's cell phone was fully charged. After Jean Savitsky left for work, Jeremy and Charles went to the Barkers. Inside the Barker attic, they found that the space to the Headstrong home was too small for them to crawl through. The hole would only accommodate the boys and possibly Chole. Donnie had a key to his back door, so the group entered his home. There they found the space to the Headstrong house was blocked, covered with new wood. Charles said he could kick a hole in the wall, but the noise would surely alert neighbors up and down the block. Instead, piece by piece, they pried enough wood away to make an opening. It was no larger than the one in the Barker home.

"I thought it was bigger," Donnie said.

"Me, too," Jeremy agreed. "I don't know how the vampire filled the gaps without anyone hearing the noise."

"Looks like we're back to square one," Ned said. He seemed somewhat relieved they could not reach the Headstrong home.

"Now wait," Charles said. "If all these homes are nearly identical, there might be another way."

Charles crawled to the center of the eaves. He pushed up on a hatch that led to the roof. Light poured in as soon as he lifted off the hatch and set it on the back roof, which was nearly flat.

"Bats!" Ned called.

Three small bats that had nested inside the hatch lip fell to the attic floor. Charles scooped up the rodents with an old towel, one by one while they were disoriented, and tossed them outside into the air, where they fluttered away.

"We might be able to get the Headstrong hatch off, if it's not locked, and get inside," Charles said. He boosted himself out on the roof and moved cautiously to the Headstrong roof. He lifted the Headstrong hatch and dropped it immediately.

"Wasps!" he cried. "Make room." Charles dashed across the roof to the Savitsky hatch, dropped inside, and pulled the hatch closed.

"You're pretty fast for a big man," Ned said, smiling. He handed Charles his flask.

"Fast as I need to be," Charles said.

He took a pull on the flask and caught his breath. After a minute, he crawled inside the eaves and stuck his head outside the hatch. The wasps circled the Headstrong hatch, annoyed, but they hadn't followed Charles.

"I'm allergic to stings. Have to be careful," Charles said.

"Have an EpiPen?" Chole asked, tapping her thigh.

"Used to, but they got too damn expensive. Now I take my chances."

"We have to get in that hatch," Chole said.

"We have spray," Donnie said. He went downstairs and returned with a can of spray insecticide. "It's from last year."

"It's almost empty," Charles said, shaking the can. "I guess it will have to do."

Charles offered the can to Ned.

"I don't do heights," Ned said. "Sorry. I might pass out."

Charles explained the plan and then walked cautiously to

the hatch, setting down the spray can. The nest was quiet now. He jerked off the hatch and flipped it over. The wasps attacked immediately. He turned to pick up the can but kicked it instead, sending it spiraling toward the roof's edge. He chased the can, but it picked up speed on the downhill pitch and fell over the end. He changed directions, darted across the Barker roof to his hatch, yanked it open, and dropped inside. After five minutes, Charles emerged from his hatch.

"You okay," Chole called. There seemed little point in trying to be quiet now, after the madcap races across the rooftops.

"They got me a few times. I can take one hit but no more. I'm woozy, have a little trouble breathing. I take another hit and my throat will close. You'll have to go on without me."

Chole boosted herself to the roof and walked to the edge. The heat was intense. The sun's reflection off the metal roof, painted silver, blinded her. She expected to see the spray can on the ground, but the rain gutter had caught it. When she kneeled to retrieve the can the metal roof burned her hands and knees. She plucked the spray can from the rain gutter and stood quickly. The heat and brightness dazzled her, and she half fell back toward the hatch.

Thankfully, the wasps had settled down again. Occasionally, one of the wasps left or arrived at the colony. She approached the Headstrong roof cautiously, shaking the spray can. The nest lay in a corner of the hatch interior. Chole approached the nest slowly. She aimed the can and depressed the nozzle. The insecticide sprayed over the nest. The enraged wasps, already dying, took to the air in a cloud. Chole dropped through the hatch to the floor and scurried into the attic, breathless, the smell of insecticide in her nostrils. She waited several minutes. Then she poked her head above the roof. Dead wasps lay scattered about. A few circled at a distance. Ned poked his head through the neighboring hatch. He smiled.

"How's Charles?" she said.

"He's okay, but still woozy. I talked to him on the phone."

"Bring me the crossbow and stake. And your flask."

Chole dropped inside the hatch and sat cross-legged on the floor. The heat inside the eaves was intense as outside on the roof. Sweat ran down Chole's back, dripped from her armpits. After several tedious minutes, there were light footsteps on the roof. A hand reached in the flask. Chole grabbed it and took a long pull until she choked. The crossbow and stake followed. Then Jeremy dropped inside, brandishing the sharpened broomstick.

"What are you doing here?" Chole said. "Where's Ned?"

"He thought you could use my expertise on vampires," Jeremy said, smiling.

"Your expertise!"

Chole looked above the hatch. Ned was at his post.

"You son of a bitch," Chole called. "Sending a kid over here. What were you thinking? Keep that goddamned hatch open!"

"The kid knows the layout."

Chole dropped inside.

"Let's go before I lose my nerve," Jeremy said.

First, they examined the blocked hole. Neither could remove the new boards that closed the hole. "The vampire must have done this," Jeremy said. "They are known to be very strong."

"You ought to wait here at the hatch, on the roof, in the daylight," Chole said.

"But I know the way. It will be over in no time. Remember, a vampire is powerless during the day. He, or she in this case, *must* stay in the coffin."

They walked slowly to the attic steps and descended even slower. "Watch your step. This place is full of shit," Jeremy whispered."

"Shit?"

"Junk."

"Oh."

Chole engaged the crossbow string and loaded the stake. They tiptoed up the hall. "That's the door," Jeremy whispered, pointing his stick. "Get ready!"

Chole stopped near the door. Her lips were dry. She moistened them with her tongue. She looked at Jeremy and nodded. He nodded back. She waited a moment and cried "Go!"

They charged inside. Chole wielded the crossbow from side to side. Jeremy cried out and impaled the mummy with the sharp tip of his broomstick. He pulled out the point with a grimace. Shredded paper fell from the hole in the mummy's chest.

"Papier-mâché," Chole said. "The fucking thing is papier-mâché."

Jeremy looked at her seriously. "One down and one to go."

"I thought you said the vampire was in here."

"It was. It must have moved the coffin to another part of the house. A place it thought was safer. We'll have to look through the whole house."

"Maybe it's gone," Chole said.

"I don't think so. It would have to drag the coffin away to another place. And with no legs..." Jeremy spread his arms to make his point.

"Headstrong said it was staked while it transitioned. Maybe it went back to human form."

"A possibility," Jeremy said, raising his finger, "but from what I know about vampires, I still think she's in the house."

"What you know about vampires? What you know about vampires comes from B-movies."

"Do you know anymore? Now let's go."

They moved through the rest of the second floor, searching closets carefully, nodding each time before they tugged open a door. They kneeled almost silently to inspect under the beds. It was a painstaking, long process. Once the second floor was cleared, they covered the first floor equally thoroughly and took turns opening kitchen cabinets, in the chance the creature still had no legs and folded itself inside one. Satisfied the vampire was not in the house proper, only the basement remained to be explored.

Chole opened the basement door and was met immediately with a stench of rotting flesh. She gagged but held down her stomach's contents. She reached inside the basement stairway, found a light switch, and flipped it on. It did not work.

Chole turned to Jeremy. "You'll have to go back up over the roof and have Ned get us a flashlight. It's too risky going outside. You might be seen."

Jeremy turned to leave. He had a worried expression.

"And tell Ned to make sure the flashlight works."

Jeremy scampered away and up the steps. Chole sat on the floor, her back against the basement door, cupping her head in her hands. It seemed like an eternity before Jeremy returned with a flashlight. He flicked it on and off to show Chole it worked.

"Ned wants his flask. He said I should bring it right away."

"Tell Ned that if he wants his flask he can...never mind," Chole hissed. "We wasted enough time."

She stood and opened the basement door an inch at a time. She turned on the flashlight and proceeded down the steps, taking one at a time, stopping to listen in between. Jeremy followed. Both choked on the stench.

Finally, they reached the basement floor. Chole moved the flashlight beam this way and that, checking all facets of the basement, including the joists above them as they proceeded. She used the long light to knock down cobwebs.

Jeremy sidled next to Chole, touching her side. He whispered, "Dirt floor. Not a good sign. I wouldn't be surprised if that vampire can tunnel through the earth like a fish swims through water."

"You see that in a movie?" Chole whispered.

"No, but it makes sense."

"I don't buy it. I thought you said a vampire is powerless during the day."

"Supposedly, but I saw movies where vampires move around during the day. *Bram Stoker's Dracula* was one of them."

Chole looked for a moment at Jeremy in disbelief.

They stopped their slow progress in front of the gas boiler when it fired noisily, causing them to step back quickly and stumble. They sat heavily, still side by side on stacked wooden crates that splintered under their weight.

"You okay?" Chole whispered. She was breathless and, after a moment shined the flashlight on Jeremy's face. He nodded. "Me too," she added.

"I think I'm stuck in this box," Jeremy said. "I broke through it and can't get up. The wood is holding me."

"I'll pull you."

Chole set down the crossbow and flashlight, groped for Jeremy's arm. "Let's go. One, two, three!" She tugged. Even in the basement darkness, Chole knew Jeremy remained seated.

"Push with your free hand," she said.

"I pushed with both hands."

"I have your arm."

"No, you don't."

Chole held onto the cold limb, picked up the flashlight, and snapped it on. Her hand encircled a woman's thin bare calf just above the ankle. She dropped it immediately. Then she dropped the flashlight but managed to fumble in the dark and catch it before it fell to the dirt floor. The flashlight was off, and she struggled to turn it on again.

"You have my arm now," Jeremy said, with some relief.

"I don't. I'm trying to turn on the flashlight," Chole hissed.

The flashlight snapped on. Chole moved the beam around and saw the naked female vampire sitting in the small coffin, its new legs extending to the floor. It had a voluptuous body and long dark hair. Its eyes stared at Chole. The creature's hand gripped Jeremy's arm. Jeremy's eyes were as large as saucers. Above and to the right, Viola Barton's body hung from the rafters, upside down, bloody and bruised, her clothing shredded after being torn through the walls.

The fiend licked its lips. Jeremy winced and then moaned

when she tightened her grip on his arm. Chole aimed the flashlight at the vampire's eyes. It screamed and dropped Jeremy's arm. He pulled himself from the crate and scrambled away. The creature threw its hands up to protect its eyes. Chole kept the beam focused on the vampire's face and reached for the crossbow. As she raised the weapon and fired, the vampire slapped the crossbow away. The stake rang off a heating pipe above and hit Viola's sizable rump with a thump.

The fiend shrieked again, stood, and grabbed Chole by the throat, lifting her off the floor. It licked its lips and looked up and down Chole's hanging body. It cocked its head while Chole struggled for breath, kicking her legs and shaking her arms. It pulled Chole against it, as if savoring her warmth, and licked her cheek. Chole's grip on the flashlight loosened as she lost consciousness, but the beam still illuminated her and the vampire.

The creature changed its grip to the back of Chole's neck to expose her vulnerable throat. Chole gasped for air and screamed in pain as the vampire's hold clamped on her vertebrae. Chole's feet swung off the floor. She raised the flashlight to strike the vampire, but the vampire pulled it from her hand with ease and threw it aside. The flashlight landed among the broken crates, but it still illuminated the creature. The vampire held Chole away from her for a moment, focusing on her jugular, which visibly thumped wildly under the skin.

The boiler fired again. The vampire looked toward it. Jeremy advanced with his pointed broomstick. The creature laughed, a hollow, otherworldly laugh, and swatted it away. Jeremy stood frozen. The vampire smiled at him. Charles charged from another direction and impaled the living corpse with the silver stake. The thing shrieked in surprise, groped for the stake to remove it, but Charles pounded the end with his fist and drove it through the heart and out the other side.

The vampire moaned deeply, looked at him in disbelief, and fell back into the little coffin.

"You're so beautiful," Jeremy said, as the corpse withered in front of him. He touched the smallish round breast beside the stake hole. "Wait until Donnie hears about this."

Chole managed to stand, massaging the back of her neck. She pulled Jeremy away from the coffin.

"She was hot, but now she's rot!" Jeremy said.

Jeremy pulled the flask from his back pocket and handed it to Chole. "I figured you could use one of these."

VAMPIRE VS. NEIGHBORHOOD WATCH

THE EXPLOSION ON MARLIN AVENUE ROCKED THE neighborhood in the middle of the night. Firefighters, police, and paramedics were on the scene within minutes, their flashing lights and squawking radios made the street surrealistic, a scene from a modern slasher movie. Thunder rumbled in the distance and lightning lit the distant mountainside. Marcie (not her real name) recorded the event on her cell phone from her front lawn. She was dressed in pink onesie pajamas that had a hood with little pink ears. The hood was raised to hide her sleep-disheveled hair. Her bare feet were wet from the dewy grass. Every time one of the rescuers moved her back toward her home, Marcie inched back toward the street. She ignored her parents' call of Jewell (her real name) from their front porch.

Marcie was first on the scene when the explosion ignited the split-level home across the street. She ran to the sidewalk with her phone recording. "It's *Marcie in the Mousetrap* outside my home in Mammoth. That's Pennsylvania for those of you who aren't geography scholars. This is a special video I'm making *live* of an explosion and fire across the street. I have to be careful, because the blast blew out the windows and there's glass all over." She panned down to show her feet. "I didn't have time to put on shoes, so here I am surrounded by glass. I can feel the heat on my face from the fire. The grass is cold. What a combination!" She panned back to the fire and the flames licking through blasted-out windows. "This is like something from a horror movie. Eli Roth, are you watching? Your star, Marcie, awaits. And here comes the first fire truck. I can't see it, but I hear the sirens, see the flashing lights in the distance. No. It's an ambulance. Here comes the fire truck around the corner with Barkley Ave. I hope they don't collide. What a catastrophe that would be."

Marcie hopped up and down. The ambulance stopped in front of her.

"Asshole! I was here first. You're ruining my shot!"

"Get the hell back kid," the ambulance driver berated. "And get that phone out of here."

Marcie turned the phone toward her face. Blond hair rimmed her face inside the pajama hood. She made a face, twisting her mouth. "This is Marcie in the Mousetrap, reporting from Marlin Avenue in Mammoth, PA. There's a legit fire across the street from my home. And here come the police."

The cruiser passed the ambulance and pulled to the curb."

"Sorry, faithful. I didn't have time to attach my gimble, so the video might be a little shaky but, nonetheless, more dramatic. Remember *Blair Witch Project*. Maybe my mom can run upstairs and get it for me."

Marcie turned toward her home and called amid the noise,

"Mom, where are you at? I need my gimble." She returned to her audience. "There're more people on the sidewalk." Marcie panned her phone to the sidewalk. "Everybody's in their pajamas. No night owls on this street. The police are out of the car and chasing them back. Meanwhile I'm going around this ambulance that has blocked my view.

"Aw! Ouch! Fuck! I think I cut my foot on glass." Marcie lifted her left foot and showed her begrimed sole to the camera. "False alarm, everybody. No blood. It was only a stone, thank God." She hollered, "Mom! Get my shoes when you get the gimble!" She returned the camera to her face and adjusted her hood. "Where the hell did she go. Mom! Mom? Oh well, again I apologize for any choppiness in this video, but this is raw footage from the scene. You won't get any better. Was this an accident or was the explosion carried out on purpose? Time will tell. I expect the bomb squad was called, too. You can't be too safe. I've heard bomb squad guys are really cute, so I'm looking forward to seeing them arrive."

Marcie walked to the back of the ambulance with its open doors. "Hey everybody, this is the inside of an ambulance. I hope you never have to take a ride in one. But if you do, they have a lot of shit inside that might save your life."

"I told you to get out of here before you get hurt," the paramedic screamed, as he came around the back of the ambulance and saw Marcie.

"Don't let this guy haul you away," Marcie said, pointing her phone at the man. "He's mean. You'll never make it to the hospital. He'll take you to an asylum, where they'll experiment on your sex organs. Give you endless electric shock treatments. Keep you in a straitjacket."

The paramedic waved his hands in front of her phone. "If you don't go home, I'll call the police."

"All right, Mr. Malpractice is making me move away from the ambulance, everybody. I'm going across the lawn. The Gossetts cut their grass today. Now my feet are green. Aww! My toes look like Swamp Thing." Marcie panned the phone down to her feet again and the wet pajama bottoms before sweeping back to the fire. "I can tell you now the firemen have their hoses out...Oops!...Not those hoses, but the fire hoses." Marcie panned back to her face and giggled. "You know what I mean. Everybody! It was an innocent mistake. A slip of the lip. Cut me a break. I just woke up. Now I'm going to let you watch the firemen in action." She inserted a finger in her hoodie ear. Pretended to scratch the interior, pulled out, and examined her fingertip, made another face, flicked away imaginary ear wax. Then she smiled.

Marcie turned the camera's attention to the firemen who had their water streams trained on the open windows which exhausted billows of black smoke. She was silent for a minute. Then she coughed. "The smoke is intense when the wind blows this way." There were shouts from the street. The rescue vehicles were silent, but their lights flashed. Bright lights now illuminated the home. Eventually, the flames diminished.

The camera returned to Marcie's face. She smiled, showing her perfectly straight, white teeth. "I hope nothing's stuck between my teeth. I had a bowl of caramel popcorn earlier, while I watched TV. You know how I love horror movies. But I flossed, brushed, and rinsed before bed." She sang, "As always! Or somebody inside will have a meltdown." She pointed with a thumb behind her back.

"You should remember the video I did a few weeks ago on my nighttime routine, the one I shot with the bathroom mirror. It got a lot of positive comments, especially where you could see my face twice—in the camera and in the mirror. Very avant-garde. Let me tell ya, that took a lot of work to set up. I had to put the fricking tripod in the bathtub. The tripod left black marks in the tub. Mom had a meltdown." She sang, "As usual! It was a good thing I made the video in *my* bathroom." Marcie returned to her speaking voice. "What I didn't tell you then was that video was proof I'm not a five-hundred-year-old beautiful vampire. Just a crazy teenager who has a camera and a reflection in the mirror." She pushed an index finger into her cheek and spun her hand.

"Wowee, everybody! We're on fire again!" Marcie aimed the cell phone camera back at the house. "We caught it here on *Marcie in the Mousetrap*, two firemen just broke down the front door and entered with tanks on their backs. No! They're not setting up for a kegger. I heard a cop say they didn't know if anybody's trapped inside. Well, let me tell you, if anybody survived the fire, they're drowned now by the tons of water they shot through the windows. Still, they *have to* look for bodies. This is getting so Stephen King because if there's a body they don't get out, it will come back to life. If the body is burned beyond recognition, to ashes, a ghost will emerge. Everybody, it's gonna be *supernatural!*" She sang again, "And guess who lives across the street? *Marcie in the Mousetrap*, now made smelly by all the smoke. I probably stink like a cheap cigar.

"Have to go, everybody! The evil stepmother has me by the sleeve and is dragging me back inside. I think the fire is out anyway. It looks like some of the trucks are pulling out. Later!"

Of Marcie's 350,000 subscribers to her channel, she didn't realize one stood dressed in black down the street, hidden in an arborvitae's shadows, watching her live feed of the fire, intent on every word, moistening his lips every time she turned the camera on herself and her face was illuminated. His own youthful face was illuminated dimly by his cell phone's screen. This man, young by vampire standards, crossed several states to come to Mammoth. He was tech savvy and had watched Marcie's channel for more than a month. Binge watched every episode. He was enamored with her, as many teenage boys were, judging from the male name commenters left on her channel. You could never tell when she would model bikinis or underwear for the camera. She had even taken a discrete bubble bath on screen and shaved her legs.

Discovering Marcie's hometown and address was easy for the vampire compared to making the journey, traveling at night, hiding in complete darkness during the day, often using his vampire's strength to break into old graveyard mausoleums. He lay in the graves imagining her flat stomach, slim legs, and pubescent breasts while he rested in the daylight hours. How he wanted to smell her long, blonde, highlighted hair!

It was still dark when the last emergency trucks pulled from the fire scene and the street returned to its normal silence. Marcie switched on her camera and whispered, "This is a follow up on the fire, everybody. Lucky my bedroom is in the front, and I can see the burned home from the window next to my bed. So, I had to take a shower and change pajamas. My pink ones got wet because of the dew and there was a mist in the air from all the water that didn't shoot through the windows. My cow pajamas—the ones I'm wearing now—have a trap door in the back, but I can't open it now for ya. Maybe another time because," she sang, "because I'm wearin' nothin' underneath! I don't want my platform expunged for porn."

Marcie giggled. Her camera sat on her desk and was aimed at the bed and the window. She spun on the bed to show her backside and pointed at the buttons. Then she spun back. "I have to whisper because Mom and Dad are down the hall doing God knows what. Probably not sleeping. Probably spying on me. Maybe having sex. I know they do *it* because sometimes they act pretty frisky at foreplay. Even around me.

"So, the thing I don't like about firemen's gear, the clothes they wear to fires, is that they are too baggy, very bulky. You can never tell if a guy is fat or buff, young or old, especially with those helmets and face shields. I propose that firemen wear *gear* more fashionable. Let me know in the comments if you have any ideas. I would like to see tight-fitting briefs—wet of course —nothing else, so you can get an idea about their Johnsons. That might not be safe, but...Yes, there are female firefighters, and they can wear a bra in my dream. I know the firemen clothes are heavy to protect them from heat. Please, no comments. I don't read anything sarcastic or nasty. You know the purpose of this channel is to have fun and entertain you guys.

"One more thing before I go, because there is school tomorrow and I must go. When I came in from the fire, I got grass clippings on the carpet and then in my bathtub. Mom had a meltdown." Marcie sang in a slightly louder whisper, "As usual. That's why I *must* go to school tomorrow." She returned to her normal voice. "Anyway, I ruined my polish scrubbing the dirt off my feet. Maybe tomorrow we'll do a *paint video*, even though I've done a few this year. We can look at some new colors. Let me know in the comments. Ciao for now."

Over the next few days, the State Police Fire Marshal determined the blaze across the street had a suspicious origin. An accelerate in the form of gasoline was found on the first floor. The homeowners, who only recently moved in, had disappeared and could not be traced. Rumors swirled in the neighborhood. The explosion was caused by either a natural gas leak or a meth lab. The homeowners escaped with the clothes on their backs or were blown to smithereens, without a trace left. The couple might have been the targets of a mob hit, after being fingered in the Witness Protection Program, or they were inept drug makers. The smashed-in front door and the blown-out windows were covered with plywood. Utilities to the home were cut. The front, side, and backyards were littered with glass and other debris that firemen hauled or hurled outside. Caution tape strung around the house fluttered and twisted in the breeze.

After a black-clad man was seen at night prowling along Marlin Avenue and surrounding streets, Marci's father Gregory Barton decided it was time to resurrect the Neighborhood Watch Program. He would be captain again. No one disagreed. Marcie did a segment on making fliers for the first meeting, allowing her subscribers to select type styles, font sizes, and colors. She typed meeting details with the camera rolling. She even changed copier ink as part of the program. The video became wildly popular and different from Marcie's usual fare because it showed her face in concentration with her tongue sticking out at the corner of her lips. Her subscribers agreed she was cute. New followers were added.

The vampire, who subscribed to Marcie's channel as *I got U babe,* commented that Marcie was "cute as a button," and Marcie shared that with her ardent followers. Marcie was cute. Her videos started as a way to pass the time. She offered girl talk and solutions to girl problems, including things like how to know when a guy likes you, how to attract a boy you like, how to get rid of a boy who likes you when you don't like him, etc. However, Marcie herself didn't have a boyfriend. Her parents were strict about dating and good grades, and they didn't follow her channel much at first. Marcie's stepmother Joan was a third-grade teacher. Her father owned a dry cleaning business. It didn't take long for Marcie's perky attitude and sometimes outrageous comments to attract an ever-growing number of viewers.

"He runs all night on the wheel, keeping me awake," Marcie complained in one video about her hamster Sheldon. "Then he humps my hand. Just like a guy. Look at him go. I love horny boys." She stroked the rodent and kissed it. Inserted Sheldon's head in her mouth. The video went viral. "That's my Ozzie impression."

Marcie applied makeup, painted her nails, and modeled her favorite clothing. More and more subscribers followed, and she picked up internet advertisers. Stores sent her products to discuss and try on camera. She did remote videos from stores in Mammoth where she modeled clothing. She hiked, rode a specific bicycle, ate at certain restaurants with her friends, where they talked about boys and giggled a lot. She got paid for almost everything she did on camera. Her parents took notice and started a college fund. Next, Marcie had an accountant. Although Marcie's parents came to micromanage most of her videos, she still managed to stream silly things with her dancing in her bedroom, eating doughnuts, washing her hair, and playing with Sheldon.

"Sheldon's inside his exercise ball, rolling across my bedroom floor. I hate it when he goes under the bed. He's so hard to get out. Yes, Sheldon is always hard, the little pervert. I hope there are no dust bunnies or dirty underwear visible under there." She sang, "I'd be so embarrassed!" She turned the camera back to her and made a face. "I hate to clean, but Cinderella's wicked stepmother makes her do it much too often. I'm waiting for Sheldon and his exercise ball to turn into a coach and driver to whisk me around Mammoth. Maybe to attend a ball. You might see me."

The lingerie video from Bella's hooked the vampire. She filmed it inside the exclusive women's store in Downtown Mammoth. The night after it was posted, the vampire began his trip to Mammoth. He moved into the burned-out house as soon as it had been inspected, analyzed thoroughly, and condemned by the city. He entered and exited through a basement window from which he had pried off the plywood cover. He watched the Barton home from an upstairs window and a hole he painstakingly drilled with his fingernail through another plywood cover. He watched Marcie's bedroom from morning until the second she turned off her light and went to sleep. Then he hunted.

Meanwhile, Gregory Barton held the first Neighborhood Watch meeting in his basement. Some men would have accepted beer from Gregory's draft tap system, but none was offered. The meeting was all business. Neighborhood zones were laid out. Zone lieutenants were appointed. Cell phone numbers were exchanged. Patrols were scheduled with teams of two walking or driving the streets. The watch members carried pepper spray and Louisville Sluggers. Some, even a few women, had concealed carry licenses and packed. Whenever possible, patrols would extend from sundown to sunup.

Otherwise, late and early evening patrols were scheduled. The Barton home always was available for coffee. Each team carried an *itinerary*—Marcie's choice—which named the patrollers, the dates and times they were on duty, and ample space for recording suspicious activity observed. The itinerary was designed, of course, with suggestions from Marcie's subscribers. Thousands of loyal followers volunteered to travel to Mammoth and join patrols. Marcie graciously declined the offers, knowing those thousands would end up lounging in and around her home.

"Everybody, this is serious stuff. No goofing around. No stupid remarks," she scolded on one video. "We had an arson across from *my* home," singing, "recorded exclusively by me." With her normal voice, she added, "And now there's a sketchy character dressed in black prowling the streets. It's supposed to be a guy. What's he up to? Everybody wants to know. It could be he's looking for another house to burn down. That's my opinion. Better not be mine. I also believe the neighborhood watch will take him down. That's why I need your help. Since everyone works and not all patrols cross paths, so to say, we need a way to cross reference what goes on at night. Thus, the itinerary.

"What I need from everyone are ideas what to include on the form." Marcie pointed her two thumbs toward herself and added, "I've been tasked with designing and maintaining a data base of the patrols because," she sang, "I'm the computer nerd!

"So, let me see what ideas you have. I'll put the form

together and post it, so everybody knows what it looks like. Everybody! Thanks for the help!"

Marcie received more than four thousand replies and suggestions. She did another video of her designing the itinerary and printing copies for the watch patrollers from her father's printer at the dry cleaning store. Another video showed her shopping in skimpy shorts, her midriff bare, large sunglasses with lenses shaped like hearts, for binders to collect the itineraries. She mounted her camera on her shopping cart. An online version of the information would be available to all watch members. Another video showed Marcie in her cow pajamas entering information into the online database.

"All caught up. Good night sweet princes and princesses," she cooed before signing off, climbing into bed, and turning off her bedroom light.

The vampire noted every move from across the street, peeking through the second-floor window, an eye pressed against the hole he bored in the plywood cover, sitting in a half-melted computer chair, amid sagging sheetrock, spongy carpet, and a still-wet and dripping ceiling. How he wished Marcie's bathroom had a window.

When he didn't hunt at night, the vampire visited a coffee shop in Downtown Mammoth to recharge his cell phone, which was paid for by fake credit cards. His allure as a vampire opened many doors, as long as it was at night. The coffee shop was dark and mostly illuminated by computer and telephone screens. He ordered coffee and sometimes a cookie but never consumed them. Neither did he talk to any shop patrons. He sat alone, his head bowed, his face obscured, absorbed—like most others—with his phone's contents. When his battery charged fully, he slinked from the shop unnoticed, so intent were the other patrons on their own devices. After walking a while, he poured his coffee into a storm drain, deposited the cup into the closest trash can, and tossed any food item into shrubs. Then he returned to the burned-out house.

Marlin Avenue, as were other parallel streets, was a dead end. The streets melted into a swampy area part of protected wetland and then state game lands. The wetland was impassible most of the year. A meandering stream and pond in the middle were habitat to honking geese and a variety of other birds and creatures. It was strange, as Marcie reported in a video, that the surging rabbit population, a plague to local gardeners in recent years, had almost disappeared since shortly after the fire.

"It's a shame in a way, not that I like rabbits so much, even though I got this cute bunny-ear hairband at Bella in Downtown Mammoth. Check out their site." Marcie stroked one of the hairband ears, brown with pink linings. "Aren't they cute? Back to the real rabbits. These rodents, because that's what they are, destroyed most of Mom's flowers, killed Dad's fruit trees, and poop all over the place." Marcie pointed at the camera. "You don't want to step in rabbit poop when you think it's safe to walk barefoot in the yard." She shuddered on camera.

"At first, the watch patrol thought there was a fox dec...im... ating the rabbit population," Marcie sang. "Like that word came from the mouth of a teenager. Neighbors did see a red fox last year, and you might think that by now there would be more foxes. That's what those critters do in the wild, but now it is apparently gone. Without a fox, you think the rabbit population would explode. Rabbits *you know what* like...rabbits." Marcie moved her hands up and down in front of the camera, as if she were juggling several small objects.

"No fox. No rabbits. That's strange. What's stranger is, you know, they never found the people who disappeared from the burned-out house. I think their name was Miller. I don't remember. Maybe they are victims, too. Everybody, let me know what you think. It takes me a long time, but I read every comment. There are so many now, I can't respond to all of them. Sorry." Marcie brushed her rabbit ears again for the camera and smiled.

"I will tell you that it's been pretty dry here for weeks, maybe longer, and the wetlands have mostly dried up. That's what my dad says. You can actually walk through it, where you couldn't walk before. I might have to go on a bunny safari soon, before school starts back up. Don't forget, we are going school clothes shopping soon. Hang in there. I have to make arrangements with the stores. I'll keep you posted. And I'm getting a new computer. You won't want to miss that. I'm gonna grill the tech nerds in the store to make sure *we* understand what we're getting with our new laptop. Everyone, you're invited on the bunny safari. I have new boots and a backpack to show you. Perfect for safari and even school. Our destination on bunny safari is *bunny central*. We'll find out hopefully why the bunny population is down. Not that we really care."

Then Arlin Bottoms noted on his itinerary, "Haven't seen many squirrels around lately, or the feral cat that hung around our yard. Anyone else have similar observations? For that matter, the goose population seems to be down, too. They seem to have a flight path over my house to the marsh. There's a lot less honking. It used to rain poop sometimes. Is it me, or have the geese migrated early?"

Marcie set this itinerary aside, highlighted the comments, for her father to bring up at the next Neighborhood Watch meeting, when most of the patrols would gather in the Barton basement.

Mark Sweep piped up at that next meeting. "What about deer? Anybody see deer lately? I had a big buck come into my yard every evening—a twelve-pointer—and now he's gone."

"Probably chasing doe," another man said. "They'll be going into the rut soon enough."

"I ain't seen a deer in a week," another man said. "They had a trail along the back of my yard."

"Me neither."

"If you ask me, it's poachers. Illegal trapping. There's got to be a natural explanation."

Marcie raised her hand with a question, but thought better, and pulled her arm down.

"What about those geese?" Mrs. Sweep said. "To me, there's less honking. You know the racket they make. Can't flap a wing without a honk."

Marcie took notes and made a video the next day on the diminishing wildlife.

The weather remained dry. Marcie appeared at the back of her yard, where the lawn transitioned into underbrush at the edge of the wetlands. "We're live with *Marcie in the Mousetrap*. This is the bunny safari I promised. First, though, I have to show you my boots and backpack." Marcie panned down to her boots, then hoisted her backpack from the ground. "Last but not least, how about this killer pith helmet?" Marcie showed the camera her new hat, then pulled out a tube of sunscreen. "No bunny safari is complete without skin protection." She opened the cap and squeezed out a generous amount on fingertips. Then she applied the lotion to her face, explaining why an even covering was necessary. Finally, she put on her hat and heart-shaped sunglasses. "You don't want your face cracking and peeling...like Boris Karloff as *The Mummy.*

"All right, we're ready to march. Because we're live today, I'll read some of your comments while I go. Again, because so many people follow me, I can't respond to every comment. There's already five hundred plus watching. There's no other way to start than to plunge into this underbrush. It's very thick. I see nowhere to go without a fight. I hope it gets easier as we go. As George Clooney said in *Dusk to Dawn,* 'Okay Ramblers, let's get rambling.'"

Marcie waved at the camera. "Hi, *John G.* Thanks for the five bucks. Everybody, I appreciate all your donations. It's going into my college fund."

Marcie stormed into the brush and bounced back. "This shit is tough. I have a machete that belongs to Dad. He told me not to take it because I might cut myself swinging it around. It's sharp as hell."

Marcie hacked at the brush and soon made a path through the tangle of vines and thickets that knocked off her hat repeatedly. She emerged winded some twenty feet in and stopped. "Just as I thought. The growth here is lower and not as thick. I'm sweating like crazy. There are a lot of small trees—saplings you could say—all over and brush. I'm surprised there aren't more rocks. Maybe they sank into the bog when it was boggy."

Marcie intoned mysteriously, "I'll be careful, *Becky.*"

To another subscriber, she said, "I hope there's no quicksand, *Honey Bunny.* What does quicksand look like?"

Marcie directed the camera in the distance and pointed with her arm. "There's a great big dead tree in the distance that I'm going to use as a landmark to find my way back. It has a huge limb that points this way, right toward my house. The tree itself stands high above all the rest. You can see it from anywhere. And, as you can notice," she sang, "It's dead. Been that way for a million years."

Marcie trudged through the undergrowth to the tree. "Okay, this is our landmark, everybody, brave safari members, and that's the limb that will guide us back. You can see it's very creepy looking, like a dead arm pointing. A zombie arm. I don't expect to see much wildlife, because, unfortunately, I make a lot of noise when I walk, with the bushes and dead leaves underfoot. Anything wild will probably avoid *me*. I just pray I don't see a snake. Let's just say I'm afraid of snakes more than anything in the universe. Even aliens, who might or might not periodically abduct and experiment on me. That's a good idea for a future video. Dad says there are water snakes back here. He has killed a few in the yard. Probably with this very machete. They can look like copperheads, but they're not poisonous. Still, they can be aggressive, according to Dad. We have already discussed in another video what he knows." She sang again, "Everything, so he thinks."

"The other announcement I have is that Dad will be starting my driving lessons soon. I'm not sure when, but you can guarantee I'll be videoing the whole experience. I already told Dad I want an SUV, the kind that looks like a mini hearse. You know what I mean. A black one, of course. Dad says NO!, but we will see."

She turned the camera back to her face, sweating and red.

"Okay, everybody, we're leaving behind *the* tree to explore more. There's kinda a narrow path here we'll follow, because it will make walking easier and quieter.

"I know *Sally*. You don't like the crunching, either. Sounds like eating Frosted Flakes without milk."

Marcie smiled for the camera before saying, "I'll let you look at the surroundings while I continue. Everybody, single file on the path. I wouldn't want to be the last one. The last one is always the first to go when you're in a horror movie. LOL. Everybody, you are all safe as long as I'm safe. No lions, tigers, or bears in these woods. What else might be here we'll have to learn on our own." Marcie turned the camera on herself and shivered.

"Vampires? Really? *I got U babe*? Thanks for the ten bucks. You're so awesome. Vampires don't come out in the day, in the sunlight, silly. A vampire out here now would start a brush fire in a second as it exploded into a big fireball. I don't plan on being here after dark. Where will I be? That's for you to find out, *I got U babe*."

Marcie continued on the path for a few minutes. "Everybody. I'm stopping for a water break. The heat and sun are intense." Marcie swung off her backpack, opened the flap, and took out a purple, refillable water bottle.

"Don't worry, *I got U babe*. I will stay hydrated. By the way, this is a great backpack. I love mine. It has lots of room and it's on sale at *Bella*. Tell the girls there yours truly recommended it."

Marcie continued. "As you know, we're friendly to the environment. This baby is insulated to keep your water ice cold.

And reusable. They're on sale at Boscov's. You know the drill. Tell them I sent you."

She took a long swig of water and burped. "Excuse me, everybody. I didn't try to burp. Didn't plan on it. As my Nanna says, 'Better out than in.' Eventually, I'll need a pee break." She sang, "You won't see that one!"

Marcie frowned. "No way, *I got U babe*. I wouldn't trust you to turn your back while my pants are down. Geez Louise!"

Marcie put away the water bottle and slung the pack on her back. "As you can see, the ground here has changed. There're small patches of some kind of grass, very green, and the ground is cracked. Almost like a mosaic. It looks like the skin on my Nanna's arms. Sorry Nanna. Hope you're *not* watching this one." She turned the camera to her face and dug an index finger into her cheek, rotating her wrist. "I'd guess this ground is usually wet, probably muddy, but with the drought it has dried up. I see some tracks." Marcie focused the camera on the ground again. "These look like rabbit tracks. Over here is a deer hoof print. I recognize it from the ones Dad showed me in our yard. Dad is such a pilgrim. And here is a poop pile. Possibly rabbit. Possibly deer.

"I agree *Sammy Slammy*. It must be the world's largest rabbit. Let's confidently call it deer poop. Thanks for the buck, *Sammy*. Or should I say dollar, so no one thinks you sent me a male deer.

"Now I smell something." Marcie spun the camera back on her face. She pinched her nostrils with a thumb and index finger, crossed her eyes. "Smells like something dead. I'm not sure. Maybe it's a pool of stagnant water. That can get gross. I'm going to continue on," Marcie said in a nasally twang. She continued, "Look at this. Human footprints. Looks like a sneaker or running shoe. It's a big print. Probably a guy. You know what they say about guys—big feet, big…Ha Ha!"

She took a few steps and stopped. "Oh no. It's a dead deer all right. I'll bet it's the one with the big rack that visited the Sweep property. It's a real stinker. The hunters will be sorry. I'll get a closer shot, despite the intense aroma." Marcie panned the camera over the deer's body. "It looks really dried out. Must have been here for a while. You can see its dead eye and its little tongue sticking out.

"Isn't *I got U babe* the smarty pants? *Exsanguinated!* That's a college-bound word, indeed. Exsanguinated. That's what it looks like. All the blood is gone, so it bled to death, but there's none on the ground." Marcie zoomed in on the deer's neck." These holes look like puncture wounds. There's a bunch. And just a little trail of blood on the fur. Here's a close-up of the punctures. I'd say something killed this deer. The holes could be bullet wounds. Maybe buckshot. What do you guys think?

"*I got U babe*! They're not teeth marks. Can't be. How could someone chase down a big deer like this and bite it?

"*Barney Rubble* said maybe a mountain lion. Possibly. But there are no other marks on the deer. No claw marks.

"Turn it over? Really? *John the Arc*. I couldn't touch it. Besides. I don't have gloves. Who'd bring gloves when the temperature is like ninety degrees? Anyway, even though it's dried out," she sang, "*exsanguinated*, it's still a big deer. I don't know if I could flip it over. Even with gloves. No, *I got U babe*. I'm not touching the antlers or even a hoof.

"I'm moving on. This smell is getting to me." Marcie walked away from the carcass.

"Just when the smell goes away, it's back again. I'm trying to follow these human footprints." Marcie panned her camera to the left. "There's some kind of pile over here."

A half dozen large crows took off screaming, scaring Marcie so much she almost dropped her camera.

"Fuck! Did you see that! What the fuck. Crows are a bad omen, I think. That pile looks like a big fur coat. Everybody, look at this. I hope nobody's inside it, but who'd wear an expensive fur coat out here on the hottest day of the year? It's not a coat. It's rabbits." Marcie touched the pile with the machete blade tip. Then she twisted her mouth and crossed her eyes for the camera.

"All dead. All stiff. Yes, *I got U babe.* All exsanguinated looking. All very stinky. A banquet for crows. This is very Edgar Allen Poe. Where is the man when you need him. He and the rabbits are nevermore.

"Moving on again." Marcie quickened her pace. "Smell's gone, finally." She spun around and pointed the camera. "Just so you know, I can still see the big tree. Our beacon to get home. We're definitely taking another route on the way back to avoid these stinky dead things. I don't care how thick the underbrush is." She pointed the camera back at her sweating, flushed face. She took off the pith helmet, wiped her forehead, and replaced the hat. She looked around nervously and bit her lip. "It makes me wonder what else could be dead out here. Not sure if I really want to know. Animals die and are killed in the natural world all the time. It kind of depends where something is on the food chain. Nobody notices in a place like this because nobody's around to witness it. But these things weren't killed for food, for meat. I feel like they were killed for their blood. What would do that?

"Where am I on the food chain? Shame on you, *I got U babe*. This is a friendly channel We don't tolerate unkind remarks. Send another one and I'll block you from my videos! That goes for everyone. This is a serious safari."

Marcie wiped an imaginary tear from her eye and pouted. "Everybody, let's move on. I'd like to reach the lake before we go back. I've never seen it, except on Google Maps. It must be close because I can hear geese honking. Some have flown over, so we know the geese are still here, not drained of their blood, lying in a pile.

"Incidentally, the dead deer could be a natural thing. Maybe it was rundown by a predator or shot. It could have died of old age or disease. The rabbit pile is another thing. That is most unnatural. Rabbits don't die in piles. It's not like an elephant graveyard in an old Tarzan movie." She sang, "By the way, I love Tarzan because he has no underwear."

Marcie walked on. "Good news for a change, everybody. Cattails and mud. Water must be close. I'm just going to wade into the cattails and see what I find. They're very thick here. As you can see, visibility is poor. Only a foot or two. It's like walking through a cornfield." She spun the camera on her face, smiled, crossed her eyes, and wagged her head. "You know, walking through a cornfield, knock on the door, peep in, turn the latch, walk in, chin chopper, chin chopper, chin chopper! Mom did that to me when I was little." She panned the camera back to the ground. "I still see the human footprints." Marcie turned the camera back on her face. "So, the footprints are deeper here. That tells me a couple of things.

"That's right, *Cougar*, you must think like Sherlock Holmes. Basil Rathbone was the best Sherlock, in my opinion. So, either the dude weighed more than me—that's a no-brainer because most dudes with big feet will outweigh me—or he walked through here when this place was wetter, muddier, and sank in. Maybe both. Maybe a week or two ago, maybe longer. Get my drift?"

Marcie chirped, "We'll see, *Barnstormer*. Maybe you can be my Doctor Watson. I wouldn't mind having a Doctor Watson about now."

To *Sally Lou*, Marcie said, "You got it. A big, strong Doctor W. Of course, he would be handsome."

Marcie stopped, trained her camera to the right. "Everybody, over here it looks like something crawled." She pointed to the mud.

"That's right, *I got U babe*. It looks like something could have been drug through here. You're very astute, *I got U babe*. I hope you're cute. It was something rather large. Maybe another deer?"

Marcie crouched, moved forward, slid on the mud. Almost lost her footing. She smiled for the camera. "Did you see that. That was a close one. Almost went on my ass."

The cattails got thicker. Marcie hacked at them with the machete. She duckwalked through the morass. "This is really tough going. I don't know if I'll make it to the water. Every step gets muddier. Slicker. I'm sinking deeper. Wait until Mom sees these new boots. Still, I can see the drag marks. I'm going to chop over here and follow them as far as I can."

Marcie was still crouched. She swung the machete. The

blade struck something solid and sank in. It wouldn't pull out. "This mud is like cement. Maybe it's a rotten log."

Marcie stood. Grabbed the machete handle. Before she pulled, she separated the cattails in front of her and let out a blood-curdling scream. She had plunged the machete into the body of a prone naked man. A naked woman lay to the dead man's right. In the length of time the scream lasted, Marcie saw both decomposing bodies were exsanguinated like the deer and rabbits.

In that instant the smell of rot hit Marcie's nose, and she knew she had found the missing neighbors from the burned-out home, the Millers, or whatever their names were. She turned and ran. Her feet slid in the mud, first sideways, then back and forth. Although Marcie didn't realize her camera was still recording, the video caught the action of a cartoon character trying to escape a menace, feet and legs spinning without making progress. Finally, her begrimed boots caught, and she sprinted away through the cattails. Eventually, she hit dry ground and ran along the game trail. Marcie leaped over the dead rabbits, vaulted over the buck. A boot tangled in the antlers, and she fell heavily on the ground. The fall knocked the wind out of her.

A black snake—the video later revealed—slithered across the path inches in front of her face. She wanted to scream. Couldn't because she lacked air in her lungs. She gagged on the stench of death while her lungs sucked in as much air as they could in little gasps. The video showed her lips scattering clouds of dust along the ground. Dirt got in her eyes.

Eventually, she staggered to her feet and limped to the dead tree, with its ghastly, specter-like branch pointing toward home.

She leaned against the tree and vomited. She cried. Coughed. Tried to catch her breath. The machete and pith helmet were gone. The pack still clung to her back. Her hair and clothes were stuck with nettles and burrs. Her face was scratched by vines. Somewhere along the way, she managed to sprain an ankle. Probably on the antler. As fast as possible, she made her way through the underbrush, tracing the trail she made earlier, as crows followed her, screaming overhead. Finally, she fell through the last obstacle and landed in the grass in her back-yard. Marcie wretched again. Dry heaves.

After her stomach quieted, Marcie said into the camera, "The only time I ever barfed like that was last Christmas when we had a sleepover at my friend's house. Natalie! You remem-ber! We got into her dad's boilo and, oh baby. I was able to sleep it off with nobody knowing—especially my parents, thank God. That's the first and last time I touched alcohol. I really don't recommend it—boilo or anything else. We'll have to continue this later, Everybody. I'm going to fade out now."

The rest of the day was occupied by the police. Marcie called her father. He came home from the dry-cleaning busi-ness, retraced her path through the wetland, which was easy, with her boot tracks, bent grass, and flattened brush. He called 911 from the site of the bodies, returned to the Barton backyard with Marcie's machete and pith helmet to wait for the cops.

Then he returned with the cops to the body scene. More cops were called in. Crime scene investigators combed the wetland. The deer, the rabbits, and the Millers—they suspected —were photographed and prodded. Samples and evidence were collected. Casts were made of the footprints. The Bartons, espe-cially Marcie, were interviewed. Finally, after dark, the corpses were excavated from the wetland mud and removed for identification and autopsies.

Marcie was hugged—some overly friendly—kissed, slapped on the back at the Neighborhood Watch's emergency meeting later that night, as she limped around the Barton basement with an Ace bandage wrapped on her ankle. She felt dazed by the day's events. The entire membership attended, along with strangers. The basement was filled and noisy. Joan Barton had to make an emergency run for coffee. A second coffee maker was set up. Doughnuts and cookies were brought in and arranged on a long folding table. The patrollers gobbled sweets and slurped coffee, scattering crumbs and java on the area rugs.

Gregory Barton was flushed and eager to tell what the police allowed him to say, which was not much, despite Marcie's blow-by-blow description of the wetland that went viral. He made his rounds through the crowd, smiling and chatting. You might think he was running for office. After the meeting was called to order, the membership immediately was disappointed. There were no photos of the Millers, the trophy deer, the heaped rabbits, or the male footprints, not even the black snake, to pass around or pin to the walls. Sam Johnson, owner of a Mammoth shoe store, said with confidence he could identify the shoe brand *if* he saw the footprints.

The locations of the bodies, the deer, and rabbits would remain a secret, even though their locations were cordoned off by bright yellow police tape. The state police closed the wetland to the public. More forensic investigators would comb the locations starting at first light. Motel owner Clyde Barnes confirmed all his rooms were booked. His parking lot was filled with black SUVs and TV news station vans with satellite dishes. Still, he couldn't get one word from the investigators as they wandered into his office to ask about good restaurants and places to buy toiletries. Clyde figured some investigators were called to Mammoth on a moment's notice, without time to pack even a toothbrush and deodorant.

"Don't kid yourself," Gregory Barton chimed above the clamor. "I can't answer any of your questions. I know more than the police are going to release, simply because I viewed the scene, but Marcie and I were told to divulge nothing. I repeat. Nothing that could hinder the investigation."

The membership released a collective groan and grumbled. They had a right to know investigation details. Their families had to be protected. Gregory Barton used the moment to pull out new patrol rosters.

"We believe two murders have been committed and wildlife mutilated. We want to patrol this area around the clock," Gregory yelled. "Who wants to help?"

The crowd cheered and pumped their fists. Men and women stepped forward to join the group. Existing members said they would take more patrols, even if it meant turning down overtime at work. Gregory smiled widely as he filled out the paperwork, until the Barton basement half-bath toilet refused to flush and the crowd, awash with coffee and with sticky fingers, were directed to Marcie's bathroom upstairs to empty their bladders.

Marcie had slipped away from the meeting, tired of being manhandled, jostled, and retreated to her bedroom where she locked the door and changed into pajamas. There were too many people in the basement. Normally she liked the attention her celebrity status brought but tonight was different. Most of these people she didn't know, and they circled the basement like vultures, spilling coffee and dropping food on the floor, noting the lights, the decorations, the furniture, her dad's liquor bottles, as if they were casing the place for a robbery they planned. One guy was different. He was tall, dark-haired, and dressed in black. He stood motionless across the room, staring at Marcie. He was hot, someone she had never seen before. Perhaps he had recently moved to Mammoth. Imagine if he turned up in one of her classes in September. She dreamed of tutoring him in algebra—Marcie was a whiz—leaning over his shoulder, smelling his body wash, inspecting the back of his neck, feeling heat from his body rising to her face.

Marcie was aghast when her bathroom toilet next to her bedroom flushed time after time, and watch members jiggled her door handle as they lined up to pee.

"Everybody, it's *Marcie in the Mousetrap*," she whispered. "Tonight, it's Marcie in the *house* trap. Dad's having a Neighborhood Watch meeting in the basement, which I narrowly escaped because now I am more of a celebrity," she sang, "if such a thing is possible!

"Apparently, the toilet downstairs broke and the overflow—no pun intended—is using the toilet in *my* bathroom across the hall. How gross. I'm calling Stanley Steamer in the morning. By the way, the half-bath off the kitchen—the one I did a video on around Christmas because Mom had crowded so many decorations inside you had to practically wipe yourself with garland—has the water shut off because Mom is having it renovated." She sang, "Great timing, Mom!"

"Anyway, this is a live feed, kind of spontaneous, so feel free to comment and I," she sang, "*as usual*, will read some of the remarks. Everyone says the missing Millers from across the street are dead and were the bodies I found this afternoon in the wetland. You'll read about it in the Mammoth Sentinel tomorrow, but remember you learned it first from *Marcie in the Mousetrap*, where all the good news is.

"Now, I saw these Millers when they moved in, whenever that was, even waved to them, but they don't look *now* like they did that fateful day, if you know what I mean. For one thing, they wore clothes when they moved in. I see you all have a zillion questions about the bodies, but the police said they will take my camera, freeze my account, if I mention anything about the case. Everybody, can they do that? Any lawyers watching? The coppers have a gag order on my dad, too. Speaking of the cops, they confiscated my boots and my backpack, even my camera's memory chip of the bunny safari. But you all know that was a live feed and is already uploaded.

"Thank you for the money, everybody. Two bucks from *Swing chick*. A single from *Bobby Bee*. Oh, and five bucks from the *green dragon*. Another fiver from *I got U babe*. Thank you one and all. Everybody, I'm kind of exhausted and will sign out for now. Sorry *I got U babe*, I like talking to you, too, but I need sleep. I'm just peeking out my bedroom window. I love these mini blinds. They should be called *clandestine* blinds. Slide one panel up and you have just enough space to spy. Some people are leaving my house. The meeting must be over, thank God. I know because my toilet hasn't flushed for a while. I hope that *it* isn't broken, too. Use your own facilities, people!

"One last look outside before I go. Hey, there's a pinhole of light coming from the burned-out house, the boarded-up window, second floor, directly across from my bedroom. I wonder. It just went out. The whole place is dark now. That's strange. Everybody, any ideas?

"*Kitten mitten?* Hey, long time, no hear from ya. Really? You think someone's spying on me? *Me!* Who could it be?" Marcie's voice trailed off. "But that's impossible. The place is empty. I promise. I will be careful. Maybe we'll do something creative in the next video. I've wanted to paint our mailbox. Dad has nixed the idea, but we'll see. I can get the paint for free. Good night, all, sweet dreams."

Marcie turned off her cell phone and clicked off the light in her room. She returned to her bed and the window, slid up a blind panel, and peered across the street. The burned-out house was dark. Was the light she saw a reflection from the street, a shiny nail head in the plywood, or was it a flame, another fire that might have smoldered all along, suddenly flared up only to die out again? Where there's smoke, there's fire, she told herself. Surely smoke would have escaped from the house if there was a second blaze, even a smoldering one. A flame would have a yellowish flame. The light she saw was silverish, like from a cell phone. That was impossible, too. Who could stand to be inside the house without a respirator? Even when she was outside, there was a heavy odor of charred wood that almost gagged her.

In bed, Marcie slept fitfully. She dreamed she awoke in the morning and found a note pushed under her door. The paper was stained and folded in half. The paper stuck together and was difficult to open. Carefully, she slid a finger along the page and pulled it open. Inside was a note written in letters that flowed elegantly across the paper. Still, Marcie had difficulty reading it, because it was in cursive, a form of writing with connected letters she hadn't been taught in school. With difficulty, placing a finger over one letter at a time, she managed to read the note.

Marcie,

You should know I love you. I have watched your videos for some time and am enthralled. The last word was a killer and took considerable time to decipher. Marcie had to transcribe each letter in block print at the bottom of the page. *I especially like when you wear bikinis. Please do more. Your account of the fire was better than the television news and more accurate than the Sentinel's newspaper story. I hope you will go away with me. I can promise you a life that is very different from the one you have now, but you will never grow old. You always will be young and beautiful. I will take good care of you. We will be on the run, hunted by those who would destroy us, but I know how to survive in <u>this world</u>. I have been doing it for a long time.*

I have already been inside your home (as you can see from this note placed under your bedroom door). I have watched you sleep, which is wonderful. Sometimes you make strange and wonderful noises. I could have eaten you alive, but didn't, because I love you so much. I have other plans for you.

While you slept, I packed some clothes in your new suitcase, including bikinis. It's the suitcase you did a video on. It is in your closet ready to go. I will be around after sundown today. Please be ready to leave, to come with me. Again, I love you more than life itself. You will see!

Your immortal beloved,

I got U babe

Marcie dropped the letter on the bed. *I got U babe* had been in her home during the Neighborhood Watch meeting, climbed the steps, maybe flushed her toilet, stood outside her bedroom door, slipped the note inside her room. He might have talked with her parents in the basement, drank coffee and ate cookies—*no, he's a vampire*—rubbed shoulders with her neighbors. If he told the truth, he had been in her bedroom. He stood over her while she slept. He knew how to get in and out of her home, despite the deadbolt locks and alarm system.

Perhaps *I got U babe* squatted in the burned-out house. Maybe he killed the Millers and started the fire. *It was possible she knew him.* Did he go to school with her? Was he in her classes? Had he been on the swim team she quit because it interfered with her videos?

Marcie looked toward the window. She realized suddenly it was already dark. She had slept through the day. Marcie tiptoed to the bedroom door and opened it a crack. The house was dark. She opened the door more and stuck her head into the hall. The home was quiet. She closed the door and locked it. Turning back to the room's interior, she saw her open closet door. She never left it open. Considered it bad luck.

The end of her new suitcase stood partially inside the bedroom, just enough to notice, just enough to prevent the door from closing. The case was heavy when she lifted it. She threw it on the bed and opened it. Her clothes, mostly ones she introduced in videos, spilled out. There were toiletries, too, collected from her bathroom. Everything was packed haphazardly, nothing folded, as if thrown in while in a hurry.

Then there was a soft knock on the door. The doorknob giggled. Marcie woke, jumping off the bed, shouting "No! I won't go!"

Her mother was outside the door. "Honey, are you awake? I'm going for groceries. Do you want anything?"

Marcie realized it was morning, not night. Her closet door was closed. She ran to the closet. The suitcase was missing. Probably in the attic, where such things were stored.

"I'm okay, Mom. You woke me. I was having a bad dream."

"Open up."

Marcie unlocked the bedroom door.

"Sorry, Honey. Do you want to talk about it?" Joan hugged Marcie.

"No. I've already forgotten it," Marcie lied, not wanting to get into it. She smiled at her mother. "I'll be all right. I can't remember it, but I was scared."

"You ought to take a break from this Neighborhood Watch, especially all this stuff with the wetland, the Millers, that burned-out house."

"You're right, Mom. I have to clear my mind of all this," she sang, "crazy stuff!"

"That a girl," Joan said, hugging her stepdaughter again, before she left for the grocery store. "You're getting a pimple on your nose."

Joan moved lightly down the stairs, then exclaimed, near the bottom, "Oh my GOD!"

Marcie rushed to the top of the steps. "What's wrong, Mom?" she called down the steps.

"Some idiot tracked mud in here last night." She looked at Marcie and shook her head. "Your father and his deadbeat patrols. Whoever it was probably tracked it all over the house. There might even be mud upstairs. I didn't see any in the hall. Let me know what your bathroom looks like."

After inspecting the bathroom the meeting attendees had used, *her bathroom,* Marcie returned to the top of the steps and chirped, "Just some pee on the floor. What do you expect from guys? Otherwise, everything looks good up here. No mud."

"Thank God. I'll inspect the basement when I get back from the store. You might want to clean the toilet before you sit."

"I promise. Maybe whoever had the mud realized it and took off his shoes," Marcie said, smiling at her mother.

"Really?" Joan turned and left the house.

Marcie returned to the bathroom wearing long-sleeved gloves, cleaned the toilet, outside and inside the bowl. Then she cleaned the floor around the toilet. "I'll have to do a video on the way guys pee," she said to herself. "Not that I'm an expert, but I have seen the results. I don't think I'll have a problem getting volunteers."

Marcie took a long, hot shower, steaming up the bathroom because she neglected to turn on the ceiling exhaust fan. She was ready to wipe the moisture off the mirror to inspect the nascent pimple on her nose when she noticed a message written on the mirror.

Come see me. You
know where I am.
I got U babe

Marcie poised her hand over the steamy mirror and decided not to disturb the message. She turned on the exhaust fan and returned to her bedroom to towel off. Marcie dressed and washed down two cherry Pop-Tarts with a glass of milk. Her father was at the dry cleaning business or on patrol. Her mother was in her glory—shopping. She sat at the kitchen table for a few minutes, sorting out things in her mind. The meeting. The dream. At the front door she found mud, identical to the kind in the cattails, dried now, on the mat and smeared on the hard-wood floor.

Marcie left her home through the front door. The street with its dead end against the wetland was quiet. The only traffic on her street tended to be residents and Amazon delivery drivers. Marlin Avenue ended with a rickety, moss-covered split-rail fence perpendicular to the roadway a few feet off the asphalt. No one remembered who built the fence or had ownership. Mammoth City Council said it was not responsible for the dilapidated fence. It would never stop a vehicle barreling down Marlin.

The neighborhood remained silent. Marcie looked up and down the street. No neighbors were visible. She wondered whether multiple security cameras had caught her image crossing the street to the burned-out house. Marcie ducked under the wagging police tape and walked along the side of the home, getting her first close-up view of the fire damage. She immediately noticed the gray, sticky mud where cattails grew in the wetland. The odor of burnt wood was strong. She followed the mud trail along the house until it disappeared. Then she saw a single footprint, like the ones she followed on the bunny safari, just outside a basement window.

After looking around, she tugged on the window's plywood cover and found it swung open easily. All the window glass had been cleared out. She bent over and slipped through the window. When she dropped to the basement and its muddy floor, she knew immediately it would be more difficult getting out. Glass shards crunched under her feet. The smell from the fire was intense, made her cough, then sneeze. The footprints appeared immediately again in the light from her cell phone.

They tracked back and forth across the floor between the window and steps, as if someone had crossed and recrossed the basement floor.

The home was quiet. Occasionally, a water drop, a remnant from the fire company's deluge, worked its way down through the interior and dropped to the floor, hitting something metallic. Marcie stood at the bottom of the steps, a hand on the rail. She was undecided whether to continue. What if the cops or city officials arrived for another inspection? The house had already been condemned. What if the damaged structure under the weight of thousands of gallons of water-soaked building materials collapsed on her? A gallon of water weighed about seven pounds. What were the chances of that?

She would feel better if she were recording. Talking to her camera always steeled her nerves, but she couldn't make a video inside the home. She could get in trouble. The house was off limits. Marcie cleared her throat, as if interrupting someone who hadn't noticed her approach. She pressed up to the first step, as if testing the stairs' strength. She listened and then followed the same pattern, taking one step and listening a few seconds before climbing the next. She finally reached the top. She turned around on the landing and surveyed what she could see in the basement. All mud. Her and the stranger's footprints. The basement door was blown open, partially charred.

Marcie stepped into the kitchen. The tile floor was still wet and slippery, tracked with mud. The water cannons had blown pots and pans from their hooks, smashed knickknacks, knocked over chairs, and soaked everything. The living room's carpeting was soiled and still squishy. The walls and ceiling were scorched from the roiling flames, smutty with smoke stains.

Firemen had axed apart furniture to hunt down hotspots. The whole house smelled of dampness and mildew.

Marcie righted a small table so she could open a closet near the front door. She heard a noise there. The closet was empty and dripped water from the floor above. A heap of soaked drywall lay on the floor. She moved to the second-floor steps. Some handrail spindles were missing or had been broken and left with jagged ends. Others that remained had discolored or bubbled paint from the fire's intense heat. She pried out a broken spindle that had a point.

This is the last thing someone should do in a horror movie, Marcie thought, move deeper into an abandoned house. She took one step at a time, always stopped to listen before moving up. She thought she heard a noise upstairs—something moving —but told herself it was nothing. Perhaps a curtain remained at a blown-out window and moved in the breeze. The stairs' carpet was soggy, the individual fibers either burned or crusty from melting. Marcie's palms were soon black from soot when she grabbed the handrail or steadied herself against the grimy wall.

Finally, she reached the top of the steps. The second floor was dark. All the windows had been boarded over. Only a few slices of light showed through where there were gaps in the plywood. More soot and scorch marks. One burned area looked like an immense devil that crawled up the wall and across the ceiling like a menacing shadow. Marcie imagined the horns, jagged teeth, claws, and a forked tail. She had goosebumps on her arms and stifled a cough.

Why am I doing this? Why did I come here? It's dangerous. I could get in trouble. What will my subscribers think? Me, whole-some little Marcie, breaking the law. Will a conviction hinder my chances of getting accepted at a good college? What will become of the tuition I already accumulated from the channel? Pay legal fees?

She knew she should return to the basement, find something to stand on, and climb through the window and safety. Her mother would be home soon. Perhaps she was already unloading groceries into the refrigerator and kitchen cabinets. Still, just like the heroine in a horror movie, she continued down the hall, peering into rooms, ignoring the little voice in her head, fascinated by the fire damage.

She could see the ceiling caved in on what would have been *her* bathroom in her own home. She heard another noise. Did something scurry in the front bedroom that faced her home, the room where she saw the pinpoint of silvery light last night? Had rats already moved into the house? Did a rat watch her through a hole in the plywood? She carried the spindle across her chest like a rifle; its point charred to hardness in the fire.

Marcie continued down the hall. The door to the front bedroom was open only a crack. She approached it cautiously, pressed a palm on the bubbled paint, which crackled under her hand. There was resistance when she pushed the door. Something inside was against the bedroom door. Perhaps the firemen knocked something over. She could tell the room was dark. Its two windows were boarded over.

Marcie put her weight against the door, and it crept open slowly. Suddenly, the door sprang open. Marcie lost her balance and stumbled into the room. The door slammed shut behind her. Standing in front of the closed door was the young, dark-haired man she had seen in her basement last night. He stared. A lock of hair fell over his forehead.

Marcie said, "You're..."

"*I got U babe.* You recognize me." He smiled.

"You were in my home last night. I saw you in the basement."

"I was there."

"You were watching my house through a hole in that boarded-up window." She pointed the spindle at a window. "I saw the glow from your phone."

"Guilty as charged."

"You turned off the phone when I mentioned it on my video."

He chuckled.

"You tracked mud into our house. My mom had a conniption."

"The same mud as in the marsh. Just enough mud for you to see, to know I was there. The same mud I left outside this house, so your curiosity would get the better of you, that you would sneak inside to investigate."

"I had a dream about you."

"No, Marcie. I gave you a dream. Put it up here." He tapped his temple. "The letter you read in the dream is true. I could have left it for you under your bedroom door. But what if you missed it on the floor, walked over it, and one of your parents found it. Then they would know there was an intruder in the house. They think you are too young for a lover, but I know different.

"I put the dream in your head to ensure you got the message, to prepare you for our new life together." He stepped toward Marcie.

Marcie stared at him and said, "How did you get in *my* house. Who invited you?"

The young man smiled. "I stood on the front porch and rang the doorbell. Your father invited me in."

"You are a vampire. I understand everything now. Never to grow old. Never die, never even be sick. I'm ready. I'm not as innocent as I might seem, as you might think. I am ready to join you in the dark world." She smiled. "I need to know your name."

"It is Arturo. What you would call Arthur."

"Arturo is much more beautiful. I will always call you Arturo." Marcie cocked her head. "Not Arthur. Not Art. Not Artie. Always Arturo. It sounds so wonderful."

Arturo smiled. "It is a big step to take, Marcie. To join me. It will be painful at first, until you adjust. It is painful to die."

"I'm ready."

"You must actually die and be reborn. Just as I was. But once you join me, life, or I should say death, will be wonderful, exquisite."

"I said I was ready." Marcie bounded up and down on the squishy carpet.

"You must leave behind everything you know. Your parents. Your home. Your friends. Your school. Your videos and the celebrity they give you. You must give it all up to be with me. And I must kill you."

"I'm tired of all this bullshit. This so-called *life*. I'm tired of making videos. Pretending I like the people who send me a few dollars. The girls who want to be like me, dress like me, talk like me. If we went to the mall right now, you'd see girls all over talking, raising their heads, to sing a few words, just like me. It's nonsense. And the guys who lurk on my channel. They send me money and jerk off. Disgusting. Find a real girlfriend, because I'd never give them the time of day.

"I don't want to go to college. What's the point? To study four more years so I can have what? A house like this or the one across the street." Marcie spread out her arms to emphasize the room, the house. "Please! Make me gag!"

"I was one of those male lurkers. I jerked off when you came out in a bikini. When you brushed your hair. Put on lipstick and smacked your lips. I even sent you money."

"I remember. The thing is Arturo, now you can have the real thing. Without the bikini."

Arturo moaned. His lips quivered.

Marcie laughed and looked around the room. "Is there any part of this place that's dry? Do you have any idea how long I've waited to do *it*?"

Arturo showed his fangs.

"Come to me," Marcie said.

They embraced and kissed, somewhat awkwardly.

"You feel cold from being in this damp house. You smell like...but I don't care."

Marcie pulled him closer. He was almost a full head taller than she was. Arturo moaned with passion. He wrapped his arms around her. Then he shrieked.

Marcie aced AP Anatomy. She placed the spindle perfectly and drove it under the xiphoid process at the bottom of the sternum, between his lungs, and into the dead heart. They locked their eyes for a moment.

"You smell like the dead, like a fucking vampire! Or, at least what I imagine one would smell like." Marcie stepped back.

"Marcie, I love you."

"Love this!" Marcie rammed the spindle with her palm until the bottom was flush with his chest.

Arturo sank to his knees. He took one last look up at Marcie. His mouth opened, as if he wanted to say something more. The spindle's jagged tip was visible in the back of his throat. His body turned to jelly, collapsed, then liquified, spreading across the already soaked carpet. Marcie jumped out of the way. Only Arturo's foul-smelling clothes were left. Marcie looked at her Fitbit. "I was going to do a video this afternoon." She raised her head and sang, "I'm so behind. Now, how to tell Dad we don't need the Neighborhood Watch anymore. And he was so into it."

THE ART OF HOARDING

Silas Barry moved between the back of his SUV and his garage interior, unloading today's collection bought at three yard sales around Mammoth. He collected anything and everything. At sixty-four, the rotund, balding man, prone to wear flat driving caps, even inside, had difficulty moving about his home. He was not that big or his home that small. However, over the years the house he grew up in and still occupied was packed with what he collected.

Silas's father had been a bank president who had a penchant and certain acumen for investing. As a result, Silas was left a fortune and never worked—didn't have to—although he called his collecting his *job*. Silas's mother died of cancer when he was a teenager. After she was gone, he and his father settled into an odd-couple-like relationship. Like two old men, they shared meals in the dining room and talked little. High school graduation came and went. There was never a discussion about higher education, or even work. Silas seemed content to waste his time around the house and around the town. He never had many friends. It seemed no one came around the house— boys, or especially girls—to hang out. Silas never announced to his father that he was off to see a movie with a friend, attend a party, or had a date.

Silas was an odd duck, so people in the neighborhood agreed. He was always portly, walked in a strange manner with his toes pointed out, and had a sloping forehead that seemed to extend to a longish straight nose. His head appeared to be a caricature painted by a sidewalk artist.

After so many years of going to the bank five days a week, the old man seldom left home after he retired and his many investments were secured in long-term holdings, preferring to watch television and smoke his pipe from a corner not taken over by Silas's junk. Meanwhile, Silas brought in ever-growing armloads of things and carried them to the attic. The old man watched Silas waddle up the steps and shook his head. Anything the old man said was under his breath. He didn't want to get into an argument with his sharp-tongued only child. Senior never bothered to ask Silas what he was doing or why he collected so much.

Silas did little to specialize in specific categories like stamps, old books, art, pottery, knickknacks, or guns. He brought home anything that tickled his fancy on any given day. At first, he kept like items together, books in stacks along an attic wall, old tools in the basement, old-fashioned toys arranged in an attic corner or in his bedroom.

His father employed a cleaning woman, who came in one day a week. He had known Sally from the bank. Neighborhood gossip claimed Sally cleaned more than the house while Silas was on one of his frequent forays, but only the old man and Sally knew for sure. Eventually, Sally died. It was rumored the old man paid for the funeral, but there was no proof. A replacement for the cleaner was not hired, because it was said the old man did not want the general public to know about the home's true condition. Another bit of gossip claimed Sally died in the home—possibly in bed—and was covered with a pile of Silas's eclectic junk and soon was lost and forgotten.

After his father died and Silas inherited his father's estate, his collection grew at an increased rate. As rooms filled with the oddities, Silas saw no reason to clean them. There was no longer space to run a vacuum across the floor or dust shelves, tables, and counter surfaces. Navigating through rooms to clean became tedious, even hazardous. He let the dust accumulate and covered it with layers of more items.

Silas hated to see old things go to the dump or ruined. He'd snatch an old toy from a child's hands, because he knew the boy, especially boys, would soon break the toy and it would end up in the trash. If he were at a yard sale and the sky threatened rain, he would scoop up old books and silverfish-eaten magazines, regardless of their subjects, even though he would never read them, rather than see them waterlogged by rain and thrown away.

After the house filled, Silas had a garage built at the end of his property and an asphalt driveway poured to it. The three-bay garage with automatic overhead doors and additional space for a workshop was an auto mechanic's dream, but it never housed any vehicle. There was never a tire mark on the interior's pristine concrete floor, because the garage was intended to store more stuff.

On the outside, Silas's home was trim and tidy, if not a little rundown from neglect. Paint peeled on the wooden windows and some bricks needed repointing. A landscaper cut grass, trimmed bushes, and shoveled snow. Therefore, neighbors never complained about his hoarding. In fact, they only suspected he filled room after room, starting with the attic, with an assortment of junk he brought home almost daily. He unloaded his car after dark, often late at night, to avoid detection. Since the garage had been built, Silas spent so much time there some neighbors believed he was a motorhead, perhaps restoring an old muscle car, even though they couldn't remember hearing Silas revving a supped-up engine.

Silas never missed garage and yard sales, flea markets, or auctions. Auctioneers knew him by name as he waddled into their venues. Homeowners who held annual yard sales expected him, too, often asking, "What are you looking for this year?"

"I don't know," Silas would answer coyly, with a smile, perhaps even blushing, "but I'll know it when I see it."

Even though Silas had lived his entire life at the same address, none of the neighbors knew him—even the longtime neighbors. They tittered about the pear-shaped man who never seemed to have had a sweetheart or been on a date, so they imagined. They waved at him coming and going and he waved back, although they seldom talked.

Exchanges were limited to such things as "It's a scorcher," or "Did you hear that thunder last night? Almost knocked me out of bed," or "Nice day for a picnic." When they did exchange words, neighbors later imitated Silas's odd, high-pitched voice. These same neighbors even rifled through his garbage set at the curb for collection when he wasn't home. His diet of microwaveable, processed meals and diet soda was evident. As the years wore on, Silas bought ever larger vehicles to haul more treasure. Treasure it must have been for his face showed an evil delight as he unpacked his car.

The neighbors shook their heads and said, "That Silas. At it again. He ought to find a nice girl to straighten him out. One who likes to put her money in the bank instead of collecting junk. A good, home-cooked meal and time between the sheets with a honey would turn him around. Too bad that Sally died so young."

After a time, neighborhood gossip swirled around Silas. There was a story that said he had a girlfriend who died and left him heartbroken. Another tale claimed his girlfriend disappeared on a camping trip, possibly abducted by satanic cult members, even a Sasquatch. Silas barely survived. His own crippling injuries caused his funny walk. Brain surgery gave Silas's head its odd shape. However, the best was that he murdered his girlfriend after she threw away some bobble he had just bought. Supposedly, she remained buried somewhere amid all his junk, possibly in the same room where Sally was interred.

Now there were only a few long-time neighbors left. The days were gone when a couple bought a home and lived out their lives there. Now, people came and went. They had plans to buy a home, save money, make a few improvements, and move to larger digs after a few years. Or perhaps they had dreams to live on the West Coast someday, in a big city, in some quaint New England town. Whatever jobs they chased, most people were gone within a few years. Silas never knew their names but suspected they spied on him.

Some neighbors wondered, *How could someone not work and apparently have so much money to spend?* Silas bought a new and larger vehicle every few years. He had built an expensive garage and never parked a car in it. No one was allowed inside. If someone came to the door, he immediately stepped outside, regardless of the weather. He was seen sometimes picking over clothes in department stores, smiling over stacks of sweaters and trousers, examining the details on hanging belts, twirling silk scarves around his neck, trying on suits, Homburgs, overcoats. Salesmen fawned over Silas, brushing imaginary threads from his shoulders, smiling, almost genuflecting, because they knew him to buy expensive items in quantity. He would buy not one suit, but two or three if he could not decide among the solid colors, pinstripes, or plaids. Their commissions would be large. Occasionally, he was seen dining alone at an expensive restaurant. A Manhattan was followed by an appropriate glass of wine with dinner. Dinner was lobster or select cuts of meat—all expensive—all at market rates. Desserts followed.

Although he seldom interacted with other people and appeared to have no living relatives, Silas never considered himself lonely. He was occupied with his passion, collecting. Neither did he think about what would become of all his loot after he died. He never thought about dying, even though he knew everyone died eventually. After all, he was the last member of his family. The Barry line would die out when he passed.

Silas moved from one bedroom to another after the closets and bureau drawers filled to bursting and there was no more room for him to sleep in the beds, which became covered with mounds of stuff, sets of sheets, towels, drapes, clothing, blankets, comforters, bric-a-brac wrapped in newspaper. He installed a clothes rack in the upstairs hall, through which his pear-shaped body could hardly squeeze. The attic steps were impassable. He had piles of stamps in sheets, candles, teetering stacks of books he didn't read, a collection of odd lamps without lightbulbs, a half dozen ceiling fans on the floor in their boxes, unopened air fresheners, scores of lightbulbs, volumes of old mail that spilled on the floor, a mountain of newspapers, mounds of bags, their contents unknown, bottles of whiskey and wine he didn't drink at home, flatware, china, and goblets, and stockpiles of outdated canned food he didn't like, especially tuna, carrots, and peas that had been on sale, televisions and radios that were never plugged in, music and movie CDs in their original packaging. There was no end to this enormous deposit.

After he unloaded into the garage a carload of yard supplies that would never be touched—tools and bags of grass seed, fertilizer, mulch, and weed killers—because soon they would be covered by more stuff, Silas stood and stroked his chin, catching his breath. He mopped his sweating brow with a yellow, tattered handkerchief, even though he had bought six packs of new handkerchiefs last week. He no longer knew where he put them. The garage he had such grand plans for was almost full. He closed the overhead garage door with his remote and locked it in his new SUV.

After dinner one night, his few dishes washed and set on the counter because there was no room in the cabinets and the automatic dishwasher was filled with unopened cleaning supplies, Silas sat at the kitchen table, its surface narrowing with its ever-growing pile of junk, to read the newspaper. Among the classifieds, which he scanned religiously, an advertisement caught his eye:

1956 Cadillac hearse, all original, mint condition, new tires, recently inspected, great for camping, road trips, storage. A real conversation piece.

The word *storage* caught Silas's eye. Travel had no allure. Like his late father, Silas was a homebody. He called the telephone number in the ad. The owner picked up immediately, said he was negotiating already with two people, a rock band member interested in carrying drums, speakers, microphone stands, guitars, and the like to the group's gigs, and a DJ wanting to haul his equipment. Both parties thought the hearse would make their businesses unique. *Who's playing? The band that travels in a hearse. Oh, yeah. They're fabulous.*

Silas offered $250 more than the prices the DJ and rocker haggled over. With the deal sealed, he planned to pick up the vehicle the next day. He took his first Uber ride to the location, an old funeral home in a neighboring town.

"This hearse better work, or I'll need another Uber ride home," Silas said to himself after he departed from the Uber's cramped back seat.

"You know, this place has been closed for years," the long-haired, bespectacled young man said as Silas prepared to close the car door. "I hope you weren't thinking you were arriving for a funeral."

"So I've heard, but I have business here," Silas said, as if he were Jonathan Harker pointing to Castle Dracula. "Not a funeral."

"They won't bury anyone for you," the driver said.

"I'm not looking to bury anyone," Silas answered curtly.

Like a Romanian peasant of old, the Uber driver gave Silas an uneasy nod and roared away in his little car.

Silas approached the old funeral home, which still had a faded sign: *Moore Home for Funerals*. The grass was long, and the sign hung on chains that creaked in the summer breeze. An assortment of Amazon packages littered the porch. After Silas knocked, a tall, middle-aged skeletal man answered the door. He remained in the shadows while he looked up and down the street before admitting Silas. He and Silas collected the packages, brought them inside, and stacked them on the floor.

"I suppose you're here for the hearse?"

"Yes," Silas said. His excitement about the vehicle showed.

"I'm Tommy. We talked on the telephone yesterday."

The man had longish hair and wore shorts and a T-shirt under a long, soiled terrycloth robe that might have been white at one time. Silas found the man's grip oddly cool when they shook hands. His fingernails were long and sharp. Tommy led Silas on his spindly legs down a long hall, passed a large viewing room, smaller sitting room, and cluttered office. It appeared the place had not held a funeral in years. There was a toppled light, two church trucks for moving caskets, one on its side, dead, brittle looking flowers in vases. The rooms had closed, heavy drapes, which made them dim, but still visible was stained and peeling wallpaper.

"You'll have to excuse the place," Tommy said. "I'm having some work done."

"Not a problem," Silas answered. "I know what that's like. I have an older home."

Both men chuckled. However, Silas knew the clutter was the work of a fellow *collector*. Silas did not like the word hoarder. Silas thought this man could not bring himself to throw out anything. Although he probably had several new bathrobes, he couldn't stand to part with the old one, regardless of its condition, the frayed cuffs, the worn elbows, and the greasy fabric. Silas would have liked to take his time going through the old funeral home, with its high-ceilinged rooms, see all the stuff, perhaps make an offer on some interesting items, but there was business at hand. Silas had brought his checkbook, a credit card, and a sizable wad of cash.

"This was my parents' place, my grandfather's before them," the man said, craning his head over his shoulder to talk to Silas. Suddenly, he stopped and turned around, paused to scratch his unshaven cheek with long, dirty nails. "Personally, I never had a taste for the *business*. After he was too old, Dad employed a mortician for a few years, a young guy, but he left, claiming there wasn't enough *action* here in town."

"Oh?" Silas looked up at the man.

"Let me tell you something. There's absolutely no action in the funeral business. You'll never get laid. At least that's what I found, unless you're into necrophilia."

"I see your point. Everyone is either dead or mourning." Silas shuddered visibly and raised a skeptical eyebrow.

"Exactly," the man said. "Although one time there was this widow. I shouldn't talk about it." The scarecrow of a man continued toward the back of the building. They walked through two rooms filled with junk and a teetering stack of empty Amazon boxes and entered a room with a concrete floor.

"This is the mortuary where they embalmed the bodies,"

the tall man said. "Everything still works. There's even embalming fluid in that cabinet." He pointed toward the wall with his bony, long-fingered hand.

"Is it still good?" Silas asked.

"What do you think? It's going in somebody dead. It won't hurt them, if that's what you mean."

"Of course. I see. You took part in the..." Silas asked.

"Sure. I never went to mortuary school, but my father taught me. So, when I said I didn't have a taste for the business, I know what I'm talking about. I picked up bodies, handed out funeral cards at wakes, moved cars around the parking lot in back, filled in as a pallbearer. I did it all, and I hated it all. Plus, I wasn't very good at makeup—on the bodies, that is. Dad was a whiz, though. An artist. You need to be part artist, part longshoreman in this business. You're either painting on an eyebrow or hauling some fatty up a couple of flights of steps. After Bob left—the other mortician—I closed the place. I didn't have a license, anyway. That was five or six years ago. Now I just live here. After the renovations, I'll probably sell, that way I can let the equipment go with the house. I hope another funeral director buys it, although there were some kids in town interested in making a haunted house attraction." Tommy shrugged.

Silas smiled. He knew the man would never sell the joint. He was only starting to fill the place. Silas strayed from the man and looked around the room. "What's this?" he said.

The man chuckled. "It's a cadaverous injector. It injects the embalming fluid, a mixture of water and up to two percent formaldehyde. You know, this one is almost new. I hate to let it go."

"And these?" Silas said, moving further along the wall.

"Trocars. They're used to remove various fluids from body cavities and organs."

"Very interesting," Silas said. "And this, over here?"

"The hearse is through that door," Tommy interrupted. "In the garage." Tommy seemed to want to end the tour early.

"Oh, yes" Silas smiled. "That's what I'm here for."

They entered the garage. The hearse sat, dusty, but in beautiful shape. Little pleated burgundy curtains, faded but still pristine, hung from the side and back windows. Silas walked around the vehicle. There were no rust or dents. "Amazing," he said. Even the tires looked new, clean wide whitewalls, just as the ad had claimed.

"I didn't get a chance to go to the car wash. It rained and then..."

"Not a problem." Silas smiled. "I'll pass one on my way home. Maybe throw a coat of wax on it tomorrow, weather permitting."

"You need wax?" the man said. He rummaged through a cabinet on the wall. "Dad had a guy wax the car a couple times a year. The guy didn't drive. Imagine that. I had to pick him up and take him home. Dad would always have a glass of bourbon with him inside after the car was waxed. It was about the only time Dad drank. But the old guy died. Hit by a drunk driver walking home from the liquor store. Really mangled him. Dad used a ton of makeup on his face, just to make him presentable. I don't think the car's been waxed since." He added quickly, "But it's been in the garage all the time, unless it was out to the cemetery. It was never much in the sun. The curtains look new. Hardly any fading."

"No worries," Silas said. "I have car wax at home."

In fact, Silas had at least a dozen cans and bottles of automotive wax, if only they were still good and he could find them. Too bad he hadn't acquired any embalming fluid, which apparently had no expiration date.

"Well, let's start her up," Tommy chirped. He opened the overhead garage door, then climbed inside the hearse. The engine fired immediately and settled into a purr. "I started it regularly to keep the battery charged," Tommy called from the driver's seat. "The battery's only a year or so old. And it's a good battery. It should have lots of life. The warranty's in the glove box."

"Excellent," Silas said. "I plan to use it more than you did."

The man grimaced. "The other thing I wanted to do is clean the thing out. I didn't have a chance. I've been...busy. Never thought there'd be so much interest in an old hearse, and it would sell so fast. I should have sold it sooner." He waved his creepy hand toward the back of the hearse, which was filled almost to the ceiling with bags and boxes. "This stuff has been in here forever. I couldn't tell you what's back there, or if it's any good."

Silas smiled again, raising a finger to his lips. "Not a problem," he said, slowly, pronouncing each word with a slight pause in between. "I'll go through everything. It'll give me something to do while the wax sets up." This was an unexpected bonus, Silas thought.

"Okay," the man said. "I guess we're finished. We have a deal."

"We are finished," Silas said. The men smiled at each other. Even though the man rubbed his hands together briefly, his handshake to seal the deal was clammy. His nails were like daggers.

Silas made out a check on the hood of the hearse and handed it to the man. Tommy borrowed a pen and transferred the title to Silas. Then Silas dug in his pocket and pulled out a fifty-dollar bill. "This is for the stuff in the back."

"That's not necessary. It comes with the deal," the man said. "But thank you."

———

THE NEXT MORNING, Silas's longtime neighbor, Mrs. Rollins, almost fainted when she saw the shiny old hearse in the Barry driveway. Silas must have died overnight. She wanted to scream but couldn't. She opened her mouth, but no sound came out. She took a step back from the window, caught her balance, and moved forward again. Who found the body? Who made the call? She rushed to the front door, expecting to find at least one police car or a wagon from the coroner's office. There was nothing. No traffic at all.

She hated the idea of not being the first to spread neighborhood gossip, especially when it might concern Silas, but she would call the neighbor on the other side of Silas's home. She might know what's going on. She returned to the kitchen, peered out the window. There was Silas, wiping the hearse's back door, removing the last of the dried car wax haze. Silas appeared heavier than when she last saw him several months ago, but nevertheless, in good health. And he appeared rather spry as he moved around the vehicle in his silly trot bent at the waist.

SILAS COLLECTED his polishing rags and threw them into the garage. He returned to the back of the hearse and threw open the door. Several small garbage bags and a box toppled to the ground. The box's corner struck Silas in the forehead, drawing a drop of blood. Silas cursed. He closed the hearse door, picked up the fallen items, and carried them inside the garage. Carefully, thoroughly, Silas went through the contents as if they were delicate papyrus scrolls from an Egyptian tomb.

There were figurines—one broken—balled up newspaper, candles in jars, long tapers in boxes, tea towels with Christmas motifs, partially melted wax fruit, and two old telephones, complete with their long, knotted phone cords.

Silas smiled broadly. He saved everything, including the wadded-up newspaper and broken figurine. He set the figurine aside to fix when he found glue. With difficulty, he turned the hearse around and backed it toward the open overhead garage door. This would make it easier to empty and obscure its back from prying neighborhood eyes. He was too excited to wait until after dark to empty the hearse. He began immediately.

Silas opened the hearse's back door again. More bags and boxes toppled to the ground. He lifted these inside the garage. Between trips inside the garage, he peered around the hearse to ensure no one sneaked up on his new vehicle. It took Silas most of the day to barely put a dent in all the junk and examine each piece thoroughly. Sadly, there was nothing he didn't already have, but he was delighted his car wax supply was replenished, even enhanced by a can of paste wax, a bottle of liquid car wash, and a three-pack of shammies.

Silas called it quits after the car product discovery, which probably had been intended for the bourbon-guzzling old geezer run down by a pickup. What pleased Silas most was that he had another day of exploration through the hearse guaranteed for tomorrow. He ate his microwaved dinner with gusto and turned in early after a cursory examination of the Mammoth Sentinel newspaper.

———

THE NEXT MORNING, Silas was up early and out in the garage. After he opened the hearse's back door, he saw more packages and boxes had spilled from the top and lay on the vehicle's tail. He pulled these away from the main pile and discovered a silver metallic corner that sat on a track inside the hearse. After much grunting and huffing, Silas managed to spill more of the hearse's contents on the garage floor. This he waded through, like a man trudging through high snow, to return to the hearse.

To Silas's surprise—or horror—there was a casket inside. He staggered away from the hearse until he backed into the garage's mountain of collected junk. He covered his mouth with a palm. He rose and fell on the balls of his feet. He pulled the ragged handkerchief from his pocket and mopped his sweating fore-head. Pulled the hat from his head and fanned his face.

"Oh my! What will I do?" Silas hissed to himself. He ran outside to see if anyone was watching. His first impulse was to call the funeral home. Demand the man there take back the casket. Then Silas remembered the man's final words. "It comes with the sale." Meaning the hearse's contents was now his. He and the clammy-handed Tommy shook on the deal. That's how the collecting business was conducted.

He could call the police. Never. He knew city officials would not look kindly on his vast collection. They would call it a fire hazard and him a hoarder with mental problems. Silas knew how the system worked.

Silas sweated more. He ran his hands over the top of his bald head. He cleared newspapers from an old cane-back chair and sat down. "How do I know there's a body inside? After all, it might be empty. A coffin that was never used. It must be valuable. I could sell the thing to another funeral home or place an ad in the newspaper.

CASKET FOR SALE — NEVER USED — PREPARE FOR THE INEVITABLE — PRICE NEGOTIABLE.

Silas said out loud, "That's more like it. Now you're thinking. No need to panic, old boy. We might want to drop the NEVER USED part, because any buyer would know it would have to be never used."

Silas sat for a few minutes and wiped his head dry, patting the ragged handkerchief over his face and head. Finally, he returned to the hearse, climbed in and over the casket, pulled back all the stuff, bailed it into the garage without thought for any fragile items. Finally, he dropped from the vehicle back to the concrete garage floor. His chest heaved. His back ached. He was not accustomed to hard work. Most of his hauls were small and light, took little effort to carry inside.

Again, he sat in the old chair, inspecting the casket, its polished handles, the pewter metallic finish. Compared to everything in the vehicle and its exterior, the casket was not dusty. Was the casket shiny because junk covered it and collected the dust over time? Or was the casket placed in the hearse recently? Silas stroked his chin and scratched his head.

Finally, Silas mustered the courage to inspect the casket more carefully. He approached the hearse, decided to partially pull out the casket for a better look. He ran his fingers over the handle on the casket's end. Lifted the handle and let it drop. He did this several times. Then he lifted the handle with both hands and pulled.

The garage floor was level, he knew, because he had tested it with several levels he had in his possession. Silas expected the casket to roll out smoothly, as he had seen at funerals through the years. It didn't budge. He pulled harder. Still the casket did not move. Silas didn't know what an empty casket weighed. He tugged on the handle furiously until his hat flew off and he was breathless.

Something must be lodged under the casket to prevent its movement, Silas thought. Some gewgaw. Some cheap trinket. He stood staring at the casket until he caught his breath. Then he tried to lift the casket over the obstruction. Still, it would not move an inch. Silas rocked the casket back and forth. Then he tried rocking the hearse. The vehicle barely budged. The casket did not move. He panted again. The day was growing warm, and he sweated profusely. His bushy eyebrows couldn't hold back the torrents of sweat that stung his eyes.

Silas leaned against the hearse, looking down. Then he saw it. The hearse peg, inserted in the floor rail against the back of the casket. It was metal, silver in color, and had a rubber pad, which fit against the casket. He pressed a button on the hearse peg. It released and came off in his hand. Silas touched the casket, and it moved easily on rollers in the hearse's floor, as if it had been greased.

Silas shook his head in disbelief. Smiled at his folly. All that work for nothing. The tugging, the grunting, the sweating. Silas grabbed the casket's handle and moved the casket back and forth, a few times to his delight, using a single finger. He lifted the casket and felt it was heavy. Did it contain a body, after all, or was it filled with more stuff? Silas thought briefly of calling Moore at the funeral home, but then the man might want the casket returned. The casket was obviously worth more than the fifty dollars he had offered and, in his mind, became more valuable by the minute. The more Silas thought he was convinced the casket contained more stuff, possibly fragile items, valuable things, placed inside so they wouldn't break, so they wouldn't tempt would-be thieves. Surely the funeral home would never leave a body in the casket, no matter how inept the family might have been, especially Tommy. There were laws to prevent such things. Paperwork. Records to be audited. What about a grieving family? Relatives would want to see a body and see whoever it was laid to rest.

What to do next, Silas thought. He needed to get the casket out of the hearse and open it. He had seen Mrs. Rollins watching him from her sidewalk across the street. He would take the casket inside to the basement, where no one could intrude on his privacy. He had several dollies in the garage. He could lift the casket down on the dollies, one end at a time, roll it through the yard, and ease it down the exterior basement steps. He'd wait until night for the actual move. He couldn't chance a neighbor seeing him roll a casket through the backyard.

Now to find the dollies. He had bought several over the years at various yard sales. He thought he would need two—maybe three—dollies to move the casket. While he rummaged through the garage, squeezing through piles of accumulated material, looking for the dollies, literally burrowing into the collection in some areas, he found a new cloth painter's tarp, dark green, with which he would cover the casket to prevent its shiny surface from being noticed while it glided through the yard.

Silas dug through the mess in the garage like a cadaver dog. During his quest for dollies, Silas broke several old glass milk bottles that slid to the floor and poked and scratched himself while moving some twenty plastic garbage bags filled with empty aluminum cans. After an hour, he held up two dollies triumphantly.

It was well past lunchtime, and Silas decided to take a break. He warmed up crab cakes, spooned potato salad on a plate next to them, added a slice of cake, and a can of Coke. He carried it all to the garage and ate in silence, not wanting to leave the casket alone. After lunch, he added his begrimed paper plate to a stack of old newspapers and sat on the cane-back chair a while, fanning himself with his hat. He had several little battery-powered, handheld fans, but he didn't have the energy to look for them and fresh batteries.

With his strength somewhat restored by lunch, Silas positioned one of the dollies under the hearse door. He leaned the other against the vehicle's bumper. Wearing a pair of new work gloves he found while tunneling through the mountain of tightly packed junk, and a straw hat that was cooler than his wool driving cap, Silas took hold of the handle and carefully rolled out the casket. Finally, it reached a point where it started to tip toward the floor. Mustering all his strength, puffing all the way, Silas eased the casket down on the dolly. He placed the second dolly where the first had been and let the dolly supporting the casket roll slowly, an inch at a time, away from the hearse. When the end of the casket approached the lip of the hearse floor, Silas moved his hold on the side handles to the end handle. The casket cleared the hearse and suddenly rotated away from him. Silas caught the movement with great effort and let the casket fall to the dolly. The casket pivoted back and rested on its bottom.

Silas leaned against the hearse door, gasping. He imagined something moved inside the casket when it spun away from him, rolled against the interior side and then back to the middle. He thought he heard and felt the movement, but he couldn't be sure. Did he imagine it felt like a body inside? Maybe it was just the stuff inside.

Silas unfolded the painter's tarp and covered the casket. He was tired. He closed the overhead garage door with the remote, locked the hearse, and returned to the house. He turned on the window air conditioner with its remote and sat on the only chair available in the living room, his father's old recliner. He wanted to take a nap until nightfall and time to move the casket.

Although he slept fitfully, Silas dreamed. He returned to the garage after dark. It appeared a storm was brewing. One of the overhead doors was open and the painter's tarp was thrown aside. The wind, Silas thought, but he saw the casket was open and empty. Silas ran to the garage exterior. He looked around. The driveway and yard were empty. He expected to see thieves carrying his valuables away in a wheelbarrow.

He paused a moment to listen for the clink and clank of heirlooms as they were bustled away. Hearing nothing, he ran through the yard in his funny gait to the front of the house and looked up and down the street from the sidewalk. He didn't know the time. He figured it must be the middle of the night, those quiet hours when no one walked or drove. The homes were dark. The street was empty in both directions. No getaway car waited with the engine running.

Ominous clouds covered the sky, blotting out the moon and stars. Streetlights flashed on and off at irregular intervals. Trees swayed in the wind. Then he heard the first scream up the block. It was blood-curdling. Then the next and the next. Silas placed his hands on the sides of his head. This couldn't happen. It sounded like his neighbors were being slaughtered.

He stepped forward to the curb. The slightest trickle pulsed down the gutter. The stream was dark and no thicker than a pencil. It throbbed regularly while it moved forward, as if it were pumped by a giant heart. The shrieks, the cries for mercy, continued, grew closer, could now be heard across the street. Old Mrs. Rollins was surely another victim. The stream of dark liquid in the gutter grew larger.

Silas bent over and touched the liquid with an index finger. It was warm. He rubbed the thick fluid against his thumb. He sniffed his fingers. It was blood. He reeled backwards. Now it flowed in the gutter across the street. Both gutters soon filled with torrents. There was more blood in the street than all the inhabitants of the block held, more blood than if they were all exsanguinated at once and hung upside down with their throats slit.

Silas was horrified.

He thought he would be next. Despite his terror, Silas found it difficult to turn and run for the safety of his home. He moved in slow motion. The screams came ever closer. Now he heard them across the street, directly opposite him. He had just managed to pivot and face his yard. He pumped his arms for locomotion but managed only one slow step at a time. Silas looked over his shoulder and saw a large sanguine man with long gray hair, dressed in a black suit, emerge from a house with a smashed front door. The suit was soaked in blood.

Silas cried, increased his efforts to run, but could move no faster. The man appeared to have a knife, but Silas realized in an instant his hand was a knife, and he closed the distance to him. Between gasps for breath, Silas howled with the rest of his neighbors. He sensed the man's footsteps behind him. Silas craned his neck to take one last look. The street was empty. The wind had stopped. The screaming halted. The gutters were dry. The man in the blood-soaked suit was gone, too.

Silas panted. He leaned against the side of his home to catch his breath. He straightened. Lights went on in a few homes across the street. Pajamaed figures appeared at the upper windows and peered into the street. His arms spread, Silas pressed himself against the house like a miniature, espaliered plum tree. He waited that way until the lights across the street blinked out. Then Silas walked normally to the garage. The overhead door was closed. He opened it with the remote he had left in his pocket. The door tracked open slowly, almost silently. The casket lay on the dollies covered with the painter's tarp. Silas rushed to the casket, ripped off the tarp. He pulled on the casket's half lid. It opened slowly, revealing a pale figure with decaying flesh. Silas jumped back.

He fell from the recliner to the floor. Slowly, Silas raised himself and sat again on the chair. Silas held a palm against his forehead. It was wet with sweat. Now would be the time for a good stiff drink, Silas thought, but he couldn't remember where he had stashed the bags of bourbon, scotch, and vodka he carried home from the liquor store in a buying spree a few years earlier. It was 11:15 p.m. Silas went directly to the garage, let himself in through the service door, and turned on overhead fluorescent lights. He had blacked out all the windows after the garage was built and knew the neighbors wouldn't see him. Silas kneeled with difficulty next to the casket and pulled off the tarp. He felt around the casket lid's top section, gently inserted his fingers, and pulled. The lid wouldn't budge. He stood over the casket to get more leverage and pulled again. Still the lid wouldn't open.

Silas cursed to himself. Then he remembered. The casket had a lock. The thing was locked. He couldn't call the funeral home. The man there would know he had a casket. There had to be an easy way to open the thing. He had several crowbars in the basement, collected over the years, but a crowbar would damage the lid, reduce the casket's value to nothing. Possibly ruin an airtight seal. Silas tapped his chin with an index finger and looked toward the ceiling. Of course! He would Google the question. *How do you open a locked casket?* Silas covered the casket again and trotted back to the house, but not before he turned out the lights and was sure the garage service door was locked.

Because he hadn't used his desktop in several weeks, it took Silas a tedious minute to move the junk that covered it and his computer chair. Once he was comfortably enthroned, Silas typed in the Google search engine, *How do you open a locked casket?* Silas typed with his index fingers but still managed to hit several wrong keys. He cursed and hit the backspace button furiously to erase mistakes. Sweat dripped on the keyboard, stung his eyes.

Finally, the question was posed. He hit the enter button. The answer appeared in an instant in the form of several articles and three videos. Silas clicked on one of the YouTube videos. A young, dark-haired woman, dressed in black with dark nail polish, appeared in the video by a casket holding a contraption that looked like a ray gun Flash Gordon would carry. After introducing herself and her morbid channel, she explained this universal key would open practically any locked casket. As she talked, she demonstrated the key's use.

"All you have to do is go to the foot of the casket, unscrew this little cap, insert the key, and turn. The lid will pop open. Just remember, righty tighty, lefty loosie." She smiled at the viewing audience. A close-up revealed dark eyes and very white teeth made brighter by red lipstick. She went on to discuss a casket's construction, but Silas ended the video before he heard more details. He was too tired to look for a key now. After all, he had been through the back of the hearse. He doubted there was one there. The search would have to wait until tomorrow. Silas went to bed disappointed.

In the morning, Silas ached all over from his exertions the day before. He ate cereal, Frosted Flakes, one of eight boxes in his pantry. He ate quickly and carried coffee brewed in one of a half dozen makers he had on the kitchen counter. Three were still in their unopened boxes. One he thought might not work.

Once inside the garage, he put the coffee cup on the floor

and opened the hearse's driver's side door. He climbed in and searched for the key. He hadn't noticed anything unusual on his drive home from Moore Home for Funerals, but he was not looking for anything special. He was consumed with his good fortune and what might lie in the back. He slid across the seat, checked the glove box, where there was only a crumbling owner's manual, a maintenance schedule written in an elegant hand, and the car battery warranty.

He checked above the visors. Nothing. He climbed out of the hearse and felt under the driver's side seat. What funeral director would not have a casket key always at hand for emergencies. His hand found something loose, thin, curved, metallic. It might be a long-forgotten child's toy pistol. Perhaps it was Tommy's. Silas pulled it out and found it was the casket key, exactly like the one held by the woman in the video. He jumped up and down with joy. He returned to the kitchen with the key and his coffee cup. Once inside, he sat at the kitchen table and caught his breath. Then he poured more coffee. He turned over the key in his hand. Felt its weight, wondered about its composition, as if it were a centuries old artifact. He drank more coffee. In fact, he consumed the whole pot while he imagined what waited in store for him.

Silas returned to the garage on his tiptoes in the strange gait he exhibited when in a hurry. The walk amused the neighbors who took every opportunity to imitate him. He had just closed and locked the service door when it hit him. The urge to pee. Coffee did that to him. He returned to the house, the casket key safely hidden in his side pocket, and climbed the steps to the second-floor bathroom. The coffee, running back and forth between the house and garage, had made Silas sweat. He mopped his brow while he relieved himself, removed the straw hat he now wore, and wiped the top of his head. There was a toilet on the first floor, one his father had installed after it got too painful to climb the stairs for his frequent trips to the bathroom, but the diminutive powder room was now filled with junk and unusable.

Silas returned to the garage, where he locked himself inside again. He pulled the tarp from the casket. He went to the foot of the casket and located the nub. He repeated the video woman's words aloud and screwed off the silver cap. He looked inside the cap and then inside the lock, kneeling to press his eye close to the hole. He pursed his lips and blew into the keyway several times. He pulled the key from his pocket, examined it again, and inserted it in the lock.

"Let's see," Silas said. "Righty tighty, lefty loosie." He turned the key to the right. It wouldn't budge. "Sealed tight as a drum," he added, smiling.

Silas pulled out the key and dropped it in his pocket. Patted the key against his leg. He pulled up on the casket and found the bottom heavy. This pleased him, too. "Lots of good stuff," he said.

Silas imagined he knew what Howard Carter felt like when he had to wait to open King Tut's tomb. He had read and now owned several books on the subject, including a first-hand account Carter wrote himself. The delay would be worth it. After all, Carter didn't use a jackhammer to enter Tut's tomb. Silas replaced the cap on the key hole and spread the tarp over the casket. He smoothed it carefully, straightened it so the ends and sides were of equal length. He checked the key in his pocket one more time and returned to the house. He would wait until nightfall to move the casket to the basement, slide the thing down the three exterior steps to the inside. It would take little more than a minute to accomplish. In the meantime, he placed several planks on the basement steps.

After a sound, dreamless snooze, Silas woke at twilight. He made a quick supper of canned chicken noodle soup, one of some fifty cans of soup in his cupboards. He didn't worry about rotating his stock. He grabbed one of the cans closest to the front. Then he sat and read the newspaper, the Mammoth Sentinel. Everyone said Mammoth was the kind of place almost anything could happen. He noticed the hearse sale was no longer listed. He cut out several ads for yard sales, carefully underlining the dates, times, and addresses. He stacked them in order to ensure his rounds would be efficient. No sales would be missed.

It was after ten when Silas folded the newspaper, added it to an ever-growing stack that now teetered next to his chair at the kitchen table. The bottom-most editions were already yellowed with age. Silas washed his meager dishes and returned them to the counter next to the sink. He looked at his watch.

"Well, old boy, it's show time!"

Silas tiptoed to the garage in the dark. He had disabled the motion sensor lights that illuminated the garage, yard, and house if anyone trespassed. As quietly as possible, he entered the garage through the service door, locked it, opened the overhead door, pushed the casket outside, and closed the overhead door with his remote. He looked around furtively to determine whether anyone had noticed the door noise. Satisfied the neighborhood remained quiet, Silas moved the casket outside and locked the garage again.

The makeshift gurney sailed smoothly, silently over the driveway's asphalt with little effort, but when the dolly wheels hit the brick sidewalk through the yard, the wheels rumbled, the casket shook. The vibration traveled up Silas's arms and rattled his teeth, jostled his hat over his eyes. His rolls of flesh shimmied. He pushed harder to get the casket through the yard and to the basement quicker. He stopped just short of the basement steps and looked around the neighborhood. All the lights were out, but he imagined prying eyes peeped through window blinds.

Silas leaned the planks over the exterior steps, pushed the coffin over the steps. He caught the dolly as it lost contact with the casket's bottom and, holding the end handle, let the draped box slide smoothly down the planks. Near the bottom, Silas opened the unlocked basement door. The casket was heavy, and Silas started to puff. He sweated and grunted as the load reached the basement floor. He pulled the casket's end off the floor and kicked the dolly back under it. Silas let the casket glide down the planks and into the basement. He closed and locked the basement door immediately.

Silas panted and leaned against the basement wall.

"This better be worth it," he said aloud.

With considerable exertion and little noise, Silas had transferred the casket from the garage to his basement. He threw off the casket shroud. The casket was unstable. After he repositioned the dollies, Silas wheeled the casket to one of the few open spaces in the basement under a fluorescent overhead light. There he blocked the wheels with anything he could find—a screwdriver, a hockey puck, a clothes pin from one of several packs he owned. Silas was parched and returned upstairs for a can of Coke. He returned to the basement immediately, downed the Coke, set down the can, and rubbed his hands together with glee. He turned the cap off the casket lock and pulled the key from his pocket.

Silas inserted the key in the lock, carefully, as if he were defusing a bomb. He repeated the words, "Righty tighty, lefty loosie," and turned the key to the left.

There was a distinct click. He turned the key a little more. The top part of the casket lid opened with a pop. After a moment of silence, a mist-like ectoplasm squeezed through the small opening. Silas tried to relock the casket lid but again turned the key to the left. The lid inched open more. The ectoplasm poured from the casket, streamed down the sides, and across the floor.

"Achhh!" Silas cried.

He turned the key to the right, but it spun inside the lock.

Silas screamed. He dropped the key and threw himself on top of the casket. The dolly wheels rolled over their blocks, and the casket sped through the basement. Silas pushed on the lid. It resisted and pushed back. Silas screamed again.

"What have I done?"

The casket rolled on. A pale, long-fingered hand appeared on the edge of the lid. Its long nails were translucent. Silas kneeled on the lid, jumped up and down on his hands and knees. His hat flew off. He wanted to catch the fingers in the lid, cut them from the hand, if necessary. The casket stopped when it ran into a stack of junk, spilling boxes and bags on Silas. The lid flew open. Silas was thrown from the casket. He burrowed into the pile. He heard the casket roll away. A strong hand caught his ankle as he was about to disappear into the mound—

an artificial Christmas tree, yards of garland, several wreaths. Silas was hauled out like a child and dumped on the floor.

"No! No! No!" he screamed.

Silas rolled on his back and looked at the creature. She appeared young, had pale skin, white as alabaster, dark hair, and piercing black eyes. Her lips were full, bloodless. She was dressed in a funeral shroud, also white, yet yellow and stained with age. She parted her lips and rubbed a hand over her mouth, revealing two pointed fangs among her teeth. She smelled of death and Silas coughed.

She stared down at Silas. "You are my first meal out of hibernation?"

Silas grimaced.

"I had hoped for something better. But plate presentation isn't everything."

"You belong at the funeral home. That's where you came from!" Silas shouted.

"That was merely a layover," the creature said. "The old man..."

"He's dead," Silas sobbed.

"Of course. I killed him."

"And Bob is gone."

"Killed him, too." She grinned.

"Tommy?"

"Hardly worth the effort. One taste of his blood was enough. Stagnant." The creature made a face of disgust. "Is he still alive?"

"That's where I got you. You were in the casket. In the hearse I bought from him. It was a business deal." Silas edged away, crawled like a crab.

"Stop!" the creature commanded. Her voice was loud, hollow-sounding, and echoed off the block foundation walls.

Silas complied. He lowered his head a moment, then returned his gaze to the creature.

"Stand."

Silas stood with difficulty and faced her. She stepped forward until she was inches from his face. They were the same height. She sniffed his neck and then licked his cheek. "Not bad."

Silas fainted.

Silas woke in the recliner. He was soaked in sweat. It was still dark. "Another dream," he mused aloud. "How many dreams like that can I take? I wonder if that casket is worth the trouble. I'm parched," Silas said. He walked to the kitchen for a Coke, wishing again he could remember where his whiskey stash was.

She sat at his kitchen table, in his chair, three dehydrated mice in front of her.

Silas gasped.

She looked over her shoulder and nonchalantly said, "You have rodents downstairs. Just as well. Their blood has prolonged your life, at least temporarily."

Silas reeled back and slammed into the refrigerator. The door popped open and some of its contents fell to the floor. A plastic bottle struck him and spilled milk over his head.

She sniffed the air. "The milk's no good, anyway," she said. The soured, clotted milk made a trail across the floor. "Well, clean it up."

Silas stared at the woman a moment. He found paper towels

and mopped up the mess. Then Silas noticed she had his check-book and his folder of financial statements open.

Silas pulled his cell phone from his pant pocket and raised it toward his face. "I could call the police."

The woman grinned. She disappeared in a blur, noiselessly appearing at Silas's side. His phone smashed off the wall across the room.

"My phone!"

The woman looked around the room. "I'm sure you have another. You have a lot of *stuff*." She held him in her arms and squeezed. "You are soft and weak, Silas." She sniffed his neck again.

"I can't breathe," Silas choked. Her body was cold and hard, like a statue's. She released her grip. Silas took a deep breath. Then she clasped his neck and lifted him off the floor.

"If you like to breathe, you will not try to double cross me, Silas. Do you understand?"

Silas couldn't breathe. He kicked his legs. His eyes rolled back. The woman released him. Silas fell to the floor. He gasped for air and rubbed his neck.

"Do you know what a double cross is, Silas?"

"I know. I would never do that to you."

"That's what they did at the funeral home. First it was Thomas, the old man. He tried to wheel me into the sunlight, but it turned cloudy suddenly. By the time Bob was drained, Tommy got the point." She chuckled. "You don't like my joke?"

Silas looked at her in horror. She picked him up like a doll and sat him on the kitchen chair. Silas still rubbed his neck.

"So, the Moores were supposed to keep me in the funeral home in a locked casket during the remainder of my hibernation—twenty-five years in all. It lasted only seven. I was to rest amid a display of other caskets they offered families. Mine was locked. The others were open. The Moores were paid handsomely to keep me safe."

"I don't care," Silas interrupted. "You're going to have to leave my home. Your... otherworldly problems are not mine." He stared up at her with as much resolution as he could muster.

She was at his neck in an instant. At least Silas could breathe this time. "You know what I am?"

"I have an idea."

"I could break your fragile neck like an eggshell." She sniffed Silas's panting breath and stopped suddenly. "I could... You are a virgin." She dropped her hand.

"No," Silas moaned.

"Yes." The creature smiled. "I can smell your virginity. A virgin's blood is the sweetest elixir known to vampires. I would take a sip now, but I am thirsty. I don't know whether I'd be able to control myself. I'd drain you in seconds. After I feed you will be my dessert."

"No. You can't. I won't let you." Silas stood.

"You will do anything I say, Silas. You will be my fat little happy slave to the end of your days. I will determine how many days you have. You will serve me. I will decide when to drain the last of your virgin blood."

Silas recoiled in horror and knocked over the chair. He fell backwards on the table, scattering much of its contents to the floor. She picked him up in an instant and held him by the shirt close to her face. He choked on her rank odor.

"Your virginity has saved you, Silas. The first thing you will do is take me to Tommy's funeral home. Tommy must die for his family's broken promise. We will go tomorrow. Meanwhile, *we* will sleep in your basement."

"No! I AM A VIRGIN," he screamed. "If we..."

"You will remain a virgin if you sleep only with me. After all, I am a corpse." She giggled.

Silas fainted.

The next evening, Silas woke and immediately choked on fetid air. It was dark. He was naked and on his stomach. He felt the vampire's cold body under him. He recoiled in horror, sprang from the casket. The basement light was on. Although the windows were blacked out, he could tell it was not quite sunset. His clothes were torn to shreds and lay on the floor. The naked vampire lay in the casket. Her black eyes stared. Silas felt lightheaded. He stumbled to the stairs that led to the kitchen and sat. His head spun. His leg hurt. He saw a wound on the inside of his thigh near the groin—two puncture wounds surrounded by bruised tissue. His privates were sore, chafed.

She had bitten him after all. Drank his blood. That explained the lightheadedness. He thought he was doomed to live the same life this creature had. He held his head in his hands and sobbed.

Silas returned to the casket. He stared at the vampire. "I killed her. She's not breathing," Silas wailed. "I can't have a dead body in my house. What can I do with her? What will the authorities say?"

Silas placed his palms between her breasts and started chest compressions, the type of CPR he had seen on television. When it was time for him to lock his lips over hers, to fill her lungs with air, he recoiled. He continued with the compressions.

"You have to breathe. Take a breath. Please breathe for me."

The casket rolled on the dollies. Silas followed it across the floor, continuing the compressions, stepping sideways to keep up, half hopping, half skipping. His rolls of fat giggled with each compression. The vampire's face showed no reaction. Finally, the casket stopped after it bumped into a support pole. Silas was exhausted. He reeled back to the steps and collapsed.

The creature stirred and sat up. "There you are, Silas." She smiled. "What were you doing to me just now? Going at me again? How nice. You were a tiger."

"Trying to revive you. You weren't breathing."

"Foolish pumpkin. I'm a vampire. I don't breathe, but I appreciate your effort. Did you ever have a sweetheart, Silas? A girl you kissed and fondled? I must tell you. You are—how do they say it—a wonderful lay, although somewhat inexperienced for a man your age."

"I couldn't have. Don't remember. Wouldn't have."

The vampire frowned. "Unfortunately, that is the price for having sex with a vampire, Silas. No memory. I can tell you this. There is a whole generation of female humans who have missed a wonderful experience. You are well endowed."

Silas shook his head. "No. It wouldn't be possible for me to..."

"Get it up for a corpse?" she said coquettishly.

"Well, yes."

"You are my slave, Silas. I control your mind *and* body. Do you want to know how many times we did *it*, my aging Lothario?"

"No! I don't want to know! You bit me!"

"And you bit me, Silas," she countered, laughing. She

turned to reveal human teeth marks on her left buttock that were already healing.

Silas groaned. "Not your ass!" He wagged his tongue outside his mouth and spit. In a flash she was seated beside him on the wooden steps. She cradled him. "My little round pumpkin bit me. How I enjoyed it, but I didn't let you drink my blood, for then you, too, would become a vampire." She tickled his hairy back, twirled the long strands on an index finger.

"You drank my blood," Silas cried.

"I couldn't help myself, little pumpkin. I'm not sorry. A virgin's blood is extremely sweet and highly valued among my kind."

"I need a shower," Silas moaned. "Oh, God."

"Later, Silas. We have a murder to commit." She licked his cheek with her foul-smelling tongue. "Get dressed."

"You ruined my clothes."

"You have many more."

———

Silas left Mammoth, driving the hearse west, with the fiend beside him. She had discarded her shroud for jeans and a polo shirt she found among Silas's clothes. All were new, still with the tags connected, and much too large. The jeans were cinched to her waspish waist with a belt. She was still barefoot, because all of Silas's shoes fell off when she walked. She looked out the window, scanning the roadside with interest.

"The first two things you will do for me, after we kill Tommy—"

"I didn't bargain for murder when I agreed to drive you," Silas said, his voice rising, showing contempt for the vampire.

"You will do what I tell you, Silas," she commanded. She pronounced her words slowly. "Your days of squeamishness must end tonight. You will find it necessary to do much that is unpleasant by human standards, but you will do them because I say so. Eventually, you will enjoy it."

Silas shot a glance at the vampire. Her face was beautiful. She reminded Silas of a girl from high school, Margaret "Peg" Border. She was nice to Silas and smiled at him when they passed in the hall. However, Silas was too shy to ask her out. His weight did not make him a popular student. Boys made fun of his pudginess. Peg had been slim like the vampire. He wondered where she was now, if she were still alive, if Tommy might have embalmed her, seen her naked.

"Tomorrow, you will procure me clothes that fit. I can't go out in public in my burial shroud. And I can't wear this outfit. That will include some shoes. I can't look like a peasant."

"I never bought women's clothing. I wouldn't know what sizes to get."

"There's a first time for everything, Silas, as you found out earlier. You may measure my body for clothes later."

"No. I won't have it."

"The second thing you must do is teach me to drive."

"You don't drive?" Silas looked incredulous.

"I never needed to," she said.

"You'll kill yourself."

The vampire laughed. "Silas, you have forgotten again one small detail. I died a century ago."

Silas pulled down his cap, turned his attention to the highway, and was quiet the rest of the ride. Eventually, he pulled into the parking lot behind the funeral home. A pole light there blinked on and off. Silas parked in the shadows.

"*You* can go in the back, into the garage, or go to the front," Silas whispered. "The back might be better, where no one will see you."

"Mmmm," the vampire cooed. "Tommy already knows we are here." She turned and stared at Silas. "You are coming with me."

"I can't."

"You will accompany me, and you will kill him for his family's betrayal. Let's get this over."

Silas turned to her. "You could kill him much easier than I could," he choked. "I've never murdered anyone."

"I can't kill him," she said, matter-of-factly. "He's a vampire already. I turned him. It would be, how should I say it?"

"A code of ethics?"

"Of course not, little pumpkin. Vampires have no codes. No morals. It would be like killing a family member. On the other hand, it would be a rite of passage for you. A final submission to my will."

They climbed out opposite sides of the hearse. The vampire slammed the door.

"We'll have to be quiet," Silas hissed. "I wouldn't have the strength to kill someone. Tommy's skinny, but he's what you would call wiry. Plus, he's a vampire."

"You might surprise yourself, little pumpkin." The creature smiled at him and raked her fingers down his back.

The vampire walked toward the funeral home in front of Silas. Silas's jeans made her ass look like a large balloon puffed out under the belt. She paused at the garage door and listened for a moment.

"This door is heavy it will be difficult to..."

She took a step back and delivered a powerful kick, splintering the door, knocking it off its tracks. They walked inside. The vampire picked up a sharp, wooden shard and handed it to Silas. She picked up another for herself.

"I told you he expected us," she said. "Bring that machete, too."

"I'll bet he sharpened this blade today," Silas said, hefting the machete in his hand. "It's a good one. I have a few myself."

"Be ready!" the vampire hissed. "He might attack us from any hiding place. There could be many in a building this old. I need to feed. My strength is waning." She sauntered down the hall and entered the viewing room."

Silas followed at a safe distance and whispered, "Tommy told me he was having remodeling done."

"He's a liar. He has tried to mask his presence from me with the heavy perfume in the air."

"It's overpowering," Silas said.

"It's cheap."

They had reached the front of the funeral home. There was no sign of Tommy. The vampire sniffed the air and retraced her steps. She sniffed at the steps to the upper floors, turning her head sideways for a moment, as if concentrating. She moved back to Silas and twisted her face. "He's in the basement. This way."

"Maybe he's out. We could leave," Silas said. "Make a plan. We have no plan. Come back another day. I always think you should have a plan, one that's well thought out."

"Tommy is here. He expected to spend eternity buying things online and collecting them, storing them here and at other places," she said with disgust. "That was his ridiculous plan for a future."

After a short pause, Silas looked at her and said, "Really? Collecting forever? Ridiculous? It might have some merits."

The vampire shook her head. "Humans." She led Silas into one of the auxiliary rooms.

"Eternity?" Silas said. "Collecting?"

"Stay focused." She motioned to a door. Silas slid his back along the wall and stopped next to the door. The vampire approached the door.

"Please don't kick it," Silas whispered.

She turned the knob and pulled the door open. Carefully, she led Silas down the basement steps in the dark.

"Do you mind?" Silas whispered. He flicked on a small flashlight he had brought on the ride concealed in a pant pocket. "I can't see a thing."

"If it helps."

The blinking pole light outside provided intermittent flashes of light through basement windows, but it helped little, throwing confusing shadows on the walls. Silas waved his beam of light around the basement. A half dozen display caskets were arranged around three walls. All had their lids closed. Behind the caskets were two closed doors. Silas stopped, pulled a new handkerchief from his back pocket, and mopped his forehead.

The vampire sniffed the air. She moved from casket to casket. As she approached the fourth, the lid sprang open, Tommy leaped from the interior, roaring, brandishing a stake in each hand. Silas reeled backwards, fell into the sixth casket, which toppled off its church cart and hit the floor, dislodging the corpse of a young woman. The body landed on Silas's prostrate form. Silas screamed. Tommy roared again and attacked the vampire. He swung his stakes like a ninja. His filthy bathrobe fluttered like a cape.

Silas struggled to get from under the stiff, nude body. He clawed at the floor. Cried for help. The body moved back and forth across his fat back like a rolling pin through dough. The dead face, frozen in horror, came within inches of his own. The vampire grabbed Tommy by the throat, lifted him off the ground, threw him across the room and against the wall. He crashed into the wall, splintering the paneling, but landed on his feet and charged her immediately, both stakes raised.

Silas pushed the body aside and scrambled toward the steps. In the instant the vampire looked back at Silas, Tommy struck, driving both stakes into her chest. Neither hit her heart. She howled. Tommy's mouth frothed with delight. Silas found the machete and the flashlight on the floor. He turned to the vampire. Tommy pulled out the stakes, prepared to strike the vampire with a lethal blow. The wounded vampire slumped to the floor. Silas staggered to his feet. He panned the flashlight beam back and forth. Long shadows leaped around the room.

"Nooooo!" Silas shouted, lunging toward Tommy.

Tommy spun in an instant, driving one stake into Silas's shoulder. Silas screamed. Pain seared through his body. He staggered backwards.

Tommy returned to the female. He grabbed her by the neck and picked her off the floor. Her blood streamed over's Tommy's robe. Tommy held the vampire a moment, smiling, sniffing her. She stared back at him with contempt, with cold, black eyes. He gnashed his teeth. Curled back his upper lip to expose his fangs. Tommy raised the second stake over his head.

There was a swoosh so silent it was heard only by the vampire and preceded the loud thwack of the machete separating Tommy's head from his body. The head rolled across the room, blood pinwheeling from the neck. The skull burst into flames after a couple turns and continued to roll, growing ever smaller, until the fire went out, leaving a small pile of ash. Tommy's body collapsed and burned, his robe smoking, stinking. Silas limped to the vampire. He helped her stand. Already her wounds had stopped bleeding, had begun to heal. Silas's had not. She tore his shirt open and drank from his wound. Just enough to regain her strength. They helped each other up the steps and through the darkened funeral home. Silas stopped her at the viewing room. He hated to do it, but Silas pulled a disposable cigarette lighter from his pocket, limped to the windows.

"Couldn't we wait for another day?" Silas said, a look of pleading in his eyes. "Just to see what's here."

"Do it now!" the vampire commanded.

Silas opened a flame and set the heavy, dusty drapes on fire. The old fabric ignited immediately and became great conflagrations, which caught the peeling wallpaper and furniture aflame.

There were sirens in the distance by the time they reached the hearse. "The whole place will go up," Silas told the vampire. "There'll be no evidence. What a shame. We'll never know what's in a place like this."

Silas mustered all his strength to start the engine and pull out. He navigated the road's dips and turns, the corners, in great pain.

"Hurry, Silas. We must return before sunup."

Silas grimaced. "I'm trying."

The sky had turned from black to a plum color. Dawn was minutes away when Silas pulled into his driveway. He and the vampire hurried to the house and into the basement. The vampire tore off Silas's baggy clothes and settled into the casket. Silas sat on the wooden steps. He was drenched in blood and sweat.

"Come to me, Silas," the vampire said. She patted her flat, porcelain stomach, showing she was already healed.

Silas stood to obey and collapsed. He groaned.

"What is it, my pumpkin?"

"I have a pain in my chest. If only I could burp. I think it's gas. I'll get a Coke upstairs."

Silas stood, turned to go up the steps and sank again. He moaned and clutched his flabby chest.

"Your heart is erratic," the vampire said. "I hear it. I think it is a heart attack."

Silas gritted his teeth. "Can't be."

The vampire left her casket and came to Silas's side. She placed a palm over his heart. "You are dying, Silas. I know this feeling. Your skin is gray. Your lips are purple."

"No. Too young. Too young." Silas shook his sweating head. "Dad was much older."

The vampire sank her fangs into her own wrist with a succulent pop. Blood poured immediately. She placed her wrist over Silas's lips, so she would bleed into his mouth. "Drink, little pumpkin, and feel well." Silas sucked greedily at the wounded wrist and passed out.

———

After his transformation was complete, Silas trotted back and forth between the naked vampire, who stood still as a statue, and his tablet that lay on the kitchen table. She was radiant. Her wounds were healed. There was not a blemish on her body. Silas used a cloth dress-making tape, one that had been his mother's, to measure the vampire's feet, heels to toes, her waist, inseam, bust, arm length, and neck. Today he took great pleasure in touching her dead flesh and tickled her often. She nibbled on his neck, fondled his privates, while he measured her. Despite the thrills, he managed to transfer the exact measurements from tape to paper.

"The pain in your chest is gone?" the vampire asked.

"I don't know when I felt this good," Silas said. "Not in years. Maybe never."

She pressed her palm over his heart. "That's because your heart no longer beats. It is as dead as the rest of you, but it must be protected at all costs."

"My shoulder's better, too." Silas moved his shoulder about and stretched his arm. "I'm a new man."

"You are a new vampire."

Eventually, Silas dressed. It was not yet sundown, but heavy clouds rolled in, accompanied by thunder and lightning. He would be safe. His skin tingled in the indirect sunlight, filtered by clouds, but did not burn. Silas drove to Downtown Mammoth in his SUV and marched into *Bella*, an exclusive women's store, with his list of measurements. The place was empty of customers. Within moments, the employees, including the large-bosomed elderly owner in ridiculous high heels, two red circles of rouge on her cheeks, descended on Silas, surrounded him. They smiled and giggled. They waited in apparent anxiousness for Silas to speak, as if he were the first man to ever enter the shop. The store was quiet and packed with stacks of clothing, dresses on racks, jewelry displays, cosmetics, handbags, and shoes. Perfume scented the air.

Silas was not accustomed to dealing with females, unless it was with sweating, overweight women he haggled with at yard sales and flea markets. He felt an attraction to these women that was similar, he imagined, to their interest in him. They seemed enchanted by this round little man.

"I have a friend," he began hesitatingly, his voice nervous, "a young friend, a beautiful friend, who has no clothes."

The store employees looked from one to another.

"I'd say she's the lucky one," the shop owner said. Her beehive of a hairdo was stiff and unmovable. Her circles of rouge disappeared momentarily on her apple cheeks but soon returned. The other women laughed. They surged to surround Silas.

"You don't understand," Silas said. "There was a fire. It was rather tragic."

"Yes, I see," the shop owner said, straightening his shirt collar with a be-ringed hand. Her enchanted employees watched.

"Well, she needs new clothes, everything from underwear to...outerwear," Silas said.

"Perfume?" a hawk-nosed, heavyset employee said.

"Of course," Silas said. "Everything. Imagine she stepped off a spaceship from another world."

The women nodded in agreement. Smiled.

"She should have come in herself to try things on," the matronly owner said.

"I'd be afraid she'd be arrested for indecent exposure before she made it through the door," Silas said. "She literally has nothing to wear. She's at my home now, wrapped in a bedsheet, fashioned like a toga." He raised a hand dramatically in the air. "She looks like the wife of Caesar."

The women raised their eyebrows in unison, as if they imagined Silas was holding her against her will. Still, they seemed fascinated by him.

"How are we to help then?" the owner said, with a smile.

Silas pulled out his paper. "I have her measurements."

"I hope they're exact," the shop keeper said, with another smile, this one wider, trying to look at the list. "We don't like taking clothes back that have left the salon. Making refunds. You understand, of course?"

"I took the measurements myself," Silas said.

The women tittered, moved closer to Silas.

"We should know how exact. These are fine clothes. They don't have cheap elastic waistbands," the store owner said. She shot a glance at the hawk-nosed girl. "Did you take these measurements with or without the toga?"

"Without, of course," Silas said. He cleared his throat and smiled at the women.

They laughed and drew still closer to Silas. They surrounded him. Waited expectantly for his next words. One put a hand on his shoulder. This was a new experience for him.

Not one woman, but four, smiled, flirted, and batted their eyes at him. They crowded around him. Silas sensed their individual heartbeats. Despite their heavy perfumes, he could distinguish their individual scents. The old lady snatched Silas's paper, held an index finger to her lips, and read over the numbers.

"Lily, size seven shoe."

Lily, with her eyes made up like a pharaoh's queen, glided toward Silas. "What does your friend like?" she cooed. "Something like this?" She raised her leg to show Silas her foot and sandal with bejeweled straps. "Or boots? High heels or flats? Sneakers are popular, too, depending on the rest of her wardrobe, which you told us she doesn't have. We even have work boots for girls who like a *very* casual attire." She smiled. "Our clientele don't actually work in them. The boots are for things like hiking, picnics, or camping, making s'mores, if you like that sort of thing."

"I think it would be too warm for boots, but I'll see what you have. I think she'd like the sandals."

"Some flip flops, too?"

"Of course," Silas said. "Pajamas and bedroom slippers, also. And a robe for the bedroom."

"Very good!" the store owner shouted. Her face reddened again, and the rouge disappeared. "Girls, attention," she added with a clap of her be-ringed hands. Bracelets slid up and down her sagging arms.

In quick succession, the matron called her employees by name, gave them sizes, and clothes to show Silas. While the summer thunderstorm raged outside, and the overhead lights flickered several times, Silas was tugged from department to department, shown more clothes than he thought the small shop could hold. The women's hands stroked his head and back. They giggled. He loved every minute of it.

Eventually, Lily took his hand and guided him to the shoes. He sat in a chair, his lap piled with clothes to consider, his erection hidden, while she tried on shoes to show him, pair after pair. Lily giggled and wiggled her painted toes at Silas between modeling shoes. Silas was enthralled and chuckled until his fat giggled like a Jell-O mold. A fierce thirst grew in him. He imagined draining the young woman's blood. He could throw himself on her, gag her screams with a hand, palpate her flesh with his tongue, find an artery, and bite. His imagination tasted the hot young blood, guzzled it. Its heat coursed down his throat.

He felt no twinge of remorse over killing her. No sympathy for Lily's family and its loss. Lily was, after all, merely food. Silas felt that if he didn't leave the shop soon, he would murder all the women, suck them all dry, if that was possible, if he could consume that much blood at once. It would be worth a try, he thought, with a sly smile.

The other women fawned and pawed at Silas, ran their long nails down his back, pinched his sagging cheeks. In the end, he bought eight pairs of shoes, four dresses, six pairs of slacks with coordinated blouses—three with sequins—enough socks, stockings, and underwear for two weeks, four silk scarfs, three bottles of perfume, and an assortment of rings, necklaces, and dangling and stud earrings. His purchases bagged and boxed, he stood by the store's front window among the women—one goosed him and he suspected Lily—watching the storm die out. The sun set just as the clouds parted. This man, who had been so hapless his entire life, at last had the male vampire's allure that attracted women, or so Silas imagined. Despite his dumpy appearance, he was irresistible.

"You know," Silas said slowly, drawing out the words, "I'll definitely be back. Next time I'll bring my friend. I believe she would enjoy your store."

The women cheered and rubbed against Silas, mussing his little remaining hair.

After the rain, Lily helped Silas pack his purchases into the back of the SUV. Meanwhile, the owner cleared her cash register, and the other women folded and returned to stock clothes Silas didn't buy. It was past closing and dark now. They all seemed extremely happy, as if they had just served a celebrity and in doing so inked a contract to supply women with clothes for an epic movie with a cast of thousands.

When the last of the packages were piled in, Lily said, "I don't believe it. There's still a little room left." As she bent forward into the SUV to push the last packages forward, her dress became tight against her body and caught Silas's eye.

"Just enough room for you, I'd say." Silas smiled. He imagined her wearing only a ball gag and her Egyptian makeup, spreadeagled on his bed, full of puncture wounds from where he and the vampire feasted on her blood day after day. He already had a plan for disposing of her exsanguinated body.

Lilly laughed and offered him her wrists, ready to be cuffed.

Silas giggled in return. He licked his lips.

"What is it you do that makes you so generous with your friend?" Lily chirped. "I'd think you're a lawyer or something."

"I'm a collector. I'm always acquiring new things."

Silas took her hand in one of his, cupped her elbow with his other hand, and admired the inside of her slim, white arm, watched the veins in her wrist pulsing under the skin. He delighted in his new powers.

"That must be expensive and take a lot of time," Lily said with a wag of her head, letting the handholding continue.

"Not when you have lots of money and all the time in the world."

ONE PUNCH MASSACRE

They used to call it a one-punch massacre, a haymaker, a single devastating clout from a hard fist the victim never saw coming. It ended a fight almost before it started. It was such a blow that took the life of Rhonda Simmone in January just short of her forty-first birthday during a prolonged cold snap caused by a polar vortex. She was tall and athletic. A college volleyball player, she also had been a finalist in the Miss Pennsylvania Pageant twenty years earlier and still retained her pageant looks with the help of good genes and a personal trainer named Hector. Her husband, Dr. Jack Simmone, was a DO who had a family practice in Mammoth, Pennsylvania. He had been quite an athlete himself; a division two college football lineman called the "Ox."

It was Doc Simmone who delivered the lethal blow, a force that twisted Rhonda's neck so violently her spine snapped. She died instantly and dropped to the floor, spinning in a semi-circle while her knees buckled. She came to rest on her back, her open eyes appearing to stare at the ceiling.

Jack opened and closed his right hand, examined his bloodied knuckles. He felt no remorse for the murder. He stood and grimaced over his wife's body. He worried about explaining his damaged hand, Rhonda's imminent disappearance, and the need to dispose of a body under frozen ground. He stroked his graying goatee and ran his undamaged hand through thinning hair.

His first act was to move the body to their home's attached garage, where leaking body fluids could be cleaned up more easily. He grabbed Rhonda by the wrists, pulled her to the garage, and laid her on a piece of opaque plastic left over from a living room paint job a year ago. Jack examined Rhonda's clothed body. Then the crime scene. It appeared no fluids leaked from the corpse inside the home—no blood, saliva, vomit, urine, or feces. The plastic, meant to be a floor protector, was never used and had no paint spots that could be traced, the Ox thought. Blood now seeped from Rhonda's nose and ears. In addition, there were two blood spots on her turtleneck at the throat. Her mouth hung open at a disjointed angle, as if in a silent scream. Her tongue, stained with red wine, lolled over her lips.

Jack flipped a corner of the plastic sheet over Rhonda's face.

He stood for a moment over the corpse and returned to the dining room to inspect the table where their dinner remained, the nearby credenza, and the wall behind, the area where he struck her. There were no apparent signs of blood, spit, or splatter anywhere. Just to be safe, however, he got a cleaner and a roll of paper towels from the kitchen and cleaned the entire area. He worked thoughtfully, scrubbed well beyond the area where any fluids might have splashed.

Satisfied he had cleaned the dining room thoroughly—carpet, walls, and furniture—Jack sat down to finish his dinner and poured himself another glass of cabernet. Then he cleaned Rhonda's plate, forking its contents onto his plate, and ate them. He transferred her wine to his glass and sat back to think what he would do next.

There was no panic. He was safe in his home. Even the argument that preceded the one-punch massacre would not have been audible to his neighbors, even if they and he had open windows. This was winter. Freezing temperatures. All the homes were closed against the frigid air. Even the homes themselves were set far apart in this exclusive, well-heeled, and gated community. There were no children. No relatives to speak of. Neighbors went their own ways, leaving occasional waves or head nods when they crossed paths. No one ever needed to borrow a cup of sugar.

The body would have to disappear. Thanks to the long-lasting polar vortex, the ground was too hard to dig an adequate grave. All the ponds, lakes, and waterways suitable for dumping a body were frozen thick enough to allow ice fishing and skating. Before rigor mortis set in, he'd roll Rhonda in the plastic, fix her in a fetal position, and bind it all with rope, otherwise, her tall body would not fit in the trunk and barely lie across the back seat. He could cut her in half like the Black Dahlia, but that would be too messy. Jack retrieved a second wine bottle, opened it, and poured a glass. Before he drank any, he cleared the dining room table, filled the dishwasher, and turned it on. Then he returned to the dining room and sat in *his* place. While he pondered what to do with the body, he also replayed the dinner.

It was a Thursday, and Jack had no office hours. Although he normally worked in his home office on Thursdays or played golf at the Mammoth Country Club, he started going to his clinic in Downtown Mammoth since he learned about Rhonda's affair with Hector. He reviewed test results from a half dozen patients, called his accountant, and talked with his divorce attorney. The divorce would cost him plenty. Jack stopped at the Parkway on his way home for a drink, bourbon on the rocks.

The place had a few barflies scattered along the dark, dingy place who apparently had no better place to be, despite the bitter cold. They avoided Jack, who was dressed, as usual, in a tie and camel-colored topcoat. The first drink he downed quickly, and ordered another. He nursed the second bourbon. He and Rhonda had decided to split. She would get the home and cash. Their separate lawyers were working out the details.

With help from an old flame who was a real estate agent, he was already looking for a condo. She could arrange for a decorator to furnish the new digs. Over the years Jack had grown fond of sleazy bars like the Parkway. Their age, the worn atmosphere, dim lighting, and odor of stale beer appealed to the Ox. Reminded him of the dives he and his teammates frequented during college. Even when filled, the Parkway was the type of place you could sit with your thoughts, talk about sports with some old codger, or listen to the conspiracy theories that were rife. They were still talking about John and Bobby Kennedy. Jack considered another drink, but he collected his coat and scarf and drove home. The last thing he needed was a DUI. There was a time when a doctor with a bit too much under his belt was paid professional courtesy, let off with a verbal warning and a wink. The inebriation was chalked up to a bad day. Not anymore. Most of the cops were merciless.

It was 6 p.m. when Jack arrived home. Rhonda had dinner ready. She was dressed in a turtleneck sweater and jeans. A salad, baked haddock, and green beans were already on the table, as if she had known when he would return. Red wine was poured. They always had wine with dinner. They split a bottle and rarely uncorked a second. Their life together was predictable. Although the fish would indicate a white wine, which Rhonda preferred, Jack liked reds, and she had opened his favorite cabernet from a case that rested in the garage.

Rhonda had stopped cooking weeks ago when Jack served her with divorce papers, although she bought food he could prepare himself. Mostly, however, he ate out alone. This meal was a mystery. Rhonda must have an ulterior motive, Jack thought. Perhaps she had broken off her relationship with Hector. Maybe he had moved on to someone younger, someone with more money, and she wanted to come crawling back. Jack remained mostly silent. Still, he thanked Rhonda for the dinner. They ate together in silence. The wine bottle was placed where both could reach it.

Jack wondered what Rhonda saw in Hector. He was an immigrant. Barely knew English. Was almost a head shorter than she. Of course, he was young, fit, and probably could fuck like a monkey. He doubted their fling would last, but he would not take her back. Screw the house. Screw the money. His practice was booming. There was plenty of money to be made. He was still young.

"I talked to my lawyer today," Rhonda said, waving her fork in a small circle over her salad plate.

"So did I," Jack said.

"Oh?"

Jack looked up to meet her stare. She looked surprised. "That is, I talked to my lawyer. Nothing new to report."

After several seconds, Rhonda said, "Well, my lawyer thinks I should get more cash, some stock, too, and the new Mercedes. You like the old one anyway. It's bigger."

"That's not what we agreed to," Jack said. He rested his fork on the plate silently, wiped his mouth with a napkin. He continued to stare at Rhonda. His face flushed.

"You still would be in the surgery center partnership. And I don't want your gun collection." She dropped her eyes to the plate. "You know I don't like guns, and despite their value and historical significance, I'm not interested in breaking up the collection."

"You'll never get my guns," Jack said. His voice was tense. He raised his head, pointing his square chin at Rhonda, looking over the top of his glasses.

She looked at him and raised her voice slightly. "That's what Art recommended. He said I gave up my chance to have children, which—you remember—I wanted. I gave that up for you. Now I can't have kids."

"What kind of mother would you have made?" Jack raised his voice louder. "You only worried about keeping your trim figure."

"That didn't seem to bother you when you paraded me around as your eye candy. No invitations were turned down. Now we don't even go to the movies."

"That's because all you do is bitch."

"And by the way, I would have made a great mother."

Jack dismissed her with a wave of his hand. He threw down the napkin, picked up his glass, and downed some wine. "You can tell your lawyer the original agreement stands. I'll agree to no more. No amendments. Who suggested this new deal? Art, so he can bilk me out of more money? Or your boy toy Hector, who can retire and lie around my pool all day? Let his migrant worker family run through the grounds. Take over the house, fill all the rooms with relatives, make it smell of refried beans."

"He and his family are not migrant workers. They have been in this country for several generations. They had businesses in the South."

"Taco Bells?"

"Hotels."

"Brothels?"

"You're an idiot, Jack," Rhonda screamed and stood. "What changed you?"

"Nothing changed me. I'm the real deal. I'm the OX!"

"You used to be." Rhonda balled her slim hands into fists and squeezed so hard they shook. "Tell me why we have no friends anymore. When was the last invite we got from anyone?"

"Because you're peevish, Rhonda. Everyone is sick and tired of listening to you and your gym routine, and your darling trainer Hector. How hard he works you, even to exhaustion. You never worked a real day in your entire life." Jack stood, moved a step from the table, and faced her.

Rhonda raised her voice louder. "No! Maybe it's because everyone knows about the secretary you fired for stealing pills, when it wasn't pills she stole, it was you who knocked her up. She disappeared with a chunk of *our* proceeds from the surgery center. Bought her out. That's what you did."

"Fuck you!"

"That secretary has a sister who goes to my gym," Rhonda shouted, leaning toward Jack. "Guess what? By chance we became friends—hot yoga class—and, when she found out who I was, she spilled the beans. Then I spilled the beans, you son of a bitch! You're as guilty as I am."

Jack had made a fist, too, and it fired out, catching Rhonda on the chin. He felt the bone crunching under his hand, heard the neck snap, saw Rhonda whirl in a semicircle like a dervish as she crumpled to the floor.

Jack looked at his wife, her eyes staring.

"Case closed. No Mercedes. No stock. Not a fucking thing."

Jack realized he had drunk the second bottle of wine. He would have to dispose of Rhonda's body on the weekend. Too much wine to try it now. He decided to wrap Rhonda in plastic, tie her in a fetal position to conserve space, and dump her body late at night off Route 125 in Mammoth Township, a desolate road outside the city. He needed time for his hand to heal, the one with the devastating punch. During his football-playing days, bruised knuckles were a badge of honor. So was inflicting pain on the opposition. Nothing to worry about. Displayed with pride. Now, however, Rhonda's disappearance and his injury might raise alarm. His plan was set, and he felt good about it.

Jack entered the garage to discover Rhonda and the plastic she was loosely wrapped in were gone. He couldn't believe it. He reentered the house and went through the fight, standing where he had stood, then where she had stood, even swinging in slow-motion the punch that killed Rhonda. He stared at the spot where Rhonda lay on the floor. He saw the traces where her heels drug across the carpet, two thin lines. He ran back to the garage. Saw where the plastic originally had been stowed on a shelf among paint cans.

It was gone.

He stood over the place where he had set the body. He looked around. Even the rope was gone he had planned to use to truss up the body. The overhead door had not opened, because he would have heard it. The service door on the garage's side entrance was locked from the inside. They hadn't used it in years, and it was covered with gardening tools, shovels, rakes, hoes. Two bags of cement lay in front of it. The window next to the door was locked and had not been opened in years. Cobwebs draped over the glass like a flimsy curtain. No one could have taken the body out of the house while he sat in the dining room. They would have passed by him. He knew she didn't get up and walk out. She was dead.

Two days after the murder, Jack reported Rhonda missing. He told the investigating officer he had no idea what happened and cooperated fully. He came home from his office, and she was gone. He turned over his cell phone to be analyzed. He admitted the crime scene investigators to go over the home. He stayed out of their way and answered their questions. He never mentioned consulting his lawyer. In the coming days, he appeared on local television news, asking Rhonda to come home and pleading for anyone who knew about her disappearance to come forward.

Jack received sympathy from the medical community, patients, friends, and strangers, even as details of the couple's marital woes became public. Rhonda's gym friends were less kind to Jack's character. Meanwhile, he kept his hands covered with gloves. No one suspected with such cold weather. After a week, he went back to work. He wore latex gloves in the office, which was not unusual. Also, police said they found no evidence of foul play in or around the Simmone home.

Police believed Rhonda might have been abducted outside the home, even though her new Mercedes, the apple of her eye, remained in the garage. Jack appeared on the TV news again, interviewed by the 6 o'clock anchor. Again, he pleaded with Rhonda to come home, for anyone with knowledge of the case to speak up. He sobbed before the cameras and covered his face, keeping his right hand in his pocket. All was forgiven, he promised on air. Police said the Ox was not a suspect in Rhonda's disappearance.

A month passed. The polar vortex shifted above Pennsylvania, bringing in warmer southern air. A false spring arrived in time for the Mammoth Lions Club plans for a roadside clean up along the interstate. No one expected Jack to show for the club's annual community service, but he had organized it and arrived early on a mid-February Saturday. It was a beautiful, cloudless day. Cold but still warmer than the weather they experienced last month.

Club members now offered Jack condolences because there had been no funeral, no memorial service. Still, no one expected Rhonda to come home alive. A few expected her to never turn up. The Lions spread out on the interstate's wide grassy median and the highway's shoulder, like a poorly formed civil war picket line, with their garbage bags and pointed sticks for spearing trash. Large boulders and clusters of trees were scattered along the way. It was difficult walking on the medium's incline. The Ox had grown out of shape over the years and lagged in the center of the volunteers who stabbed trash and transferred it to their plastic bags.

Suddenly, Guy Pierce called. "Hey Jack, give me a hand with this big piece. I need the *Ox*."

"Coming," Jack said cheerily as he half jogged uphill. He approached a large piece of plastic. He was winded. "Christ, who threw this here?"

"Probably blew out of a truck," Guy said. "Hold on a sec," Guy said. "I gotta take a whiz over here by the trees."

"Take your time."

"Coffee and the cold air don't mix. I think it's an aging thing."

The Ox smiled. "You got that right."

Jack approached the plastic. He recognized it immediately. He unfolded a corner and saw Rhonda staring at him. Her body was naked and shriveled, dried out. She looked like a mummy, Jack thought. This was impossible, even for someone out here in the cold for more than a month.

Guy returned and froze when he saw Rhonda. He called the other club members and pulled out his cell phone, and called 911.

Rhonda's discovery would hit the news on Sunday. The fact that Jack found his missing and dead wife put a strange twist on the case. TV anchors and reporters in the field grimaced as they broke the news. Jack would be a person of interest again, especially in the press. Could it be possible that he kept Rhonda's body hidden for more than a month? Placed it himself on the interstate with the intention to discover the corpse himself? What kind of fiend would do such a thing?

An autopsy revealed Rhonda's broken neck, smashed jaw. What was more interesting and not released to the public was that the autopsy found postmortem ligature marks on Rhonda's ankles. The medical examiner said she was hanged upside down, and her blood and body fluids were drained through a gash in the neck. Her brain was extracted through a hole in the roof of her mouth, and the inside of her skull was cleaned as if by a tongue. The cranium was empty when the ME sawed through the skull, its interior buffed to a dull shine.

Jack holed up in his home for another week, while the press hounded him. Reporters camped out on the sidewalk, waiting for him to retrieve the mail or a newspaper. He received few calls and no visitors. After the autopsy's lurid details leaked, the media theorized only someone with medical training could have sucked the life out of Rhonda Simmone. It was a strange occurrence, indeed, but Mammoth residents were not too fazed because their city was the kind of place where almost anything could happen. On Saturday, a week after the body's discovery, Jack sat in his home office most of the day, blinds drawn, staring into space. After dark, he fired out of the garage in Rhonda's sporty Mercedes, almost running over a female reporter thrusting a microphone at the car, while others screamed a cacophony of unrecognizable questions while the herd moved toward the opening overhead garage door. Some remained at the door as it closed, filming the garage's interior. Wearing old sweats and sporting beard stubble, Jack bought bourbon at the state store and picked up takeout food. No one recognized him with the Eagles stocking cap pulled over his eyebrows.

He flew back to his home, opening the garage door remotely down the block and firing into the garage before coming to a screeching halt. Reporters accosted him again, this time from a safer distance, but he remained inside the car until the door closed behind him.

Jack sat in the car for several minutes while he calmed his nerves. He had almost driven the powerful little car through the garage's rear wall. He noticed Rhonda's scent still hung in the car's interior.

Jack entered his home through the garage to discover a man sitting in the living room.

"It's you," Jack snarled. He raised his closed fist.

"No sense in that, Jack," Hector said. "I didn't come to fight."

"Fight? You fucked my wife!"

Jack charged Hector. He drew back his arm to deliver another haymaker. In that moment while rage drove Jack across the room, he knew he had a trespasser he could kill in self-defense. Meanwhile, Hector stood and waited. Hector was a head shorter than Jack, but lean and muscular. His features were sharp. His skin a flawless brown. Jack swung. Hector caught his fist, stopping it in midair, and squeezed. Jack shrieked as his knuckles popped, and he dropped to his knees in pain. Still squeezing, Hector lifted Jack to his feet, pushed him backwards, and forced him into a seat at the end of the sofa. Jack moaned, panted, and examined his hand, which had barely recovered from the punch he delivered to Rhonda.

"What do you want?" Jack said as he winced, trying to move his fingers. "Jesus Christ, you're strong."

Hector smiled. "The strength of many men, Jack. Many men. And older than many men's years added together."

"What are you talking about?" Preoccupied with his hand, Jack wasn't paying attention. He worked his fingers, opening and closing his fist. Then he glared at Hector.

"I'm here to repay a favor," Hector said. "A favor your wife asked me."

"You were fucking her."

"Yes. She was going to be mine, but you killed her."

"I didn't kill her. Don't you know? She was missing. Somebody murdered her. Drained the blood. Nobody knows what really happened to her. The police haven't charged me. They can't. There's no evidence." Jack rubbed his hand. He looked furtively around the room, as if in search of something to use as a weapon. Sweat rolled down his face.

"Don't try to escape, Jack, or attack me again, because it is useless."

"What are you doing here? How did you get in?"

"Like I said. I'm here to pay a favor Rhonda asked. I came to kill you."

"You're crazy. I didn't touch Rhonda."

Hector laughed. "You killed Rhonda with a what, a one-punch massacre? I heard it on the news when a reporter explained the autopsy findings. You left her in the garage while you finished your and her dinners, drank her wine. I know. I was in the garage and heard you argue. I waited that night to kill you, as she had asked. She was going to make you dinner, and you were going to disappear. She would say you decided to go out to your bar and never came back. But you killed her, and I carried off her body through the garage window and locked it again from the outside. Vampires are clever that way."

"You drained her blood?"

"Yes," Hector said. "And removed her brain. She was an extraordinary woman. She was going to live through the ages with me."

"You're insane."

"You don't believe in vampires? Neither did Rhonda at first. After our training sessions became intimate, I invited her to a meeting with my followers. She became a novice, one who would serve me, and I would turn at the right time. In some cases, that time never comes. At first, I didn't think Rhonda was suitable. Still, I drank her blood, a sip here and a sip there. This weather made a perfect season for turtlenecks to hide the wounds. After all, you didn't pay much attention to her anymore. You would hardly miss her for the rest of your brief, pathetic life." He smiled and shrugged. "The *Ox?*"

"You would have killed her," Jack said. "You are a murderer. I made a mistake. I never intended to hurt Rhonda. I agreed to a divorce settlement, but she wanted more. She was greedy."

"I would not have killed Rhonda. Not kill." Hector wagged a finger at Jack. "I offered her eternal life. Vampires don't love. But we share a common bond. Survival. We would have survived for ages."

Jack looked terrified. How could he escape this fiend who had the strength of many men?

Meanwhile, Hector looked more relaxed. He said, "After Rhonda knew I was a vampire, but before I thought of turning her, one evening she said, 'How hard would it be to kill Jack? I want him to disappear. I believe he's going to contest this divorce, and he has a good lawyer. I don't know if I could get half of everything. To be honest, I'd rather have it all and be rid of him.'"

"Rhonda wasn't like that," Jack said, shaking his head. "I don't believe it."

"That was the moment I decided to turn her. She was a survivalist. All she wanted was to survive. So, we made our plans. She would make you a nice dinner, which she hadn't done in a while. She'd lure you into the garage to look at a blemish on her new car, and there I would kill you. I would turn her—she was ready—and I'd drain your body of blood. One of my novices would arrive early in the morning while it was still dark, and we'd load your body into his trunk. Your body was the one that was supposed to be dumped along the interstate, to lie there until someone, as Hamlet said of Polonius, nosed you out."

Jack sat stunned.

"Nothing to say?"

Jack was silent for a moment. Then he said, "Could I become a novice?"

"That's impossible," Hector said. "I could never trust you. My novices are completely loyal. They would die for me in an instant, because they have the promise of eternal life. I do not need an *ox*."

"I could be like that, too," Jack implored, reaching out to Hector. "Completely loyal."

Hector smiled and shook his head.

"There's got to be a way."

"Through the ages, vampires have been vilified. We were

abominable. Hunted down to the graves where we slept and killed. Exposed to sunlight. Decapitation and stakes through the heart. We may not be desirable to the living, but a promise is a promise. Rhonda won't drink your blood, but I will."

MILE MARKER 66.6

"Paramorsels?"

"Yes. That's it," Derek said.

"Para, as in paranormal?"

"And morsels, as in food. Good food. Gourmet food." Reid leaned back in the car seat and looked at his boyfriend Seth Bonney.

"That's a stretch," Seth said. He stroked Reid's clean-shaven cheek. "Maybe for a Halloween special, but a weekly show? I don't know."

They sped along in the dark on Route 125 in Mammoth Township, west of the city of Mammoth, in Schuylkill County, Pennsylvania. Seth was a front man for the television show *Paranormal, Anyone?* and investigated program ideas before hosts and crews were sent in with all their equipment. Not all projects fared well on film, and Seth decided whether an idea was worthy. Unlike most paranormal shows, *Paranormal,*

Anyone? producers insisted on using the real people involved in the unusual incidents, not actors, whether they encountered Bigfoot, were abducted by aliens, knew of demon possessions, or witnessed a host of other paranormal events.

The producers wanted raw emotions.

They considered episodes with hysterical crying the best. The real people didn't have to be Hollywood types, but they had to have a presence on camera—including most of their teeth and no visible needle marks—be well spoken, and mostly believable. If an idea proved to be farfetched or a downright hoax, its details might be manipulated. The interviewees could be coached to make their stories more credible. After all, they were paid non-SAG-AFTRA wages, and the show's credits rolled through a series of disclaimers that blew by in fine print when the show ended.

This time Seth was on the trail of a cult whose blood-guzzling members were rumored to live eternally. They were not vampires, per se, but something else. Perhaps demons were involved. Cult activities occurred years ago, which made the story more enticing, because there was no one alive to repute lurid, blood-curdling claims, and anyone with a remote personal knowledge of incidents would have foggy memories at best and difficult to find. Seth had a limited budget. He didn't look for trouble.

Reid was not a part of the show but was along to keep Seth company. They had been partners for almost a year. When the two men started traveling together to scout episodes, Seth had to keep Reid's expenses separate from his own. Now, no one seemed to notice. The couple shared the room Seth would have anyway, and the two were rarely extravagant.

"I was thinking you could pitch the *Paramorsels* to Benny when we get back," Reid said. "If this cult episode proves to be the slam dunk you predicted, Benny should be more receptive."

"You'll have to put something in writing," Seth said. "Benny likes show proposals on paper so he can present them to the other producers. I can't go in and wing it, because I wouldn't be able to answer questions. And I don't think you're ready to face Benny. Not yet. Not alone."

"That doesn't say much about me, does it?" Reid said.

"I didn't mean it like that. Let's face it. The only reason I got this job is because nobody else wanted it. I haven't had many high-profile projects. They're all backwater ideas used to fill in after bigger segments, when viewers are already hooked for the hour." Seth smiled at Reid. "We'll get you on board. All you need is the right idea at the right time. Your day will come. So, what's a *paramorsel*?"

Reid became excited. "The way I see it, you get a celebrity chef, maybe a different one each week, to cook something special in a haunted kitchen. What chef wouldn't want to do a show like that? Lord knows there's enough haunted places around. They could be kitchens in exotic places—New Orleans, castles in England or Europe, famous haunted inns, if the budget allows. Otherwise, it will be Small Town, USA. Just as the chef starts his meal, something crazy happens, like the lights go out."

"What are the chances of that?" Seth said.

"Like we don't fudge anything," Reid said.

"So?"

"So, the staff has to drop everything, and while still filming, find candles for the chef to see. The next week, the gas could shut off. The chef would have to move outside and cook over an open fire. No precise temperatures for something like a soufflé. Wing it and see what happens. Test the chef's skills. Get my point?"

"I think so."

"You seem skeptical," Reid said. "Don't forget, a mean-spirited poltergeist could knock a mixing bowl off the table, and the chef would have to start over. There'd be a time limit on completing the dish. We could have spooky music and spooky sets. Guests, or even judges, might be dressed as zombies. The opportunities are limitless. Imagine a panel of judges who *look* dead."

Seth sighed.

"You don't think it has merit?" Reid said.

"It's not that. I'm tired. Put it all in writing and I'll give your idea to Benny when we get back."

"Yes!" Reid said. He slammed a fist into his palm and then slapped his thighs repeatedly.

The two-lane highway, which had twisted, turned, rose, and fell, suddenly opened on a level, straight stretch. Large trees crowded close to and overhung the highway. The terrain next to the roadway rose sharply on their right to the east and fell into darkness on the west. Seth's rental had a direction indicator on the dashboard.

"Look at that," Reid said. "Mile marker 66.0"

"That means there's a mile marker 66.6. We'll have to visit that spot in daylight. It might have some creepy value for the segment. You never know when we need a few extra spooky seconds."

"You're the best, Seth."

"You have good eyes, my friend."

"I have more good news," Reid said. "We just passed one, two, and there's a third roadside memorial."

"There's one and two on my side," Seth said excitedly, as if they were trying to spot out-of-state license plates on a long, boring trip.

"One more on my side," Reid laughed. "And it's lit up. At mile marker 66.6."

"One, no two more for me," Seth said. "This has possibilities."

"Two more over here," Reid said, incredulously.

The road began to rise and turned sharply to the right. "That's it. Mile marker 67.0."

"That's incredible," Seth said. "The nicest piece of roadway for miles, flat and straight, recently paved, new lines painted, and it seemed to have the most accidents. Fatal ones evidently."

Seth thought something was wrong. "We should have reached the B&B by now. I'm pulling over for gas. We'll need it anyway. I'll get some directions."

"What's with the GPS? It hasn't chirped for a while," Reid said. "Is the girl asleep at her map?"

"No wonder. No signal."

Seth pulled into a convenience store and stopped at the pumps. His *Paranormal, Anyone?* credit card wouldn't work in the pump, so he trudged into the store. He gave the cashier the card and smiled.

"You'll have to leave the card here while you pump your gas," the cashier said. "Sorry. It's policy." She had dark hair and a pretty smile. It appeared her jeans were painted on her slim legs. "Who's the cute guy you're with?"

"My boyfriend," Seth said defensively.

"Ouch!"

"I'll be back for the card."

The girl sniggered as Seth left the store. When he returned after filling his tank, Seth bought bottles of mineral water and avocado salads. He asked the girl for directions to the Forever Hideaway B&B.

"Everybody gets lost." She pointed at the roadway. "You go back to mile marker 65 and hang a left. It's Forest Lane. Forever Hideaway Inn is on the left, about a mile from the intersection."

Seth nodded, as if he understood the directions.

"Pleasure trip?" she asked, apparently trying to be friendly.

"Business. We're advance scouts for the *Paranormal, Anyone?* TV show.

"No way!" The girl laughed. "I watch that show. You doing a part on the Blood Path Cult?"

"We're considering it. You know about Blood Path?"

"Everybody does. Blood Path is Mammoth Township's claim to shame, as they say. But you're not a show host?"

"I work strictly behind the scenes."

"Smart. You won't get typecast."

"I suppose. What's with all the memorials along mile marker 66? They're on that one-mile stretch of road."

The girl emitted a long, slow whistle. "You noticed, huh? That's just the tip of the iceberg. People have died along that road for years. It's only in the last few years that the memorials started going up. I knew kids who were killed there."

"Really?"

"I placed one marker myself and helped put up two more." She leaned across the counter. "All kids from my senior class." Her breath smelled like peppermint as she chewed gum nervously. "Every year it seems there's a death around graduation. The state is baffled. The road is perfectly straight. They pave it every few years. Replace the lines every year. There are reflector stakes along the road and grooves in the asphalt make noise when your tires roll over them. If a mile marker sign goes down, it's replaced in a day or two. DOT seems paranoid. Always doing something to improve the road."

The girl looked around the empty store, as if someone might be listening.

"There is a kind of legend. When the road wants to take someone, fog drifts downhill. The fog is icy, and has ice crystals suspended in it, even in the summer. People say the road can move, throw a car onto the bank or downhill. Or one of those big trees can slide across a lane and cause an accident. Then everything goes back to normal. The fog disappears. The road straightens and the trees move back in place. The road surface looks perfect after an accident. Brand new No cracks. No divots. No bumps."

"That's incredible," Seth said. "Still, it's just a legend."

"I know." She touched Seth's hand as Reid walked into the store.

Reid cleared his throat.

Seth pulled back his hand. "I got water and salads," he said.

"So, I see," Reid said, moving next to Seth.

Seth introduced Reid.

"I'm sorry," Seth said to the girl. "I didn't get your name."

"It's Bonnie," she said.

"That's my name," Seth said."

"You have a girl's name?" Bonnie twisted her face into a frown.

"No. Let me explain. My last name is B-o-n-n-e-y. Like William Bonny. You know. Billy the Kid."

The girl nodded in agreement. "My first name is B-o-n-n-i-e. Bonnie Cleaver, as in *Leave It to Beaver*. What a coincidence! Are you related to Billy the Kid?"

"No, but we did a *Paranormal, Anyone?* episode on him two seasons ago."

"That's so cool," Bonnie said.

Reid rolled his eyes.

"Would you be willing to show us around the highway?" Seth said. "You'd get paid. We might even interview you on camera, if we bring the whole crew in."

"No way!"

"Yes, really," Seth said.

Bonnie grinned. "I'll show you. I'm off tomorrow." She bounced up and down, clapping her hands.

"This might not fit into our plan for the cult, but it might work," Seth told Reid. "Offer an interesting twist to the case. Who knows? We might find a connection. Or it might be worth a separate segment. We have to come back with something."

Seth and Reid smiled and nodded to each other.

"I travel over that very road every day to work," Bonnie said. "So, I know the area well. Never saw anything crazy, but I can tell you something else strange. Some people who crashed disappeared. Their cars were wrapped around a tree or flung down the bank. But no bodies."

Seth looked at Reid. They smiled.

"Locals say the cult took them for special ceremonies,"

Bonnie continued. "Kept them alive until a full moon or Witches' Sabbath."

"What kind of ceremonies?" Reid asked.

Bonnie leaned over the counter again. "Special." She raised an eyebrow. After a pause, she said, "The police claim the injured hit their heads, crawled away, and fell into crevasses."

"I didn't think *the cult* existed today," Seth said.

"Well, no. It doesn't. It couldn't. I don't know if it ever did. But accidents still happen. There was a guy who went missing last month. There were search parties and cadaver dogs. He never turned up. You have to understand this area is pretty wild. Everything was under ice eons ago. The glaciers weighed a zillion tons and dug up huge rocks as they moved south."

Bonnie used her arms to simulate the scooping action. She said, "I remember it from science class. The rocks were carried for miles inside the ice. Eventually, the ice melted and left the rocks behind. There're all kinds of crazy formations around. Huge slabs piled up high. Some are famous, at least around here. When I was in high school, we had keggers inside them. If it wasn't football season, somebody'd say, 'There's a kegger tonight at the coven, or the cathedral, or the Flintstones.' Everybody'd know where to go. It was a bitch climbing up to those places, especially in the dark. It was even worse coming down with a buzz on." Bonnie laughed. "Guys from the football team were always in charge of getting the beer, carrying it up the mountain."

Seth made arrangements to pick up Bonnie the next day at the B&B. He and Reid retraced their route along Mile Marker 66. They stopped at Mile Marker 66.6. Seth put on the four-way flashers and exited the car. Reid followed him. They stood in silence. The air was still. The forest canopy blotted out the night sky. They walked a few yards toward a memorial just off the road. Their small flashlights illuminated the way. The memorial was a wooden cross with plastic flowers, blue and white, stapled to the wood. The name Jean Delmar and RIP were painted on the crosspiece.

"How sad," Seth said. "Jean never got to live her life. I wonder how old she was."

"She picked a creepy enough place to die," Reid added. "I hope the B&B is this quiet."

"There's the cross that has lights," Seth said, motioning ahead.

They walked farther up the road to a bank where there was a white, wooden cross with a solar disc attached to the top. Rope lighting bordered the cross's edges. The men looked skyward to a patch of sky in the forest canopy.

"That's where the light comes in during the day," Reid said, pointing upward. "Just enough to charge the battery."

Suddenly, there was commotion in the woods. Something moved downhill toward the roadway. It crashed through the undergrowth at breakneck speed. Seth and Reid backed up slowly. Their bodies touched. Seth pointed his flashlight in the direction of the noise. They were a good fifteen yards from the car. A large doe bounded from the trees onto the highway and stopped to look toward them. It breathed heavily and appeared frightened. It snorted several times.

The first wisps, fine filaments, of fog followed the deer from the woods, spreading slowly over the ground, then the road. The cloud rose higher as it moved toward the animal, its vapors roiling slowly. Seth and Reid backed toward the car. Just as the first finger-like foggy tentacles reached the deer, the animal snorted again, lifted its legs, as if walking through deep snow. Suddenly, it charged away. Its sharp hooves slipped on the asphalt, and for a moment, its legs raced in place like a cartoon character, the deer going nowhere, its hooves scraping loudly on the road surface. Suddenly, the hooves caught, and the animal bounded away, crashing into the woods again and disappearing downhill.

Seth and Reid looked at one another and laughed. Reid put an arm around Seth's shoulder.

"I thought we were goners," Reid said.

"Bigfoot?"

"Who knows, at mile marker 66.6."

"We'll do that on another expedition."

Seth trained the flashlight back to where the deer had stood. The mist had stopped there and changed direction toward them, inching its vaporous trail to engulf them.

"Let's go!" Seth said. He sprinted away.

Reid's leather shoes slipped on the asphalt, and he fell to one knee. He rose to run and stumbled again, this time on both knees. The cloud, about knee-high, floated toward him. Seth returned and pulled Reid to his feet. He guided him back to the car. By the time Reid closed his door, and Seth circled the vehicle's rear to reach the driver's side, the fog enveloped them. Seth jumped in, gunned the engine, and pulled out.

"That fog must be made of ice crystals," Reid said, "like Bonnie said. I'm freezing."

"I got a lung full and now I have trouble breathing. It hurts."

Seth stepped on the gas.

"Not so fast," Reid said. "I don't want to get wrapped around one of these trees."

Seth slowed the car to the speed limit. Together, they counted the road markers until they reached 65.0. Neither talked about the highway, deer, or fog, and drove in silence. Seth followed Bonnie's instructions, made a left at the intersection, and drove a mile to Forever Hideaway Inn. The B&B was larger than the quaint inn Seth had envisioned. It was built of three stories of stone and had white wooden trim. The path to the door was well lit. Wooden wind chimes hung in the trees and clunked in a light breeze. The wind moved the rocking chairs on the front porch. People on the patio laughed.

A bell tinkled when they walked through the front door with their bags. A middle-aged woman, plump, with a beehive hairdo, approached down a hall.

Seth introduced himself.

"Check-in ended an hour ago," the woman said matter-of-factly.

"Sorry. We got lost and then detained," Seth said.

"Police detain you?" the woman asked.

"No police. We got lost and stopped to get directions and gas."

"You're the movie producer?" she asked.

"I'm not a producer. I represent a television show. *Paranormal, Anyone?*"

"Can't say I heard of it. Don't watch much TV myself. Have over a thousand channels and still can't find anything interesting. Come over to the desk," the woman said. "Mr. Hardwick, the owner, will check you in. Just so you know, the kitchen and bar are closed. We don't tolerate barflies."

"That's fine," Seth said. "We have food."

She gave them an odd look and led them to the desk, old, ornate, and mahogany. Mr. Hardwick was a tall, gray-haired man. When he turned toward him, Seth was struck by his pale face and what appeared to be peeling skin—like a sunburn without the redness. The old man smiled, revealing yellow and worn teeth.

"Yes?" the old man intoned, raising his furry eyebrows.

"We have a reservation," Seth said.

"Check-in ended an hour ago."

"We heard. I'm sorry. We got lost and had to stop for directions."

"I see."

The woman hovered nearby, flipping through a stack of mail, flipping the same small stack repeatedly. "I thought you were detained," she said.

"We were," Seth said. His arms moved in small circles. "We stopped for gas and asked for directions from a girl at the convenience mart. She told us about a curiosity on Route 125, mile marker 66, where people die in traffic accidents and some go missing."

"Really?" The man seemed surprised. He turned to the woman, who stopped shuffling the mail. She shrugged. "Never heard of anything like that, and I've lived here my entire life."

"Me too," the woman chirped. "You know young people," she added, rolling her eyes at the old man. "Maybe we have to get out more."

"This girl said she helped set up some of the memorials along the road," Seth said.

"She knew some of the people killed," Reid added.

"Well, I think those memorials are akin to dumping trash," the woman said. "After a few years, they're falling over and decrepit. The people who place them move away or get on with their lives, forget about the dead. We're left with an eyesore. The state doesn't touch them. That's one thing about the dead; they'll be forgotten before long."

Seth and Reid exchanged glances.

"You gentlemen are from a television show," Hardwick said. He smiled again. "Not much interesting on television. Never was, in my opinion."

"We're investigating the so-called Blood Path Cult," Seth said.

"How interesting," Hardwick said. "Honestly, I doubt such a cult ever existed. Imagine that. Everlasting life here on Earth. People would be lined up for miles."

The woman tittered as she shuffled the mail.

"Sorry to say I'm not familiar with your television program," Hardwick said. "But we have all the latest accommodations here for those who do. Cable TV, Wi-Fi, all that jazz. It seems rather silly to go on vacation and sit inside to watch television all day. Don't you think?" The old man smiled. "There's so much to do outside. It's a lovely night. Look at the people on the patio."

"We appreciate the modern conveniences," Seth said.

"We do have a problem, though," Hardwick said. "I have only one room and *it* has one standard double bed. We're pretty full. The reservation was in your name only. I didn't know you were bringing a...friend."

"A co-worker," Seth said. "He was added at the last minute."

The old man stifled a cough."

"We'll get by," Reid said. "We can double up."

"Very well," Hardwick said. "We have a lady from the Associated Press doing a story on something. Pretty young thing. Drinks like a fish, though. But that's none of our business, and it's not our livers affected." He gave the woman a sly smile. "Then we have the usual tourists. Two rooms are being remodeled and, of course, we have our permanent residents."

"Permanent."

"The third floor has two apartments with kitchens and their own bathrooms. We have a Mr. Heil on the north and Mr. King on the south." Hardwick pointed overhead in the direction of the apartments with his pen. "Both are retired gentlemen. Mr. King is from the South. Has an extensive record collection. Mr. Heil is German and came to us from Argentina, where he lived for many years after *the* war."

"What would attract them to Mammoth?" Reid said.

"Solitude," the woman interjected. "They both value their privacy." She pointed her stack of mail at Seth. "I told that newspaper woman not to bother them. And that goes for you, too."

Hardwick smiled. "The AP writer saw them in the hall and thought interviews might produce another story. Both men declined, because they are quite reclusive and go out only at night."

"You'll meet the AP writer, I'm sure, in the bar," Hardwick said, with a sneer. "She is quite attractive."

"She's a snoop," the woman said. "You think every young woman is attractive. In my opinion, she's a barfly. Talk about a happy hour. The first to arrive and the last to leave. Imagine that?"

Hardwick cleared his throat and checked in Seth and Reid,

told them they would have to carry their own bags to the second floor, and said smoking of any kind was forbidden inside the inn. As Seth and Reid turned to grab their bags, Hardwick said nonchalantly, "Who gave you the directions here? The girl at the convenience store?"

"Her name was Bonnie Cleaver," Seth said. "Do you know her?"

"I know of the family," Hardwick said casually with a wave of his pen. "Bonnie is pretty. Dark hair. As I recall from newspaper accounts, she was somewhat of an athlete when she was in high school."

"Yes," Seth said. "I can imagine that."

"Too bad she didn't leave the area. There's no future here," the old man said.

"She might own that store someday," Seth said.

"Perhaps"

"She's going to show us around the area," Reid added.

Hardwick smiled, revealing his worn and yellowed teeth again. "I see. How nice you made a friend already." He looked toward the woman who still shuffled the mail.

"Too skinny, if you ask me," the woman said. "The same as you two boys. The three of you should go out for a couple of good meals. Don't miss the complimentary breakfast in the morning. Fill up on those waffles. It's an old recipe. We have real maple syrup. You can't get that everywhere."

Seth picked up the keyed cards for their room and led the way upstairs. He noticed Hardwick and the woman watched them from below when he looked down the staircase. Their room was near the stairs to the third floor. Seth stopped at the door when he heard a third-floor step creak. He turned to see a pair of legs dressed in blue, pin-striped trousers and shiny black cowboy boots scurry up out of his eyesight. As Seth paused, the steps on the stairs stopped, too. He waited a moment before opening the door. Seth dropped his bags on the floor inside, returned to the door, and opened it slowly a crack.

The hall and stairs were quiet. From the third floor he heard music, barely perceptible, "Love Me Tender," as sung by Elvis Presley, but an older, deeper voice seemed to sing with the recording. Inside the room they found the air conditioning turned on the lowest setting. The room was small and stuffy and had a strange odor, as if something foul was masked by the perfumed air. The curtains and matching bed spread appeared old. The room had one aged, winged back chair with threadbare cushions. There was also a scarred writing desk. A small, flat screen television, the only modern accouterment, sat on a worn dresser.

The closet was small and dusty. Seth surmised most people didn't bring much clothing to the inn, except perhaps Mr. King and Mr. Heil. He examined the drain, heating, and water pipes concealed in the closet that led to the third floor.

"Do you want to eat first or go at it," Reid said.

Seth smiled. "Let's eat later."

The next morning Jill Piranna of the Associated Press joined the men for the continental breakfast in the inn dining room. She introduced herself and asked what their television show wanted in Mammoth. She had been at the inn for several days and seemed to know all about their business. The alcohol she consumed the night before hung on her breath. Seth was noncommittal, saying they were interested in potential paranormal activity in the area.

"I got sent here to do a feature on a cadaver dog trainer," Jill said. "Just as I got into town, he got called away for an old man with dementia who walked away from home, so I've been cooling my heels here until he gets back. We have another appointment this morning. I'm trying to tie in global warming to the need for his services. At least that's where I'm going with it."

Without asking, Jill tore a piece from Reid's croissant and helped herself to coffee from their carafe, rather than returning to the buffet table. "How long will you be in town?"

"It's hard to say. We have some research to do," Seth said. "You know how it is."

"Yeah. Pain in the ass. I'm pulling out tomorrow. You want to go bar hopping tonight. Mammoth even has a gay bar."

"Why would that interest us," Reid said.

"There's nothing wrong with that. But it shows. Some fucking complimentary breakfast. You can't even get a Bloody Mary."

———

After breakfast, Seth and Reid waited outside for Bonnie to arrive. She parked her car in the visitors' lot and left with the men in Seth's rental. They drove to mile marker 66.0 and parked where the berm was wide. Seth had a pack with bottles of water and protein bars. Bonnie brought food in a bag from the convenience store, which she stored inside the pack. They walked one side of the straight highway, recording the memorials, names, and their locations in a notebook. Reid photographed each memorial from several angles and every mile marker sign. Some memorials were simply a bouquet of plastic flowers deposited on the ground. Others had vases and stuffed animals. One had a toy firetruck attached to a stake. Most had a cross with a name painted on it. A few had dates. Some were nailed to trees. One had a faded football jersey attached to a large tree. Many had small piles of white rocks. The most elaborate was the one at mile marker 66.6, which had the solar disc and rope lighting, under one of the few breaks in the forest canopy to catch direct sunlight. The name on the cross was "Bottoms Up."

There was little traffic on the road. Most people were at work at this hour. School was out for the summer, and it was too early for senior citizens to be out and about. A few cars stopped and the drivers asked if the trio needed help. When they reached mile marker 67.0, they crossed the road and returned on the other side, the one facing the downward slope. In places the terrain had steep drop offs and guardrails near the highway. Other areas had slight grades that descended slowly. At midmorning they reached mile marker 66.6 again. The day was already warm and muggy.

They decided to walk down the slight slope into the woods, where the fog had crossed the road the night before. Scratches from the deer's hoofs still marked the asphalt, where it tried to propel itself across the road the previous night. Seth told Bonnie about their encounter with the deer and the fog as they waded into high grass.

"I've never experienced the fog myself," Bonnie said. "Just heard about it and the fact that it's cold, even this time of year."

"The deer seemed to try to avoid the fog by high stepping out of it," Seth said. He moved his arms like a prancing deer.

"Oh, yeah. There's a lot of wildlife around here," Bonnie

said. "It attracts hunters from all over. The Forever Hideaway is packed during hunting season. You know, hunters have gone missing over the years, too. They walk into the woods and never come out. Sometimes their rifles or packs are found. I don't know too many guys who will leave their rifles behind."

"More crevasses?" Seth said.

"You got it," Bonnie said. The ground flattened out, and Bonnie took the lead. "This looks like a game trail. Let's follow it."

Really?" Seth said.

"My dad's a hunter and he tried to get me interested in it when I was a girl. It wasn't for me, but I learned some things. This *is* a game trail. Animals use it so much it tends to wear a path in the brush."

"Lead on," Reid said, with an exaggerated wave of his arm.

"Anyway, even though this forest goes a long way in all directions, and it connects to state game lands and more forest, if you got lost and walked in a straight line, you'd have to come out somewhere, encounter civilization again, eventually, even if it's a road or a farm. Plus, I think it would be easy to spot a hunter's fluorescent orange in the bush."

"I think it's possible to get disoriented, even if you don't hit your head, and walk in circles," Reid said.

"There's this guy outside Mammoth who trains cadaver dogs," Bonnie said. "He's supposed to be the best. He goes all over the country, even other countries, to find people lost in mudslides, earthquakes, that kind of thing, and his dogs turned up nothing here. I repeat, nothing."

They continued along the barely discernible path in the

knee-high grass, avoiding low limbs and saplings. There was a low wet spot where cattails grew on the left.

Bonnie said, "What's that smell?"

Reid caught the odor next and finally Seth, who brought up the rear. They moved off the trail, fanned out, and cautiously walked toward the smell.

"It's very dead," Reid said. "Whatever it is."

Seth shot him a glance. Suddenly, Reid went down, sprawled over a dead, ripped open deer. He screamed and shot to his feet. His jeans and shirt had gore on them. All three backed from the carcass.

"Mother fucker!" Reid shouted. "Look at this mess."

After Reid assured them he was all right, they approached the deer again.

"Do you think it's the deer from last night?" Reid said.

"Could be. We didn't get a good look at it in the dark," Seth said.

"The fog got it," Reid said.

"We were in the fog, and it didn't get us," Seth snapped.

"Coyotes," Bonnie said, matter-of-factly. She leaned over the carcass and poked it with her foot. "Definitely a pack of coyotes. This wasn't your deer from last night. This deer 's been here a while. Look at the maggots. Too much stink for a fresh kill. Your deer got away, but the coyotes will be back to finish this one."

"Let's get back to the road," Reid said. "I can't believe I fell over it. I didn't even see it."

Bonnie picked several maggots off Reid's back and showed them to him in the palm of her hand. In one quick move, Reid stripped off the shirt, wadded it up, and threw it as far as he could.

Bonnie smiled. "I'm waiting for the pants."

"You won't see that."

Bonnie laughed. "You're too much, Reid, and way too cute."

Seth took off his pack and picked through the contents before pulling out a rolled-up T-shirt. He tossed it to Reid. Seth walked into a copse of young birch trees to pick up the discarded shirt. He stopped suddenly and pointed. Reid and Bonnie joined him. There was an ornate wrought iron arch, leaning with age, which opened to a long-neglected cemetery of old stones. They approached the graves with caution. A crow cawed in one of the treetops. It was answered by other crows deeper in the forest.

"Was the warning for the birds or us?" Seth said.

"Holy shit!" Bonnie said. "I never knew this was here. Make a great spot for a bush party and easier to get to than the Flintstones."

They separated again and picked among the old grave markers, some of which leaned precariously. Others had toppled and lay flat on the ground. The engravings were difficult to read. The grass in the cemetery was low. Not that it had been mowed, but the grass was dried out and appeared not to grow. One family plot had a leaning wrought iron fence around it. The entire cemetery was surrounded by a low stone wall that Bonnie sat on. She looked toward the blue sky and watched the big trees sway in the breeze. The crow flew to a closer tree, perched for a moment, and cawed. Soon it was joined by others that sat silently, looking over the graves and them, seemingly with some interest.

Bonnie patted the top of the wall, indicating Reid should sit next to her. Reid joined her, and Seth plopped down next to Reid.

"Good day for a picnic," Bonnie said. "Nice spot, too. Let's break out the food I brought. Burgers."

"We're vegetarians," Seth said. "Sorry."

Bonnie reached inside the bag she had brought. "Don't be sorry. The store has a vegan section. They're plant burgers."

"You think of everything," Seth said.

"I usually get stuck eating the avocado salads before they go bad. When you bought two last night, I thought..."

"It's the food gay guys eat," Seth said.

"No. I thought anyone concerned about what they eat might appreciate a plant burger."

"Sorry. No offense."

"None taken," she said, passing out the burgers. Seth handed out water and protein bars.

They ate slowly and silently on the cemetery wall. The crows remained silent. Bonnie elbowed Reid in the ribs. Seth elbowed him from the other side.

"Reid Ruth! So hungry he swore off vegetarianism and feasted on a deer carcass the coyotes left," Bonnie said in a deep voice. "Now he runs with...the pack on moonlit nights."

"Vrooom! Vrooom!" Bonnie shouted after a pause.

Seth joined her and sang, "He's the leader of the pack!"

They laughed, and Bonnie and Reid leaned closer until their heads touched.

"I'm going to call you Babe, though," Bonnie said. She stroked his cheek. "You have such a baby face. Babe Ruth."

The crows squawked and took to the air, wheeling away

deeper into the forest. One bird remained to watch the cemetery. The trio collected their garbage and replaced it in Seth's pack. They studied the stone wall that surrounded the graveyard, especially where stones had tumbled from the top. Bonnie said the wall must be considerably old because there no mortar was used in its construction. They continued examining the gravestones. Bonnie took the notebook and recorded names she discerned that were still familiar in Mammoth, including birth and death dates. Reid snapped photographs. The television show liked using creepy photographs in episodes, regardless of the fact that they had nothing to do with the episode. Seth separated from his friends, imagining potential video shots and the placement of lights to make the area eerie at night. The producers loved shots of light piercing gnarled, old trees. The show could always use it as stock footage that could be added to any program.

"Over here," Bonnie cried, pointing to a tombstone. "Alphonse Hardwick. Born 1800. Died 1860. This is the guy who built the Forever Hideaway Inn. Originally, it was a stagecoach stop on the old route, with a tavern and hotel. And it was one of the first post offices. A little history lesson."

Bonnie stood on Hardwick's grave, copying the tombstone's information, when the ground collapsed and her feet disappeared underground. She squealed, looked around, and was swallowed to her knees. She felt herself balanced on a root. She swayed back and forth. Dirt from the surface spilled into the grave opening. The root snapped. She fell in, threw the notebook, and caught her hands on the sides. She clawed at the falling dirt, caught some thin tree roots. Her feet swung below in empty space. She smelled the dirt, decaying wood, and damp earth. She cried silently, unable to scream. She sank deeper into the pit. Dirt fell in her mouth. She coughed and struggled to breathe. The roots broke in her hands. She tried to find new ones as she clawed to stay above ground. Seth and Reid rushed to her side, stepped carefully near the collapsing ground, caught her under the arms, and with difficulty hauled her to the surface. The three lay on their backs between the tombstones, breathless, watching the crow look at them curiously with a cocked head.

Slowly, they crawled to the grave's edge and peered inside. Below, the sides of a rotting coffin stuck to the edge of the pit. Some fifteen feet below in sunlight from above, were the smashed boards of the coffin, top and bottom, lying in ruin on a mound of dirt. The coffin's stained and rotted cloth interior mixed with the shattered wood.

"It's a good thing we pulled you out," Seth said. "I wouldn't want to be stuck down there. It looks like a..."

"A mine gangway," Bonnie said. She spat more dirt from her mouth. "It goes left to right, back toward the highway. I'll bet you could walk through there." She turned her head to look at the two men on the grave's other side. "This area is honeycombed with old mine works. Most of them aren't on mining maps. They were called *bootleg* holes because the miners worked secretly underground in crazy places, so they wouldn't have to pay royalties to whoever owned the mineral rights to the land."

"Seems crazy and dangerous," Reid said. Seth wiped a smudge from her cheek.

"It was a way to make money," Bonnie said. "Life wasn't

easy here for most people. Then there was the Depression, and before that, labor troubles and strikes."

"One thing I didn't notice," Bonnie said, crawling again to the grave opening, "was remains. You'd think there should be at least some bones and a suit. Especially the femurs and a skull."

The men crawled to the grave's edge, too, and surveyed the ruined coffin. Any remains could be under that dirt," Seth said. "It looks like the miners tunneled under the cemetery without knowing bodies were above them."

"That's gruesome," Reid said. "Imagine having body fluids dripping on you."

They moved away from the grave and lay in the graveyard grass for several more minutes before gathering their things. Bonnie washed out her mouth with bottled water and removed a shoe, and emptied dirt from it. She and the men washed their faces. After they brushed the dirt from their clothes and hair, they retraced their steps back to the road, passed the dead deer, the cattails, and found the game trail. Finally, they scrambled up the bank to the highway and continued the now arduous job of logging the roadside memorials as they walked toward the car, still a half mile away. They were exhausted when they reached the car. Bonnie promised to show Seth and Reid the strange rock formations up the mountain where she had partied as a high schooler. Rain was forecast for the next day. The guys planned to do research at the Mammoth library and historical society. Bonnie had work.

Hardwick frowned from his spot behind the desk when the men entered the inn. "Did Miss Cleaver show you around?" He raised an eyebrow.

"How did you know?" Reid said.

"A little bird told me," Hardwick said, smiling. "The bar's open. You look like you need a drink."

"You're right. By the way, what is your first name, Mr. Hardwick?"

"You may call me Al."

"Al in Alfred or Alvin or...Alphonse?" Seth said.

"Just Al." The old man narrowed his eyes and then smiled. "Al is easier to remember. Nicer on the tongue."

Despite the small stall, the men showered together, dressed, and went down to the bar. There, they found Jill Piranna already with a few martinis under her belt. She greeted them nervously.

"Did you see the two old codgers who live on the third floor?" Jill said, helping herself to the bowl of peanuts just placed at their table. "They were trolling through the hall when I got back from my interview this afternoon. I don't think they wanted me to see them. Now, I think they're after me. Hardwick, too."

Jill looked around for anyone within earshot. She smelled of alcohol when she leaned close to Seth. "Mr. Heil is fucking Adolph 'Heil' Hitler," she hissed. "I know it. His head and mustache are shaved. Bald as a cue ball, but he's...so old, but there's no mistaking him. He came from Argentina, where the Nazis fled after World War II. Hardwick's old lady, or whatever she is, told me. I kind of trapped him when I ran up the steps to the second floor. He had nowhere to go, so he bowed and squeezed by me without a word. Then he went up to the third floor. The other one made it up the steps before I got a look at him.

"Last night they were moving through the hall, back and

forth, trying the doorknob to my room. Several times," she said, gnashing on a mouth full of peanuts, finally swallowing, and washing the nuts down with a swig of martini. "I could hear them mumbling. When I had enough of it, I went to the door and threw it open."

Seth shot a glance at Reid.

She reached for more peanuts.

Seth laughed. "Is this a joke?"

"Fuck no," Jill said. "I'm serious. It was the other one, Mr. King. He was nervous as hell. He said to me, 'Sorry, Miss, I am mistaken. I thought I was at Mr. Heil's door. We sometimes play Mahjong in the evening.'"

"And who is Mr. King? Elvis?"

"Exactly!" She slapped her palm on the tabletop, spraying spit and bits of peanut on the surface. Other drinkers looked their way. Old Hardwick and the woman chuckled from the bar doorway. "*Mr. King* is gray. Wrinkled like a prune. But it's *The King*. He plays his music all night. Sometimes he sings along with it. The voice is gone. You had to hear it."

Seth smiled. "Can't say that I did."

"You will hear it. And they peel. Like snakes. Just like Hardwick, only worse. Did you see his face? There were pieces of skin outside my door, even stuck to the doorknob. Little strips of skin on the carpet. Thin as onion skin. Later, the old lady saw me inspecting them. I was on the floor, poking them with my pen. She pulled a vacuum out of the closet and cleaned the hall immediately. Sucked up everything before I got samples."

"It's impossible. Elvis would be at least ninety. Hitler would be what? More than a hundred and thirty."

Jill raised her arms. "Hardwick is even older. He built this inn in the 1840s. I found a photo of him at the historical society. I think they're on to me. I'm leaving now. Booked a room for the night at another place. I gotta go. My car's already packed and I checked out." She picked up a large purse and left the dining room.

Reid raised his eyebrows.

"I think Ms. Piranna has a drinking problem," Seth said. "There goes our bar hopping with her. It would have been nice to see the gay bar."

Seth and Reid ate in the inn dining room, Caesar salads, without chicken, and beer. They returned to the room. Again, Seth saw legs in black cowboy boots moving rather quickly up the steps to the third floor. He found a thin strip of skin-like material hanging from the doorknob. It came off in his hands and disintegrated when he touched it. He traded stares with Reid. They stood outside the room and listened. A door upstairs opened and closed. They went inside and listened with the door cracked open. Another door opened and someone sneaked almost silently down the steps, stopped suddenly, and returned upstairs. Eventually, the door upstairs closed with a creak. Then they heard three distinct voices. One had a German accent. Another had a southern drawl. The third was Hardwick's. They seemed to argue, but the conversation was muffled. They had not seen Hardwick go to the third floor. Seth wondered if there was not another passage. After the muffled conversation stopped, they listened at the door for another fifteen minutes. Hardwick did not come down.

Seth and Reid sat on the bed and poured over the notebook's small script Bonnie recorded all day. They viewed the photographs on Reid's camera, including surreptitiously captured photos of Bonnie and Jill.

"Just for fun," Reid said. "I knew you'd want ones of Bonnie to show Benny as a potential witness on the show."

"Good thinking," Seth said. "She'll make one of our most photogenic *Paranormal, Anyone?* guests. I like her a lot."

"Me, too," Reid said. They hugged.

The next morning, the men drove in drizzle toward Mammoth to do their research when traffic was backed up at mile marker 66. State police, firemen, and an ambulance were at the scene near mile marker 66.6. Several cars in front of their vehicle, Bonnie Cleaver stood near a police cruiser talking to a trooper. As they approached, the trooper left Bonnie and walked past the fire truck.

Bonnie saw the men and jogged to them. "There's a car down the bank," she said. "Must have happened last night. I saw skid marks on my way to work and stopped. Then I called 911. The trooper said no one was in the car. Whoever it was must have walked away from the accident. Maybe got a ride."

"Or fell in a crevasse," the men said in unison. Seth looked from Reid to Bonnie. They remained silent.

"It's too uncanny," Seth said, finally. "Did you see the car?" he asked Bonnie.

"It was a red Toyota. Looked pretty new," Bonnie said.

"That's what Jill drove," Reid said. "I saw her car at the inn's parking lot.

"She was scared and wasted last night," Seth said. "We shouldn't have let her drive. She could have stayed in our room. I hope she's alright."

"I feel sorry for making fun of her. She was frightened," Reid said. All three looked at the ground in silence.

Eventually, the trooper called. The highway would reopen. The ambulance and then the firetruck pulled out.

"I'm on the other side," Bonnie said, pointing at the line of traffic in the opposing lane.

"I'll see you tomorrow morning at the inn."

After traffic moved, the trooper pulled out, too. Seth and Reid returned to their car and drove to the place they parked the day before, where the berm was wider. Seth wanted to look for evidence Jill didn't return to the road but in a confused state walked toward the cemetery. Seth and Reid slid down the bank from the highway and picked up the game trail. They walked, slowly, scanning the high grass.

"What exactly are we looking for?" Reid asked.

"Clues," Seth said. "Any evidence Jill came through here?"

"I don't see any evidence we came through here yesterday," Reid said. "This is a waste of time. We should have Bonnie here. All we're going to find is mud. End up wet again."

"Just look, okay," Seth said.

"You got it, Sherlock."

They passed the wet area with its cattails. The deer smelled just as bad, so they avoided it. Eventually, the cemetery came into sight, and they entered through its elaborate, leaning wrought iron arch. A crow perched silently above them, high in a tree. There was no sign of Jill. They separated and picked their way carefully among the tombstones, weaving back and forth. Reid was in a line with Hardwick's grave, which he saw in the distance. He noticed two lines in the ground where the grass receded to dirt and followed them. Nearing Hardwick's grave,

Reid motioned for Seth to join him. Ahead in the dirt was a woman's shoe.

Seth picked up the flat shoe, examined it, and turned it over in his hands.

"That wasn't here yesterday," Reid said. "We were all over this place." Reid pointed to the faint lines. "It looks like they continue to Hardwick's grave."

"See this," Seth said. "The heel is scuffed, as if it were drug. I wouldn't call that normal wear. I don't think you'd get that kind of scuff from a carpet or even hardwood."

They approached Hardwick's grave with caution. Seth feared another cave-in. They moved cautiously over the wet grass to the grave's lip. The coffin's remains were gone below. The pile of dirt in the gangway was trampled, covered with footprints. Another black flat shoe was half covered with dirt.

"Do you think she fell in?" Reid said.

"Jesus. She could be wandering around down there in the dark," Seth said. "But why would you walk into the dark without shoes?"

A noise behind startled them. Both turned quickly. It was a police officer accompanied by two men wearing jeans and plaid shirts. Both had scraggly beards. Seth stood and approached the officer. The cop said he was Mammoth Township Police Chief Mark Barton. Seth explained who he and Reid were, what they were doing in Mammoth, and gave the officer the shoe.

"There's another shoe in the open grave over there," Seth said. "It looks like a match to that one."

The trooper and two men walked to the edge of Hardwick's grave and looked into the gangway below. The crow had been joined noiselessly by other birds that now kept a silent vigil overhead.

"I don't see a shoe," the trooper said.

Seth moved to the grave cautiously. He was afraid they would all end up in the gangway if the earth gave way. When he peered in, the shoe was gone.

"I saw a shoe down there," Seth said. "So did Reid. We both saw it."

Reid nodded his head in agreement.

"There's no show there now," the cop said. "Maybe you imagined it."

"Maybe dirt fell in and covered it," Reid said. "That's more likely."

"We were here yesterday with a local girl who's been helping us with research," Seth said. "The ground collapsed under her. We were just able to pull her out. There was wood from a coffin in the hole yesterday. The shoe we found today was not here yesterday. We would have seen it. We ate lunch over there on the wall."

"And what about the drag marks I found?" Reid added quickly. "They weren't here yesterday."

"We know a woman named Jill Piranna owned the car over the bank," the cop said. "We think she was driving it. So, you think she dragged herself through the woods, into the cemetery, lost a shoe in the process, and fell into the collapsed grave."

"I don't think she dragged herself," Seth said. "Look at the heel on that shoe. See the scuff mark? I think *she* was dragged through here and thrown into the grave."

The cop lifted his wide-brimmed hat and wiped his forehead. "What would be the point in that? Anyway, you'd see her at the bottom of that shaft instead of a second shoe."

"Suppose she hit the soft dirt in the hole, got up, and walked along the gangway," Seth said. "There are a few possibilities."

"Even if she had a flashlight on her, the gangway probably doesn't go far," the chief said, removing his hat and scratching his scalp vigorously. "It's pitch black down there once you leave that little patch of sunlight. Years ago, miners dug along coal seams, which twisted up and down from the earth, shifting millions of years ago. Any gangway might go up and down, like most of Route 125. The low areas are probably flooded. The upgrades are near the surface and might have collapsed. If you walk around these hills, you'll see the depressions; they're usually round and might go down anywhere from a couple to twenty feet deep. Maybe deeper. They're easy to spot. They look like bowls."

"Somebody moved the body," Reid said. "I think it's rather obvious."

"After she went in the hole?" the chief said.

"Not necessarily," Reid continued. "Suppose they just drug her away. Threw the second shoe in the grave when it came off. Maybe they didn't bother to look for the first one, even though it was over there." Eid pointed toward the drag marks.

The men in plaid shirts sniggered.

"Old Man Hardwick said she was staying at the inn," the chief said. "She was drunk last night. There was a commotion upstairs in the hall. He thought she might have had an argument with you two. Then she checked out and left in a hurry. He thought there might have been something going on among you. Hardwick called it shenanigans."

"That's crazy," Reid said, stepping forward to face the cop. "*We* are a couple."

The men in plaid shirts sniggered again. Seth shot them a look, and they quieted.

"Jill was here before we arrived," Seth said. "She was doing a newspaper article on a local guy who trains cadaver dogs."

"That would be Bill Morrison," one of the guys in a plaid shirt said. "Good man."

"As far as I know, she got her interview and was going back to the AP office in Harrisburg, where she was headquartered. She might have been a little tipsy yesterday, but she intended to get another room in Mammoth for the night. If there was any commotion, it was between her and Hardwick, possibly a couple of his guests who tried to get into her room."

"Hardwick said she harassed two elderly gentlemen who live at the inn. She wanted to write stories on them. Take their photos," the cop said.

"That's incredible," Reid said. "She was frightened, especially of them, when she left."

"Is that your car parked off the highway?" the cop said, pointing over his shoulder back to the road.

"It's a renter," Seth said.

"Where'd you pick up the damage on the front end?" the cop said.

"There was no damage." Seth looked toward Reid. "Was there, Reid?"

"That car was a cherry for a rental," Reid said.

"Not anymore. Let's take a look," the cop said.

The chief started back toward the road. He told the men in plaid shirts to continue combing the woods for any sign of Jill.

They retraced their steps with the cop in silence. As they clambered to the top of the bank near the road's edge, Seth saw the rental car had a dent on the left front fender.

"Fuck!" Seth said. "That wasn't there when we parked."

"You think somebody stopped along the road and backed into you?" the cop said.

Seth thought the chief sounded skeptical.

"I have no clue what happened," Seth said.

The chief asked about the men's plans. He said he had already asked the state police crime scene investigators to take paint samples from the rental's damaged front fender.

"You can't believe I forced her off the road," Seth said. "We were at the inn all night. There must be witnesses. She left yesterday. We were at the inn all night."

"We're checking into that. Among others, the two elderly men Piranna allegedly harassed are giving statements through their attorneys."

"Their attorneys!"

"They were so upset that their doctors advised them neither to leave their rooms nor accept guests. Even their Mahjong games have been put on hold."

It was noon when Seth and Reid reached the Mammoth Historical Society. The building was closed for lunch. They waited an hour until it reopened. The curator and two volunteers on duty had already heard about the accident on Route 125. The men dug into the archives. They sat at a table usually reserved for genealogists and read various materials, including local history books and letters, taking notes through the afternoon. There was a book of old photographs preserved in clear plastic sleeves. Among its pages were photos of old buildings, including the one-time stage stop that was now the Forever Hideaway Inn. Photos showed it under construction in various stages, including with workers who stopped for lunch. Curiously, one sleeve was empty. Seth checked the index and found that the photo should have shown Alphonse Hardwick, who built the stage stop and tavern in 1840. Seth asked the curator, Mrs. Delores Witherspoon, about the missing photograph.

"Not another one," Mrs. Witherspoon said. She scratched out a note on her tablet. "I was a teacher for thirty-seven years and then was convinced to take this position."

The volunteers traded glances and disappeared into the exhibits. Witherspoon was tall and thin, with a blouse that covered her neck in ruffles. Her auburn-colored hair was thin, which let her glossy scalp show through. Seth thought she looked like a peevish old maid.

"It was supposed to be a part-time job, a couple of days a week, but now it's full-time plus. I never saw so much theft since I arrived here."

"The photo?" Seth said. "Is there another copy?"

"Of course not. It was an original," the old woman said. "There was a pretty young thing here a few days ago asking about it. I wonder whether she slipped it out of here. You know, she's the one who drove her car down the bank on 125 last night. Drunk, I suppose. Maybe they'll find my photo in her luggage."

"I hope not," Seth said.

"Hope they don't find her luggage?" The old woman raised her eyebrows.

"I hope she didn't take your photograph."

Seth and Reid walked to Mammoth Free Public Library,

arriving an hour before it closed. Abbreviated summer hours. The library had fewer items that interested them. With the help of the reference librarian, they were able to get through the documents before the library closed. They decided to eat downtown and avoid the inn's dining room and bar. When they returned to the inn, they went directly to their room. The strains of "Love Me Tender" were barely audible, drifting down the third-floor steps. Seth returned to the bar to buy a six-pack of beer. Hardwick, behind his desk as usual, motioned for Seth to join him. The man looked different. There was color in his cheeks, and his skin no longer peeled but looked almost youthful.

"I heard Miss Piranna was lost in an accident," he said. "Such a shame." He fanned himself with several envelopes.

"She might have got a ride back to Harrisburg," Seth said.

Hardwick gave Seth a startled look. "Oh, yes. I hope so, but that stretch of highway has a reputation of being unkind to travelers."

"We'll hope for the best."

"Indeed, Mr. Bonney. You know, the chief of police inquired about you and your...friend. I suspect he will want to talk to you."

"We already talked to him this morning."

"Wonderful," the old man said, nodding his head. "Good luck with everything." They traded stares for a moment before Seth returned to the room with the beer and placed the writing desk's heavy chair under the doorknob for extra security.

The men sat on the bed and went over their notes from the afternoon. They talked about a logical explanation into the disappearance of Jill Piranna.

Finally, Reid said, "We haven't done too much work on the Blood Path Cult."

"I know," Seth said. "I think these disappearances are a bigger story."

In the morning, Seth and Reid met Bonnie in the inn parking lot. They loaded another lunch into Seth's pack and drove in Bonnie's Jeep to mile marker 66.0. At mile marker 66.4 Bonnie pulled off the highway and entered an old mining road that rose slowly and paralleled Route 125. The dirt road was rutted and narrow. Sapling limbs slapped and rubbed the jeep's sides as they drove slowly, rocking side to side as they maneuvered around large holes and small boulders. A shiny black snake, a four-footer, slid across the road in front of them. Farther up a rabbit zigzagged back and forth, stopping several times for a second, before finally darting into the bush.

"It's a good thing we brought your Jeep," Reid said. "Seth's car would have bottomed out on the first curve. What's in the cooler?"

"Yuengling Lager. We're going to Flintstones. For old times' sake."

Eventually, the road opened onto a grassy field that sloped upward. To their right was a large spill bank, black with coal silt as fine as sand and rocks and slate of all sizes, an ugly reminder of the discarded refuse of anthracite mining. It reminded Seth of a moonscape. Bonnie turned the car around in a wide circle, plowing through the high grass, and parked near a rusted dragline bucket, a relic from strip mining days.

"This is it, boys," Bonnie said. "We walk from here. Just be careful where you step. Snakes."

"Christ," Reid said. "Are any poisonous?"

Bonnie laughed. "Probably not. Mostly black snakes. Make some noise with your feet and they'll get out of your way."

"Great," Reid said.

"I'll go first," she said. "You want a beer before we start. It's another hot one."

"Probably not," Seth said. "We're on the clock."

Bonnie said, "If we were in a nice restaurant, not the Forever Hideaway Inn, and I was giving you a killer paranormal story and wanted a drink, would you join me?"

"When you explain it that way, break some out," Seth said.

Bonnie pulled sixteen-ounce lager cans from the cooler and snapped them from their plastic rings. They opened the beer and touched cans.

"To the hunt!" Reid said.

"To the hunt!" chimed Seth and Bonnie. They smiled at one another.

Seth and Reid applied sunscreen lotion and passed the bottle to Bonnie. Seth pulled on his pack, and they followed Bonnie uphill, skirting the spill bank. The dirt soon gave way to rocky soil, then boulders. They climbed around and over boulders until they hit a path Bonnie took.

"Game trail?" Seth said.

Bonnie turned her head to him and smiled. "Old beer trail."

The climb grew steeper, the boulders larger. Several times one of the explorers slipped.

"I see what you mean about coming up here in the dark," Reid said.

"We used to have a long rope on this part," Bonnie said. "You could hold on, and it helped keep anyone from getting lost."

They reached a flat area where they finished the pounders and crushed the cans. The empties went into Seth's pack.

"We always had a fire here," Bonnie said, stopping at a ring of stones and the charcoal remains of an old fire. "It was a signal that the party was on and already started."

Above, up a short rise was another level area where a fantastic array of giant flat rocks, piled and toppled on one another, spread out over the top of the hill, as if they grew from the ground. One gigantic slab sat across two huge boulders standing on end, making a space ten feet high underneath. The ground in front of the opening was smooth and appeared to have been cleared intentionally, and around this space in a circle were piles of rocks and boulders of all sizes, too large to have been placed there, some ground smooth by the glaciers' immense weight and force thousands of years ago.

"This is what was left over after the glaciers melted," Bonnie said, pointing proudly at the piled rocks. "The Flintstones! Do you see a resemblance to the cartoon architecture?"

"This is insane," Reid said. He turned on his camera that was slung around his neck, and started to shoot.

Bonnie smiled, as if a flood of memories had suddenly returned. "We always had a fire here, too, where you can still see the charcoal. Sometimes we roasted hot dogs and potatoes. That hole over there, which you can barely see now, was where the keg went, covered with ice in the summer, of course. One of the guys who could weld made a special cart for the kegs, which made it easier to roll them up the hill."

Bonnie turned in a circle. After a moment's pause, she said, smiling, pointing, "Around the back, up there, I can show you the spot I had my first *experience* with a guy. It was a night in

November, after a football game, and cold as hell. A week later, that highway took him, my first love. Lately, I keep my boyfriend in my bedroom dresser."

"Really, Bonnie. That's more information than we needed to know," Reid said, rolling his eyes.

"Did your boyfriend disappear like Jill?" Seth said.

"No, he was in the car with two other boys. The welder and our quarterback."

"What did your boyfriend do?" Seth said.

She smiled a moment and said, "He was funny. He made me laugh." Her smile turned to a frown. Tears welled in her eyes and flowed down her cheeks as she turned away. "I'm sorry, guys."

Reid stepped closer, turned Bonnie around, and embraced her.

Bonnie wiped tears from her eyes and cheeks. She kissed Reid on the cheek. "Thanks, babe. It seems so long ago, but I still get emotional. I haven't been up here since after my high school graduation."

They explored the Flintstones interior and returned to the edge of the hill. Bonnie pointed to other rock formations below, the cathedral and the coven, smaller and not as popular as the Flintstones.

"What's over the top?" Seth said. "Above the Flintstones."

"I don't know. Never been there," Bonnie said. "Although there is supposed to be crevasses up there and somewhere a rattlesnake den. I don't know anyone who went over the top. I don't know if any of it is true. It sounds like the kind of things you'd tell a high school girl to scare her."

Seth wanted to see what was on the other side, get a view of the terrain below, and the likelihood that someone could wander undetected. They picked their way up the rocky slope. Reid snapped photos all the way. They ate their lunches at the summit, and each had another beer, warm by now. Starting downhill, Reid spied a concrete structure below, partially covered with vines.

"It's an old ventilation shaft," Bonnie said. "The mines were like the atmosphere on another planet—pockets of methane, which is flammable, even explosive, and black damp, which is a mixture of carbon dioxide and other gases you can't breathe. They can kill a person in seconds."

"That sounds pleasant," Reid said.

"In the old days, large swinging doors were installed that could be opened or closed to increase ventilation. Eventually, big fans were added to move the air."

"So, they ran electricity up here?" Seth said.

"They did, through the mines. It was a shorter distance. After the mines closed, the fans were removed or fell inside," Bonnie said.

"We should explore," Reid said.

"I don't think so," Bonnie said. "They're dangerous.

"How so?" He looked peeved, as if she were trying to spoil his fun.

"Well, for example, there can be cave-ins, which you're already familiar with, and unbreathable air in spots. A candle won't burn in black damp because there's not enough oxygen. If a mine opens on the surface, maybe a bear or other predator might make it a home. It's also the perfect place for spiders and snakes and that sort of thing."

"Maybe even Bigfoot," Seth said, smiling, winking at Bonnie.

"How do you know about that theory?" Bonnie asked.

"We did a Bigfoot episode near Seattle a few years ago," Seth said. "I was new on the job, so they sent me on the shoot."

"Interesting," Bonnie said.

"Not really. I was the go-for queer hoping to keep a job. You know how many coffee shops there are in Seattle? Some of the guys were homophobic, especially the local rubes they used to haul our stuff. It wasn't one of my favorite assignments."

Seth remembered the trip with bitterness. His luggage was lost and he was air-sick on the flight west. Benny declined to replace his bag and clothing, claiming he was careless. Seth, however, blamed the homophobic roadies.

They reached the concrete bunker, about ten-feet square, with the top and downhill side open. The concrete was thick. Rusted rebar jutted from the cement where it had crumbled. Inside the bunker was a yawning black hole. Seth dropped rocks into the darkness, but they never seemed to hit bottom.

"No fan," Bonnie said. "The state filled or capped most of these shafts, so nobody'd fall in. Looks like they forgot about this one. It's not very accessible."

"Do you hear that?" Reid said. "A noise from the pit."

The trio moved close to the edge and listened.

"I don't hear anything," Seth said.

"Listen!" Reid hissed.

"I hear it now," Bonnie said. "It's a chant. Sounds medieval. Gregorian, maybe."

"Yes. So do I," Reid said. "Sounds diabolic."

"I don't hear a thing," Seth said.

They listened another minute before pulling away from the hole.

"Where's it coming from?" Reid said.

"Could be from far away, echoing off the rocks, time after time," Seth said. "Shit, it could be some spelunker's CD playing."

"This is too weird," Bonnie said. "Old coal mines are not a place for spelunkers."

"Are there any ventilation shafts closer to Mammoth?" Seth asked.

"No open ones I know of," Bonnie said.

"It should be worth investigating," Seth said.

They took one more look in front of them, a forest that extended to the horizon. No roads. No clearings. No homes. They climbed back over the summit and headed down through the Flintstones and back to Bonnie's Jeep; then crossed the high grass and drove down the switchback mining road to Route 125. It was late afternoon, and they were tired, hungry, and thirsty. They stopped at a bar outside the city, Route 125 Pub, and took a booth away from the bar. They ordered plant burgers and drank Yuengling Lager. With hours of daylight left, Seth said they needed to return to the cemetery and caved-in grave.

Revived after lunch, Bonnie drove them back to Mile Marker 66.6. They parked on the wide berm and plowed downhill back to the cemetery. The graveyard was quiet and cool, despite the day's heat. A single crow sat on a treetop like a guardian for the dead. Its head bent toward the trio as they walked through the wrought iron arch. They had little trouble finding the hole. They kneeled and crawled cautiously to the lip. Immediately, they heard the chant, louder, clearer, closer now.

"It sounds like Latin," Reid said.

"You sure? I can't make it out," Seth said.

"I'm sure it's Latin. I was an altar boy when I was in Catholic school," Reid said.

"You in a robe. How sweet," Seth said. "If we only had a way..."

"I know how to get down there," Bonnie said. "I'll meet you at the inn tomorrow morning."

———

THE NEXT MORNING there was still no news on Jill Piranna. She had not returned to her office in Harrisburg.

Seth and Reid waited in the parking lot when Bonnie arrived. She showed them a collapsing ladder they could use to reach the gangway from the cemetery surface. It was her dad's. She also showed them oxygen and explosive gas detectors she brought from home.

"My dad was a mine inspector before he bought the store," Bonnie said. She wagged her head. "Somehow, he forgot to give these back and I knew where they were. They're charged and calibrated. Thank you, Bonnie!"

They drove to Mile Marker 66.6 and parked the Jeep. Seth carried the compact, telescoping ladder while they retraced their way to the cemetery. A half dozen crows sat in various trees surrounding the walled-in cemetery. The trio moved around the grave carefully. There was no audible chanting.

Bonnie gave each of the men a baseball hat purloined from

the store and a detector that pinned to their shirts. She placed a hat on her head, too. Seth extended the ladder and eased it into the grave. Dirt fell from the sides as he positioned the ladder. It was necessary for them to lie on their stomachs, inch backwards, and extend their legs into the hole to catch the top rung. Carefully, slowly, they climbed down the ladder, dirt falling from above on their heads, and stepped on the dirt pile. Bonnie handed out flashlights. A cool breeze flowed through the gangway. Water dripped from above.

The gangway sloped down across the cemetery above. Their flashlights shined on puddles, then a pool covering the floor that extended to the limits of their flashlights.

"Who knows how deep it gets," Seth said. "I don't want to fall into one of those pits. Let's go up the grade."

"I'm not a swimmer," Reid added. "I vote for uphill."

"Good choice," Bonnie said.

They proceeded uphill into the darkness. They found the remnants of the smashed coffin, which splintered more when they stepped on the wood.

"Well, we know what happened to this stuff. Somebody moved it," Reid said. He pretended to surf on a long piece of wood until it broke under his weight. He jumped but his feet got tangled in the coffin's cloth interior, and Seth caught him before he went down.

"I see you don't surf, either," Bonnie said.

"The only water this boy gets into has to be in a bathtub, hot tub, or highly chlorinated swimming pool—shallow end, of course," Reid quipped.

Their monitor lights remained green, which indicated there was sufficient oxygen and no explosive gases. The air moved in the direction they walked. The flashlights illuminated the walls and ceilings, including large, old tree trunks acting as columns at the tunnel sides that supported cross timbers that held up the ceiling. Water dripped on their heads. The ceiling, floor, and walls were moist. Occasionally, rocks littered the floor where the walls partially collapsed. At one point the gangway rose steeply before eventually flattening out. The patch of sunlight from the grave opening was no longer visible. They stopped to drink water from plastic bottles. More rocks fell from the wall when Reid leaned against it.

"We must have passed under the highway," Reid said. "We've been walking for a while."

"Thirty-five minutes," Bonnie said. "I'm keeping track."

"Hell, we could almost be back to the inn," Reid said. "Wouldn't it be funny if we came out in Hardwick's wine cellar. Drinks are on me."

They continued until the tunnel split. They took the left leg, which turned and rose sharply. "Looks like the miners followed a coal vein this way," Bonnie said. "Look, the ceiling drops and it ends. Probably the coal ran out or wasn't worth digging."

They returned to the gangway and followed the right tunnel, continued upward. Suddenly, in the distance an orange glow was visible. The chanting started again. The three stared at one another.

"Don't shine your light down there," Seth whispered. "Someone might see it. One flashlight. Keep it pointed at the ground in front, so we don't trip. Cut the light if you hear a noise."

They held hands and proceeded slowly along the gangway.

The tunnel had leveled and turned slightly to the left. The turn had obscured the light. Now it appeared they were much closer to its source. The chanting grew louder. There were voices ahead. The tunnel opened to a larger space illuminated by torches. A partial wall collapse pushed wooden wall supports across the tunnel, providing a place to hide. Seth turned off his flashlight. They peered through the spaces between the heavy timbers.

The chanting stopped. Bonnie gasped. Jill Piranna's naked body lay on a large, flat stone in the middle of the opening. The abdomen was opened with a ragged gash and the organs removed. The body cavity was filled with a thick, dark viscous liquid. Jill's body had withered, as if drained of blood. Her skin was glossy, as if it had been basted for roasting. Jill's feet were dirty and bloody after being dragged across the cemetery and then through the mine. The space was lit by torches and black candles. Behind the altar stood a large stone goat-like creature that leaned out from the wall. The face seemed to leer at the dozen people dressed in black robes who faced the altar with their backs to the trio. The worshipers were silent.

Dressed in a long red robe, Hardwick moved behind the stone and taking an ornate ladle, he spooned the thick, dark cavity liquid into a similarly ornate chalice. He raised the chalice as a priest would during communion and turned to place it as an offering for the hoofed devil. He prayed silently for a moment and turned back to the altar.

"You may approach and receive the youth of this young one," Hardwick intoned, "in the name of our god."

The worshipers filed forward to the altar. One by one they kissed the corpse, bit a piece of flesh from it, and held out a goblet, which Hardwick filled from the ladle with the syrupy concoction contained in the body cavity. Seth gagged. Finally, Hardwick filled a goblet for himself. After all had been served, they raised their goblets in unison, as Hardwick had done, in tribute to the goat god.

"We drink to thine service," they chanted in unison, led by Hardwick.

They drank the foul-looking liquid and filed around the back of the altar, where each genuflected, rose, and kissed the goat's hooves.

"We are anointed, revived, and made youthful again," Hardwick said. "Drink all you can hold of the master's brew."

Suddenly, the mass appeared to have ended, while the robed people gathered around the corpse, as if happy hour had been declared, and refilled their goblets.

"Das scmeck immer so gut," Mr. Heil called, smacking his lips and dancing a few steps of a jig. He smiled widely, revealing the kind of discolored teeth Hardwick had.

The aged man did indeed resemble Hitler, Seth thought.

Mr. King stepped up to the corpse and looked down, as if he mourned the reporter's death, even after he tried to force his way into her room.

"Thank you. Thank you very much, Missy," Mr. King said, as Hardwick refilled his goblet with a smile.

Bonnie had turned away from the tunnel opening in disgust and tried to avoid vomiting, her hand cupped over her mouth. Reid was transfixed. His eyes stared. His mouth hung open. Seth had been present for an exorcism during his first season with the show and saw a demon tear itself from a boy. He, too, was absorbed with the proceedings.

As the worshipers mingled, Seth recognized the police chief, squeezing Jill's nipple. The old woman from the inn patted and examined Jill's foot. The police chief's cronies, the men with plaid shirts, were recognizable in their robes, refilling and clinking their goblets.

Mr. Heil placed a hand on top of his head, griped the scalp, and pulled it forward. The skin came off in his hand like a mask, revealing new pinkish derma. The disintegrating skin that included his entire scalp resembled a snakeskin in his hand. He examined it for a moment and dropped it on the ground. Then he pulled his arms inside the robe and vigorously rubbed his torso and arms while his head shook. More skin sloughed to the ground from under the garment. Others started to peel their skins. Then they helped one another with back skin, leg skin, stomach skin, lifting robes to tear off shedding epidermis. The worshipers howled in delight as a pile of peeled skin accumulated on the ground.

They grinned and returned their arms through their sleeves, so their pinkish hands were visible. They returned to the altar and drank more, gulping the heavy, dark liquid as if it were a drug, until the body cavity was empty. A few licked at Jill's sides or scraped their cups against her spine to capture every drop. They laughed and bellowed long, loud burps, which seemed to please them, but the foul smell of blood and rotting flesh filled the chamber and seeped down the gangway. The odor made Bonnie and Reid vomit.

Seth recalled a similar stench when he witnessed the exorcism. Still, it took a great effort to hold down his lunch from Pub 125. Seth guided Bonnie and Reed down the gangway. They pulled out their flashlights and moved quickly back toward the open grave. Water dripping from the gangway ceiling increased. Little rivulets ran down the floor ahead of them. Water also seeped from the walls. As they approached Hardwick's grave, thunder crashed above ground. Lightning flashes lit up the ground for an instant in the shaft under the grave. Rain fell in gray sheets through the hole. Water filled the low spot and was knee deep when they reached the opening. A cave-in from above farther down the slope dropped another old coffin in the water. It floated half submerged and bumped against the ladder, threatening to knock it over.

Seth pushed the coffin away, caught the ladder, and forced Reid up. Reid climbed quickly, panting, moaning, sending a torrent of mud and water on Seth's head. Next, he got Bonnie on the ladder. She crawled up slowly, lifting one leg at a time and pulling up the other one painfully slow. After she finally scrambled over the grave's edge, sending down more dirt, Seth climbed. He lost his grip several times on the wet metal rungs and slipped down. While he hung on for a moment, the floating coffin was back, rapping against the ladder. Suddenly the ladder pitched sideways, but Bonnie, who lay on her stomach on the ground, was able to swing it back and let Seth finish the climb from the grave. Seth and Bonnie lay on the ground panting. Reid stood nearby, bent over, hands on his knees, gasping for air.

More thunder crashed, and lightning lit the cemetery. Hail fell. The larger pieces hurt, slanting in from the west and the trio found shelter behind a large tombstone. The storm raged for another fifteen minutes before it stopped suddenly. A single crow flew from the forest and perched on a limb over the cemetery. It cocked its head and cawed lowly, as if interested in the muddy trio. They pulled out the ladder and collapsed it. It was almost dark as they gathered their packs and returned to the highway over pooling water. They sat in Bonnie 's Jeep, trying to catch their wind. They drank bottled water and ate protein bars.

The car windows had steamed up and they didn't see the police car approach. It stopped on the highway next to the Jeep. The police lights alerted them, and Bonnie rolled down her driver's side window. A young officer asked if they had broken down.

"I had the boys up to the Flintstones," Bonnie called. "We got caught in the storm. We're just taking a breather before we go back to town."

"Make sure you de-fog those windows before you pull out," the cop said. "You don't want to get rear ended out here."

Bonnie smiled and the cop turned off his lights and drove away. Bonnie returned the guys back to the inn. They were all tired and already sore. Bonnie drove off, heading for home. The inn's front door was open. The large building was silent. The bar and dining room were closed. The men crept behind the front desk, which Hardwick had always guarded with his presence, as well as the door behind the desk. Seth opened the door to what appeared to be a long, narrow closet, but it was empty. They followed another door at the back, which opened on a staircase that led down. The basement, Seth wondered. They proceeded slowly down the steps. Seth tried to imagine an excuse should they be discovered in such an obviously out-of-bounds spot. Perhaps he could tell Hardwick they were looking for a creepy set to conduct on-camera interviews. That might work.

The basement was dark and smelled dusty. Old furniture

was covered with tarps. There was a teetering stack of suitcases, some old, some newer, visible under one tarp. Seth lifted the corner to get a better view. Reid took photos. Seth lifted the top suitcase to the floor. It was heavy and contained clothing. He pulled out another, older valise, from the middle. It contained clothes, too, old-fashioned dresses, a bra, and deteriorating girdle.

"What the fuck," Seth said. "Where'd all this shit come from? Some of it looks like it's been here for years."

Reid shrugged.

Next to the suitcases was a pile of purses, some showing extreme age with creased and cracked leather. Then they heard the chanting. It sounded the same as they had heard in the mine. They followed the sound through the basement, winding their way around and between old furniture, stacks of folded clothes, and shoes thrown haphazardly in a pile. Again, some shoes seemed old. Included were sneakers, hiking boots, and running shoes. Eventually, they reached a large wooden door. With difficulty they opened it a crack and listened. There were more downward steps. They stood there for 10 minutes. The chanting seemed to be at the bottom of the steps. Suddenly the chanting stopped. There were voices, even laughter.

"I'll bet it's fucking choir practice," Reid said.

"Then it's noon tomorrow," Hardwick said from below.

Seth pushed the door closed and they moved back through the basement and up the steps to the inn lobby. They went directly to their room, showered, and feasted on protein bars and leftover beer.

———

THE NEXT MORNING Bonnie's Jeep was found crashed into a tree on Route 125. She was missing. News of her disappearance arrived with the mailman. Hardwick took the news in silence behind his desk as he thumbed through the mail. The old woman tsk-tsked from her perch nearby. Hardwick's complexion was pink and younger looking. Age lines had vanished. His wrinkled skin and eye bags were smooth.

Seth heard the news as he walked into the dining room for breakfast, a few minutes after Reid. The mailman had paused for a quick cup of coffee and told what he knew between sips. Seth and Reid stared at each other for a moment and left the inn immediately. They stood in the parking lot next to the rental car.

"We can't go to the police," Reid said. "The chief is part of the cult. Do you want to drive to her car?"

"That would take too long," Seth said. "We know where she is. We have to get back into that basement, without Hardwick knowing, before it's too late. At this point we can't trust anyone."

"Maybe there's a window or an old coal chute. Even a door to the basement," Reid said.

They walked behind the inn along a serpentine path. There was a short box hedge beside the path and other neatly trimmed shrubs and beds of growing lilies. They crossed a newly cut lawn and hugged the inn's side, where hostas grew in the shade along the stone foundation. A Bilko door leading to the base-ment on the back of the building was locked. Two windows had bars over the glass.

Hardwick appeared from around the inn's corner and surprised the men.

"Looking for something?" he intoned, sounding friendly.

"Just shooting angles," Seth said.

"I see. The inn is historic. You must believe you have a story here then?"

"Definitely," Reid said.

"Have you contacted your producers yet?"

"Not yet," Seth said. "We have a few more details to work out before we give the boys back home our report."

"How wonderful technology must be," Hardwick said, showing his discolored teeth. "It's all a little beyond me. I only know enough to operate this inn." Hardwick backed away from the men. He bowed several times. "Excuse me, gentlemen. I hope you find what you're looking for...that is, the perfect camera angle."

Hardwick walked off briskly. Seth and Reid continued to circle the building. On the side facing the road was a round wooden cover in the lawn. Seth moved to it cautiously. The wood crumbled in his hand, and he picked off the cover and threw it a few feet away. A pipe underground almost two feet in diameter pointed downward.

"This must lead to the basement," Seth said. He looked around to see if anyone watched them and slipped into the pipe feet first. Reid followed. The pipe was surprisingly clean, and they slid down slowly, trying to make no noise. They dropped out of the pipe and onto a coal pile that had a thick coating of brown dust. They hadn't seen this coal pile and the nearby defunct boiler when they explored the basement last night. In the dim light they saw the mountain of suitcases in the distance and moved toward it. They picked up their trail from last night and moved by the stacks of folded clothes and heap of shoes to which was added on the top a new pair of muddied hiking boots.

Seth pointed to the pile and said, "Bonnie."

Reid shook his head.

They tugged on the wooden door until it opened enough for them to squeeze through. A wan light shone from the bottom of the staircase. The air was still. As they proceeded down the steps, Reid stopped and held up a finger. Then he pointed downward. Seth heard mumbling from below. They continued down until they reached the cult chamber opening. Mr. Heil and Mr. King sat at the base of the altar, munching thoughtfully on the discarded skin from the ceremony. Across the room was an old gurney to which a naked Bonnie Cleaver was strapped. Reid gasped. Bonnie was unconscious, but Seth could see she was breathing. Mr. Heil rose and looked around, as if he thought he had heard something. He motioned toward the stairs and Mr. King followed.

Seth and Reid retreated and squeezed into the shadows under the stairs. Mr. Heil and Mr. King stood near the stairs, as if straining their ears to hear. Seth and Reid breathed in short, soundless breaths. For the first time Seth got a look at the two old men. They did indeed appear to be older versions of Adolph Hitler and Elvis. Both had pink complexions. They licked their lips as if they were children expecting a dessert that was now visible before them. Mr. Heil motioned with his head toward the stairs. Mr. King nodded in agreement. They both pulled tasers from their pockets and tiptoed up the steps.

As soon as they heard the heavy door close, Seth and Reid ran to Bonnie. They shook her shoulder, and she moaned.

Slowly, she regained consciousness while Seth and Reid unbuckled the straps.

"You feel cold," Seth said, rubbing her arms and legs.

"I'm numb."

"We can't go back up the steps," Seth said. "At least not yet. We'll have to hide in the mine."

"They'll look there," Reid said.

"Then we'll have to go through the flooded area beyond the grave. It's our only chance."

"I'm so cold," Bonnie moaned.

Seth said, "I'm going back and getting her shoes and some clothes." He returned up the steps, pushed open the wooden door, and crept into the basement. There was no sign of Mr. Heil and Mr. King. He pulled dusty clothes from the stack of folded garments and picked up Bonnie's hiking boots. He ran back through the basement, down the steps, and into the chamber. Bonnie went behind the altar under the goat statue to get dressed. The men turned away from her.

"Not that you didn't already get an eyeful," Bonnie said, fighting whatever drug she was given. "I'm glad you guys are gay."

"You think that matters," Seth said.

"No, it doesn't. You just saved my life. We should have left the ladder in the hole."

"Shoulda, woulda, coulda," Reid said. "Let's get in the mine."

They crossed the chamber and fled into the gangway, passed the wooden wall they had hidden behind during the cult ceremony. Seth and Reid each held Bonnie under an arm to help her walk. In places her feet dragged or she tripped over rocks. Most of the water from the storm had receded, but the floor was muddy, and their shoes left noticeable prints. Water dripped on them from overhead. It seemed they walked for hours, Seth thought, and he wondered if they had not taken a wrong turn, even though there weren't any. Their exhaled breath came in little plumes of water vapor.

Then a shaft of light appeared in the distance from the open grave. Although the water ahead had receded somewhat, the intact coffin still bobbed in the black water and shards of Hardwick's shattered coffin surrounded it like so much flotsam. They had to cross the water to reach the grave. The men loaded Bonnie on the floating coffin and pulled it across the flooded area. The water rose to their armpits, and they stumbled occasionally over unseen debris on the mine floor. Eventually, the water level lowered, and they were able to get Bonnie back on her feet. They walked silently, stopping occasionally to listen for noise. About one hundred yards after the open grave, the water level rose again, this time to the ceiling, making farther progress impossible.

"There's no way to know if there's any pockets of breathable air down the shaft," Seth said, pointing at the ceiling.

Bonnie nodded her head in agreement. Still woozy, she could make a sane decision.

"We'll have to wait it out here," Reid said, "and hope they don't follow us through that other pool."

In the distance there was a noise. Voices and the sound of an aluminum ladder extended.

"They're coming down the hole," Seth whispered. "They think they can cut us off from both sides of the gangway. This might be our chance."

Seth and Reid helped Bonnie toward Hardwick's grave. The sound of voices receded. Where the water receded, they walked Bonnie through ankle-deep water under the grave. An aluminum ladder was in place under the shaft.

Seth said, "We'll climb out of here and go back to the highway, flag down a ride, and try to get back to Bonnie's store. We'll be safe there."

Bonnie nodded in agreement. "So cold," she managed to say.

"It'll be warmer above," Reid said. "You'll see."

She nodded again and hugged Reid.

Reid climbed first. Bonnie followed immediately and Seth went third, trying to keep her in motion and prevent her from falling. Their progress up the ladder was slow and laborious. The ladder legs sank into the muddy floor. Bonnie's legs were like rubber and her fingers had difficulty gripping the rungs. They advanced a step at a time, waiting a moment in between for Bonnie to balance herself. Eventually, Reid clambered over the top. He pulled Bonnie up and over, with Seth pushing her buttocks from below. Seth flopped out of the hole and all three lay on the ground panting. They got up as soon as they caught their breath and started toward the highway. Seth and Reid each took one of Bonnie's arms.

"Sun feels good," Bonnie said. "Can't wait to get a bath. Wash that cemetery off me."

"I'm going to shower for a week," Reid said.

The walk through the grassy flat land was easy, but they struggled again up the embankment to the highway. They walked toward the convenience store. Bonnie still needed help walking. Before long a car pulled up. It was the peevish librarian.

"My stars! What happened?" the woman said. "All three of you are wet. Climb in."

"Mrs. Witherspoon. Can you drop us at the store?" Bonnie said, her speech slurred.

"Certainly. I'm driving right by it. What happened?" she repeated.

"It would take too long to tell you," Reid said. "You'd have to drive us across the country."

"My stars," the librarian said.

"Do you mind driving a little faster," Seth said.

"I don't like this part of the highway," she said. "A lot of bad things have happened here. In fact, there's a car up here. I'm pulling over for a minute. Maybe they need help, too."

"No, don't," Bonnie said.

"It'll only be a second," she said, slowing, coasting off the road to a stop near the car. "I wouldn't want to be stranded out here alone."

"No! Pull out," Bonnie managed to scream.

Seth and Reid looked out the back window. Fog rolled down the hillside, enveloping the car rising over the windows.

"I do hate this fog," she said. "Can't understand fog out here on the highway, especially during the day."

The passenger side doors opened. The men with plaid shirts stood outside. They aimed tasers at the trio, smiled, and fired. Jolted by the shocks, they flinched and collapsed motionless in their seats. The men in plaid shirts tipped their hats to the librarian and closed the doors. The librarian nodded, smiled back, and turned around the car to head back to the inn.

———

As he woke slowly, Seth was undressed, lying on his back on the altar. Try though he did, he could not move. Through blurred vision he saw Bonnie and Reid, both naked and unconscious. Bonnie was strapped to the gurney again. Reid was hogtied on the floor.

A large crowd of hooded figures were assembled. After they arranged themselves in rows they began to chant, led by Hardwick. He chanted and they responded. Seth struggled but still could not move. The chant seemed to continue for a long time. Eventually, it stopped. The crowd immediately began to mingle. They laughed and joked. Goblets were arranged on a table beside the altar.

Mr. Heil and Mr. King stepped from the crowd. They removed their robes and placed them on a chair. Mr. Heil slapped Mr. King on the back. They smiled broadly.

Hardwick waved and called to the men, "Gentlemen. With this much elixir, you will soon be boys again."

"Not necessarily boys," Mr. Heil said. "But young men to conquer the world!"

ABOUT THE AUTHOR

Dean Alan Conrad is a former newspaper reporter and columnist. He is a graduate of the Pennsylvania State University with a degree in English. He lives in Pennsylvania and always has been interested in everything spooky.